W900

A novel by Tom McNulty

Disclaimer

All the places and people in this story are totally fictitious, any
resemblance to 'real life' is bogus.

Contents

Chapter One

More, or should that be Less?

T here was the sound of a vehicle pulling up outside and Hovis' heart began to race. "It's here, it's here," he squeaked in a muted, yet vaguely strangulated way. Simultaneously gripped by fear and anticipation, Hovis' torso set to move, but his backside remained rooted to the kitchen's authentic, 1950's gold and burgundy leather, Washington Redskins swivel stool, that he'd bought for a snip at auction. His brain was telling his legs to go to the door and see who it was, but the legs in question were having none of it and the cheeks of his posterior, for the moment, remained comfortably unclenched.

Then came the sound of somebody approaching in heavy boots, scrunching purposefully up his gravel pathway, followed by a sharp rap at the door.

Hovis held his breath.

"Delivery for Mr. Monk. The last man on The Hill."

Hovis forcibly reswallowed his heart and laughed at himself, 'Christ, calm down man, you're gonna give yourself a heart attack. Shit, this living alone up here is really getting to me…'

"Open the door Monk, and don't try anything smart, we've got the place surrounded," said the deep brown voice outside.

Happily, it was only Lee Kelso, the regular postman who'd been delivering to 'The Folks on The Hill,' as he called them, for thirty or more years. He'd become quite a friend to Hovis, due to his unconventional approach to his job.

"You'll never take me alive, Copper," responded Hovis, finally rising from the burgundy and gold swivel chair and heading for the front door, while fully expecting another slick piece of repartee to come flying in his direction.

"Oh, come on 'Hove,' I'm dying for a drink. Let me in and get the kettle on.... It's terrible cold out here, Sir," he added in a passable Dickensian. Obviously well pleased with his Oliver Twist moment, Lee tried it on again. "Would Sir be a wantin' me to clean your chimblies, while 'am 'ere?"

Hovis just stopped and looked wryly askance at the shimmering figure through the frosted glass on the front door,

"If you promise to shut up, you can come in but if we have any more of that Long John Silver voice, you can stay out there." There was a moment, purposely left vacant for consideration of Hovis' ultimatum, before Lee came around to his way of thinking but he couldn't resist putting him right regarding Long John Silver.

"It was Fagin, or at a stretch Bill Sykes but there was no splicing of the main brace involved."

"Whatever," he dismissively opined, grinning widely as he opened the door. "What do you fancy on this fine morning, Mr. Kelso? We have Tea, Coffee and a rather impudent drinking chocolate, courtesy of Mr. Cadbury. Take your pick?"

"Got any chocolate biccies?" Lee stepped inside, "Cos if you have, then I won't settle for anything less than a Diabetes Special and go for a 'Double Chocolate Holocaust.' I could call it lunch! I mean, who wants to live forever? After all," he added, "this is my last day, I go on holiday tomorrow, then it's a new route after that."

Hovis greatly valued his irreverent relationship with Lee Kelso but he knew that it was unlikely to survive the final closure of The Blue Yonder mine. Lee had previously mentioned this would be his last day, so he'd secretly stocked up on the chocolate biscuits he favoured and decided to have some fun with him.

"Come on in you old tart, and sit yourself down," he politely invited, while trying to see what Lee had in his hands. Was it his winnings from last week's auction? Unable to contain himself any longer, Hovis had to know what Lee had brought him,

"Okay, make with the parcel," he demanded and put both of his arms out in front of him, as he did when he was a child.

"I haven't got a clue, what this one is," said the postman, as he 'weighed' the parcel, in his right hand, just out of reach. "Not a clue," and for good measure, bounced it a couple of more times, before he placed it in Hovis' anxiously outstretched arms.

"Come on then, let the cat out....,"

"It's something very special," Hovis answered mysteriously. "Go on, have a guess. I'll give you three chances," he generously offered. "You'll never get it." He said those last few words with such surety, that Lee, looking at him askance, was prompted to enquire,

"What do I win, if I guess it?"

Hovis simply looked pitifully at him,

"You won't," his eyes strayed back to the package. "Fire away, be my guest," he taunted. "Believe me, you'll never get it." Then, just to rub it in, he triumphantly enquired, "And what do I get, when you inevitably fail to come up with the right answer?" At this point he was so sure of victory, that he offered a tiny crumb of assistance to the helpless Postman. "D'you want a clue, it won't help but if you want to eek this out, then be my guest."

Hovis' cruel streak was starting to enjoy this one-sided game.

"Well," said Lee, ignoring Hovis' failure to provide winnings, "that much bubble pack and stiffener generally means we're dealing with something fragile, perhaps porcelain, or maybe a mechanical item, a clock perhaps, or at least something like that....... But it'd have to be a very flat clock........"

Lee Kelso was now standing and peering at Hovis through two narrow slits that passed for his eyes, probing Hovis for any tell.

"It's a posh watch." Lee nodded his head arrogantly.

"Wrong," squeaked Hovis gleefully, as he poured the hot chocolates into two large mugs. "Strike one, now guess again."

The Postman's look changed completely with the denial of his guess, he peered suspiciously at Hovis. There was a certain, sixth sense involved in being a postman. It was something that the dark practitioners of the envelopic arts, gradually acquired after many years of squinting at badly written addresses and gauging the weight of appallingly wrapped packages.

"Go on then, give us a clue," Lee squinted furiously at Hovis, who was just standing there, imperiously, one hand resting possessively on the package, looking calmly out of the window.

"Okay then. One clue coming up." Hovis was considering that maybe his offer of a clue was perhaps folly but he pressed on. "There are many of them but this particular one is, or I should say always will be, unique, due to the laws of time and motion being immutable."

He was well pleased with that and smiled stupidly at Lee K, as he squirmed a little under the increasing pressure of this dual of wits.

"Ah, come on, that could be anything," Lee protested loudly and looked at Hovis through accusatory eyes.

"I never claimed it would be easy, that's hardly the point of the exercise!" He chuckled wickedly, made it even more intriguing by adding, "What's it got in its pockets's, Precious?"

"Okay you win. I don't suppose, that it's a gold ring or a record, is it?"

"Nope, t'aint!" Hovis triumphantly crowed. "And that's two guesses in one! Do you give up, or do you want a final guess?"

"Bugger more guesses, where's my biccies," Lee bleated. "Okay, okay, you win.... What is it?"

Pregnant pause, hardly covered the extended moments of silence that followed.

"If I tell you, what do I get?" Insisted Hovis, now confident in his victory.

Lee's answer brought Hovis crashing back down to earth.

"What does it matter, Man? Very soon now, you and I may never meet again, unless that's in the queue to get into heaven, or hell maybe, which would seem more likely." Seeing Hovis visibly deflate, he changed tack, "Tell you what man, I'll do you a compilation USB of my favourite ever tunes and when you get settled, email me your address and I'll pop it in the post to you," thus leaving a ray of hope for Hovis to cling on to. "You never know, we may meet again and always remember 'Hove,' stranger things have happened, not often but they have," he ended optimistically and smiled, as if he'd just informed his friend that he'd run his dog over on the way up here this morning. "Have you had the date of your final dismissal yet?"

"No, not yet but they informed me verbally, 'that my services were no longer required by The Company,' last Friday evening and told me I had a month to vacate the cabin. So, I imagine that one of those pieces of mail you've got in your hands right now, is the Coup de Gras," Hovis dejectedly replied to the postman's rather depressing question. "They usually give you a few weeks to come to terms with the news, just to make sure that you don't die of shock, or something equally inappropriate, while you're still on Blue Yonder property." He added wryly.

Looking at the stack of multicoloured mail's in Lee's right hand, Hovis pointed,

"Pass me the shit coloured one would you and never let it be said, that we poor workers were never warned about bad news."

"So, this really is goodbye, isn't it...?" Lee sighed plaintively, as he sorted through the various envelopes in his hand, knowing the reply to his question before he'd finished asking it. "Here you go, one shitty brown envelope addressed to Mr. Hovis Monk," Lee passed it to him.

"Dump the rest of those pieces of advertising in the garbage can, would you. I can't imagine I'll be wanting any of the crap that they're trying to sell me, so you may as well just junk it," Hovis mumbled, nodding his head to indicate the bin and tore the top off the envelope Lee had just handed to him.

"What's it say?" Lee called, while dumping the rest of the mail over in the recycle bin.

"Just what you'd expect," Hovis' stomach churned, "it's my official redundancy notice. They want me to leave the keys to this place and vacate the property, ready for clearance at the end of the month, so around three weeks." He headed to the kitchen for the biscuits. There was a certain finality to that word, 'clearance,' which wasn't helped by the knowledge that No.37, his world for so many years, would soon just be a pile of charred matchsticks.

The Firm always moved fast where 'clearances' were concerned. Hovis smiled ironically; while as a human being he envisioned the calamitous fiery death of his beautiful log home, as a company accountant, he appreciated the efficiency his bosses employed to dispose of the site, along the now semi-deserted A470.

"It's quite depressing, really, " Hovis muttered, returning with his Red Setter, Cheech, and parked a plate of chocolate biccies next to the two mugs of steaming chocolate, resplendent on their last surviving Washington Redskins Coaster's, which he'd had for years and if his memory served him well, Lee had delivered all those eons ago. It was just like the various Redskin's teams they represented. The player's aged, retired and in one, or two cases, died, as did his Coaster's. So, soon, like the great Washington team of the 1981-2 season, their 'on roster' numbers slowly declined and these two were the only survivors of a once pristine set of six. Wisely, their topside only had an impression of the famous Native American Helmet Decal on them, so unlike the player's, they'd had a career spreading over the decades, but not for much longer. Hovis was planning to leave them to their fate, when he and Cheech closed the front door for the last time, at the end of the month.

"Hail to The Redskin's," toasted Lee, trying to lighten the moment as he and Hovis picked up their drinks and like two mirror images, clanked the metal mugs together and then took a cautious, first tentative sip of the sweet brown liquid.

"Hail victory," responded Hovis in the acceptable manner. "This music O.K?"

Chapter Two

'I Want you, Love.., Want me too, Love.'

L ee nodded, "It's fine by me. D'you ever listen to that guy, Ken Alexander, on Radio Two?" He waited impatiently for the reply but he was on a roll, "Anyway, I was listening to 'The shipshape sounds, of the Ken Alexander show' and don't laugh too loudly but he played a really groovy track, by some ancient band called, 'The Lurch,' or something like that and anyway........." He stopped right there, as he realised he may have just blown his musical cred. Fortunately, Hovis wasn't really listening, so he blundered on anyway,

"Whenever I get into the region of The Glyder's, then Radio Two is all I can get. I know it's usually complete shit on that station, a real 'Dad Rocker's' favourite tune in 'n all but this morning, or lunchtime, or whatever time it was, that prick Alexander, played this really good track…., 'I want you, Love.., You want me too, Love,' …. Or something."

Hovis almost choked on a biscuit, spluttered, then recovering with a smile offered, "I think you're maybe talking about 'The Fester's'"

"Yeah, that's it," squeaked Lee, "The Fester's! I knew it had something to do with The Addam's Family, nice one Man." He enthused, "I don't suppose you know what it was called do you? Reckon I'll see if I can download it tonight. I'll stick a copy on the USB I'll keep to send you…."

"It was called, 'I Want you, Love.., Want me too, Love.'" Hovis answered confidently.

"Wow, Mister Memory strikes again. How d'ya remember that one?" Lee took another sip of his rapidly cooling drink, then stuffed another choccy biccy into his cavernous mouth and slicked back a blond cowlick.

"Oh, that's easy," A smug look spread across Hovis' face. "I was the Bass Player in The Fester's, many moons ago but this is probably the highlight of an inglorious history! So, I'll just wallow in the reflected glory for a moment, if you don't have any objections," Hovis flopped back in his chair, grinning. "Good track wasn't it?" He glanced at Lee's nonplussed face as he reached forward, picked up his mug but didn't take a drink. He was waiting for his ego to be stroked by Lee's response to this wild revelation.

"Really?" Lee asked incredulously.

"Really," insisted Hovis. "It was our initial release, on Deaf Bunny Records and it sold well, that is until The Frankie's let 'Relax' go later that same week, 'n then it sank without trace. It never resurfaced, as far as I know, until earlier on today. To tell you the God's honest truth, I didn't recognise it at first, when that dick, Captain Birdseye, played it on his show."

Lee, who by this time was just sitting there, looking incredulously at his soon to be, ex-buddy on the hill, exclaimed, "Well who'd have thunk it?! I've been mates with a genuinely forgotten legend for all these years and I didn't even know it," he gasped, then chuckled as he noted that Hovis had also been listening to Radio Two, but let it go. "Wow, Man, why d'you never mention it? All these years I've been bringing your mail up here......."

Hovis just looked at him, "It was years back...... I put all of that shit behind me before I started working here, eons ago. It's just not something I've ever really thought about since the band split. If that prick Alexander had just let things slide on by........."

"I thought they sounded really good but I suppose it might have been the surroundings," Lee murmured, unsure whether he'd just said that out loud, or was it just another of what he called his 'schitzorama' moments, where his 'other' brain seized control of his senses. "Did I just say that, or did I just think it?" Queried the postman.

"What?"

A worried look passed across Lee's face on hearing Hovis' response to his very reasonable question.

"Fuck off will yer'!"

Hovis laughed. "I was joking. I always thought you were bonkers, so what's new this time and anyway, Mr. Kelso, what do you think happened?"

"Oh, you're just trying to confuse me now," Lee growled, rising to the bait.

"Sit down and drink your chocolate," Hovis almost commanded. "And anyway, who cares if you're losing it a little? We're all getting older, Man…" He nodded knowingly, as he imparted that useless piece of information to his soon to be, ex-friend.

"Christ, you're a barrel of laughs today," complained Lee, "I'll recall this conversation, come the day when I can't remember my name and it's soup again for the evening meal in the 'Bide a Wee' rest home!"

"Now who's being a buzz quencher? It's no good you trying to slide around the surface, the facts of the matter aren't going to change one iota. When I've gone from here, it'll more than likely be, forever." Hovis concluded, weightily.

"Yeah, I know," sighed Lee with a tinge of genuine sadness in his voice, "but before you go, what say you and me have another hot chocolate and finish these biscuits for old times-sake?"

"It's a deal," responded Hovis, trying hard to cover up any sorrow in his voice. "I'll send you my address, when I've got one but this place," he said casting his eyes around No.37, "this place 'll be returned to dust, that's what the company does. We'll all have gone by then, hopefully to better climes."

"You taking Cheech, or are you handing him on again? Cos, I'd be happy to take him, if you've no other option." Hovis now realised what a good friend Lee Kelso really was.

"Thanks, I really appreciate the offer but I think we'll both be O.K, together. I'm pretty sure I'll find something before the end of the month. There are plenty of places to hire on a long lease basis, so I don't reckon we'll have much trouble on that score. But I'll bear the offer in mind if I do.... Thanks again, Man."

"No problem, just remember, the offer still stands, should you ever need it."

Hovis silently nodded his acknowledgement of Lee's offer. Then, turned his head to take a look at Cheech, who was lying on the rug and twitching slightly in his sleep, dreaming doggy dreams, totally oblivious to the preceding conversation regarding his future.

"Don't reckon the old boy, could take another period of disruption at his age, the move will be hard enough on him," Hovis casually observed and smiling, reached for his drink. Then, changing the direction of the conversation, he gently enquired, "What are you going to do now?"

"With Blue Yonder going, there'll be no reason for me to come over to the mountains. You are the last reason any driver from the Bangor Bunker will ever travel down the A470. I'm getting shunted to some other area of postal….., I'm just hoping it won't be Anglesey, or The Llyn Peninsular. Those two areas are fine for tourists but a nightmare to work in…, like these mountains…., long distances between drops, freezing in winter and full of tourists in summer. There's so few people living out here that I don't think it'll be long before they're forced to pick up their mail in the nearest town......"

"It doesn't sound like the future's too good, to me," Hovis interrupted his maudlin polemic.

"It's not," Lee snapped back and then on reflection offered, "Sorry Man, that wasn't necessary, it's not your fault. It's just that it can get a little weird up here in winter and it's always the Postman, who's the first on the scene."

Hovis could see Lee was bothered by something so encouragingly mumbled, "Go on," which Lee was only too happy to do.

"You know Atomic Slate closed their doors for the last time?" Hovis nodded silently, almost dreading the next few words to come flooding from his friend's mouth.

"I don't suppose you remember the old Parry place at the back of Bethesda..." he paused just long enough to register Hovis' blank expression. "..... Well anyway, Deryk Harrowby, one of ours from Bangor, went out there this morning with a Flange Sprocket, or something, for the old fella's Seed Drill and what he got was a vision straight from hell. The Parry's had relied on the money that their six lads made from the Slate workings to keep them 'n the farm afloat. Well," he paused, ensuring he had Hovis' rapt attention, "it seems old Emlyn took his shotgun and blasted every living thing on the farm into oblivion. Katie, his wife, the six lads, even his young daughter, were all shot dead…., just piled up in the kitchen. Then, it seems he went around the whole farm and killed every living animal.

When he'd slaughtered everything, he blew his own head off, with two barrels to the kisser."

Hovis was about to respond but there wasn't enough time to get a single word out, before Lee continued,

"Can you imagine it?" He stared wildly. Hovis, still dumbstruck, simply shook his head in response.

"All those Dog's, Cat's and Kin just piled up on the kitchen table, like so many anonymous victims of some crazed killer. The larger animals were found in the barn. The family's much prized Dairy Herd and all of their sheep, sixty-eight animals in all, dead, piled up against the rear wall. The weird thing was, Deryk could see a river of dried blood that had leaked under the back door but he still knocked and then, when nobody answered, he went in…. Christ man," he shook his head, "can you imagine being faced with that carnage. Jesus man, happy Christmas, or what?" Lee threw his hands in the air and understandably fell silent.

"How long had he been working on that route?"

"Only six months, just enough time to get to know them all……. It makes me think of jacking it all in."

"What and miss all those potential years of envelopic and parcel excitement? I think not," joked Hovis, humourlessly.

"That's a good one," countered Lee, sarcastically. "I could tell you stories, that would make your blood freeze but those tales aren't for telling right now. Maybe one day, over a pint if we ever get together again but I don't want to be remembered for some sordid story of another dead farmer….."

"Okay then, can I interest you in another superior packet of Sir's favourite chocolate biscuits?"

"Sure, why not," Lee responded, "but can I choose the music, this dirge that you've got going at the moment, isn't exactly lifting the 'feeling' in the room, if you 'dig what I'm saying.'"

"Let me guess shipmate," chuckled Hovis, "if I'm not mistaken, that's a genuine 'Ken Alexander,' complete with a touch of the 60's, thrown in for good measure." He smiled and looked over to the Postman, for some sign of confirmation.

"Spot on, dude," Lee stayed in character. "In fact, I believe that he used it this very day, just before he 'spun' The Fester's on his turntable. Don't suppose, that you've got a copy of it, have you," he asked, more in hope than expectation.

"Shit no," gasped Hovis. "Christ, I didn't even recognise it until it was nearly over. One decade's a long time, let alone three. I guess you'll have to revert to Plan A 'n download it, that's if anybody's bothered to put the thing up somewhere. Might be on YouTube I s'pose…."

Standing up, in order to change the music, Lee turned towards Hovis and shook his fist at the clouds.

"Damn you, Frankie Goes to Hollywood," he almost spat, then chuckled. After a quick look on his friends iPod, he chose an inoffensive mixed programme, then sat back down, waiting for his extra biccies to arrive.

"Nice choice," commented Hovis on return.

"If you don't mind me asking, why did the band split up?"

Hovis placed another plate of biccies on the Washington Redskins coaster in front of him.

"I don't know what they call it these days, but back in the day they used to call it, 'Musical Difference's.' But that was just a catch all really, it could mean anything……"

"Musical differences?"

"Yeah, it's shorthand for all the shit that happens when you spend too much time on the tour bus. The band gets far too tired and strung-out.... So, yours and everybody else's emotions get a little, uncool." Hovis realised that this talk of his 80's exploits was colouring his language with phrases that today were decidedly uncool.

Lee had been listening intently, right up to the point where the particularly beautiful, slow and ringing finale to Steve Miller's 'Seasons' cut in and distracted him. That mesmeric diversion let Hovis prattle on uninterrupted.

"Christ, listen to me, 'tour bus'!" Hovis laughed, as the word's left his lips. "It was a crappy old Transit van. It was always breaking down, well actually, failing to start would be a more accurate description…, but it was all we could afford," he added with a shrug. After an extended moment, to allow the pictures to form his 'audience's mind,' he carried on with his tale.

"Oh Man, I can laugh now but there are many occasions I can recall quite vividly, just standing outside some poxy service area, being on the verge of violence as Preston, the American who played the drums and occasionally tinkled the Ivories in the band, messed around under the 'hood', as he called it and with the will of some good she devil that he prayed to, got the bitch going again. Sometimes, things got really desperate. I remember one night after a gig in Carlisle, we pulled into Killington Lake Services for a hot drink before we slogged it on down the motorway, heading for Hereford. Or so we thought. In just those few minutes while we grabbed a drink, the fuel had frozen in the tank and we were going nowhere fast……"

"Go on, so what happened next?" Pleaded Lee, like some child whose mother actually read to him, asking for more.

"Preston decides that the situation can be saved but only if we are willing to put opportunity into the ring with total disaster." Lee's face was a picture and Hovis figured that his Mother must have read to him a lot.

"And?" The man-child was about to spill his drink on the rug.

"And," picked up Hovis...... "Preston explained this complicated carburettor-based idea he's had about the 'getting the truck going, thing,' as he so eloquently put it."

"Stoned?"

"Yup, and some," confirmed Hovis.

"Hmmm," mused Lee and chomped on another biscuit while he waited for his host to continue with his tale.

Hovis took a sup of his drinking chocolate, put his feet up on the coffee table and picked up where he had left off. "This dubious idea entailed all the members of the band getting their lighters out, lighting them in unison, then directing this makeshift flamethrower onto the carb, until he, Preston, told them to stop. I suppose you can see the inherent danger in his plan?" He tried to gauge whether his munching guest was still paying any attention to his rambling story.

"Go on," Lee leant forward, like some eager schoolboy, leaving Hovis little chance to avoid recanting the whole yarn for the benefit of an audience of one.

Fourteen minutes, several detours and twenty-seven seconds later, his tale drew to an end........

"And unbelievably, it worked! Just enough fuel was thawed out to get the engine turning over and we made it to the gig, which incidentally was one of our better ones, if I remember correctly......"

It was Lee who spoke next.

"Have you ever considered getting The Fester's back together, or maybe taking them back on the road?" He reached over to recover his mug from the table directly in front of him.

"Not much chance of that," Hovis smiled as the last biscuit disappeared into Lee's gigantic mouth. "I haven't got a clue where any of them are these days and you know, to be honest, although that fucking idiot Ken Alexander played it on the radio, I'd not heard 'I Want you, Love.., Want me too, Love,' for over thirty years! Now the dickheads got it on his band play-off thing on his next show. When, get this, it'll be up against 'Aphrodite's Child's' '68 hit. Jesus, how the mighty are fallen," he exclaimed dismally. "Normally, I couldn't give a damn about shit like this but to lose in a popular vote, to a piece of blatant Eurotrash like that abomination, would be even more than I can take! I mean, 'Rain n Tears' couldn't punch its way out of a wet paper bag," he cried passionately and folded his arms, with a "humph," added purely for extra gravitas.

"Bet your Dad did that frumpy last bit, when you were a kid, a sort of final word thing, didn't he?"

"I was about to tell you, what a pleasure it's been to know you, Man but I don't think I'll bother now," Hovis grinned broadly.

"See if I care," Lee replied using acceptable male badinage and finished his now cold chocolate with one glug. Then he stood up, holding his hand out, for his hillside buddy to respond and shake it.

"Mates forever," he said as Hovis gripped his outstretched hand.

"Mates forever," a small tear stung his right eye. "Damned eye infection," he casually wiped the liquid from his eye socket. "Looks like you've got it too," he pointed out to Lee.

"Must be contagious, I reckon," The Postman moved towards the front door.

"Don't forget to send me your address when you get settled and I'll send you a newly pirated copy of The Fester's greatest hit, free of charge. Oh, and make sure you get something for that eye, things like that can turn nasty if you don't look after yourself."

With that, Lee Kelso, gregarious postman par excellence, walked outside of No.37 for the last time, got back in his van and started the engine,

"See you around, Man. Happy trails to you, old friend."

Hovis fired back, in typically male bravadic script,

"Not if I see you first." However, Lee was right on the ball that day and as his red van accelerated down towards the Rat Road, he casually threw out,

"It's been really average knowing you," and with that he was gone, leaving Hovis, open mouthed and frustrated.

He slowly turned and looked at Cheech.

"Every time, every fucking time, he gets the last word in and then conveniently, pisses off," Hovis affectionately commented, then sighed with a smile as he turned back towards the A470 and watched as Lee Kelso's van took a left at the base of the Rat Road, before accelerating off for the last time, towards Bangor.

"He always had the last word, Cheech and he was my best friend up here," he whispered but the mere telling of this truth to the barely corpus mentis Setter, stirred something in Hovis.

"Bye, Man." He pitifully added and promptly burst into tears. His eyes stung and his nose blocked up but that ridiculous display of male emotional discharge, only lasted for as long as it took him to selfishly remember that Lee had also brought a mystery package with him, and it was still sitting over there, on the dining table. He chuckled as he realised they'd never finished the guessing game.

"You'd better be, what I think you are, or this will be a rather stale Hovis you'll have to deal with," he cautioned the package, blatantly tempting him.

Chapter Three

One week earlier…..

"What d'you fancy for tea?" Hovis asked Cheech, as he hung his jacket on one of the vacant pegs in the hallway and made his way past the recumbent Red Setter, to the kitchen. "I don't know about you but I reckon I'm settling on something simple, like a bowl of soup and a prawn sandwich." Cheech opened one eye and watched as Hovis shuffled past again, heading into the lounge.

His first port of call was the coffee table with its computer, just waiting to be given life. "Right then, let's see what you've got for me this time," he said hopefully and clicked onto his favourite auction site, to begin searching for that special something.

He was looking for anything distracting and unusual, some singularly special item with the power to raise him out of this soft brown fug that he'd been aimlessly wallowing in since he'd been given his verbal termination notice, just a few days ago. No.37 was now the last occupied property on The Hill. In fact, it was the last log cabin on The Hill, and both it and Hovis would soon be gone too.

On a first scan he found nothing and looked back towards the kitchen.

"Well, seeing as you didn't answer me when I asked what you fancied for tea," he regaled Cheech, "I'm afraid you've left me little choice. So, this evening you're going to have Choice Chicken Chunks in gravy, with biscuits and a small piece of Victoria sponge cake for afters. If you'd wanted anything else, you should've said when I gave you the chance."

Cheech raised his head at the sound of the word 'cake,' then softly followed Hovis into the kitchen. It didn't take long to prepare their evening meal and even less time for them to eat it.

Shoving his lap tray to one side, he returned to the computer in search of that, 'thing he couldn't do without.' After what seemed like hours of fruitless peering at the screen, he was just about to call it a day, when he ran up against, 'It'.

There 'It' was!

The single most, 'can't do withoutable' item in the auctions that evening:

The Miguel Indurain, Banesto Flame Red Onesey, as worn by The Great One, on the record breaking, one-hour time trial in 1994. During which, he covered 53.040 km's.

Now, remarkably and supposedly authenticated, it was up for auction. There was a starting bid of £783.00, which had climbed to a very reasonable, £823.50 with only fifty-seven minutes left on the auction. He felt incredibly lucky to have stumbled across this item.

He had to have it.

'The Big Mig,' was one of his all-time HERO'S.

He stood on an imaginary marble plinth surrounded by clouds, alongside his other sporting paragon's, like George Best and John Riggins the running back of The Redskins, or his compatriot Art Monk. Eager to be a contender for this prized object, he quickly checked the precise time the auction closed, 22.30.47GMT. Hovis was convinced there must be somebody or other's ghost watching over him on this auspicious day.

"Lucky, lucky! I could have so easily missed this one," he told Cheech, who remained ignorant of this prize.

Now, if he just timed this right, this precious item from the annals of cycling history could be his! 'Christ man, make a bid and see what happens,' he thought and calmly put in the minimum bid, then sat back to watch what happened.

The hiss of escaping gas as he pulled on the tab off the can of Guinness he'd grabbed from the fridge, got Cheech's attention. The Red Setter, as usual, opened just one eye, observed that there was nothing happening that warranted more than a single cursory glance, and closed it again.

Within a minute, another bid appeared on the screen and the going price of The Onesey rose by another minimum bid. That bid now held the whip hand but not for long, as bidder number two showed their hand and jacked the price up, by the minimum plus an additional £5.

"Rank amateur," commented Hovis as he took a great gulp from his can of 'The black stuff,' and belched gently. "This idiot's giving away their tactic's but the other one might prove to be a little more of a problem," he informed Cheech, should he by some chance be interested.

"Time to kick ass, I reckon," he calmly said, as he looked up at the clock on the wall and compared it's indicated time, to the absolute time the auction clock stated. For all intents and purposes, ownership of Miguel Indurain's Flame Red Onesey, like the 53.040 km's, that he covered in the one-hour time trial, was going to come down to a matter of seconds. For the best things, it always did. That was the thrill of it......

He cracked his fingers and then stood up, taking the empty black can with him. As he made his way into the kitchen, Hovis enquired of Cheech, "Were those Chicken Chunks alright?" Then, without waiting for an answer, he grabbed another can of Draught Guinness from the fridge and carried it back to the lounge.

"Let's see where we're at then," he murmured as he looked at the computer, checking to see if anything dramatic had occurred in the two minutes or so, that he'd been out of the room.

"Still the same," he commented. It seemed as though the endgame was playing out in a frenzy of inactivity. Hovis looked at the auction clock once again and took another mouthful of his stout. The relentless electronic counter, silently continued to tick its way down towards zero. Hovis knew by this lack of movement from the rival bidder's, that eventually, like any other battle of Wit's and Will's, this auction was going to be settled by the last squeak of the fastest mouse. It had that feeling about it. The extended gaps between bids and the infrequency of them, suggested that there were a low number of interested parties already past their initial Max bids.

However, their prompt responses to any bids, indicated that his rivals were dedicated, so timing was going to be a vital component in this tussle.

There wasn't a sound emanating from No. 37 as the tension rose. The do or die mental struggle between the three bidders involved in this tussle for The Big Mig's Onesey, was palpable. Hovis carefully considered his next move and tried to psych out the opposition, while keeping an eye open for any 'smash and grab raider's' as he called them, coming in with an outrageous winning bid in the dying seconds. They didn't often strike on Monday's, they tended to prefer Saturday night, late on, when the drugs were doing the bidding for them. So, tonight he wasn't overly concerned about any unwelcome intrusions wrecking this three-way punch up.

As the clock wound down and nobody increased their offer, Hovis began to sweat a little. His method of, 'strike hard and strike late,' was generally a good, reliable tactic. One that gave the opposition little time to react to his 'highest bid' but for some reason, this time it felt different. Hovis was getting the jitters. He needed more information about his competitors. Were they still waiting to bid higher; what was their new maximum bid? He needed to sound them both out....., if it was possible. He resorted to the crudest of methods for this probe.

"Eight hundred and ninety-three pound, plus.......umm, let's see......the minimum bid," he said, as he simultaneously typed it into the box and clicked OK. There was an almost instantaneous response from one of his rivals, who he'd guessed rightly, was watching this auction as closely as he was.

"Seven second rule applies," he declared and prepared for the nerve tingling crescendo to this blind struggle. Years previously, Hovis had failed at the last second during many, well most, auctions and so he'd put his not inconsiderable brain to work on the solution and it had come up with the, Seven Second Rule.

It was almost foolproof. He figured that those seven seconds gave him just enough time to get a potentially winning bid into the website but not sufficient time for the other bidding parties to respond beyond their limit, before time ran out.

"Right then Cheech, what should I bid?" Hovis asked, expecting no answer to his rhetorical question. "Surprise, comes before a fall," he said chuckling to himself and then, almost immediately started to consider the delaying factor of ugly numbers.

'The Hovis Monk Paradox,' as he'd christened it, was in effect a visual stun gun, which made most sane men stop to consider its sheer ugliness and in doing so, they hesitated, consequently ran out of time and lost the auction.

"Right then, let's see," he said to the void and then, after a little thought, came up with the ugliest numbers possible for this particularly important mental shoot out. "£917 and 83p an absolute classic," he growled to himself and Cheech, who seemingly felt the need to open his favourite eye again, just to check everything was fine with his world. "Turn to stone, baby," Hovis hissed. "Turn.........to.........stone," he repeated, an edge of impending victory in his raised voice. Content, he now prepared his coupe de gras for dispatch when the clock struck seven seconds.

"£917.83." He repeated the number, for good measure. "Oh man, that's a really gross figure," he chuckled. "I do believe it heralds the stench of my rival's demise," he added, doing a really bad Shakespearean impersonation. Hovis sat at the table, mesmerised by the ticking of the auction clock, counting down to the crucial moment when he would apply The Paradox and hopefully win, The Big Mig's Flame Red Onesey.

With just one minute and two seconds to go, The Rank Amateur made his bid for victory in his usual half-hearted manner, upping the stakes by the seemingly obligatory minimum bid.

"Too soon and too little," Hovis chuckled and rubbed his hands together. "One down, one to go," he said with a determined finality and waited for some response from the other bidder. The countdown dropped lower, second by second, tick by tick and then, with only twelve ticks left on the clock, an offer of £903.97p, was submitted by Bidder 2.

"Gotcha!" Squeaked Hovis. "I've fucking well gotcha," he cried as he prepared to drop The Paradox Bomb, on his rival's Homecoming Parade.

"Ten. Nine. Eight," he counted, his eyes firmly pinned on the ticking clock as it plunged down toward the magic number seven.

"And, ...Pow," he shouted, as he activated his pre-prepared Paradox Bomb with a theatrical click of his mouse. "Take that Sucker!"

He held his breath, eyes glued to the screen as he waited for confirmation of the result. Had his bid got there in time? Had another mystery bidder eclipsed his bid?

"Congratulations, you have won this auction," the notice stated flatly, as it popped up onto his computer screen, requesting payment for the item.

"We've got it, Cheech!.........We've got Miguel Indurain's Onesey!" Cried Hovis, as he punched the air then danced around on the floor of No.37 while making his way towards the kitchen. "Time to celebrate," he declared as he grabbed another full can of Guinness from the fridge and downed it in one gulp, then reached into the fridge for two more.

The mental image of the great Basque legend racing smoothly around the velodrome, wearing the self-same Onesey he'd just won in the nerve shredding auction, spun around in his mind as Hovis, grinning like crazy, danced back into the lounge and flopped down in front of the television.

"The Paradox, does its stuff again," he said and punched the air in triumph. "Yeah baby, you're the man," he exclaimed, burped and sitting back in the green leather seat, opened another 'tinny' and set about it with relish. This one didn't last much longer than the first and Hovis reached for the remaining can, before wobbling across the room and turning on the television.

This was becoming a common pattern of events on what Hovis had facetiously called 'Kristallnacht's,' due to the ruthless nature of auctions. Next, he was going to scroll through the list of tv crap available to him, taking it as read that most of it was painfully unwatchable. He knew he should be getting ready for bed but he was buzzing, his Adrenalin still stoked by the do or die of the auction. 'Hey man, it's not every day you get to win the Big Mig's famous time trialing onesey!' He grabbed Cheech and gave him a big kiss on the top of his furry head and rubbed his sides.

Cheech didn't care what had made Hovis happy, only that he was and nuzzled into his shoulder, wagging his tail ferociously.

Being 'the last man alive on The Hill,' definitely had its fair share of drawbacks and for a while now, the social angle had been diminishing by the week. As the Company wound itself down to nothing, there were simply less opportunities for people to celebrate or to get together, except for a few desperate leaving affairs. In the past, parties had been loud and raucous, continuing until everybody had gone home, but as the total number of employees diminished, so had the vitality and regularity of such shindigs.

So, now it had finally come to this: One man drinking himself into oblivion while his dog slept on the rug and the television played long, boring Infoverts to itself all night.

Hovis put his legs up on the settee, settled a plump cushion behind his head and sighed; celebrating the acquisition of Miguel Indurain's Flame Red Onesey, which was quite a coup, had to be worth more than this.....

"Tell you what Cheech, tomorrow, if the weather's fine, I'll get 'Dennis' out of the shed and we'll go for a ride along the valley. How's that sound?"

Chapter Four

David or Che?

Hovis Monk had been employed by The Blue Yonder Mining Company for what sometimes seemed like forever, but today had been his last working day with the concern and he'd needed cheering up. He was still having a great deal of trouble coming to terms with being summarily dispensed with and as the TV got flicked to a late-night movie, he took a good long look around the lounge at what was, in effect, his entire life laid out before him in the form of product.

"Jesus," he addressed Cheech, his second-hand Red Setter, whom he'd bought off his one-time neighbour, Johnny Geralitus, when he'd been laid off five years previously. Johnny G, who had joined the enterprise in the same intake as Hovis, had been allocated the Log Cabin next door, all those years ago.

"All these years and for what?" He asked the dog. "Thirty-two months wages and not even a fucking pension. I ask you Cheech, how long do they think that's going to last and who's going to employ an old fart like me?"

The G. Man and Hovis, had formed a bond almost immediately they moved into their Company Cabins. The advert, which they had both gleefully responded to, had asked:

'Are you a go getter, who wants a job for life?' Then ended with a rather old fashioned Kitcheneresque phrase, 'Then this Company Needs You!' It even sported a photograph of 'Old Mr. Gibson,' the Australian who had founded the company; which had originally been based around the Opel market and had only later expanded into other minerals. Gibson was portrayed proudly pointing into the distant future, with a freshly lit cigarette stuck between his fingers.

Lazlo Gibson, had long since departed this world, as in February of 1969. He had died of Lung Cancer but nobody at head office seemed to think that this was somehow ironic and so continued to use the same photo on all of their advertising, until late in 1995, when the offending cancer stick was airbrushed out of the image and a fountain pen was rather clumsily inserted in its place.

The odd thing was, that today, as he turned the key and opened the substantial front door of log cabin No.37, he'd suddenly realised that his present predicament was the inevitable consequence of signing his life away for money. The Blue Yonder Mining Company offered every worker a free log cabin and a life where all their household utility bills were paid by The Company.

For the first time, he was experienced a minor panic attack.

The Log Cabin, with all its latest gadgetry, constantly being upgraded for free, was anything but rustic. It had full central heating, a power shower and beautiful fitted kitchen. Its Satellite based Internet and TV, was also free. The roof was covered in solar panels and a small but thankfully quiet wind turbine, whirled away, day and night on the top of the chimney. So, wind and solar energy powered almost all the cabins' needs and it was yours until or if, 'for some unknown reason,' you decided to terminate your contract with The Company.

Then, of course, there was the Healthcare Plan.

The Healthcare Plan was something else.

In Hovis' case, the 23rd of January was significant. That was the date that he'd drawn in, 'The Raffle of Life,' as it was commonly known by the employees. What actually happened was based on The

National Lottery, or something very similar. Every prospective new employee was given a rudimentary check up by the sinister sounding Dr Heinrich Schultz. Then, at the end of the compulsory examination, he, or she was afforded the opportunity to randomly choose a date, for his, or her annual check-up.

Two barrels were placed in front of the confused 'victim' and then, Dr Heini stepped up and spun them around before offering them to his latest 'patient'.

"Be pleased to take one ball, from each of the containers," he'd say. Then, when 'the untermensch' had chosen, he'd invariably demand in his curious, affected accent, which was neither comedic TV German, or anything else immediately recognisable,

"Show me!"

One barrel contained red balls, while the other, which appeared to have the greater number of spheres within its confines, was populated by blue tumbling orb's. Both had numbers printed on them, so Hovis did as the strange Doctor had instructed and reached into the maelstrom of balls and withdrew one of each colour. Then, as if it were some kind of a game show, he showed them to the good Doctor, who in turn, "Umm'd and Ahh'd," as he took down the number's in his appointments book, before he curtly dismissed Hovis with a perfunctory,

"Guttentagh."

The next day he received a postcard through the post, which informed him that,

'He'd drawn the number 1, from the barrel containing the Red balls, which denoted January and 23, from the blue selection, which signified the particular day of the month he would be expected to present himself at The Clinic for his annual checkup.'

Below the explanation of the numbers that he'd drawn in 'The health raffle,' there was a section preceded by an asterisk, which instructed him to;

'Keep this number safe, as it is both the lock and the combination to open many of the functions in your cabin.' It also suggested, that he keep these numbers, 'In the Blue Cloud, which he could find on his personal computer within his cabin.'

As it turned out, Hovis found, that 1,2,3, was hardly a difficult number to remember, in fact it was almost impossible to forget.

Viewing the terms and conditions before signing the contract with Blue Yonder may have been a good idea, yet very few of the workers at the Welsh site ever did. Mainly because, when it came down to it, they were only too happy to have any employment with such immediate benefits. Working for The Blue Yonder Mining Company, for most, was like a dream come true. The phrase,

"Yours for free, until you leave the company," rolled sweetly along in their sing song welsh accents.

The reality of this had hit home hard for Hovis and all the others that The Company had let go over the last few years. When their redundancy notices dropped ominously through the letterbox, the entire worlds of so many of those unlucky employee's, hit the deck with them. Hovis was the final one to go and as of this morning, he had one calendar month to remove himself from Cabin No.37 and prepare it for demolition by The Company.

"So, old son," Hovis addressed Cheech, "in one short period of time, we will be cast off with no recourse to, well putting it bluntly, fuck all." He stopped his ingress at the door to the lounge and took a good long look at what in effect, was his entire life laid out before him, in the form of product.

When he joined The Company, all those years ago, it was as a young man with avaricious dreams of flashy cars, beautiful women and all the things that having too much money could buy. He never gave a second thought to the 'ordinary people'; he was living the dream and that's all there was to it. Feeling that way annoyed Hovis at first, growing out of his rebellious adolescence was not an easy task for him. So, to smooth his conscience, he hung a huge framed poster of Che Guevara on his bedroom wall and saluted it every night, for a few years. However, as the years passed and he and his work colleagues wanted for nothing, Hovis simply let all the injustice in the world drift on by, without ever considering the future.

The Che thing ended abruptly one summer's evening.

Karen Baker stepped through the door of, 'The Huntsman' public house, located on the road through the mountain pass and blew him away. When he'd steadied himself, he waltzed over to her and try as he might, had little to no success in attracting the attention of this 'olive skinned honey'.

"She's looking for a sugar daddy," one of the other regulars commented in passing, as he left the toilets. "You've got no chance with that one, unless you work for that mining company, Blue something or other, up in the hills." That soupçon of useful information, was the 'in' that he needed. Having very deliberately washed his hands and dried them, he made his way back to Karen,

"Say baby, what's a nice girl like you, doing in a place like this," he quipped as he resumed his place and Karen smiled.

"I work, at The Blue Yonder, what do you do?" He said, then just waited for her reply. Exactly what she said next didn't really penetrate his brain cavity. All that mattered was she was hooked and after a rather short evening in The Huntsman, they went back to his place and that's where it all started to go wrong. Her endless questions regarding the depth of his wallet, while insisting she wasn't purely after his money, would have alerted a rhinoceros.

When he finally got her into his bedroom, she totally blew it with one careless comment. Looking directly at his imperious poster of Che Guevara, she said,

"Oh, so you like David Essex, he's O.K, but he's not my favourite, I prefer Bryan Ferry, he's just classier, that's all."

The bottom instantly fell out of his ardour and after a quick grope and a little sexual solace, he fell asleep and when he awoke, to his great relief, 'The Lady' had left. Nowadays, the memory of that distant evening made him laugh out loud but there was a second, or two, when he wondered what had happened to her. Had she finally found her sugar daddy and settled down, or had it all gone wrong for her as well?

That evening, as Hovis was musing about Karen B's welfare and whereabouts, she was curled up, on her soft leather settee, definitely not thinking about Hovis Monk. She had many better things to be concerned about. She was and had been crying about the single most stupid and selfish decision that she'd ever made, which was eating away at her self-belief.

Many years before, she had married Gerald Thornley M.P. for money but her husband, had married her for position in The Party and it had quickly turned sour. For his part, divorce was out of the question, until and if, he ever lost his seat at Westminster. That was unlikely, since he had a consistent majority of 22,000 votes. His candidacy usually attracted over 65% of the votes cast. So, Gerald's position was secure, with seemingly nothing on the horizon to threaten that veritable Lily Pad. Stupidly, she had signed a prenuptial agreement which stated if she initiated divorce proceedings, then she would forfeit any claims on Gerald's estate. She had entered into this velvet lined trap of her own accord, a head full of all the things money could buy. Now, too late, she realised that freedom came at a much higher price.

*

For several months before his redundancy notice had arrived, Hovis had been remembering individuals from his past and just now, he was wondering what had become of Cheech's original owner and what had happened to Johnny's Cat, Chong?

Chong was a rather plump, yet undeniably handsome, mackerel striped Tabby that his neighbour had acquired from Bangor Lost Cat's Home, when his original mog, 'Charlie,' had died aged twenty-two. The problem he encountered with Chong, was purely down to his male gender, which made him an awful lot less predictable than his female predecessor.

The smell of bacon frying a few cabins away was ultimately Johnny G's downfall. After a few trial runs, Chong left home for good and moved in with the bacon temptress, a trainee nurse, whom The Company had recently signed up. It meant a move further down the hill for Chong but after all, there was bacon on the menu almost every day and that was good enough for him. So, one day he'd just squeezed out through the cat flap like an overfull tube of toothpaste and never returned. Not long after, the nurse, Helen Draper, was killed in a collision on the A470 and Chong, having lost his meal ticket, moved on, once again to who knew where.

*

On the Friday of the week before, he'd watched, almost hypnotised, as Alan Cuthbertson, the company's expansion director and his wife, Rosemary, drove away down the slope, leaving him and Cheech as the last survivors in the once fully occupied log cabins, which at the peak of Blue Yonder's global power, had numbered 59. Their last words to him, well hers were,

"You really must drop by, if you're ever in the neighbourhood...," but he was totally unaware of exactly where this "neighbourhood," was located. He'd worked with Alan for years but in all that time they'd hardly exchanged more than a few words in polite conversation, which were mainly about association football and Alan's abiding love of Burnley F.C.

Hovis, on the other hand, preferred to watch American Football and Rugby League. On the Gridiron he supported The Washington Redskins but if anybody cared to enquire as to why, he couldn't come up with any other answer than god's honest truth, which was he'd initially liked their kit the best and they'd won the Super Bowl that year. Watching Superleague Rugby on TV was not a matter of the colours, it was more a case of whoever played the most entertaining game this season. He didn't mind who that was, so long as they were good to watch and could hopefully give the long-hated Wigan Warriors, a run for their money.

When Alan and Rosemary were gone, more than likely forever, Hovis had returned to No.37 and on stepping through the door, had been assaulted by this exact same heavy brown melancholic fug he was experiencing today.

However, it was vaguely comforting to know that if things got too far out of control, there was always the 'Exit Option' written into everyone's Healthcare Plan, hidden away in the small print, under the apparently innocent listing, as 'Employees Extended Holiday's.'

Those particular breaks were all one-way trips.

Should he wish to partake such a journey, all he had to do was make an appointment with Doctor Schultz to be classified as, 'Suitable?' Then, put his magic numbers in the prescription machine and 'Abracadabra', a single white pill in a black velvet presentation case, would drop onto the counter in front of him. Inside was a card that proclaimed,

'Sorry to see that you've chosen the painless way out. The Company wishes you Happy Trails, as you move on to your next incarnation.'

That too was accompanied by an ancient photograph of Lazlo Gibson, smiling inanely with his thumb stuck up in the air, signifying his agreement to the one-way road which beckoned the recipient of his boundless mercy.

"Enough of these negative thoughts," Hovis said out loud, "Time for bed…"

Chapter Five

What's in a Name?

Hovis woke up the next morning, having not heeded his own advice, on the settee, with a crick in his neck, a repetitive dull thud resounding in his head and a dead leg, that any minute now was going to start tingling and jerking about. Then, as the 'fog' cleared away from his eyes, Hovis looked at the pile of empty black cans that he'd formed into a pathetic, irregular pyramid on the coffee table. Vague memories of the promise he'd made to Cheech, last night, started to drift back into his consciousness.

"A Coffee, or two first," he muttered and tried to stand up.

As his timorous foot touched the ground, a furious tingling tide, surged up his right leg and it buckled beneath him.

"God damn it," he yelped and then carelessly put his prickling foot back down on the ground again. "Oh shit, too soon, too fucking soon," he gasped as the exquisite cactile sensation shot up his leg for the second and then, third time, before he had any control over his actions. However, unwilling to delay the day any further, he attempted to deny the attack of pins and needles as he limped over to the kitchen like a broken robot, plugged the kettle into its socket and clicked it on.

Later, sitting at the table, waiting for his coffee to be cool enough to drink, Hovis had ample time to think about the future, or in his apparent case, a lack of one. 'Oh, why cry over spilt milk,' he grumbled inwardly, as he took the first tentative sip of his steaming beverage. 'You'll just have to do something else, that's all,' he thought and took another hesitant sip.

"But what?" A slight crack had crept into his voice, he sighed.

Having spent so many years securely greasing the same poll, whilst denying the inevitability of this moment, he couldn't think of a single thing.

*

Before his employment with The Blue Yonder Mining Company, Hovis had formed the dodgy alternative rock band, The Fester's. As was often the case, they'd had a very limited career. Truth was, they never really got past their first five track Mini Album; 'With the Fester's,' which they'd foolishly released on the unsuspecting public, the week before Christmas 1984. The 12" single, 'I Want you, Love.., Want me too, Love…,' also suffered from an unfortunate release date, sprung on the masses just as Frankie Goes to Hollywood released, 'Relax.'

It didn't stand a chance. Nothing would have.

Hovis always told himself that just two words were all that stood between it and success. Sadly, those two words were, 'Frankie Says'.

So, 'I Want you, Love.., Want me too, Love,' sank without trace and was rarely, if ever heard in the modern era. At the time of its release, it had reached No. 49 in the N.M. E's alternative music chart and had stayed there for a whole week, before being swept away by a slight brush from Big Country, who went on to survey greater vistas. Unlike the Fester's, who's career came crashing down amid internal acrimony or what were often euphemistically called, 'musical differences.'

Hovis drifted back; they were about to finish a tour of the mill towns in The North, where they had a limited amount of traction but could generally pull a decent crowd, when it all went horribly wrong. As the lights went down on their gig at The Barnoldswick Harvest Hall, Araf, the lead guitarist for the band, got into a heated argument with his brother Allan, again. Unfortunately, this time it was only resolved when blows were exchanged and Araf ended up in hospital overnight, needing twelve stitches in his face, to repair the damage done by Allan.

The two brothers had been more than a little tetchy in the van on the way to the gig. It hardly required the blue touch paper to be lit, for things to spiral out of control. As usual with young guy's, it was about women, or 'chicks' as the cool dude vernacular of the time would have it. 'Hot chick's,' we're a currency with barbs and by the end of a tour, the atmosphere in the van was getting a little tense.

The lead singer, was a female and as tended to be the case with bands of that era, she was a real mindblower. Above average height, with a stunning body and amphetaminely beautiful. She would slip onto the stage during the intro to a song titled, 'Sleaze Bucket'. Then, the band's one and only Super-trooper, which Preston Lancashire, the Fester's rather excellent drummer, had picked up for a very reasonable price, would light up, brilliantly framing Poe Pouree in a single beam of light, as she slithered across the stage. When she reached for the mike, the band hit their first chord of 'Twilight World Girl,' a swirling, amorphous tune that surprisingly earned its author, Hovis, quite a sum of money in the early 2000's, when it was used in a twenty-nine-minute short film, a retrospective on the 'Second Summer of Love and the Birth of the Ecstasy Generation'. Curiously, when it was viewed from a future perspective, 'a twenty-nine-minute short,' was a very apt title.

The problem for Araf and Allan, was that Poe had chosen to have a relationship with Preston and neither of them.

Hovis and Poe, on the other hand, were just great friends. As usual, he'd considered that she was way out of his league and so, he never made a play for her and anyway, she was hanging out with Preston....

Araf and Allan, were the almost identical, non-twins, born two years apart, of a union between the English Ralph Glendining, a wealthy Real Estate Magnate and Helen Phillips, a Welsh, whimsical, artistic young lady who would not have gone amiss back in the days of promenading along the seafront, taking the air.

In the fashion of the times, having toyed with several 'Straight names,' on each occasion they decided to name their son's according to their individual traits. Hence, Araf, which translated as "slow," in Welsh, was the first name they chose. That method, having turned out to be so accurate, was applied again when number two arrived a couple of years later.

If they'd thought that Araf was a little slow witted, then the second son, whom they named Allan, made him look like a genius. Allan didn't want to know about anything but escaping. One day, Ralph suggested Allan, or "Exit," in Welsh might suit him and in between fits of hysterical laughter, Helen agreed. Unabashed, she'd say, "There's dumb and then, there's our second son, dumber," if she was ever asked about his mild autism.

So, Allan it was but it wasn't their first names which bothered the lads as they grew up. No, it was the very English, Glendining bit that caused them untold problems. So, when they joined the band they took the punky decision to take the translation of their Christian names, as their chosen surnames. Hence, Araf Slow and Allan Exit, were born.

Preston and Poe, fared little better.

Chuck J. Lancashire and Peggy Lescombe, also had two sons, which only some pretty harsh anti-abortion laws, had saved. Given half a chance both pregnancies would have been terminated. It was only The Pope being so anti condom and the utter failure of the Withdrawal Method, that led to the birth of Preston and his brother, Leyland.

Chuck, the local high school Quarterback and Peggy their chief Cheerleader, had married when she got pregnant, it was the decent thing to do in a mid-west hick town. It wasn't until the boys went to 'big school' and some of the more world-wise Mothers started giggling behind her back, that Peggy even considered they may have found something amusing about the lad's names.

"Is there something that I'm not seeing, going on here?" She asked Chuck as they sat down for dinner one evening. After a hard day at the lumber yard, he was far more interested in eating, than debating names.

"Don't let them get to you, Peg," he said. "They're just jealous. Surely you remember what it was like when Preston started at The Ishmael Garton Day School and ended up being the most successful Flag Football Q.B, in the school's entire history." She smiled at the memory and nodded her head.

"Yes, you're probably right, he surely was a big 'un. Do you remember that game against Rosebud Seminary, when he just stood there and dominated the turf?" Chuck, just looked at her, smiling.

"I sure do, Honey and now it's Leyland's turn to step up to the plate. Don't worry yourself about the other Mother's, they're just afraid of their kid's being put in the shade again," he confidently stated and poured himself another cup of coffee, to wash down his evening meal.

They were not to be disappointed, Leyland sailed through his school days, greatly overshadowing his older brother in the Halls of Academia and gaining a massively overblown opinion of himself along the way.

Preston, eclipsed but ever the adventurer, took an extended gap year trip to Europe and never returned to the mid-west. Meanwhile, his younger, smarter brother, never left the shores of America and became a well-respected Financial Lawyer in San Francisco, where he defended some of the greatest rogues in history from impeachment and on occasions, much worse.

Whilst his sibling progressed up an increasingly greasy pole, to a town house in San Francisco, Preston had become the drummer in The Fester's

*

Poe, on the other hand, had a troubled childhood. She constantly challenged both her parents and schools, rules and values. Not for the first time, her parents had been called in to 'have a talk,' with Miss Jones, The Headmistress. This time, it was because Adrienne had stood up and declared to the entire class, that she had decided she didn't want to be known by her birth name of Adrienne Crabtree any more. Henceforth, she wanted to be referred to as Potpourri. No longer would she respond to people who didn't have the decency to use her declared new name, when addressing her. Later she would change it to the more phonetic spelling of, Poe Pouree.

"May I suggest, that perhaps one, or both of you are influencing young Adrienne, in some negative way?" The accusation from Miss Jones appeared to both offend and fluster her father Tristan, in equal measure.

"Fuff," he snorted. "Are you intimating that our daughter cannot make absolutely childish decisions, negative or not, on her own volition?" He grumpily continued, "She's Eight, for God's sake. She'll tire of this latest idea soon enough. Last year, over the Christmas Holidays, she was insisting that we call her Frankiscents...... all one word," he added helpfully, "but when I informed her the word she wanted, was actually Frankincense, she declared it sounded like an angry boys name and promptly dropped it."

Then, her mother Sian spoke for the first time,

"It was me, I'm to blame. I encouraged her to pick a prettier name and if she wanted people to remember it then a little prompter would help, particularly if she really wanted her friends to use it. It probably wasn't a good idea to say, 'Goodnight Poe'..... Sorry."

Miss Jones, simply smiled knowingly in Sian's direction and nodded her head. Seeing this, Sian fired her second arrow.

"Potpourii Crabtree is, I'll admit, a bit clumsy but Poe, I think you'll agree, is quite nice. I actually prefer it to Adrienne, no offence Tris but Adrienne is such a starched collar kind of a name. I agree with her, it's like having a boy's name.... and like it or not, Poe's an eight-year-old little girl, who'll never be a Roman Emperor, no matter how hard you wish it."

Miss Jones, gently clapped her hands together, twice, when Sian had finished, then looked over at Tristan to gauge his reaction.

"Okay, we'll try it," he said, smiling at Sian. "I'm not too keen on Potpourii but I do rather like the more casual, Poe," he added. "So, Poe it is," he affirmed looking at Miss Jones who grudgingly acquiesced. With that he stood up and promptly marched out of Miss Jones's office, heading for the carpark.

"Don't worry, I'll mention this meeting to The Staff, before we begin another day and I'll tell them about our agreement regarding, Poe. Just leave it to me," promised Miss Jones, as Sian stood up and shook her hand before following her grumpy husband out to the car.

The name Potpourii, went through several changes over the years but it was never lost. After reading Edgar Allen's literary works, she settled firmly on Poe Pouree and this was later formalised by deed poll.

So, as thing's worked out, eventually Preston Lancashire, Araf Slow, his brother Allan Exit and Poe Pouree, all answered an intriguing advert in 'The N.M.E.' placed by Hovis Monk. Together they became The Fester's, a notably unsuccessful Alternative Beat Combo, who disbanded due to 'musical differences.'

Chapter Six

Second Skin.

As Lee Kelso disappeared from site Hovis turned to his prize. Suddenly, in his moment of triumph, he was unsure of the parcel's contents.

Was this a fear born out of desperation? Or, maybe he was just scared of spoiling the picture of this moment that he'd spent the best part of a week building up to? Surely this crescendo wasn't going to be ruined by the intrusion of a dose of reality? Hovis considered this dilemma for a few moments and then came down on the side of bravery, which he knew he would but he just had to make sure.

"Well, here's hoping," he gathered all the preparatory thoughts required to confidently approach the parcel, still taunting on the table, unopened.

"It's Miguel Indurain's Flame Red, Time Trialing Uniform, it's got to be," he whispered. Hopefully the omens were right and the Onesey was just waiting for him to waltz across the floor and liberate it from its brown rectangular cell. There was only one more problem to overcome and that was the fact that his feet wouldn't move. They were planted, to the spot.

'Oh, for Christ's sake, get a grip, man,' he reasoned. 'It's a fucking carpet, not an uncharted piece of quicksand, just walk on it.' Taking his own advice, Hovis slowly took a deep breath and set off for the table, in that rather jerky, 'nothing's going to stop me now' fashion, but he relaxed almost immediately when he didn't sink into the quickcarpet. His once trepidatious feet, skimmed across the surface heading straight towards his goal.

He grabbed hold of the mystery package and like a child, gave it a damn good shaking, to try and gauge the truth of its contents, by weight and noise.

"Hmm," he expressed for the whole world to hear, and then shook the wrapped object again. It was suitably lightweight and it sounded like it was fairly soft as it shifted about inside. His mind made up, Hovis frantically sought a convenient spot to start his assault and not surprisingly, found a weakness on one of the ends. The top layer of paper came off the package easily but there was another, more carefully wrapped, lying almost seamlessly beneath the first. The only difference, was that this one was predominantly blue, whereas the first layer, had been a soft shade of brown.

Whoever had wrapped this package was either a Borg like perfectionist, or somebody who really cared that it should reach its new owner in pristine condition. This amount of care being attached to something, also insinuated that it was a genuine article, not a Chinese copy, or a straight forward rip off. Hovis had been turning mental somersaults since he'd paid for the Big Mig's Onesey…, was it for real, or had he been ripped off during his alcohol lubricated, melancholia session?

"We might have the real thing here," he quietly addressed Cheech, who was patiently lying in his favourite place, just inside the door, with a clear view to the rear of No.37. Cheech understood fully that it was his function to ward off any intruder's, who might for some unknown reason, have been bothered to climb up the Rat Road and now be going to break in and rob his home. It had never happened yet but it was always a remote possibility and if you were a pampered menial, as he was, then anything was possible, no matter how unlikely. It was, after all, his duty to guard his friend, food and fuss giver.

Cheech wagged his tail and Hovis, satisfied that he was listening, continued.

Next came a quickly dispatched layer of bubble wrap, which revealed a cardboard box, this required the judicious application scissors. Inside there were two other layers of meticulously applied wrapping paper, which grew more and more intricately patterned as each new layer was revealed. They finally stopped presenting themselves to him as he ripped away the last semblance of a rather fetching maroon paisley tissue paper, to reveal a plain grey plastic bag, which obviously held the object of his desires. No amount of tape, or sticky backed plastic, could hold him now he was so close.

"Only this plastic and then you're all mine," Hovis said with smug determination and tore at the final piece of sticky tape, which was all that remained between him and the once beautifully encased item.

Revealed at last in all its flame red glory, Hovis was unimpressed.

All he thought was, how small it seemed for such a large chap as Miguel Indurain. After all, he was known as 'The Big Mig' and if he'd ever had to wear this minuscule suit, then Hovis would have loved to know how he managed to get into it and still been able to breathe. 'But then again, they did say he must've had three lungs...... But still?' Mused Hovis, shaking his head incredulously at the concept.

Perhaps he'd stumbled on a long-lost Aztec based tribe, who, as part of their strange ritualistic behaviour, skinned and beheaded children, before packaging their flash-dried, freshly flayed skins and sending off to stranger's who'd won particularly intriguing eBay auctions?

He looked down at this morsel and silently wondered how was he going to fit his rather manly, middle aged frame, which had certainly seen better days, into this second skin as the Chameleons song, Second Skin, began playing in his mind.

Mentally he was holding on to what had once been, 'Hovis Monk, 28, freshly promoted, going places kind of guy, etc.......'

That very same guy was standing here right now, wondering just what trials and tribulations he was going to have to go through with the Great One's Onesey, just so he could look a complete idiot at the end of his lesson in un-natural contortion?

Before him lay this Flame Red, Second Skin, that did indeed seem to have some amount of elasticity but still, a good deal of imagination, or delusion, would be required when it came to the actual moment of truth. He held up the onesey against himself to fully ascertain the dimensional ambiguity. His heart sank and he put the onesey back down on the table. This was going to require a little thought, before he did anything.

Firstly, he had an inordinate amount of difficulty in deciding whether you climbed into it, or started by putting the top part of the infernal thing on, like a cardigan. Either option seemed impossible to Hovis as he picked it up again and laid it easily, on one of his thighs.

"Well, one thing's for sure," he muttered to himself. "It won't fit over your weekday clothes," he casually sucked his stomach in, as though pretending he was thinner was going to make something happen. When nothing did, he and the onesey made their way into the bedroom.

Hovis surreptitiously looked out the window, more than once, even though he knew he was the last resident remaining on

The Hill. Anybody out there desperate enough to be staring into his bedroom, would soon be turning away, feeling a little bilious at the sight of all that fat softened man flesh, squeezing into the onesey like some tube of toothpaste. Hovis smirked at that image, then vaguely wondered how he was going to get a good look at himself, once ensconced in the flash red lycra suit?

However, that didn't change the fact that he was going to have to get naked, if he was ever going to wedge himself within this time trialers uniform. After much consideration, Hovis decided that climbing naked, legs first into the headless child's skin, was his best option. He began this escapade, by unbuckling the belt holding his pants up and trying to kick them off with his trainers still on. Bad move. He was soon diving head first into the bed,

"Oumph!"

He rolled over and sat up, then kicked his trainers off and pulled his pants over his bare feet. His next goal, the removal of his shirt, was far more easily accomplished. With his shirt gone, Hovis began to feel the first twinge of cold biting at his naked flesh; it was his exposed genitals that complained the most. The phrase, 'Brass monkey's,' jumped to the front of his now shivering mind but he quickly reasoned it was a small price to pay for the privilege of squeezing into The Big Mig's Time-Trial Onesey, however ridiculously small it was.

Hovis stood up and rummaged urgently in the bed, trying to locate the tiny red item he'd cast there. He needed it to cover up his self-imposed embarrassment, which was growing smaller by the second, as the cold air took its toll.

"Wow! I never imagined you could shrink quite so much, or so quickly" he said with a hint of wonderment, as he held his penis delicately in between two fingers, as if they were a pair of tweezers. 'You're not going to win any prizes with that miserable thing,' he thought as he finally grasped the onesey and made the first attempt on its outer defences, by undoing the zip. He was going to get into this damned child's skin, even if it killed him! As it turned out, his initial move almost did, seeing him yet again pitching forward in a death dive onto the bed.

"Shit!" He expounded in a quilt muffled moment, before righting himself.

He knew, or he thought that he did, where this venture into the clothing quantum realm, had gone wrong. 'You rushed it in that headlong charge for glory and tripped over your own feet, or should that be toe?'

Hovis began a second attempt to put The Big Mig's Time Trialing clobber on, more slowly this time. To no avail; he suddenly realised that the Axminster was making a bee line for his head and he'd managed to do nothing to avoid the impact. In that micro second of perfect peace, where he was resigned to his fate, Hovis attempted to relax his muscle's and just roll, when he was hit by the advancing carpet.

He neither relaxed, nor rolled but he did manage to keep a tight grip on the quantum Onesey. Despite his very best efforts, he'd landed like a sack of spuds and finished his 'Routine', with a roll onto his back, a long deep groan and the creaking recital, of an ancient tribal expletive,

"Fucking hell."

Cheech, alerted to his master's distress, jumped on him and began licking his face. Muffled sounds emerged from beneath the furry mass as the naked, upturned beetle known as Hovis, flailed around wildly.

Realising Hovis was, in dog terms, still alive he jumped up, wagged his tail and woofed once, before heading to the kitchen for a drink.

Relieved of the suffocating furry pillow, Hovis just lay there, flat on his back, arms outstretched and his legs, wide apart like he imagined some jaded old tart, satisfying her last 'John' of the night might do. It may have appeared a touch sordid to an innocent onlooker but Hovis was simply getting his breath back, along with at least some of his senses.

"Choose another option, Man," he said to himself, as he sat up and started to formulate Plan 2. The long-forgotten memory of Muren Brucschtansinger, played across his still somewhat confused mind and he started to laugh.

'If only there was anybody left at Head Office, they'd love this,' he silently observed.

"Right then Hovis, baby steps this time," he advised and sitting on the rather aggressive Axminster carpet, he slipped one foot inside the headless child's skin, gently pointed his toes and tentatively pushed...... To no avail.

This was obviously going to require a little more than just gentle persuasion and after a quick look around the room, he summed up his realistic options and shuffled his naked arse, over to the nearest wall. Then, having carefully placed his back firmly against it, he grasped the Flame Red Onesey tightly in both of his hands, held it straight out in front of him like a strange and unexpected pair of underpants he'd just plucked out of a long-lost lucky dip drawer,

"Easy does it," he offered as advice to himself. Then, braced himself against the wall and slipped his right foot deep into the guts of the Onesey and pushed hard. When he met any resistance to his apparently unwelcome intrusion, he simply pushed harder. The material was proving to be amazingly stretchy and he soon had his leg encased almost entirely within this elasticated quantum world. Content with the progress so far, Hovis pressed on. Whilst he looked down at the red encased leg, he was trying to plan his next move. Then, it struck him how ridiculous he looked right now. Here he was, a chubby, white skinned, middle aged, naked man, sitting on the floor, with what looked like a red stocking stuck half way up his right leg.

"See Cheech, there are times when being alone can be a distinct advantage," he boldly professed to the returning Setter, but then blew the moment by laughing at his own self-image. Cheech, for his part simply lay down and aimed his gaze towards Hovis, who in turn was staring back at him. He always suspected that Cheech had something surreptitiously weird going on in his canine mind. These were just the matters that occurred between a man and his dog on a daily basis, but right now, he couldn't spend too much time psychoanalysing Cheech, with his undoubtedly cynical view of his owner's idiosyncrasies. No! He had The Onesey to put on.

"Now for the other leg," Hovis proposed to his rapidly cooling flesh as he lifted his left foot up and placed it into the small amount of space remaining in the lower half of the quantum onesey. "Firmly, does it," he said with determination and gave one almighty push. He'd been expecting to encounter some resistance but his left leg slid effortlessly into the outfit and came to a rest, just like the other one, when his foot encountered a built-in barrier that stretched conveniently across the opening and caught his foot, like a stirrup. He swiftly yanked the onesey over his arse and carefully stretched it over his rapidly disappearing genitals. He now had the bottom half of his body fully encased and supported in this red Lycra, super elasticated 'childskin.' Standing, he gazed at this vision in crimson, all he could think of was how his legs had never looked so good and what they would look like in a pair of peep-toed slingback's, with a wicked heel on them? He raised himself on tip toes and posed to get a better idea, then quickly cast an embarrassed glance in the Setter's direction. He was met with the fully expected, one eyed disapproving look.

"Yeah, yeah! It's alright for you to laugh, just wait 'til you have to wear one!" He threatened Cheech.

'Ok, now for the really tough bit of this whole escapade, the top,' he thought as he fumbled around, looking for the armholes of the flame red quantum onesey. As usual, this sort of blind grasping for some 'invisible' hole, was more a matter of luck than intention and his failed attempts were beginning to get annoying. 'I must be missing something fundamental,' Hovis thought desperately and then it struck him. He was treating this onesey like it was a business suit, whereas, it was more akin to a slippery eel and he should be treating it as such.

His right arm shot across his chest and grabbed for anything that he could pull closer to the front of this curious outfit. "Gotcha," he squeaked, as he managed to get a grip on the sleeve and work it towards a more usable position. Locating his left arm in its correct sleeve was the easy bit, what followed next was the natural culmination of a uniform stretched beyond its intended limits and a wearer, unwilling to call it a day before somebody got hurt. As the right arm of Hovis was shoved into the apparently quantum stretchy time trialers outfit, he struggled to settle it on his shoulders with the attendant tightening in the groin.

"Oumph!"

Then, he sucked his tummy in as much as he could and fumbled for the unseen zip end. Locating it he attempted to pull it up but after a few inches the zip encountered a hairy wall of flab and stuck solid.

"Eek!" He squealed as the hairs tweaked in the zip's teeth. Unable to raise or lower it while standing up, he resorted to lying on the bed. With one hand attempting to hold the onesey together, he yanked the zipper hard upwards, which, after a second or two, gave way.....

"Arrrrgh!" He cried as a few millimetres of tender flesh and several hairs ripped from his body. He paused a moment to let the pain subside, then carefully struggled to finish closing the zip which was accompanied by a distinct 'slurping' sound, as the rolls of flab acquiesced. Struggling to his feet he turned to Cheech,

"What do you think, eh?" He asked the inscrutable Red Setter, who registering that he was being spoken to, opened the one cynical eye again and looked for just long enough to satisfy Hovis that he gave a shit. Then slowly closed it again and fell back to sleep.

"Mirror, mirror on the wall," he absentmindedly said, as he tried to think where was the best mirror to view himself. There were only a few mirror's in the entire cabin. The company hadn't been too generous when it came to matters of personal vanity and the only mirror supplied as standard was a shaving one in the bathroom. The original Antipodean owners of The Blue Yonder Mining Company, were rumoured to be Quaker's and vanity was considered a vice. However, despite the fact that they were undoubtedly long dead, nobody had updated their attitudinal limitations. So, like all the other cabin's, No.37 wasn't overly blessed with reflective surfaces but as it was the executive model, there was one.....

Chapter Seven

The Horror, The Horror!

"Yes," shrieked Hovis, almost ecstatically. "You beauty," he called into the silent air, as if he was a kinsman of the founding fathers. "Inside the wardrobe door!" He cried as if it were a revelation from above. In fact, it was the only full length mirror the cabin had ever owned. The top row of cabins served as accommodation for the elite employee, usually an office worker. So, they had been provided with a full-length mirror to ensure they were respectfully turned out. To be perfectly honest, Hovis couldn't recall ever having used it for its intended purpose. As head accountant, he liaised between the local boss and head office, so smart casual dress was the order of the Australian day.

Hovis set off across the floor with a purpose if not elegance. He hadn't just spent the last thirty minutes or so, fighting with Miguel Indurain's Flame Red Onesey, to miss the opportunity to see just how heroic *He* might have looked, if *He* had held The One Hour Record, back in the day.

He had to admit that at this instant, the onesey did, in places feel a touch tight but he was sure it would soon stretch to fit. Hovis was feeling rather good about himself right now, he was confidently on his way to the mirror behind the wardrobe door, to gaze upon the magnificence of his physique, displayed in his hero's Banesto Flame Red Timetrialers Uniform.

A thrill rippled through his body, as he reached for the rarely opened, right hand wardrobe door and turned the handle. Now, like never before, it was tempting him to cast away his myriad ties and expose the almost pristine mirror to the light of public scrutiny. Quickly, he grabbed the string of ties, both gaudy and subtle, available in every colour under the sun, which hung carelessly over the area of the upper half of the mirror compartment, flinging them in the direction of the bed. This exposed the brilliance of this system. A mechanical marvel, which was loosely based on the crude but superbly designed, Lazy Susan.

In theory a mere flick of a switch and a full-length mirror would swing open. Hovis had discovered this 'attraction' some decade previously while looking up into the great unknown, which in this case was the built-in wardrobe's Anaglypta ceiling and which had prompted the beginning of his whole wallpaper refurbishment obsession. Every now and again, he would have a speeded-up episode of a kind of wallpaper covered Déjà vu, where Anaglypta's of various patterns, flashed before his eyes. He thought it must be similar to that moment just before you died, when your whole life played out before you, but in Anaglypta.

During his time at No.37, Hovis had never purposefully used this mirror and his memory was a little rusty when it came to opening it. However, he could clearly recall nearly jumping out of his real skin, the first time the Devil Mirror swung out of nowhere, scattering some of his ties and chewing up others. The smiling jobsworth with perfect teeth who had shown him around the 'executive' cabin, had neglected to inform him of this attraction… he'd just handed him a booklet, which Hovis trashed without reading, then left bidding him,

"A happy and long period of employment, with The Blue Yonder Mining Company."

After fumbling around for a while there was the sound of a 'click' above his head. Hovis stepped back as the mechanism snapped into action, but not quick enough, the mirror swung open with such speed it smacked him in the face.

"Fucking hell!!!!!!" Cried Hovis, rubbing his nose in raw shock, as the full-length mirror vibrated from the impact of being halted by his now widening visage.

"Jesus, what kind of lunatic thinks that's a good design?" Yelled Hovis at the aggressive mirror, which at this instant was still softly settling down, yet all matters of protest evaporated as he realised with shocking clarity the vision presenting itself before him.

He stared, aghast……..

There before him was the full-length image of a Flame Red Lycra Bug Monster and at least two stone over weight……., or possibly even more, he considered as he turned and observed this giant crimson bulbous beetlething, in profile.

You may have imagined that it was his extended stomach which revolted him the most, or maybe his love muffins but no, he couldn't remove his gaze from his horrendously nobly knees. The Lycra stirrups had slipped from his heels and ridden up his calf's, creating an inelegant bunching effect at the knees, making them look like two deflated footballs.

"Christ, look at those knees," he shrieked and futilely attempted to smooth out the rucked-up material covering his boney, middle aged joints. Then, the sight of his relaxed stomach muscle's struck home. He looked like he'd fitted the onesey over a couple of spare tyres.

"Jeez! I look like a fucking Scarlet Michelin Man…. Behold, Bibendum Rouge!"

In an attempt to try and recoup the situation, he stood bolt upright, put his hands on his hips and puffed his chest out, while holding his stomach in. This proved to be a very temporary solution, as a single breath can only be retained for just so long and as his calf's were now completely bare, thoughts of comparisons to Foghorn Leghorn, didn't help. Hovis' breath exploded in a fit of giggles,

"Tenshun!" He crowed, saluting himself in the mirror and tried to find a more flattering pose to take a photo of himself wearing what he truly believed to be, Miguel Indurain's Flame Red Banesto Timetrialing Onesey.

'Ok, not the moment for a selfie….,' he thought as he began to sweat profusely. The effort he'd put into getting the onesey onto his rather generous body, had been equivalent to a strenuous Calisthenics programme. The excess of chocolate biccies and two large mugs of chocolate were making him feel queasy. He barely had time to register these things before the overriding need to pee lit up his brain. He started to move, bad idea. Now he was beginning to leak quite badly. Similar to other drainage systems that he'd had prior dealings with, one leak inevitably led to another and this latest pressing demand, took priority.

Frantically heading towards the bathroom, grasping his tackle in one hand, it struck him in a blinding flash. The onesey! His spare hand fumbled for the zip and yanked at it, only for it to stick solid into his chest hair.

"Ouch, ouch, ouch!" He squirmed as the pain made him want to pee even more. With a desperate timescale now in operation, how could he manufacture the minutes undoubtedly required to remove himself from this onesey, before nature ran its course? A rather uncomfortable vision of what life would be like if he was encased in a figure-hugging flexible toilet, with no flushing system, flashed across his overactive synapses.

'Quick man, think,' Hovis demanded of his brain. 'This is getting urgent, so stop fucking around and find a solution!'

"The shower!" He suddenly gasped, as the small dark patch continued to spread around his crotch and despite all of his best efforts, grew exponentially.

Luckily, due to the ergonomic design employed by the firm that Blue Yonder contracted to design the cabins, Hovis only had a few steps to take, before he was able to open the shower closet and climb in. Even so, by the time he reached it the dark patch had spread down his thighs.

"Oh, thank God," he mewed as the darker area around his crotch, expanded its parameters and he sank to the floor, as much in relief, as anything else.

"Jesus! Where's it all coming from," he commented, grumpily, though without interrupting the flow. 'You're going to have to give it a good wash now,' he thought, as the damp patch spread all the way down his left leg. So, without a moment's hesitation, Hovis reached over, turned the pre-set shower unit on and casually, reached for the shampoo. After he'd liberally applied a few palmfuls of the noxious gunk to the befouled onesey, he lathered it, then rinsed for a few minutes. Hovis then sniffed the damp air to see if he could detect any unwanted, mellifluous odour's wafting by.

When he was totally satisfied that The Big Mig's Onesey was as clean, if not cleaner, than it had been when he'd first taken receipt of the item, he turned the water off and just stood there, dripping.

If he'd found it a difficult item to put on dry, then it was going to be almost impossible to disgorge himself from its jaw's, when wet.

"I'm trapped between a rock and a rubber place," he cried out but only Cheech heard his distressed bleat and as usual, he opened his left eye, just to show willing.

Twenty-nine minutes later, after applying a towel and a futile blow with the hairdryer, which just served to make him sweat even more profusely, Hovis had stopped dripping and now felt confident enough to move around the cabin, without soaking every surface he tarried too long beside. However, his feet were still causing problems. Gravity was still playing its part in this sideshow and he was leaving wet footprints all over the cabin. Now, another imperative was rising in his consciousness. Images he'd seen in the long mirror, visions of Bibendum Rouge, the Giant Red Bug Monster and Foghorn Leghorn were returning to haunt him. Surely it wasn't that bad?

He took another look. No, it was worse....

He was so disappointed by the reflection in the mirror, that he determined to do something more constructive than simply tug at a few selected tight bits of the onesey, where they were digging into his more sensitive, 'man parts'.

'But what?'

Slowly, Hovis realised that any further wrestling with the treasured acquisition was, if anything, a complete waste of time. He was already envisioning an outcome where he could quite possibly be trapped inside it forever. His mind played a video of him still wearing it in his coffin, mourners passing by in cycle onesies as a mistaken mark of respect. He chuckled at the thought, then sighed. The sheer excitement of holding The Big Mig's record breaking uniform in his hands, had blinded him to the blatantly obvious downsides involved in getting this child's flayed skin on and mores to the point, off, his ample figure.

Hovis realised that sweat was his enemy and the use of the hair dryer, to dry the Onesey had been something of a tragic mistake, only serving to make the bloody thing fit his rather plump frame, even more snuggly.

How was he going to get the damn thing off before bedtime?

Perhaps if he just relaxed and allowed himself to calm down, the Onesey would be a little more compliant?

Unfortunately for Hovis, as his prized Onesey dried, it became even more constrictive and he began to consider the dreaded possibility, that he would eventually have to cut himself free from its ever-tightening embrace. His mind envisioned a future where the use of scissors was the only rendition of a merciful release from the Flame Red Onesey's death grip. However, destroying his prize was not on his agenda....Yet!

"It may come to that but right now, I'm thinking there must be plenty of other options to investigate, before any desperate survival measures come into play," he muttered to himself and looked over towards Cheech. "What do you reckon?" He asked the Setter, earnestly. There was no reply from his best friend and Cheech's tail obstinately remained perfectly flaccid. "You're a lot of use," Hovis commented and tried once again to unfasten the Onesey's zip but to no avail. It simply wouldn't budge beyond the top of his chest where it had gorged itself on skin and his increasingly furry man hair. "I'm going to have to come up with something a touch subtler…, or maybe more brutal," he said under his breath and for good measure, gave the zip another hearty tug but once again, it just ate a few more hairs and stuck fast. Hovis squeaked and admitted defeat, at least for the time being and repaired to the kitchen to put the kettle on.

It seemed that any movement of his chubby, nae flabby middle-aged body, caused a certain degree of mature sweating, which in turn simply added to the constriction being applied by the onesey to his increasingly frantic body. Immobility seemed the sensible solution. He would take his coffee into the lounge and relax.

"Looks like we're both going to be spending this evening in front of the telly, watching a selection of remarkably dull fare," he casually said to Cheech as he picked up the TV guide and planned an evening of passivity for himself and his dog.

"Low carb's, low calories, more exercise and moderation in all things," Hovis said considering the image of Bibendum Rouge, then repeated the suggested formula several more times, until it almost became a mantra. "That's the way to do it," he declared and nodded his head towards Cheech, in confirmation. 'First though, I must take a photograph of me wearing Miguel's Onesey for the 'before' image......' With that thought still fresh in his mind, he set about trying to locate the old Kodak instamatic, which if he wasn't mistaken, was still at the back of 'The Elephant Cabinet,' next to the eight-foot African statue, which he called Emily after his aunt, not that she was African or eight foot tall, but she had seemed it to a tiny Hovis.

A quick rummage in the rear of the Indian originated repository, was all he required to locate the old camera and having grasped it in both hands, Hovis headed to the full-length mirror in his bedroom.

Momentarily stepping outside of reality as he quickly entered 'The Lair of The Mirror,' in his mind Hovis saw himself as the true embodiment of a super hero.

"Nobody expects......, The Red Avenger!" Hovis dramatically cried as he burst through the opening and mercilessly punched the defenceless air, which offered zero resistance to his hyper manly ingress. The draft he created, sprung open the wardrobe door and re-exposed the long mirror, pulling him up short. He stared at his reflection in abject disbelief, then raised the camera and looked again through the view finder,

"How did it come to this?" Coherent words failed him.

"Before," he bleated, vainly tightening his abdominal muscles and stuck his chest out but once again, unable to maintain the posture, he succumbed to the inevitable.

"After," he desperately gasped as he surrendered to the growing ache emanating from his overly straining stomach muscles.

"Jesus, I need to lose weight," he said with resignation.

Almost reluctantly, he raised the Instamatic Camera and pointed it towards the bug monster in the mirror and clicked the shutter. 'Flash!' The image was unfortunately captured for posterity. Hovis grabbed the undeveloped shot as it appeared and started waving it around in the air, hoping to speed up its final development.

"Seems the years have caught up with me," he mournfully opined to Cheech and let his stomach muscles relax fully. He took the photo and attached it to the fridge as a reminder for when he strayed from the new low carb diet he'd promised himself. Hovis looked at it and shrugged, 'might work,' he thought.

"Right, well if I want to get this onesey off before bed I can't eat much, for obvious reasons. Drinking more than the absolute minimum is not advisable, or I'll want to pee. So, let's get your dinner Cheech and then…" Hovis tailed off and went to prepare his companions tea, before his own evening of 'nothingness,' began in earnest.

By 8.30 pm, the concept of him sitting down and sharing some of Cheech's 'evening meal' was becoming ever more tantalising. "Time to find something to watch and take my mind off food," Hovis boldly said and headed for his DVD cabinet. After much deliberation he chose one of his favourites, 'Kingdom of Heaven,' then added, 'Schindler's List,' purely because they both contained very little gratuitous eating, so neither was likely to spark any sympathetic hunger pangs. On his way back to the settee he picked up a bottle of cognac and a bell glass, reasoning it would stem his hunger pangs, lubricate his mind and wet his throat without making him desperate to pee.

Hovis poured himself a glass of brandy and settled back to watch the movies. The evening passed quickly, almost as fast as the level of cognac in the bottle dropped. Gradually, Hovis became more and more inebriated and fell asleep on the settee some way through the second movie. When he woke the next morning, he was still in the onesey, it was still welded to his frame, he was desperate to pee and now he had a hangover to boot.

Groaning, he headed for the shower and repeated the peeing and soaping regime from yesterday. Feeling almost human, he grabbed his towelling dressing gown, pulled the hood up and headed for a coffee, or several......

Chapter Eight

Gwendolyn's Grove.

"Say Cheech, how do you fancy one last trip down the valley before the winter sets in and we have to move on? Times running out old son...., it's probably now or never. What d'you say?"

The well-oiled lock on the garden shed opened easily and Hovis stepped inside and looked for Dennis, his Red and Black striped bicycle, which he'd stored safely at the rear of the wooden shed, last weekend. He'd assumed it would be the final occasion he'd ride it before real winter set in and the mountain roads became increasingly treacherous. The frost at this time of year took longer and longer to thaw, until eventually at sometime soon, it became permanent ice until next spring. This was when two wheels became four, as Hovis retrieved his old Volvo from the garage, where it resided for most of the summer.

With relocation looming, if he didn't go now, who knew when he'd be able to ride this way again?

"Come on Cheech," he called as he opened the front gate. "Once more unto the breach!" Hovis cried but then waited for the Red Setter, who was scenting the planter by the porch, to appear at his side.

Cheech just shot past him, flew straight out through the open gate and off down the adopted track that ran by all the corpses of previous cabins; he knew the route by heart.

When Hovis started working for Blue Yonder, his first cabin had been about the size of a modern container and was located much further down The Hill. As he recalled, No.28 tended to flood in winter when the thunderous mountain rains came and poured down to the lake in the valley. Number 37, on the top row had been a great improvement, much bigger with a better view and no flooding!

He could see Cheech was already about one hundred yards further down the slope, chasing and as usual, failing to catch a Grey Squirrel, which outfoxed him completely.

"Tally-ho!"

Hovis pushed off and Dennis quickly picked up speed, as they rolled easily down the hill towards Cheech, who was still rummaging around, totally convinced that the infernal Grey Squirrel was still somewhere in the area. In fact, it was sitting on a bare branch of one of the many Rowan trees that peppered the hill, watching as Cheech worked himself up over a cunning prey, which had escaped long ago.

"Come on, then," Hovis said, as he sped past Cheech. "I thought you said you wanted to come on this romp?" He let a slight chuckle escape, as he rolled on towards what he called, 'Gwendolyn's Grove.'

"Woof!" Cheech didn't require a second invite, he simply turned and ran after Hovis, barking excitedly, as if he was chastising him for leaving him behind.

Applying the brakes, Hovis brought Dennis to a halt and just stood quite still, looking out over the lake, trying to log the view as a mindsnap for future reference.

'Alright, let's go before I start getting all melancholy and ruin the rest of this ride,' he thought and pushed off, allowing gravity to do its job and propel him down the now deserted roadway.

'This may be the last time anybody ever does this...., I mean, unless they develop this area, who's going to take a trip down to The

Grove, or get themselves down to the lakeside for a picnic in the summer, well, other than tourists?' He silently queried. 'Shut up brain!' He admonished himself before allowing the ambience, hanging heavily on the quiet mist, to flow over him.

When he reached the bottom of what everybody who lived on The Hill called, 'The Rat Road,' Hovis stopped again. Once Cheech had ceased skittering around on the loose gravel, he just listened to the empty silence that pervaded the motionless air and sighed deeply. The only sound he could hear was that of the rapidly flowing stream, some one hundred and fifty yards distant.

The A470 was originally constructed to transport Welsh Slate around the world during its glory years of global roofing, but that was then and this was now. The Slate from Snowdonia had been reduced to a tourist attraction; there was just one small mine in the neighbouring valley producing replacement slates and souvenirs. So nowadays, hardly any traffic used it...., just those at Blue Yonder, a couple of farms and some tourists in summer.

When the Blue Yonder Mining Company finally pulled out, he assumed the Rat Road would slowly rot away; in the inclement winter weather it wouldn't take long. At one time, the lower lake had been quite busy in the summer months but cheap flights to sun and sea, had seen all the enterprises that had sprung up along its banks, go into liquidation, gradually withdrawing from the water's edge. At one time, Llyn Garon had rowing boat's and kayaks for the public to hire, even a rather successful Yachting Club used to sail on its waters. On four, or five occasions, the rowing club were invited to the Henley Regatta, on the Thames. However, as the 1960's passed into memory, all that changed and the surface of Llyn Garon was these days undisturbed for most of the year, save for the occasional fisherman.

"Sit and wait," Hovis barked at Cheech, as they both stopped at the roadside and listened for the unlikely sound of any oncoming traffic. 'Nothing,' he thought, clicked his fingers to Cheech and started over the road with the Red Setter obediently beside him.

They were headed for the small, almost invisible gap in the tangled bushes, which Hovis had quite accidentally discovered many years earlier, when a brake failure on his first machine, Gwendolyn, had propelled him across the A470 and on, into and through the shrubbery that had grown up along the edges of the roadway.

Beyond the green leafy barrier, Hovis discovered a small glade. On first appearance, it appeared to be entirely covered in years of discarded pine needles, which gave him a relatively soft landing. As he disentangled himself from a prone Gwendolyn, he was just thankful that he hadn't picked up a puncture, or two for his troubles.

On inspection, there appeared to be a rough track running through this previously undiscovered area of the lakeshore. So, remounting Gwendoline he thoughtlessly followed it, to see where it led. Going from the available evidence, on occasions Cheech was even more foolhardy than Hovis. He charged ahead and his tail soon vanished around a tight curve in the path.

"Follow the dog," Hovis called and stuck his arm out like Superman.

He emerged into a much larger pine strewn glade, paused and slowly became aware that he was alone in this secret wooded enclave. Cheech had disappeared!

He stopped his bicycle and looked over his shoulder, trying to spot the point where he'd entered this secret space but to no avail, the screen of green appeared seamless. There weren't even any tyre tracks on the soft, needle strewn ground that he could use to retrace his passage. Then, there was Cheech to consider. A path seemed to continue on the far side.....

He slowly cycled around the margins of the clearing. It appeared the surrounding trees had completely overgrown what must have been a homestead at some time in the long distant past, but the house, with its attendant sheds and outbuildings, had long gone. Nowadays, only a stone skeleton of its former presence still existed, half buried by mosses, pine needles and fast-growing seedlings.

The air in the glade held a deep silence, one that hinted at an ominous, yet peaceful solitude. An essence of the past permeated the strangely warm breeze, which occasionally wafted through these aged Pines. 'Maybe this place belonged to a Slate Miner and his family, at one time, or another.......'

"I wonder what happened to them?" He asked aloud, just as Cheech came racing back into the glade, his tail wagging and panting in an excited way.

"Squirrel, was it?" Hovis enquired but Cheech didn't reply, he only wagged his tail more furiously when Hovis spoke to him. "Come on then, let's see where you've been," enquired Hovis and pushed off, into the needled detritus littering the pathway in front of him

*

Back in the present, passing through the glade today, had he cared to look up, high between the obscuring trunks of the tall Pines, you could just see No.37, the last log cabin on The Hill; while all around it were the charred corpses of other people's lives. Hovis knew this fate was inevitable for No.37. In a mere few weeks he would be both homeless and jobless, but today he was wearing the Big Mig's Flame Red Onesey and he was still free to dream.

Chapter Nine

Between Tick and Tock.

A t this moment, Hovis was existing in the time between 'Tick and Tock,' his stay of execution only temporary. When he moved out, the company would demolish the last log cabin and unlike the stone, skeletal remains in the glade, all trace of his years here in the mountains would be eradicated, almost in an instant.

Standing astride Dennis in his favourite vantage spot, Hovis looked over to the left, towards Llyn Garon and sighed, heavily. It was on the far bank, somewhere near that solitary Oak tree, that he'd proposed to Heidi Wilkinson. She'd rejected him out of hand and just to make it perfectly clear there was no way back, a few weeks later, she left The Blue Yonder Mining Company and moved to London, in search of brighter prospects, or so she said. Hovis' ego liked to think it was all a ruse to get away from him and make a fresh start somewhere else.

Heidi wasn't the first and she possibly wouldn't be the last female who would utterly fail to fall for his simpering charms. Before Heidi came along, Linda Hughes had been the object of his desires but that had also ended in rejection, as had his steamy affair with Susan Taylor. That liaison had lasted a relatively long time, over one year, in fact three hundred and sixty-seven days to be precise. He smiled as he recalled how it had taxed his energy levels and to be honest, he was quite happy when their sweaty relationship finally ended. Susan wrote him a very pleasant 'Dear John' letter, which stretched over five foolscap pages and then promptly relocated to the company's new Online Sales Office, recently opened in Warrington. Everything had taken a long time with Susan and the extended goodbye letter was no different. Why use only a few words, when a short story would do? She certainly had her charms but there was only so much of a good thing that any normal man could take. Like him, she was a creature of the night but everybody needs to sleep sometimes and Hovis was no exception. The fact that she ended their romp in the grass, saved him from having to do it; which he'd promised himself he would do, just once he'd plucked up the courage. Her missive had arrived in his letterbox one dull Tuesday morning, in late December but he didn't open it until Thursday evening. He'd remembered it as he was sitting down to watch the Ten O'clock News.

"Shit, that letter," he'd groaned, as he attempted to locate it in the mess on the Coffee table. Strangely, after he'd read it, even though he'd wanted the liaison to end, Hovis went through a self-indulgent period of feeling inexplicably sorry for himself. He smiled as he thought of it now.

Beyond the last few tree's, the lonely shore of the lake beckoned and Hovis found himself drawn towards it. So, he dismounted, called for Cheech to come and join him, then made his way to the water's edge and crouching down, touched the mirror like water,

"I make ripples; therefore, I am…"

Reminiscent of a scene from some eminent production of Huckleberry Finn, Hovis made his way to his favourite spot to sit, under a pine tree, in a space between two of its exposed roots, with his leg's stretched out before him and his back comfortably nestled up against the trunk. He stared out across the calm waters of Llyn Garon, to the opposite shore. At that low level, the lake appeared to be huge, even though it was only just over a mile across. From down there, Hovis thought it took on the imaginary appearance of an

American Great Lake……, but with a giant Red Setter having a drink from it!

"Here, Cheech," he called and patted his right thigh, which certainly got the dogs attention and he came bounding towards him, with a really stupid look on his face and catching his owners' melancholy mood, lay down with his head resting on Hovis' lap. A hand was soon stroking his head and he snuggled in to get more comfortable.

"So, this is goodbye," Hovis said, melodramatically, as though the lake gave a damn about his existence. His words dried up as the spirit of the place took his thought's away and deposited them in a dreamscape.

Hovis stretched his arms out, then wrapped one around Cheech, who just grunted contentedly and pressed even harder into his side.

"This is probably the last time, that we'll ever sit here," he quietly postulated, "probably the last," he repeated, as though to give the casual statement some added weight.

The air was thick with the essence of pine, as though there had been an unobserved fresh fall of needles within the last few moments. The unusually ambient temperature of the air induced a sleepiness which he found hard to resist. On several occasions his eyes lazily closed, as his subconscious mind travelled through time and visited random people and places, without him moving a muscle. Cheech gave up the battle first and started to snore, which only made it harder for Hovis to stay cognitive.

The pale, late autumn sun had an unnatural warmth to it, causing a fine mist to lap at the lakes margins and sleep lurked around the edges of this mirage. There was hardly a sound penetrating the stillness of this perfect moment, just a solitary Blackbird, singing a mournful song.

Occasionally, a vehicle could just be heard passing on the road above, heading downwards for one of the conurbation's in The South, or climbing the pass, heading towards one or other of the big Northern cities.

Every so often, Hovis drifted a little too far and awoke with a jolt, which in turn disturbed Cheech, who let out a quietly surprised,

"Yip!"

Then, the fading sound of an engine, lulled them both back towards sleep and time began to slip by.

Fleeting images of people, who hadn't changed one iota since the last time he'd seen them and small pieces of disjointed recollections, swam back and forth in his discorporated mind, adding to this seance of time, passing by in waves. Old friends of both sexes, drifted slowly in and out of focus within this private world, as Hovis drew ever closer to those elysian pastures. The ghost like echo of that now long distant vehicle, was replaced by the insistent growl of what Hovis guessed was a sport's car, going in the same direction. The driver carelessly changed gear and the engine spluttered and protested loudly. It coughed to clear its throat and then, with what sounded to his foggy brain like a renewed determination, set about the climb up to Bangor.

Before Morpheus could carry him away to some other random time, the present day got hold of his arm and led him away to safety.

"Come on Cheech, it's time we started making tracks," he encouraged. "You want some food don't you, well it's not going to happen if we stay down here, now is it?" Cheech answered the word food with a lick of his lips and sprang up, whilst Hovis struggled to disentangle himself from the annoyingly comfortable tree. Now on his feet and rubbing his arse, he looked for Dennis.

'The Menace,' was lying on the ground amidst the mass of old pine needles, exactly where he'd left him. So, with a hearty slap of his thigh and a single note whistle to get Cheech's attention, Hovis walked over and retrieved the red and black striped machine from its bed of needle's, then brushed the saddle to remove any persistent ones. Suddenly, there was a loud blast from an air horn of a truck on the road above, screaming past on its way south.

"Jesus!" He cursed, startled, then tried to see the offending vehicle, as it raced off, towards Swansea or Cardiff. To no avail, it had passed but he could still hear it and by the pitch of that engine, the driver was either desperately trying to make up time, or more fancifully, effecting some kind of getaway.

One last glance towards Llyn Garon and a couple more moments spent in affectionate recollections, only delayed Hovis for a few extra seconds.

"Let's go the long way around, eh kid," he smilingly enquired of his four-legged companion, who quite naturally just woofed in reply. "I thought you'd say that, so let's do it and then we can say a proper goodbye, to an old friend as we pass," Hovis unnecessarily explained and pushed off to the right, heading for 'Bedd-y-Gwen'.

Gwendolyn's grave was marked by a tall straight Pine, which by some miracle, still had the dead body of his once much-loved white bicycle, firmly lodged some thirty feet up in the air, clinging grimly onto its living grave marker by its front forks.

The accident, which created this curious set of circumstances, was an event that Hovis had been trying to forget for the past twenty years. He had recurring nightmares of flying through the air, looking up and seeing a jagged formation in the shape of a tree trunk racing towards him, whilst time held its breath. Within this hiatus, his lightening approach to mutilation, pain and possible death, was only halted when he was a matter of inches away from an excruciating collision and then............, whatever it was, happened?

Maybe it was the simple movement of his head as he grimaced and jerked it to one side that saved his face getting the worst of the smash. Who knew but the Company's Sleep, or in Hovis' case lack of sleep, Therapist; 'Call me Phil' Rowbottom, had said this action was,

"The key to the whole point of these sessions."

Hovis had nodded vigorously and "Umm'd" and "Ahrr'd," in all the correct places, trying to get signed off from this pseudo mental health programme, but there was no escape, not until he'd been through all the scheduled sessions. Many times, he'd thought the end was in sight but 'slightly encouraging,' was all the therapist said. Whilst 'Call me Phil' sifted through the rubbish in his brain for something diagnosable, the real reason for his disturbed nights, slipped silently by. 'Call me Phil' was trained to look for something traumatic in the patients mental set, usually from their youth, so failed to diagnose the 'sheer wonder' in Hovis' abject puzzlement. 'Call me Phil' had quietly moved on to a new victim, long before Hovis was cured of whatever was the 'deeper issue' plaguing his sleeping hours.

The event had seemed like a dream; after his face narrowly missed the tree's gnarled bark, Gwendolyn, his bike, had run straight into the fallen mature corpse of another tree, brought down by the storm of '87. She had been flipped up, tossed Hovis aside mid spin and as he was heading for a collision with the needle strewn ground, 'Gwen,' was flying in the opposite direction.

They both struck their unintentional targets, at almost the same instant. The difference being that he hit the soft ground and after rolling over, pirouetted as if he was gracefully closing an Olympic floor exercise. While 'Gwen,' airborne, had her maiden flight cruelly cut short when she smashed straight into the welcoming branches of a young tree. By a fluke of geometry, she was stuck fifteen feet up in the air with bent forks, twisted wheels and smashed handlebars; a right off.

That event had occurred over twenty years ago and now, even after all this time, there she was, many feet higher up off the ground and obviously still in need of some emergency maintenance, yet still recognisable. Suddenly, Hovis felt sorry for his old steed.

"It won't be long now, until nobody remembers exactly how you got up there and you'll just become another curiosity," he addressed Gwendolyn, attempting to signal his impending departure to her ancient rusting frame. "I'm the last one left on The Hill and now it's my turn to go," he said with a heavy heart. "Blue Yonder promised us a job for life but now they can't get rid of us fast enough. So, I won't be calling by to see you again, Gwen. My time here is almost over." Hovis, then cast one last lingering look upwards and silently said his final goodbyes to the unresponsive crumbling frame of Gwendolyn.

*

Lance Percival's 'Bike U Like' in Bangor, was probably the finest Cycle emporium in the whole of North Wales. So, it was first port of call after Gwendolyn's decision to become a living sculpture. Hovis decided to treat himself to a real killer machine. He chose this eighteen-gear, Black and Red 'Graffiti' model, which cost him the princely sum of £999.00, nearly 20 years ago.

"Keep the change," he facetiously remarked to the assistant, whose work tag claimed was called Dave, as he ostentatiously and very deliberately counted out the one hundred £10 notes and slapped them down on the counter, in front of the amazed shop worker.

Dave, suitably irked, responded in kind, asking Hovis if he wanted the bicycle 'gift wrapping and delivering, or was he in fact, going to ride the machine home?'

"If so, may I say, that Sir will be needing a helmet. However, I think that we'll be able to throw in a cheap one for free," he offered, with a sickly and sycophantic smile on his face.

"Actually," said Hovis, "I'd like the thing delivering to this address," and he furnished Dave with his card giving the location of No.37. "You don't need to gift wrap it, it'll be just fine as it is," he offhandedly added as he headed for the door.

"If you're from the mountains," said Dave looking at Hovis' address on the card. "Won't you be wanting a better-quality helmet as well? Maybe a new pair of gloves too? I notice Sir's are rather worn." Hovis stopped abruptly and turning around, started to make his way back towards Dave at the sales counter.

"You might like to try on a pair of these as well," Dave offered, holding up a pair of this years, new wrap around cycle sunglasses. "I know that it sometimes gets a little 'glarey' up there and you wouldn't want to go over the edge, would you?" He asked, while trying to tempt another sale out of his victim.

"Okay," Hovis mumbled barely audibly. "How much for the better hat, gloves and the shades?"

Dave twiddled his pen in between his fingers and made it appear that he was totting figure's up, "£123 exactly," he replied with a half-smile. "Plus, I'll throw in a couple of reflectors, for free," he added as a further tempter.

There it was again, that magic and very personal number. Was it fate, or simply pure chance? It was obvious that the figure was just randomly made up, so just how and for what reason did Dave choose 1,2 and 3?

"You're a silver tongued divil, Dave," Hovis commented with a wry grin, while counting out the required sum. "Have them all delivered, to my address please. A.S.A.P," he added sternly and walked out of the shop, feeling quite pleased with himself.

*

The legend of the Lance Percival's, was a matter of folk law amongst the Welsh cycling community. They had been there at the very start of it all and toiled endlessly to get bike riding, as it was called by most people, recognised as a real sport and not solely a means of personal transport from A to B, or for casual recreational sojourns.

In 1891 Lance Percival senior organised the very first Snowdon - Cadre Idris - Snowdon, mountain climb and therefore, he was one full year ahead of 'La Doyenne,' the Liege - Bastogne - Liege classic of today. 'The Peaks Race,' or 'El Doublee' as it came to be known, attracted many cyclists over the years it ran. However, the locals considered him to be more than just a touch insane and did their best to forget all about him and the race after he died in 1901, in the second Boer war, after being recruited as an engineer.

Lance Junior had been born a few years earlier and was brought up regaled with stories of his father's cycle exploits and military heroism.

He joined up at the start of the First World War in 1914. He went missing, presumed dead, at the first battle of the Marne. The memorial, which was erected at the end of the war, was placed right in the village centre of Cemaes Bay. The place of his birth ensured his name was included on their War Memorial, which proudly bore the names of eleven other of their finest youth, including one Hywl Monk. On the bottom of the cenotaph there was a plaque, bearing the sanctimonious words, 'The war, to end all wars,' and 'Never again,' in both Welsh and English. Unfortunately, just twenty-three years after it went up, everyone seemed to have forgotten those fine words and The Second World War began.

In reality, Lance had been injured and lost his memory. It was many years later that he finally recalled his past and returned home, only to be shunned by the villagers who didn't believe his story and reckoned he'd deserted. So, Lance took himself off to live in Bethesda in the mountains, where he re-established El Doublee, which he only rode one single time. Unfortunately, due to his age, too much wine and Welsh cheese, he failed to finish the Haute Category climb up Cadre Idris and he was forced to withdraw through an onset of ferocious cramp. In his later life, the story went;

"I was lying in a respectable fifth place and closing on the leading group, when suddenly.............!" At that point, he would take a very pregnant pause to build up the tension another notch. Then, he would stick his right leg straight out in front and grab his thigh in mock cramp. "Where was I?" He'd ask, knowing full well, just to draw his audience in. "Oh yeah," he'd glance around to check everyone was listening, before continuing with the increasingly bogus tale. "Well anyway, I was in so much pain, that I couldn't even think straight." He paused again, to give his audience enough time to fully appreciate, his ancient anguish. "I lost control of my wheel's and down I went," Lance soliloquised, fully exploiting the tension that he himself was building. "I left half of my leg up there, on those jagged rocks that litter the summit of The Cadre." Then after a deep dramatic breath, he would finish with the statement, "That devil of a mountain ended my cycling career and I've cursed it ever since." Then he would appear to relax, pick up his almost empty glass and drain it. He was of an age when storytellers still had a value in society and a good story was rewarded with another glass.

Shortly after that cramp ridden debacle, during his first running of El Doublee, he opened the shop on Bangor High Street and made a decent living from the ever-increasing public fascination with bicycle's. His cycle sales and rentals provided him with a more than adequate income, until his unfortunate 'second death' in 1947, when a sudden shower caused his glasses to steam up, the road to become slippery and he'd gone over the edge of 'The Kid,' falling two hundred and fifty-six feet to his untimely demise. The spot where his machine left the road, was for many years marked with a sturdy wooden cross but somebody stole it in the sixties and it only recently had been replaced with a heritage plaque.

Over time, the two Lances were amalgamated in the public mind, and Lance junior became known as the Father of Welsh Cycling, an error which Lance junior did nothing to dispel, as it was good for business. Consequently, a tourist pamphlet later offered the reader a candid history of Welsh cycling and pointed out the spot, where the Father of Welsh Cycling, Lance Percival, had shuffled off his mortal coil. Hovis, had visited the spot but felt it to be a little disappointing.

The final El Doublee race, was run in the autumn of 1939, just a few months before Germany invaded Poland and the world went to war again. That last outing was won by Lionel Hewson, a promising rider from the Wirrell, who was unfortunately killed during the allied landing's in Normandy, on June 6th 1944. He was cut down by a machine gun nest on the road to Caen and sadly, after the conflict ended, there was no appetite for something as trivial as a bike ride through Snowdonia. So, El Doublee was consigned to the waste bin of history.

Even though the race that his forebears had instigated was now defunct, Perrin, Lance juniors only son, kept both the shop and the family name alive on Bangor high street. In the passing years, 'Lance Percival's, Bike-U-Like,' had become a local tourist attraction and it was almost unimaginable that it could ever close.

Local legend's apart, Hovis and Cheech, still had to ride back up the Rat Road to No.37. He was hungry! His stomach gurgled its dissatisfaction. In an attempt to quell it he took a drink from his bottle, which just triggered an inconvenient response from his bladder. He reacted hastily, looking around for a place to relieve himself but that was the least of his problems. There was the small matter of Miguel Indurain's Onesey to take into consideration. 'I knew that third mug of coffee was a mistake,' he frowned.

'At least I don't want to poop,' he chuckled inwardly, as a dark patch around his groin silently expanded and appeared to dribble down his left leg.

'Well, pissing down your own leg was an option I suppose,' Hovis thought ironically, as his shoe began to fill up and his foot grew warmer.

"Come on, let's get back home," Hovis said to Cheech. "You got any idea what time it is?" He asked, never expecting an answer, after all Cheech didn't wear a watch. So, he looked up into the pale milky sky, trying to locate the Sun. He didn't really know what he was doing but he'd seen Gary Cooper do it once in a Western and seeing as the Sun appeared to be roughly overhead, Hovis hedged his bet's.

"I reckon it's around midday....ish, so let's get back up the hill and get some lunch inside us, eh?"

Silence from Cheech.

"What d'you say 'bout that?"

Cheech wagged his response and Hovis, now satisfied, set off.

When they reached the A470 crossing point, he dismounted and looked down the long slope of the road as it swept away to the South and then up as it climbed past The Glyder's, on its torturous route to the North. It appeared to be clear for as far as the eye could see. Nothing moved in either direction as they slowly walked across the empty roadway and made their way up to the tarmac trackway, that led home.

Hovis remounted Dennis, snapping his feet securely into the toe studs, to aid his climb up the Rat Run. Where that name had originated, was something of a mystery to Hovis; in all the years that he'd been using it, he'd never seen a rodent of any kind, neither running, nor squashed upon its surface.

As they began the final climb towards home, it seemed the two intrepid explorers could possibly be the last two living entities in the whole of Wales, well at least this valley. There wasn't a sound to be heard anywhere, aside from the rather heavy breathing, which was emanating from them both, as they climbed the steep hill at the end of another lengthy ride.

Chapter Ten

In Pursuit of Glory.

A s he approached the last but one turn on the climb to No.
37, the faint sound of his radio permeated the still autumn
air. This tradition of leaving the radio bleating away
whenever he went out, with or without Cheech, began after a passing
observation from postie Lee Kelso; who swore it was a great
deterrent to thieves.

Lee had inexplicably volunteered for the 'Mountain
Monster,' as it was referred to by the guys at the 'Bangor Bunker.' It
may have been a pleasant enough delivery run in the summer
month's but the weather in the spring and autumn could prove
unpredictable at best, often washing away the lanes in flash floods.
Winter was always a frigid time in the mountains and the ice could
prove treacherous. Every year it claimed lives and just because the
day may have started bright and clear at sea level, didn't necessarily
mean the same thing was true at a thousand feet, half way up a track
leading to some godforsaken and utterly isolated farmhouse. In
winter, at that altitude, it wasn't unusual to have to contend with ice,
snow, dense fog and a howling gale that seemed hell bent on wiping
the landscape clear of all natural impediment's, simultaneously.

However, this was Lee Kelso, born on a stormy night to
Mary and Dougie Kelso on their sheep farm located on the tip of The
Mull of Kintyre. It was called, 'High Clachaig' and it was a good
few miles up a dirt track, often blocked by snow from mid-
November until the end of March. Lee made the move to North
Wales when the opportunity at the Bangor site appeared, quite
unexpectedly, in The General Post Office Internal Gazette of

October 1991. He found it during one of his annual check-ups with the GPO's doctor. As usual, he'd started reading from the back of the magazine and there it was, hiding away in the 'Hard to fill vacancies.'

"Rugged mountain men wanted," it read.

'That's me,' Lee boldly asserted to himself and for good measure, added 'Rugged, was my Mother's middle name,' then, laughing out loud, nearly choked as he almost swallowed a whole Trebor Extra Strong Mint. 'Shit, that could have turned ugly,' he spluttered but couldn't resist the desire to laugh again.

*

The radio broadcast, now permanently tuned to Radio Two purely to hear if The Festers were played again, became ever clearer as Hovis drew closer to No.37.

"And don't forget matey's, this is Ken Alexander and I'm coming at you, loud and proud, on 88 - 91 on the FM wavelength. So, get yourselves there, on the dial pronto, because it's time for our new competition, the one we're calling, 'Reheat the hit.'"

"Oh, fucking great," Hovis gasped, as he approached the front door of his cabin. 'Can't wait,' he sarcastically thought, as he propped Dennis up against the wall.

"So here it is," said Ken in a very, 1960's and slightly Tony Blackburnish kind of way. *"The first rewarmed tune, from way back when and after all these years, it's back again"* he excitedly proclaimed. At that point, Ken turned up the music playing in the background, before he continued with his mundane announcement.

"Yes Werlitzerino's, from a time before the Earth cooled; it's The Fester's, with their only smash, ''I Want you, Love.., Want me too, Love.' And you're hearing this once again, on The Big T...W...O."

Each letter individually and perfectly pronounced, so as not to confuse the stations ageing listener's, he continued with his antiquated delivery,

"Psychedelic-ic-ic, baby," he declared and turned up the echo effect. *"Far out and solid,"* he gushed as the keyboard cut in and the opening refrain started, with a jingle jangle guitar and the immortal words,

"There's someone special, out there in the stars......"

Ken Alexander, sounding almost ecstatic, cut back in enthusiastically,

"Pretty groovy, eh kids. They don't make 'em like this anymore and if you want to hear it again tomorrow, all you guys out there in Radioland have to do, is vote for it in our listener's poll and remember, it's The Fester's, with their only hit, 'I Want you, Love.., Want me too, Love.'"

"Oh, the ignominy," Hovis muttered. 'Fancy being reduced to this?' He thought. 'Now we're just another forgotten band, with another forgotten single, released on a long defunct label. Jesus Christ, we've gone from The John Peel Show, on late night Radio One, to Ken Alexander's Lunchtime Regatteaux on Radio Two!'

Even so, he was still going to phone in and vote for it. After all, when your band's been gone for thirty odd years, you need all the publicity you can get.

"Well Cheech, old son," wheezed Hovis, as he closed the door to number 37, "that was a hard pull up from the lake but it was worth it, eh?"

The Red Setter, just unceremoniously pushed past him to reach his water bowl and slake his thirst.

Then, Ken was speaking again,

"Today, The Fester's go up against 'Aphrodite's Child' and their classic tune, 'Rain and Tears'. And don't forget, matey's, only you can decide who's going to win that clash of the moribund monsters."

"Jesus, people actually get paid for this?" Hovis followed Cheech inside.

Ken Alexander was still blithering on as Hovis closed the front door and made his way towards the bathroom. At times like this, when need greatly exceeded ability, expediency came to the fore and pure logic took over. The effort involved in climbing the Rat Road home, had made Hovis sweat quite profusely and even the concept of getting 'The Big Mig's Onesey' off in time, was so ridiculous that it made him laugh, which made him leak. He looked down towards his crotch and there it was again, a small dark patch, spreading inexorably through capillary action.

"Shite," he half groaned disappointedly and abandoned any pretence of getting naked, before stepping into the shower. 'Three times in 24 hours, that must be some kind of record,' he mused as he stepped under the hot jet and got the Onesey lathered up.

'I wonder how many other people, have done exactly this same thing?' He thought, whilst giving his genitals an extra dollop of shampoo for good measure, before making sure the Onesey got a good rinsing.

After last night and the previous fiasco at the lake, Hovis had taken a little time to consider the practical options when the thorny problem of rapid removal of the time trialing uniform, reared its ugly head. Apart from cutting the damn thing off, which he wasn't willing to do, not seeing how much it cost him, so far he'd got nothing.....

"How the fuck do I get out of this Latex prison cell before I need to poop!?" He yelled but nobody could hear him. Hovis began looking around for anything that could be of assistance in his bid to be free.

Nothing was overlooked.

He even had a fallback position. If the worst, came to the worst, then he would use the old Moulinex hair dryer again and give Miguel Indurain's Onesey a blow dry, but on the cool setting this time. The only flaw in this plan, was that he had no idea whether the accursed garment would get even tighter under the duress of rapid cool air drying; he could do without compounding the problem.

'The Moulinex Conjecture,' was a risky option but unless he came up with another plan, it was the only option bar scissors he'd got left in his playbook.

"No wonder that somebody or other, decided to be rid of this thing. It's cursed and a lot more trouble than it's worth," he grumped, under his breath. The thought of the Onesey passing from hand to hand, after each owner wore it just the once, before they encountered exactly the same circumstances as he was enduring right now, ran like a film in his head.

Excitement was quickly replaced by confusion, as the new owner attempted to actually wear the damn thing. Their horror and disappointment as they finally viewed themselves in the mirror. The cycle ride wearing said onesey, once only and everything else was just self-perpetuating history. The next thought, that jumped the queue and pushed its way to the front of the line, was back to the eternal showering inquisition.

'How many people have pissed themselves in it before they could remove the monstrosity?' That left field enquiry was quickly followed by the utterly pointless concept of trying to work out the number of 'Pisser's,' who had previously befouled this annoying but greatly revered piece of cycling memorabilia. It was a piece of statistical nonsense that his number addicted brain leapt upon.

To work this out, he was going to need something to eat, a drink, a quiet place to sit and

"A little warmth," he said out loud. What he'd spotted was the ray of sunshine illuminating the rear patio. It had been built as a sun trap and it's windless, undisturbed environs could often be several degree's warmer than the rest of the garden. He stepped out onto the patio,

"Well, that's two out of four demands met," he said pompously, to nobody. Hovis went inside and twenty minutes later, after both he and Cheech had eaten some lunch, emerged with a steaming mug of coffee, the radio and his iPad. Then, having selected his berth on the sun warmed stones, he started to draw up an estimated number of owners, which he hoped would provide him with the average number of anonymous Pisser's he was dealing with. He agreed to ignore the estimate of an estimate quandary.

"Thirteen years, at roughly nine resales per year and then add six for ill luck and you get a figure of?" He stopped there, to check his calculations and then after a moment's consideration, blurted out, "One Hundred and Twenty-Three!"

"Jesus, that's a lot of piss," exclaimed Hovis, sniffing the air around the Onesey for traces of incriminating evidence. "No wonder the thing has baggy knees!" He absentmindedly smoothed out the stretches around the knee of the now drying outfit. The sun was in effect, naturally testing the principals that the whole of 'The Moulinex Conjecture,' hung from. The stone slabs of the patio gave off a lot of radiated warmth and steam began to rise from the onesey. Hovis watched, fascinated,

"And I thought it was almost dry!"

It seemed there was a good deal more moisture retained in the fabric of the onesey than he could ever have guessed. "Shit, I could be here all afternoon if I leave it to natural convection," he complained bitterly and started dabbing at it with his towelling robe. "Once I've got you off you're going back on the market! Some other victim of your undoubted charms, can find out the hard way, that you're just not worth it." That emphatic proclamation, was followed by another of his father's 'that's that' kind of a "Humph," as Hovis folded his arms and nodded authoritatively towards the adoring crowd his imagination instantly arrayed before him.

Clearly inspired, he gave reign to a very passable 'Dear, dear Larry,' impersonation, complete with all the over exaggerated arms and pathos he could muster from his days studying grade one melodrama.

"Alas, poor Yorick, I knew him well," he pontificated, while apparently talking to his right hand,

"So, what do you think of it so far?"

To which he responded,

"Rubbish!"

"Well, it seems that this is it, old son," Hovis informed the Red Setter, settling back on the patio with his iPad and his radio. "We're residents of this secluded spot, for at least the next hour, so let's make the most of it, eh?" Cheech, tired from his run, was perfectly content to spend his afternoon, on the patio, drifting in and out of sleep. "Do the front first?" Hovis said quietly, as he lay back on the sun lounger and closed his eyes against the glare, listened to the music and daydreamed about the past and what the future may hold, for a plump, middle aged, redundant mining company accountant.

'Not much,' he fatalistically considered as he passed, 'steaming' into the broken and twitchy, semi sleeping stage.

"The world, is hardly going to miss me when I'm gone, now is it?" He grumpily mumbled to the universe and slunk into an uneasy doze.

When he briefly awoke to turn over onto his stomach, Hovis smiled internally as the warmed front section of the onesey, pressed itself into his chubby midriff and the slightly damp cooler back, was exposed to the soft afternoon sunshine. Rapidly, Hovis warmed up and as he did so, he fell back into his still broken but rather satisfying nap and steam began to rise from the rear of the onesey.

On the radio, Ken Alexander had given way to Pete Jones, who was doing his utterly harmless afternoon slot, which normally ran right up to the rush hour, when Dougie Newton took over with his inexplicably popular brand of inoffensive, 'Dad Rock,' to smooth out the listeners often extended passages home. He attempted, though not always successfully, to get them to their chosen destinations with the fewest number of bumps in their personal roads and with the lowest incidents of road rage possible in the chaotic outgoing traffic, or 'Bangor Stampede' as the locals called it. Whether it was crossing the two Bridges onto Anglesey, or passing through what some of the more irreverent locals referred to as, 'The Princess Diana Memorial Tube.' In both cases, the problem was the same creating the inevitable problem of tailbacks.

Lying there on the patio, drifting in and out of a semi sleeping state was very pleasant but it was just wasting precious time. Hovis only had until the end of the month to sort out some kind of a future for Cheech and himself. This thought nagged at him as Peter Jones spun Jethro Tull's, 'Living in the past.'

"Well, we're going to follow that one with today's winner of the band face off from Ken Alexander's show, here's……."

Suddenly, there were The Fester's, back from the grave once again......

'Wow! We beat Aphrodite's Child! Well, who'd have thunk it?' Hovis thought, as he sat up and reached across the stone slab, which apart from the odd design flaw, had become a useful outside coffee table.

"Come to Daddy," he somewhat creepily said to the iPad. Mister Kelso had said something about going to YouTube and seeing if there was a copy of 'I Want you Love.., Want me too, Love,' available on the site but that was in connection with bootlegging the track and burning it to a cd. That was a side of life which had passed Hovis by and he had gone straight to memory sticks and his iPod. During those years when the CD Player was a gift from God, he'd been working to climb the company ladder and secure his future. It was only when he'd obviously plateaued and the promotions had dried up, that he got back into music in any serious way.

He didn't hold out much hope when he began the search but soon enough, there it was: The Fester's, 'I Want you, Love.., Want me too, Love.' It had incurred only 239 likes and 26 anti's but that was quite an encouraging beginning. 'Hmm I wonder what this fan video is like…' He clicked play…. A series of live stills began to accompany the old acoustic intro and Preston's sleazy keyboard cut in, which had always heralded the entrance of Poe, from behind the black curtain hanging at the back of the stage.

"Dumm, der dumm dumm," mouthed Hovis, as his Bass introduced itself into the mix. At this juncture, he was playing Air Bass and his fingers seemingly had an instinctive life of their own.

Now, Poe began to sing.

"Oh wow, listen to that!" Hovis, smiling, let his fingers slip easily over his nonexistent Bass guitar. "Shit, that girl could give a statue a hard on," he said and laughed out loud. 'Wow look at that girl…. Shit! Look how young I look… And thin!'

Hovis continued playing his air bass.

'It would be nice to see her again, after all this time,' he mused and then remembering what Lee had said, 'I wonder if she'd be interested in coming to one last get together?' He continued playing and watching the video, which had been lovingly stitched together with live footage, stills of the band and memorabilia by someone called Festerette. In the past thirty years, he couldn't remember ever having read anything about Poe, which saddened him. He'd been so sure she would be a success at anything she'd wanted, maybe he'd missed something?

He still wasn't quite dry, so he decided to spend the time searching for any trace of Poe and the other members of the band, online. 'Shit, I hope none of them are dead…..'

Chapter Eleven

Sweat and Patchouli.

Only Poe Pouree and Viv Albertine, had ever had that kind of effect on him. It would surely be a sad day, if they were both beyond reach. The Fester's had played a show with The Slit's once and to be honest, got blown off stage in about twenty seconds flat. He'd run into Viv in the corridor, as her band came off stage and all he could remember about that gig was how erotic she looked all bathed in sweat and smelling of Patchouli oil. He subconsciously drew the air in through his nose, he swore he could still smell her.

'Pleasant thoughts of days gone by,' he mused, as he began to type the Fester's into the search engine. Over the years, he'd somehow forgotten the deep mesmerising timbre of Poe's voice and he noted that it had the same effect on him now, as it had all those years ago. Alongside her siren song, he'd always had to deal with the endless trouble her body created in his trouser region. When she slithered around on stage, Hovis couldn't take his eyes off her and there was no doubt he'd almost lost his timing on many occasions.

Poe used to hit the stage completely oiled up, wearing very little in the way of clothing. He'd often watched the lad's pressed up against the stage, take a step backwards as she slid towards them. Maybe this was the reason for his lifelong desire for sweat soaked ladies, who smelled strongly of Patchouli?

"Down boy," he commanded shrilly, as the onesey grew a little tighter in a sensitive region but his body was taking absolutely no notice of his orders.

'This is all very well but I could be doing something a darned site more useful, while I'm drying out than thinking about women as they once were. Unless something miraculous happens your gonna have enough time for tripping in the past.... Now ain't the time. So, snap out of it!' His fingers didn't listen, they often didn't.

'The Fester's+80's British alternate band,' was placed in the search box and then.........he hesitated. 'Maybe it's better, not to know,' Hovis thought. 'What if it's worse, than I imagined?'

In reality, he was simply afraid to discover that something awful had happened to Poe; like she was living with some lucky bloke and had a couple of sprogs back at home. Though, on the up side, there might well be a recent photograph of this fantasy female and it would certainly fail to live up to his ridiculous expectations and put an end to this useless fantasy.

"You've come this far, so there's no point in chickening out now," he expounded, purely to bolster the decision he'd already made. "Nothing ventured, nothing gained," Hovis theatrically 'thesped' and then, in one flowing movement, dramatically clicked on the 'Open,' icon and shut his eyes.

"Ninety-Eight."

"Ninety-Nine."

"One Hundred." He childishly counted and then opened his eyes again and looked at the screen.

This was better than he could have hoped for, there were five different destinations on offer, so in typical accountant style, he started at the top and slowly worked his way down the list, reading every word and absorbing the information, in case there was ever a future need to be precise.

'Jesus Man, you never used to be like this. Sure, you were solid but aren't all the best Bassist's?' He asked himself, knowing what the answer would be, even before he'd made the rhetorical enquiry.

"We've got a fan club?" he incredulously asked, as the first site informed him that The Fester's had a small but loyal following, that had never wavered in their belief that one day the band would take their rightful place in the pantheon of the truly greats.

"Perhaps a touch overstated but I won't pretend it's not appreciated," he said in his very best, 'Elvis in the bath,' voice. Below, there was an address, which somewhat confusingly read, contact Rita Metermaid57@ The Larches, Acacia Avenue, Whitehaven, Cumbria. There was also a telephone number but by then, he'd lost interest and had moved on to the Wikipedia posting.

This was more the kind of thing he'd been hoping to find. It contained section's that the compiler referred to as, 'A candid history.' There was also a Bibliography and that was followed, by a naturally short Discography but his real interest lay in the opening, 'General Information' section. He was already aware of the past, what Hovis actually wanted to find out, was what had become of the other members of the band, during the past thirty, or so years.

Just seeing their names in print, made his heart skip a beat.

His eyes slid across the page, starting just below the less than flattering photograph of the band, which for some reason, he could remember being taken by Les Tomlinson; who at the time was considered to be climbing up the international rating's. Many in the business, had tipped him to soon be challenging the doyen, Annie Leibowitz, for the cover of The Rolling Stone Fifteenth Anniversary of The Woodstock Festival edition.

Les, was unfortunately killed some years later, in a suspicious James Dean like 'accident,' on the High Wycombe Off ramp. At the time, he had been on his way to do a shoot with Transvision Vamp, before their first appearance on The Tube.

Images of Wendy James now flashed across his mind and he sighed deeply, but not because of the unfortunate and suspicious demise of 'The new David Bailey, in waiting,' whom as it would later be revealed at his autopsy, had ingested enough 'Speed', to drop a horse. The Coroner had stated,

"It was a miracle, that he could drive at all with this amount of high-grade Amphetamine Sulphate in his system." On the street, the concoction that Les had chosen to lead his suicidal dance, was colloquially known as 'Pink Frost.' A forerunner of Crystal Meth, it was remarkably popular on the music scene in the early Eighty's.

Hovis smiled to himself and shook his head ruefully as he recalled those lost woe begone days and continued to scan for present-day information, but disappointingly found none. He would have to think again.....about everything.....

Hovis was confused and disturbed by the oncoming deadlines in his life. During all his years with Blue Yonder, he had never had to take so many things into consideration. From the day that he'd started the job, the company had always taken care of all the mundanities of life. The free housing, Internet n tv, free heating and lighting together with the generous personal allowance and above all, the wages that accrued for the efforts that he and the hundreds of others had put in for the firm, were slowly but inexorably drawing to a close.

There was always a certain strange sense of loss and loneliness, which accompanied these strands of thought and he found these chaotic random memories of a rather foggy past, were intruding on his waking life with increasingly regularly as his final day approached.

"Not many days left," he said to Cheech, who again ignored him. "Humph, your no use!" Hovis' mind snapped back to the present......

'Now, where else can I look for the guys?'

He'd opened a Facebook account some years previously but had rarely visited it, as he found he had very little time for the trivia and the troll's that infested social media. He didn't care what stranger's thought about X, Y, or Z and that wasn't going to change any time soon but on thinking about it, if he was ever going to find out if the other members of The Fester's were still alive, then Facebook was probably a useful tool. He searched for each band member, using the only names he knew, to see if they had a page but found none. Disappointed he went to strategy B and returned to his own page.

"What would you put?" He enquired of his canine colleague, without ever expecting to receive, or adhere to anything that he may propose.

Numbers were Hovis' forte, not words. "What about a direct approach?" He suggested and began with the line,

'Were you in The Fester's? If you weren't, do you know the whereabouts of Allan Exit, Araf Slow, Preston Lancashire, or Poe Pouree? I'm Hovis Monk and I've got a proposition for them. Please contact me ASAP by private message if you can be of any assistance.'

Then, as a rider, he added,

'Listen to the Ken Alexander show, on Radio Two, tomorrow lunchtime. All of you latent Lurcher's may be pleasantly surprised.'

Now, in a state of near euphoria over the ease with which the message had been constructed, Hovis congratulated himself again, just in case he'd failed to fully appreciate his own genius. 'See that wasn't so hard, was it,' he chuckled and looked up at the ever-darkening clouds, gathering on the mountains. He glanced back at his message, then added,

'Don't forget, all you Lurchers out there, to vote for The Festers @ Ken Alexander on Radio TWO! Let's blow those challengers off stage!'

Then, after another quick read through he added a photo of the band on stage in their glory days and hit post. As an afterthought he quickly went to YouTube, copied the link to the single and added it in the comments to his post. 'Cool,' he thought and smiled.

Now, all he had to do was wait for the replies to come flooding in.

"Yeah right," he fatalistically commented, as he rose, gathered his things and made his way, slowly and calmly back into No.37. He was as dry and cool as he was going to get and the sun was sinking rapidly.

He had a pressing appointment with Miguel Indurain's slightly soiled but perfectly serviceable Flame Red Onesey, for the removal of said item from his chubby person.

Visions of himself getting fatter n fatter and the suit getting tighter and more threadbare by the year filled his mind. No, it wouldn't do to end up looking like a potential victim, in a trussed, red marshmallow style, fetish suit!

Chapter Twelve

Flames to fame!

There was an ugly truth forming in his head, as he made his way inside the log cabin. He just had to have one last look at himself wearing The Big Mig's Onesey, before he put it back on the market.

'Perhaps when I was younger, I might have got some real use out of this thing but now……,' he thought defeatedly, as he made his way back to the scene of his major deflation. The full-length mirror was still exposed on the back of the wardrobe door and it drew him towards it like some kind of humiliation magnet. The memory of those baggy knee's and that middle-aged man gut, taunted him. Perhaps he'd look a little more toned after his enforced overnight diet and long cycle ride.

No.

Then it occurred to him that if he took a selfie he could photoshop the result, add himself alongside the Big Mig in the same uniform.

"Cool…." He muttered and grabbed his iPhone.

"Before!" He said with authority, then just let everything relax, he even buckled at the knees and slumped his shoulders, to increase the 'Slob Effect'. Hovis snapped a quick selfie of the hideous vision in the mirror. Then, with determination he straightened his knees and stood to attention, then commanded, as if it were an official parade ground order,

"After."

He attempted to tighten, both his abdominal muscles and his buttock's in the one movement. He soon realised it was going to have to be one, or the other. Tightening a flabby gut was one thing but the saggy arse was a step too far. Mere optimism was no substitute for the ravages of the ageing process. His attempt to multi task went down in flames when he failed to hold his breath at the crucial moment and voluminously farted, just before he struck the requisite pose. In one amazingly smelly instant, his entire facade collapsed into one of wobbling cherry jelly as he shuddered with laughter.

"Cheech, how could you!" He cried, desperately shifting the blame for the green gas filling the room. 'Hmm, better get this thing off sooner rather than later, smells like a sign of things to come…..'

Cheech raised his head, his nose wrinkling with distaste, then did a quick exit from the bedroom.

"You might well run…," Hovis called after him with faux disdain.

Alone, Hovis decided it was probably best to start the process, by doing the obvious things first; so, once again he carefully gripped the front fastening zip and pulled. There was only a minute movement of the fastener, before it stuck once again in his chest hair and in frustration he grabbed the collar with one hand and gave it a good yank with the other.

"Aye Caramba!" The pain that accompanied this rather rash action, brought tears to his eyes. He expelled another cry of "Ummph" and with that gritted his teeth and determinedly gave the zipper another experimental tug, until his grasping fingers just slipped off the slider. He wheezed through the pain accompanying the 1cm increase in the total length of a newly abraded chest hair. Surely, it would only be a matter of time before the slider jammed completely on its diet of skin and hair, trapping him forever within its elasticated confines? The prospect filled him with horror as his stomach gurgled and the need to poop became more critical.

"Think!" He commanded. 'I need more purchase on the slider, something so I can yank it down more quickly……'

"A coat hanger!"

'Yes! Hook it onto the slider! Yes! It might just work…..'

His eagerness to actually put the Onesey on, had caused this situation in the first place. That triumphant and satisfying 'Zuzzy' sound, as he'd yanked the slider tab up, had blinded him to the fact that in his act of impatience, he'd managed to entangle a long strip of his bodily hair within the fastener's mechanism. With the hanger now hooked through slider, Hovis took a few deep breaths and prepared to go to Def Com One. Closing his eyes, he readied himself for the exquisite agony he knew would erupt from his chest area, once he resumed the struggle with 'Zippy'.

"No pain, no gain," he rather unconvincingly stated. Then, grasping the hanger firmly with one hand and the Onesey's collar with the other, he took another deep breath, screwed his eyes up even more tightly and sprang into determined action. With one mighty yank, he tore the Zippy all the way down, revealing his hirsute chest now sporting a well-defined bald line, running from the start of his neck, to below his waist. From there it passed conveniently through the exact centre of his pubic region, dividing the hair in this rather delicate area, into almost two equal sections.

Yet Hovis knew nothing of this.

Hovis was doubled over, hands on knees, eyes watering, squeaking and gasping for breath as the pain seared through his mind like a flame thrower.

"Fucking Hell that HURT!!!" He wheezed and he wobbled, as his head suddenly felt very light. For a few crucial seconds, he was entirely at the mercy of his vestibular region, until it rebalanced itself.

Years before, he'd learnt that fighting with his body's natural processes was a waste of time, so Hovis let it out and let it go......flopping back onto the bed like some deflated luft ballon.

Staring up at the anaglypta ceiling, he was suddenly assaulted by Cheech jumping on the bed to check he was alright.

"Ooumph! Cheech....Get off me......" his words became unintelligible as Cheech smothered him in excitable dog fur and wet noses. Then, like all over excited Setters, he jumped off and ran to fetch his softie toy for Hovis to play with.

Momentarily alone again, his senses rebalanced as he traced the patterns in the ceiling paper. Calmer, breathing easily, he relived the single vicious Zippy movement and gently stroked his freshly depilated stripe. Carefully unhooking the coat hanger, he thought of being a kid again, when it was commonly thought that the best way to remove a sticking plaster, was to rip it off in one movement, suffering a single moment of intense pain, rather than carefully teasing the Elastoplast slowly away from the surface.

"Guess I'm still a ripper then.....," he said, looking down the length of his mutilated torso with gritted teeth and a rather sick smile on his lips. "Free at last but at what cost?" He idly mused as he peered at the white stripe running down his torso, already turning an inflamed shade of pink. "That's going to hurt later on but it's worth it...... Free....Free at last!" He cried theatrically, sat up and took a deep intake of cool air, just as Cheech returned with his soft duck. Hovis reached down to pick it up and throw it......

"UhOh, toilet!"

Luckily, extracting himself from the rest of the Onesey, was a relatively simple process and fifteen minutes later, he was stepping out of the shower preparing to hang it up on the clothes rack to dry. Hovis didn't quite trust in 'Head & Shoulder's' ability to cleanse the item completely, so it required a few sniff's, just to see if any trace of Aux de Urine still clung to it. Nope, nothing but that vaguely medicated anti dandruff shampoo aroma...he smiled his satisfaction as he applied a little salve to his increasing red Onesey wound.

"Now for that food you were promising yourself for most of last night" he declared, slipping his green robe on and made for the kitchen. He'd spent most of the previous night, lying on his settee, getting drunk and watching his two chosen movies and a selection of old television programmes, trying hard to avoid any mentions of food but Eva Green alone, was insufficient distraction to stop the rumbling growing ever louder and by lunchtime Hovis had succumbed to several rounds of toast.

The sound of Pete Jones was still on the radio, only now he seemed to be having an argument with some listener, about the singing voices of Kylie Minogue and Natalie Imbruglia.

"Like it matter's," he glibly said, as he turned the grill pan on and found the pack of 'home made' beef-burger's that he'd bought at Premier last week. 'Blodwyn The Butcher's,' was an in-store franchise but they produced the finest everyday burger's available, anywhere within easy reach. Going all the way to Bangor for a few supposedly, 'Home Made Burger's', was generally out of the question. On top of that, for quite a while now he'd doubted the veracity of the name being used by the obviously large and faceless chain, who called themselves 'Blodwyn The Butcher's'. That old Welsh nome de plume, gave off a strong sense of tradition to the people who chose to shop at their emporium. Yet, there was no butcher to be seen, just one woman who worked behind the counter in the 'local' store and her name, he knew because he'd asked her, was Noreen.

Hovis had a weakness for these tough, 'couldn't give a shit' kind of women, whom he just took it as read, swore at the dinner table and farted at will, no matter how genteel the company was. They showed no man any respect and didn't care who knew it. When he'd been younger, all the virginal lad's he knew had experienced their first sexual encounter with one of them and very few had any complaints.

However, all those years ago, this meeting with Noreen over a few dozen 'home made' shop produced beef-burger's, was the opportunity that back then he'd been far too much of a rogue, not to accept. Anyway, he'd been alone for quite a while and after all, Noreen had those lustfully attractive, cold grey eyes and a voluptuous body.

Thoughts of Noreen made him recall the girl's 'off the estate' where he grew up, who went to the local High School for the minimum number of years they could. He recalled how they'd always seemed to more developed and mature. They got into Pub's more easily and they always had older boyfriends, which often led to teenage pregnancies and a life on the social. Hovis remembered that nearly all the girl's in his class at the more highly reputed Grammar school, were glad that they weren't them but at the same time, greatly desired to be like them.

His liaison with the sexually provocative Noreen, was never going to last and they both knew it. As their third date, lunch at the local pub, was drawing to a close, they'd both reached the same conclusion and at the same moment, they had both tried to express it to each other:

"This isn't working, is it?" They both said in unison and shook their heads, thus answering their own questions.

"You're a nice guy, Hovis but just not my kind of partner," Noreen offered, as a balm of sorts but he couldn't tell her what he was thinking. Suffice to say, it was very male and was distinctly physical.

"I hope you'll still be coming in the shop," she impersonally tendered, like some pre-programmed automaton, as she turned away.

'That'll teach you,' he thought to himself as he walked out of the pub, heading for the car and home. 'Short hair and a great pair of legs, doth not a relationship make.' He knew that to be true but Noreen sure did have fantastic legs and she knew how to use them. ZZ Top's 'Legs' began playing in his mind.....

For the next month, he had purposely stayed away from the franchise but eventually, 'The cry of the burger,' tempted him back into the store. Noreen, he was informed, had left in order to marry some swarthy guy called Lionel Cadaver, or something like that and he was informed that she was now, 'more than likely sunning herself on some beach somewhere hot and sweaty, drinking a Martini, before sitting down to lunch.'

These were typically Welsh ways of thinking and in fact Noreen, he never did learn her second name, was at this moment cashing up an order, on another till for, 'El Tiempo,' some overseas hypermarket. Signor Cadaver, was cheating on her with his secretary but she didn't really care, because after all, 'he just wasn't her kind of partner.'

His musings, were rather abruptly ended, when Pete Jones began to do the roundup of his show.

"And don't forget to give me a bell, on the Kylie versus Natalie thing, we'll get back to it tomorrow." Then he played an advertising jingle for the Ken Alexander Show:

"Hey there shipmates, don't forget to vote for The Fester's or Baccarat tomorrow on your favourite DJ's show, mine! Ken Alexander on Radio 2. Will the Festers sail on, or sink back into ignominy? Only you know listener's, so give the station a call on........"

Hovis, was zoning out and about to reach for the 'off' button as Ken continued,

"So, wishing y'all a brisk head wind and a calm sea, this is Ken Alexander, sailing into tomorrow and I'll see you shipmates on the other side."

In the background, the last few notes of 'I Want you, Love.., Want me too, Love,' faded away and Hovis reached for the Off button and clicked it.

"Thank heaven for small mercies," Hovis said with relief. "It's quite a trip, hearing the band again," he said to Cheech, as he sat down to watch a news report with his burgers; another easily avoidable disaster was unfolding, as usual, somewhere in Africa or the Middle East.

"Tell you what Lad, seeing as The Fester revival continues tomorrow, I'll do my bit and vote, just to see how long we can keep it going. He,he! Let's wait and see what happens." As he ate, he pondered about the fate of the other members of the band. 'It really would be interesting to see what and how, everybody else is doing...., that's supposing that any of them are still alive,' he mused and smiled at the whole concept, as it played over in his mind.

Chapter Thirteen

"Yes Sir, I Can Boogie!"

Next morning, standing there naked from the shower, Hovis was seriously considering wearing the Onesey one more time, to take him and Cheech on a trip up the Old Road to the top of 'The Kid.'

'The Kid,' was the parochial name that everybody who worked for The Blue Yonder Mining Company, called the relatively subtle peak, which appeared to grow out of the side of the Big Mountain. Snowdon was so dominant in the area, that almost anything else in the region appeared to be insignificant by comparison, though many of these lesser slopes required a certain amount of technique in order to ascend them successfully.

Hovis realised that technique was all it took to apply, or remove the Onesey safely.

'Note to self. Shave my front and legs, plus I must remember undies and to use the talcum powder, next time,' he thought and picking up his hair dryer, began to wave the thing in the general direction of his torso. He smiled as the warm sensation ruffled his remaining body hair.

Having now removed any trace of moisture, no matter how insignificant it may have been, Hovis skipped over to the all-purpose 'chairdrobe,' sitting conveniently by his bed and groaning under the weight of all the items that had founding their way onto it's every surface.

'Wonder why I felt like some kind of Muren figure, before?' He asked himself and laughed at the comparison his mind had instantly drawn, of himself campily bouncing his way across the floor, with Miguel Indurain's Onesey in his right hand. 'I'd have said, I'm more like Martin Prince...... but I suppose there's a little bit of Muren in us all,' he reflected, as he placed the now dry and reshrunk Onesey, carefully on the back of the 'chairdrobe,' picked up his favourite black T-Shirt from the pile on its seat and slipped it over his head. He added an old pair of cargo pants and shoved his bare feet in his trainers.

'Right then Hovis old chap, before we even consider a cycle ride, let's get our shit together and do this Facebook thing. You never know what you'll find when you open that particular Pandora's Box of trick's,' then, changing the subject completely, added,

"I need a good strong Coffee," and headed off towards the kitchen.

Arriving in the lounge five minutes later with his steaming mug of Coffee and a handful of Pringles', that he'd 'merely found' in the kitchen cupboard, he lay back in his recliner and grabbed his iPad. Had anyone responded yet to his Facebook message?

No.

Hovis was not surprised, 'probably too soon' he thought as his mind drifted towards Ken Alexander's suspected moronic audience. He reminded himself to vote for the Fester's before they tired of 'I Want you, Love.., Want me too, Love,' and moved on to something that was more to their natural tastes.

'I'll be amazed if those simple fools don't go for that damned Baccarat thing, just because they can all sing along with it,' he began to beat out the dreaded line,

"Yes sir, I can boogie, boogie woogie, all night long."

"Christ, we've got no chance against that," he spluttered. "It's just so brilliantly awful, that even I'm singing it! I'd best vote before it becomes utterly irrelevant and the world forgets about The Fester's again," he said turning towards Cheech, looking for some kind of silent understanding in the old dogs' eyes. For his part, the prone Setter, simply opened one eye and wagged his tail, which Hovis took as confirmation.

*

He hadn't been in contact with anybody from the band, since they all went their separate ways, back in the day. Araf and Allan, had as usual, been at each other's throats but you expected it from two brother's. Poe used to say that it was empirical proof of precognition in the womb and everything would be O.K, until the day dawned when they both woke up with the same murderous thought in their heads and decided to do something about it. Then, events would take on a life of their own and woe betide the fool who tried to intervene. Both brothers' characters were diametrically opposite to each other, in almost every aspect, except one. That one, was in the band with them and her name was Poe Pouree.

Unfortunately, Poe wasn't available. She and Preston had been a pretty solid pair ever since The Fester's formed and her best mate in the band, was and always had been, Hovis. This arrangement worked well until Araf made a play for her attentions after the Buxton Pavilion Gardens gig, during the band's first tour.

Needless to say, his galumphing Welsh approach didn't impress her and she made it clear to him, that if he wished to exercise his pelvic regions, then she was sure that there would be a Groupie available soon enough but until then, he would have to conduct a relationship with his right hand. Allan only became aware of his brother's rejection during one of their often-delayed journey's from 'The Florence Nightingale Lounge' in Ambleside, to Newcastle's 'Paradise Garden's,' when their Transit had got itself stuck in a long queue, behind a truck that had blown over in the wind and covered the road in Margarine. The interminable boredom had loosened his brother's tongue.

Even the most average of fortune tellers could have predicted, that once Allan became aware of his brother's lustful intentions towards Poe, he had to try to get in there first.

Sadly, he too received a withering put down from the woman of his fleeting dreams, so, naturally attempted to take out his frustration on his brother.

Bad idea.

Allan may have been bigger but Araf was noticeably faster on his feet and always seemed to slip out of his brother's grasp at the last minute. This ability increasingly rankled his sibling and it came to a crunching cataclysm ten days later, after the disastrous gig at, 'The Warm Leatherette,' in Stoke. The middle of August, during an un-naturally windless heatwave, was not the time to play that place. It wasn't called The Warm Leatherette for no reason. When punters entered the place, they would open the swing doors to the main hall, only to be hit by a blast of what seemed like superheated air, which almost blew them back outside again.

"The Night of The Fester's," as Preston dubbed it shortly afterwards, began at that door and ended up in the casualty department of Stoke General.

The Fester's were supposed to be the opener's that night for 'Red Lorry, Yellow Lorry' but two bands of that time, thrown together in a cramped overheated, windowless changing room no more than 10' by 10', could only lead to one outcome.

Araf and Allan, who'd been having a go at each other all day, started fighting over something so trivial that Hovis could barely recall the origin of the fisticuffs but due to the heat and the drugs, things quickly got out of control. Thankfully, the Fester's had already played their set, when all hell broke loose backstage. Araf, 'accidentally' bumped into his brother and made him 'accidentally' spill most of his cold drink onto the floor. Which naturally, in that heightened mood made Allan spin around swinging, intending to wallop his brother. However, all he connected with was the jaw of one of 'The Lorry's,' who blindly swung back at the Welshman and decked him.

Now it became a matter of family honour and like some crazed Sicilians' brother, Araf sided with Allan as all hell broke loose in Stoke on Trent.

As he sprang to his sibling's defence, Preston noticed that Allan, still a little groggy, was very slowly and rather unsteadily, trying to get up off the floor. Initially, he positioned himself to protect the prone band member, whilst Araf let fly at the oncoming horde of incensed Lorry's. One Welshman and several infuriated Lorry's, was hardly going to be a fair fight. The Festers had a gig the following night at 'The Pump Room,' in Carlisle. So, like a protective older brother, Preston stepped up to help Araf against the rapidly advancing mass of 'heavy haulage' units, whilst Hovis took up guard of Allan.

Preston was a big, well fed American, ex College American Football quarterback, ostensibly in Britain to experience European Culture, not to cause an international incident. Though at times like these, it did seem that somebody had neglected to fill him in on the finer points of that idea.

Fortunately, Lenny Dixon, the proprietor of 'The Warm Leatherette,' had instructed one of his staff to phone the nice cop's in the station next door if anything 'kicked off.'

Luckily, the police arrived in the nick of time, or else Preston could have severely dented several of The Lorry's before they could have made their presence felt. Sadly, his defence of the solo fighting

Fester, was seen by the owner of the venue as provocative and the Fester's were banned from The Warm Leatherette, for life; or until it changed hands, which incidentally it did shortly afterwards, becoming yet another cog in Sammy Pullen's, 'Empire of Fire' chain, which went on to dominate the Drag Scene a few years later.

Luckily for the liberty of the band, Poe hid their Cannabis Resin in such a very personal place, that The Police never dared look there for it.

"Nice one," Preston said, as he sidled past her and went over to the still dazed Allan, who had managed to get to his feet but was still wobbling all over the place, before collapsing out cold and ending up in A&E.

Chapter Fourteen

Rain on the Mountain.

T he sky darkened and the rain started to fall, just as he was clearing the dirty pot's away and setting the dish washer off. The first discernible drops landed on the skylight as he walked directly below it, causing him to stop and look upwards.

What began as a few large drops, rapidly grew in the ever-darkening heavens. Then, a blinding flash of lightening like you'd see in a crumby horror movie, lit up the entire sky, exposing the broiling, writhing base of an angry thunderhead, seemingly formed directly over No.37.

Before his eyes had time to adjust to the flash, a clap of deafening thunder almost simultaneously followed, forcing Hovis to duck involuntarily with the percussive force, as the peel rang out and echoed its way on down the valley.

"Fuck, that was loud," he gasped and turned his head to check that Cheech was alright. The Setter didn't like fireworks or loud noises. He expected to see Cheech cowering in a convenient corner, shaking like he'd got a severe case of Parkinson's but he was relieved to see him doing his one eye thing and weakly wagging his tail. In fact, Cheech hadn't actually heard the peel of thunder. He'd woken to Hovis' alarmed, expletive explosion. The tail thing was totally habitual but Hovis seemed to like it.

"I thought we'd take a last trip up 'The Kid' but right now, that doesn't seem like it's going to happen." The Red Setter, now had no eyes open and was starting to involuntarily twitch. "Oh brilliant, so I'm that interesting, am I?" He commented facetiously as he walked over to the lounge windows and peered off, into the dark South Western sky. Suddenly, a second flash of lightening lit up the room and Hovis began the habitual, silent count. This time it took seven seconds before the thunder reached No.37. The storm, if it could be called that, was quickly moving away to the South.

The rain was now a constant and steady downpour. After three decades of experience, he'd learnt that when the rain set in so relentlessly, it usually meant the mountains were in for a few days of steady precipitation.

"Looks like we'll be taking a rain check on any walking or cycling for a few days but don't worry, I won't forget about it," Hovis said reassuringly to a comatose Cheech. Then he returned to his fascinating task of staring at the darkening world through the ever-distorting liquid lens of the double-glazed French Window's, looking out over the panorama from the dry comforts of No.37.

The log cabins along this stretch of the hill, were built up to the tree line, or 'The Tideline,' as the occupants facetiously called it. Just beyond lay a region of heather and bracken leading up to the bare grey rocks of the Snowdonian Range. If it snowed, then the flakes usually started to settle just above the position of the final Rowan, where the march of the trees was halted by the relentless winter winds and thin desiccated soils, which prevented any hope of an adequate root system.

There was something about rainy days on The Hill, for which he'd never quite found the right words to explain. It was a feeling which seemed to manifest itself in an unfathomable and obscurely amorphous form.

As the evening passed into darkness and the downpour continued unabated, an ever-deepening silence descended upon the cabin. It enticed Hovis to play one of the Classical playlists on his precious iPod. Precisely why he always turned to melodic, 'old guy music,' was something of a mystery but it had eased his passage through some of the toughest points in his life and right now, he saw no reason to change his ways.

*

The steady precipitation muffled any sounds, including any from Blue Yonder's operations, which had almost ceased. There were just a few off-site contractors preparing for their complete withdrawal. From a workforce, which at its peak in the late 1990's had numbered 3,837 soul's, there were now just sixteen, bused-in removal crew and himself, left. Truth was, he didn't have a job anymore, he was simply passing the time preparing to leave by the end of the month. Except for the morning arrival and evening departure of the specialised removal crew, the Rat Road, was blissfully silent for long periods of each day. Occasionally, he would hear what sounded like a rather heavy vehicle, labouring a little, as it climbed the steepest section of the A470 Road, then turned towards the summit of the incline and Blue Yonder's mine entrance and their offices in the Agamemnon Building. They came to remove machinery and other items The Company deemed worthy, all else would be sealed in the mines, their entrances dynamited.

*

It was still raining and Hovis had tired of listening to music. He quite fancied something like a damn good movie, or a seriously heavy piece of serialisation, which he could lose himself in.

"Right then, let's have a look and see what's on Telly tonight," Hovis stated, as he got to his feet and walked across the panelled floor of the log cabin, clicking the remote furiously, as he went.

The fodder on offer this evening was rather disappointing but what did he expect. This time of the year was notorious for its blatant reshowing of shows that many people had missed during the long hot days of summer. However, to the avid watcher of quality television, a group to which Hovis happily counted himself a member, they were simply boring repeats, too soon to watch once more after their original airing. One day, he may decide to watch them again, for a second, or even a third time but that wasn't tonight. No, tonight he was looking for something new to get his teeth into.

As it worked out, he ended up lying on the leather settee, watching a game of football, which went to extra time and then penalties but he missed most of the game, through the intrusions of a fitful sleep. During the match, the two teams had immense trouble scoring goals but when it came to the taking of the penalties, it appeared that both teams suddenly found it a comparatively easy task to hit the back of the net. The game finally ended when somebody called Emilio Gonzales, overcooked his run up and smashed it into the crossbar, where it ricocheted off into Row G of the Home Stand. The cacophonous celebrations that followed, snapped Hovis out of his semi submerged stupor and through all the confusion, he sat bolt upright with the bewildered exclamation of, 'What?' on his lips.

The final score of 14 to 13 led him to believe, that this had probably been a rather good game but right at this minute, he couldn't for the life of him recall who these two teams were. In itself, this lapse of memory didn't matter much, as he didn't generally care for Spanish football but he did feel comically concerned for the unfortunate Señor Gonzales, who was still lying prostrate on the pitch, holding his head in stunned disbelief. Hovis reckoned that time would be the great healer and Emilio G, would have got over himself by tomorrow morning, when he found the world still revolving around the Sun. With that not so brave prediction, Hovis turned the television off, then quickly checked Facebook for messages,

"Bummer, nothing yet......" With that he lazily headed, yawning, to his bed. The gentle sound of the rain on the skylight and the endlessly repetitive dripping, rapidly lulled him back into a deep sleep, unbroken until the ringing of his alarm clock, which woke him at 7.30 the next morning.

*

"Ugh," croaked Hovis.

He instinctively raised himself from the warm cover's as though he was about to begin his usual, perfected over the years, morning 'go to the office routine'. Sitting in a lazy heap on the edge of the bed, yawning and scratching his head, reality began to reassert itself and a great sigh emanated from deep within his chest.

Outside, the rain continued to fall steadily and after taking a quick glance through 'the distorted window,' he realised there wasn't likely to be a walk or cycle ride again today. Even though he knew that Cheech would happily tag along, purely out of a misplaced Canine sense of loyalty, he wouldn't be enjoying it and neither would Hovis. Those youthful days of pounding the pedals whatever the weather, calculating times and distances, pushing himself to the limit were a distant memory. Nowadays, Hovis would happily settle for a day inside; after all, he had put out the 'Fester feeler' on Facebook, he may get a reply, he mused. His next thoughts were to start getting organised to leave. He needed somewhere to live and he needed to start sorting through his things......, both of which had the appeal of a kick in the nuts. What Hovis really wanted to do was listen to Ken Alexander and hope they won the vote.

"You never know," he whispered with a friesant of hope. "But first, socks," he wheezed, as he bent over to retrieve his casually discarded hoof apparel and sniffed them to see if he could get away with wearing them again today.

'Like who's going to notice?' He enquired of himself. 'I could romp around stark bollock naked all day, or all week for that matter, nobody's going to come calling on a day like this, now are they?' He didn't even wait for his own answer, before his mind reset the default button.

"Socks," he said again, to see if saying it twice, meant he might remember it this time and not lose himself in the scent testing of male under garments.

Fact was, that apart from giving Miguel Indurain's Onesey a wash, he couldn't recall having had a proper shower since he officially learnt he'd lost his job, last Friday and that was almost a week ago. This lack of need, led to an equal lack of desire and this perceived descent into The Land of The Morlock's, would nose dive if it was left to stagnate for much longer. His temporary cover all sins, cheap as chips, workaday L'au de Toilette, was becoming cloying.

'Too late now though,' he reasoned, 'I've got my socks on.'

*

Preparation for the coming work day, had generally taken him between forty-five and sixty minutes. In his sprightlier youth, when life had seemed so much more urgent, he could manage it in around twenty-five. In his early thirty's, he'd put up a poster of The Mad Hatter on the wall by his desk, with 'NO TIME,' printed on it in bold red letters, Helvetica font.

"No time indeed," he murmured with resignation, as he slipped on his second shoe, promptly rose from the bed and headed for the open door. His overriding concerns, were the need for him to be out of No.37 by the end of the month and the undeniable fact, that as it stated clearly in your contract,

'Unless you had put in forty-five years of full contributions to the company's pension scheme, you weren't eligible for a full payout on retirement at 65.' Hovis' thirty something years, were hardly going to provide for a luxury retirement when he reached that vaulted age, even though he'd been the longest serving member of staff at this location for quite a while. 'I really should have read that contract better, before I signed it,' he quietly cursed under his breath as the giant hole of his future now lurked ominously close. 'Good job I put all that money in the Company Save and Loan. Using the old Volvo instead of accepting the executive model company car, gave it a nice boost. At least that should buy a cool place to live...., I just need something temporary whilst I look.......'

As he reached the kitchen, the usually comforting aromas seeped their way into his nasal passages, aided by the ambient temperature of 21C that always appertained in No.37. The property had an excellent central heating system, which cost the lucky occupant absolutely nothing to run. If you managed to climb up the slippery slope and made it to the top of The Hill, you really had it made. Slowly, you withdrew from the routines of normal external human interaction, as more and more of your everyday life, required little or no concern from you on a truly conscious level. The Blue Yonder Mining Company left nothing to chance when it came to hanging on to their assets. They created a dependency culture, a Blue Bubble which their employees found themselves floating in. When you signed up to the plan, in order to confirm his or her appointment, the successful applicant was required to sign a different contract for each of the generous benefit's that the company offered.

'Offered,' that was, after you'd traversed the minefield they'd purposefully laid out, directly in your path. Question after question was fired at the successful applicant, alongside the pieces of paper that required signing, which seemed to flow endlessly below their eager pen. By the end of this section, fingers were aching and they were totally confused by the torrents of information they'd been exposed to. Whilst they were quite obliviously signing their lives' away, they'd had to decide on which model of car they wished to drive, the decor of their company log cabin and a myriad of other, totally free options on offer. This was an overwhelming introduction to life with The Company and it was made abundantly clear, even though by this point in the proceedings almost nobody was really listening, that these benefits were only applicable during the time they remained in the employ of The Blue Yonder Mining Company. Somewhere, in really small green letters, were the more salient points, which stated that the occupant of the log cabin had no legal rights of tenure and forfeited all other privileges if they were made redundant, or for some reason they decided to leave.

Chapter Fifteen

'OnceanAbutnowaP.'

T he aromas of today's coffee added to the comforting feel of the familiar kitchen. On his climb to the top of The Hill, all the cabins had provided identical kitchens, the enhancements had come in such things as size of lounge and bedrooms, en suite facilities, fitments and French windows. Hovis sighed as he realised just how much he would be losing when he left, then downed his coffee and went to pour a second cup, flicking on the radio as he passed by.

"The Fester's," he blurted out as it slowly dawned on him exactly what he was listening to on the radio. "Bloody hell! Nothing for thirty years and now I don't seem able to escape the damn thing!" He chunnered to himself, as he placed four slices of wholemeal bread in his trusty toaster and lazily dropped them into the machine for a three-minute browning. While he waited, Hovis caught himself dancing around on the tiled floor and almost perfectly mouthing all the lyrics to the seemingly reborn, 'I Want you, Love.., Want me too, Love.'

Then the D.J broke in, with another bout of inane chatter,

"I heard that one yesterday on Ken Alexander's great show. I thought that I'd give it another spin on my show this morning. I can't say that I've ever heard it before but it sure has a hook to it. Let me know what you think and perhaps I'll spin it again," he droned on, in a youngish sounding voice.

"That'll be because you probably weren't even born when it came out," barked Hovis, then took a large bite of his first slice of warm toast and to top off the sensation, followed it up with a rather large swig of his coffee. "Ahh, bliss," he sighed and swallowed heartily. "The Fester's, a bite of buttered toast and a mug of coffee, you can't beat it," he proposed to a sleepy Cheech. "Maybe I'm dead and I've gone to Heaven while I wasn't watching for a moment," he added, chuckled, ate the last piece of toast and gave its crust to a drooling dog. With that, he moved over to his company funded computer.....

"Three messages," he addressed the screen. "Well, let's see what we've got today, eh Cheech." The sometimes, one-eyed Red Setter, was now lying at his side, idly having his head scratched.

With a cautious smile and a flourish, Hovis boldly clicked on the message icon. Two messages were simply speculative shots from blatant chancer's just fishing for trade, so he deleted them both but the other one, was from somebody who signed themselves in as 'OnceanAbutnowaP,' now that one was definitely intriguing.

Copying the Safe Crackers he'd seen in the old gangster movies, Hovis cracked his knuckles, 'Spidered' his fingers and took one long steadying breath, before melodramatically opening the mystery message.

"Hi there, brown slice. Have you got it yet? No? You used to be smarter than this. Read the call sign again and when you figure it out click the link at the bottom of this note. Contact me."

He just sat there, staring at the screen and re-read the message for what felt like the thousandth time but in fact it was only the fifth. His eyes rested upon the end statement, 'Contact me,' it

126

said. He was sorely tempted to just blunder on and open the attachment, without a single thought for security but then his natural accountants caution got the better of the nervous excitement coursing through his body and he reverted to type. As he'd been advised, he looked again at the Username, or 'Call Sign,' as he preferred, because that sounded more Star Trekkie.

"Once an A but now a P," he repeated for the umpteenth time, sitting back in his chair. 'Who do I know, that an A, to a P applies to?' He asked himself. 'Who the hell's this A character?' Then it struck him. "It's not the A," he gasped almost breathlessly…….. "It's the P!"

"Poe!!!" He yelled excitedly. "It's from Poe!" His mouse searched for the promised link. It took him to a blog page about performance art. He looked quizzically for a moment then saw it was run by someone called Poe. Smiling, he searched for the 'about' box....

"O.K. Lady, let's see if my memory's been playing tricks on me again, or are you as beautiful as I remember you," he whispered wistfully. After a couple of seconds preparation, he opened it and a face from his past appeared in front of him.

"Wow! Jesus!" He gushed, as the modern-day Poe Pouree smiled back at him from somewhere within cyberspace. True to form, she was holding up a copy of a recent Times newspaper, as if she'd been kidnapped in a cheap Stephen Sagal style movie and was still alive..... "On August 10th this year" he noted squinting at the date. She was still beautiful, just older. The blue eyes still twinkled and Hovis was suitably impressed by her diligence, when it came to keeping herself in shape. Her Cleopatra like, geometrically cut jet black hair, which he'd always considered was simply another well thought out disguise to keep the true identity of the real Poe Pouree a closely guarded secret, was now an obviously expensive, rather short, Salt and Pepper razor cut. It appeared that she had almost completely dispensed with the female shackle and chains, which the use of cosmetic's applied to most women and she looked marvellous for it.

'I'd love to see you slither across that stage one more time,' he professed to the still photograph and began to consider what he might say when he replied to her communication, later on. "Can't say stuff like that, these days," he muttered to himself and then began to imagine exactly that. He again recalled how the young boys at the front of the stalls almost melted as she approached them, her cat like movements vaguely promising them all sex. Of course, this was all in their furtive imaginations but Poe sure was a sexy creature, when she wanted to be.

Many was the time, when he wished that he'd been Preston but he'd never had the confidence for that kind of a move. He could always imagine some obscure and bizarre reason for her to turn him down, so it was easier not to make the attempt in the first place. It would only 'end in tears,' as his Grandmother used to say and he could do without that, then as now. He was feeling a little fragile because of the redundancy and he didn't need his confidence further eroding by some foolish, ancient crush. No, she was probably married, or something similar anyhow, he mused,

"Never mind, only thirty years late again," he ruefully intoned and started to play the Mazzy Star programme, on his iPod.

As the music lulled him into a comfortable place, he continued to stare at the modern-day Poe. He just couldn't help himself, almost subconsciously he began replying to this woman, whom he'd not seen for over three decades.

High Poe

Looking good. Where are you? How's it going?
What you doing? Plus, a million other questions. You surprised me. I
didn't think that anybody would reply to the enquiry, let alone so
quickly. Groovy to hear from you and always remember this, you
were my favourite female member of the band. Contact me on
hovisbass@gmail.com.

'That's enough, on the first date,' he thought, which made him laugh internally and he was still jiggling, as he closed his reply with his usual 'Sign off',

Love & Peace,
Hovis.

He read the whole thing once more, just to be sure he'd got everything right, because it would never do to open a new 'conversation' with sloppy grammar, or lack-lustre spelling.

"That kind of thing, comes with familiarity, like a good blowjob," he commented, under his breath, just in case she could actually hear him and clicked on, 'Send.'

"One down, three to contact," he chirped as he sat back and folded his arms, smugly across his chest. The first glimmerings of a possible limited reformation of The Fester's flickered across his mind, as he stared aimlessly out of the large plate glass window. From his lofty position, looking south down the Welsh Mountain Valley bathed in gentle rain, Hovis was jolted back to reality.

All those dreams of his youth, were suddenly dismissed by the sound of a mighty roaring engine, which sounded as if it was struggling under a great weight, trying to make its way up the road towards the Agamemnon building in the neighbouring valley.

"Big one," he said almost automatically, as he turned and scanned the local paper online. He was looking for a place suitable for both himself and Cheech, to live. Although he'd only been seriously looking since the actual date he'd been informed of his eviction from No.37, he'd already seen a pattern emerging.

'How did it used to go?' He queried, while wracking his brains, for the first words of the phrase,

"Got it," he almost yelped. "No Blacks. No Dogs. No Irish." Even though it was no longer polite to actually air those kinds of sentiments, they somehow still applied when it came to finding a place for him and Cheech to rent. Although in their case it was more, 'No Blokes, No Dogs. No English'.

"Perhaps we need to look for something a touch more rural and give up on the idea of living a semi-urban lifestyle for now," and promptly changed the search parameter's from, 'Town,' to 'Country.'

That said and the new search logged into both the computer and his brain, Hovis seriously got down to the task of finding a place for them to put down some roots, at least for a while. He needed to reacclimatise himself to the world of men, after floating about in the Blue Yonder Bubble for decades. He looked at cottages situated in the middle of nowhere first. However, even though there were many dogs out there in the farming regions, it didn't seem noticeably easier finding a place willing to give a home to him with Cheech.

If he'd had more time he could have considered buying a property, he'd held off from that, fantasising that he'd be offered a transfer to another Blue Bubble, hopefully somewhere warmer and sunnier, like Australia but that bubble had burst. Still, he comforted himself that he'd have the cash for a nice place of his own soon. He just needed his bank transfer to come through from the Save and Loan Company scheme, he'd so diligently invested in. He made a mental note to chase them up about this again. His last email requesting information on withdrawal from the scheme seemed to have been ignored.

*

He was just about ready to give up and call it quits on the search for now, when the sound of the big truck's engine invaded his ears once again. It was louder this time and obviously pulling an even greater weight, as it hauled its way out of the depression that housed the main body of the mines and offices. Hovis sat there with heavy eyes and listened to the invisible truck changing down a gear as it reached the pinnacle of the short slope leading up from the main, ludicrously named, Agamemnon Building, moving towards the Rat Road and drove on for the freedom of the open road ahead of it.

*

The driver of the truck, who incidentally was called Glen, had initially intended to pick up the entirety of the company's 'special' load in one hit. Unbeknown to him, it was a secret stash of gold ingots and other bullion, that the founders had deemed necessary to hold in hidden reserve, after the Wall Street crash had almost wiped the company out. The consignment was also to include the contents of the Save and Loan vault.

This gig in the mountains suited Glen to a tee. Most of his work time was spent endlessly trucking up and down the M6 and M5 motorways, in heavy traffic, between Bristol and London. This was a nice change.

He'd originally got this day out in Snowdonia because he just happened to be a few minutes late getting into the dispatch office, due to unexpectedly heavy traffic on his way in to work. By the time he got to the counter, all the other available drivers had had their pick of the runs on offer. The Blue Yonder Haulage Company's method of reward for being 'early,' was a well tried and trusted doctrine, which was roughly based on the Feral System of, 'first come, first served.' When he'd looked in the tray which held all of the day's runs, there was only one sad, dog eared, coffee stained docket left. He'd picked it up, looked at it and couldn't believe his good fortune.

The chance to get out of the polluting motorway fumes by taking a trip to the Welsh Mountains, would have been his choice if he'd been the first in the line, not the last. It was a pity about the rain but a little moisture wasn't going to spoil this welcome day out. He only wished that there were more of these 'jobs'.

There were three pick-ups on the docket that he peeled off the bottom of the tray. The first was at Arbuthnot & Jones Ltd, in Frodsham. The second was new to Glen. He'd never even run across this Company, before. They went by the name of, Wolstenholme, Harvey & Sackville and reputedly, they had interests in Southern Africa and then thirdly, the part that he was most looking forward to, finding the:

BYMC Agamemnon Building, Number 1, The Rat Road, Bethesda, Snowdonia.

This wasn't your typical kind of location name and there was no post code either but he thrived on a mystery like this. He'd typed it into his sat nav and obtained a general route to Bethesda but it cut out when he was in the mountains due to lack of signal. In the end he only found it by accident, one which involved almost running down two Farmers, one of whom only spoke Welsh and refused to communicate in any other language and his friend, who couldn't have been more helpful and had a black and white Border Collie at his side.

"Pay no attention to him, see. The bugger's not even Welsh, he comes from Workington," and then amongst all the infectious grinning, he added, "he's only doing it because he thinks it makes him somehow more Welsh but believe me, most of what he says is rubbish. I think he makes most of the words up as he goes along." Glen smiled back at him and prepared to leave but the farmer asked if it wouldn't be too much trouble, could he take himself and his collie up the road a 'tad' and he'd point out 'The Rat Road' to him. "You could drop us at the corner, we'll walk the rest of the way, from there," he added, helpfully.

"Yeah, why not...., jump in."

"Thanks man, I'm Callam and the good looking one, is Ray. Don't mind us, it's only a couple of miles up the road and we'll be leaving you but thanks a lot anyway, for giving us the ride," he added, while climbing easily into the wagon and patting his left thigh. In response to the single command, Ray's rather impressive black and white form, was up, sitting on his master's knee and looking impatient to be on their way to the Rat Road.

"It's a funny thing nowadays, most folks won't even stop and have a word if you've got a dog with you. I reckon they think your dog's going to bite them, or something, so they just look the other way and hurry on by…, I suppose it's just modern times…., I reckon," he continued, as he fastened his seat belt and got Ray securely settled on his lap.

Glen only had the pleasant company of Callam and Ray for roughly eleven minutes and then, they were gone. He watched them, through his wing mirrors, as they crossed the A470 and vanished down what appeared to be an invisible track, which led to what he imagined was an old farm house, located in a clearing, somewhere within the tree's. However, at this moment, he didn't really have time for any more of this romantic musing bullshit. So, with a tug on the trucks horn, he turned left and slowly headed towards The Blue Yonder's Head Office, which as he was soon to discover, revelled in a huge neon sign saying, 'Welcome to the Agamemnon Building.'

That name had been chosen by some pompous old men, who lived on the other side of the world and were presently engaged in the systematic rape of a large area of the Australian interior, searching for Opal's. Within the Company they were known as, 'The Committee' and were the overprivileged sons of the men who had once gambled everything on a new find, of what would later be called Marquisette. This sensational, exotic looking, dark crystalline gemstone was a true sensation for a while, before it was discovered to be massively overvalued, due to its overabundance in the earth's crust and the bottom fell out of the market. Leaving many men of established status, in a somewhat embarrassing wasteland. They had gambled great fortunes on Marquisette, hoping for another phenomenal return but great fortunes, were lost in mere seconds.

Before the great cry to "Sell," went out and the slightest hesitation bankrupted all but the wildest of broker's, the then 'Committee' of The Blue Yonder Mining Company, had quietly liquidated almost all of their Southern Hemisphere stocks and relocated them to Britain, thus escaping the worst ramifications of that particular crash.

*

However, Glen knew nothing of this as he parked up below the neon sign. He went inside to gauge the size of the consignment, which was to be taken in the vaulted compartments within his truck, to a location he would be given in Aberystwyth. He quickly realised that it couldn't all be taken in one load, there was too much for his compartments and he already had heavy loads on, filling the back. Indeed, the consignment was much more than one full load of his truck, on its own. This was a cock up. After much messing around on phone lines and internet, passing blame and solutions around, it was eventually agreed by those higher up the food chain, that Glen should take as many of the lighter 'bales' as would fit in his compartments today and return, at a date to be arranged, with an empty vehicle. After this second pick up, like today, he would be given a route to follow, sent to him by phone from Blue Yonder head office. He was to go straight there without deviation and he would receive a bonus for his troubles.

'Hmm, very cloak n dagger,' thought Glen, 'but hey, it's another day out in the mountains and I know how to keep my gob shut and pocket the hefty bonus to boot.'

"Yes, Siree," he grinned. 'And you never know, it could be sunny too.'

Chapter Sixteen

No Blokes, No Dogs, No English.

Hovis listened to the truck's engine as it reached the junction of the Rat Road and the Old Road which climbed up the side of 'The Kid,' it halted for a moment and then, it turned right and curiously headed upwards instead of heading for the A470. Even from this distance Hovis could hear the strain the incline was putting on the engine.

"That'll teach him," he said. "One slip on that road and you're a dead man."

As the sound died away, his mind drifted back towards The Fester's once more. Suddenly, he found himself pointlessly wondering if they'd won their battle with Baccarat's ridiculously catchy ditty? Had they emerged victorious from that dual? If so, then who could tell what tomorrow's challenge would be? That decision, it seemed, was purely in the hands of Ken Alexander. Hovis felt his heart sink when he considered the pantheon of schite from which the DJ could pick as their next opponent.

Then just to depress himself just a little more, he began singing the opening verse of 'Yes Sir, I can Boogie.'

"Yes Sir, I can boogie and if you stay, you can't go wrong,

I can boogie, boogie woogie all night long,"

He wailed as the first involuntary tears, moistened his eyes and Hovis dropped his head and wept for himself, realising just how much he'd lost in the passage of the years.

"Christ man! Pull yourself together! It's not the end of everything......."

He wiped the tears away gruffly. 'Focus on the future..., you can choose where you live now, you are free to do new things......Thank fuck for the Save and Loan......'

All the unspent money from his allowances were languishing in an account with Blue Yonder Savings Limited. The 'Save and Loan' scheme, was based on employees not spending all of their living allowances, the excess being held by the company for a rainy day, in their savings account. Hovis had been a diligent saver, adding monthly to his nest egg. It was this money he was now banking on to buy a place somewhere, for him and Cheech to live and to tide them over until he found other employment. At 55 that wasn't going to be easy, visions of being just another aged shop worker at the local hypermarket in Bangor already gave him nightmares. First though, he needed to get his pay out via bank transfer. In the meanwhile, the hunt was still on for rented accommodation..... Well it would be once he stopped drifting...,

'Saving a Sum at the Save and Loan is so easy,' had gushed the ever-smiling D List actress, while waving her hand gracefully over an image of two smiling children, patiently waiting for both of their nonsmoking parents, to get in their obviously expensive vehicle.

'This could be you,' she'd threatened, as the supposed parents approached the vehicle and smiling sycophantically, unlocked the doors, got in and drove away. The whole family waiving as they disappeared from the cheesy advert.

Just then a mail appeared in his inbox and broke Hovis' reverie. He clicked on mail, hoping it was a message from Poe. It wasn't. Hovis sank a little then perked up when he realised it was a reply to his message to the Save and Loan department asking when his money would be transferred to his bank account.

He opened it,

Dear Redundant Employee,

The Blue Yonder Mine Company, Snowdon Division, has declared Bankruptcy. As such, all monies hitherto within the Save and Loan scheme held by the stated Snowdon Company, will be used to pay creditors. It is not anticipated that there will be anything remaining after the liquidators have finished but you can lodge a payout request pertaining to a share of any remainders with T. E. Jones. Details in the attachment below. All further correspondence on this matter should be directed to T. E. Jones.

Consider this your formal and legal advisement of the situation.

Best wishes for your future.

The Blue Yonder Mine Company

Please note this is for information only and cannot be replied to.

"What?" Gasped Hovis, staring open mouthed at the screen. "They can't do that! It's MY money! I had plans for it!" He reread The Company's blunt e-mail again. Not one word changed, no matter how many times he read it, just his outrage built to an incandescent crescendo.

"You fuckers! You miserable fucking shits! Arrrrrgggggh!!!" He slammed his fists down on the table, startling Cheech who jumped up barking, desperately looking for the threat.

"Whoa Cheech, it's ok boy, just your dad freakin' out. Come here......" he slapped his side. Cheech cocked his ears, listened, then decided Hovis was right and after all, it looked he like he could cop a bit of attention from that outstretched hand.

Hovis hadn't retired, he'd been booted out and now, as the e-mail so clearly stated, he had absolutely nothing to fall back on, except his Lloyd's current account, a few premium bonds and a second-hand Red Setter. All those years of saving for a home and a secure retirement, now seemed utterly meaningless.

The Company had stolen all the money he'd stashed in their Save and Loan Scheme. His plans for a new home, free from rent or mortgage, lay in tatters. Suddenly, he was staring at a possibly poverty stricken 'tomorrow' and on into the future. Hovis just stared at the screen blankly, The Blue Yonder Mining Company, had completely shafted him.

The only sensation he felt was Cheech's soft nuzzle in his right hand.

Hovis stroked the Setter's head,

"You and me, eh boy. You and me….."

*

Maybe it was Poe that had set his mind off on this unfathomable and amorphous tailspin, coming as it did during this seemingly chaotic period in his life. Hovis had studied chaos theory, initially attracted by the psychedelic fractal patterns and the numbers behind them. Like most, he'd wound his way through life on that slippery path between chaos and order, until now.

Now he'd taken a sleigh ride into the psychedelic realms of chaos and disorder. For some reason he'd yet to comprehend, he was feeling more excited than he had for thirty years. The challenge to find something positive from the experience, had awakened an old friend.

"In chaos there is opportunity," he said to Cheech with a smile on his lips.

*

He had just so many days left, before he had to find a new home to rent and apparently, nobody wanted him and Cheech.

"No Blokes. No Dogs. No English," he said scornfully, as he looked towards his computer again, with renewed urgency after the Save and Loan e-mail. First, he checked to see if anyone had been in touch while he'd been lost in space.

There was one from a Mrs. Dugdale in Llanbadrig and almost unbelievably, it was much welcome news.

"Hey, hey Cheech," he yelled. "We've been accepted by that nice lady I contacted last Saturday! We've got a new home!" Hovis threw his arms open and sat back, "Shit! That's a relief eh guy? Next month we'll be living in an isolated Welsh Crofter's Cottage, not far from Llanbadrig but with a lot of space around for you to run, not bad eh lad?" He looked over to Cheech, who was blissfully unaware of the intended move but opened one eye to show willing. Hovis folded his arms and gazed up at the ceiling, tracing the anaglypta roses with a broad smile on his face.

"Thank-you God and a very special big one for you, Mrs. Dugdale, you've just saved our bacon," he slowly and very thankfully intoned to the four winds. Cheech, who had seen all of Hovis' histrionics many times before, simply closed his eye again and went back to sleep.

'Please be good news,' he said to himself, as he opened the next e-mail.

This was a polite apology, issued by the company,

Please bear with us but we are removing vital equipment to more secure surroundings and we expect the work to be completed in two, or at the longest, three days. We apologise for any inconvenience, that this restructuring may cause.

Hovis cursed and consigned it to the trash along with a couple of spam mails. Then, he noticed another Facebook, or as he called it, Facefuck message had arrived. It professed to be correspondence from somebody who laid claim to the illustrious title of, Llewelyn's Ghost.

'Seems unlikely,' Hovis thought but he was intrigued. "Nothing ventured, nothing gained," he mumbled as all previous moments of doubt were instantly dismissed in the wave of excitement that Poe had initiated with her message.

'It could be another Fester related correspondence!' He paused momentarily, 'OK let's see whose ghost you really are then,' and clicked 'open' with a flourish.

"Araf Slow, bloody hell," squeaked Hovis. "Well I never."

This was far better than he'd expected when he placed the enquiry about The Fester's on his rarely thought about, Facefuck page. "Two replies already," he confidently stated, as he perused the second offering.

Howdy Doody, Hovis. How are you doing old man? Long time no see dude but then again, this might not be you. If it is, we must get together. Write me at llewelynsghost@yahoo.co.uk.

Araf

'Hmm, short but sweet, typically Araf,' he commented and loaded mails. His second correspondence was much the same as the one that he'd sent to Poe.

Now he'd had two responses, he was greedy for more.

"Two down and just two to go," he said expectantly but judging from what he knew from previous experience, he imagined Allan was probably sitting around some place, watching a football match, surrounded by a million kids and his worn-out wife, who had undoubtedly contemplated suicide on many occasions.

Preston, on the other hand, was more than likely back home in The States, holding down a good job and doing very nicely for himself, so he too may never reply. Time alone would tell but two, within just twenty-four hours, was 'well cool' and tomorrow may be just be as kind.

Looking out of the large back window, he could see that the murky weather, was closing in and putting a dampener on the remains of an already dingy day.

Then suddenly, with absolutely no warning, Hovis jumped up.

"Eureka!" He cried, "Eu-bloody-reka!! Brilliant too, even if I do say so myself," he thought out loud. "You're a fucking genius, Man" and with that, he nodded his mental confirmation, sat down and sighed deeply. Cheech nudged his hand for confirmation that things were ok,

"Poe might know a thing or two about Preston and Araf, might know the same kind of stuff about his brother. Good thinking eh Cheech?" Hovis stroked his head, then quickly sent them both an email requesting info about Preston and Allan. For all he knew, Araf might have killed Allan and done away with the corpse years ago. Hovis smirked at the concept but didn't completely dismiss it from his considerations. Araf and Allan, might well have been brother's but both considered that the other was always the favoured child. There was no logic in their mutual animosity. Neither was habitually placed ahead of the other in their parental super-hip mind.

Araf Slow and Allan Exit, were two gloriously Punk names. They had both chosen outstanding bilingual nom de plumes. It had taken Hovis a few minutes to get the social joke but when he did, it made him laugh for weeks and judging by the ridiculous grin on his face at this moment, it still did.

The Fester's were all either blessed with curious names at birth, as with himself and Preston or adopted them. It wasn't Preston's fault that he was born in America and his parent's thought that giving him that moniker, somehow made them appear to be a little more cultured than their neighbours. They were so immensely pleased with themselves, that Mr & Mrs Lancashire, gleefully named their second son, Leyland.

'I wonder if they ever found out, or are they still oblivious as to just how amusing their two lads' names are, to the British,' he pondered?

"Hmm," he grunted. "I've got no room to talk," he said to Cheech, who didn't hear a word of it. He'd been asleep since Hovis had stopped petting his head. "What kind of a name's Hovis to saddle a young chap with," he queried. "Talk about malice aforethought. Jesus, nowadays that's almost tantamount to child abuse; possibly somewhere on the cruel and unusual spectrum," he moaned pathetically.

*

When Poe called him "Brown slice," there was an essence of affection in it but when the bully boys and the one bullyette, had picked on him at school, there had been no humour in it.

After months of merciless torment about his name, Hovis was, as usual, sitting alone at the school dinner table around the time of the Christmas festivity's, when he was approached by Janice Etchells, the self-appointed, Head Bullyette. She was quite something, in his eyes. For starters, judging by the length of her skirt, she'd brazenly turned a double fold over in the waistband. Her pristine white blouse, always unbuttoned one too many, made it obvious she was fashionably bra less and most importantly, she was his first stop on The Masturbation Highway. As a youth, he'd spent many happy hours in the imagined company of Janice Etchells and he'd never apparently, gone the slightest bit blind.

He was entranced and when she sat next to him and offered him one of her Corned Beef Roll's. He was so taken in by this whole charade, that refusing her offer was impossible. He blindly took one of her bread roll's and bit into it. He chewed on the 'Corned Beef' once and then, horrified, spat it out onto the floor.

"Ugh, shit." Hovis yelped, "What was that?" He asked and then spat again, to make sure, that it was all out of his mouth.

"A brown slice butty," was all she managed to get out, before she dissolved in a fit of cruel, hysterical laughter. Hovis heaved violently, which only made Janice laugh even more, to the point where she started to cry.

"A brown slice roll, for Brown Slice," she wheezed. "Delicious, just fucking delicious," she repeated and collapsed in a heap.

The incident with Janice, had stayed with him for quite some time but over the years it had become a reasonably humorous event from his earlier life. He again dismissed it with a crooked smile.

Chapter Seventeen

Desire Me...

Coming back to the present, Hovis searched then clicked on Ken Alexanders' Facefuck page. For a moment he could hardly believe it.... The Festers had beaten Baccarat! He checked again, then punched the air,

"Yeah! Take that you Spanish Babes!" He yelled and fell back laughing.

Cheech opened one eye...

"Hey Cheech, we won! Time to celebrate.... How do you fancy eating the rest of that cake? I sure do...and a coffee too....."

Fifteen minutes later, both stuffed with cake, Hovis and Cheech were back sitting in front of the computer.

"Right, let's have a look," he said as he optimistically opened up the mailbox. A piece of trash from some guys who went by the name of, Cooke & Braithwaite, who were trying to sell him some Horsey Stuff, such as a grooming kit, which they claimed left your steed,

'Ready for anything,' whatever that meant?

"Oh yah, I really must get one of those," he said and in one swift movement, dispatched the e-mail to the trash. Next, was the almost obligatory plea from some charity, or other. These fishing mails always annoyed him because he gave to his favourites by monthly bank order and cash locally; if he responded to all he'd be even more bankrupt! Hovis didn't even open this one, it went straight into the bin. He was now almost hypnotically staring at the last three pieces of mail and deciding which one to open next?

There was one from The Green Party, which more than likely featured 'My favourite Munchkin,'

"Not right now Caroline," he said, almost apologetically, as though she could hear him dismissing her with a click of the mouse, as he saved it for later. 'The Munchkin,' was always nice to look at but the title in the subject box, 'Two years to save the oceans,' didn't exactly fill him with glee and his Chakra had taken enough of a beating recently.

"Not now," he insisted, dragging away his hovering mouse.

"Next," he forcefully requested, as though the mouse was actually listening and his eyes slid across the remaining two mystery mails. The first one was from some dude who claimed he'd won a massive sum of money on some lottery but for some spurious reason, needed to let the cash rest in Hovis' account for a couple of months, before he could access it.

"Funny how they're always from Nigeria, or somewhere like that," he said to himself as he junked that e-mail too. "Just how dumb, do they think we are?" He moved along to the last item, in his Inbox. The sender was somebody, who wished to be known as, theredroseyank@gmail.com.

"The Red Rose Yank," he said, reading out loud, a long and heavily pregnant pause followed, then in a flash of inspiration, he got it. "Preston, you old dog......., I think?"

'Is Preston the new de facto capital of Lancashire?' Hovis asked himself? "Not unless I missed something," he added, aloud. 'Lancashire's the red rose county, isn't it?' His inner child asked, knowing the answer full well and then he lost patience with his brain. "So, this is what happens to you, left to your own devices,"

Hovis whispered never expecting an answer. 'Perhaps, I'm going utterly crazy up here on my own with Cheech….. But who gives a shit anyway?' Again, his offending grey matter, failed to reply to his taunts and he drew this stupid instant in time to a close, as he shut his eyes and clicked on the 'Open' icon.

Had he just released the proverbial bats, or possibly awoken the world's worst ever virus, that was about to destroy the Blue Yonder's entire data system?

'Howdy ex-partner, how's it hangin'?' The subject matter box said and Hovis laughed, then immediately pressed on, impatient to see what his old drums and keyboard playing colleague, had to say.

I knew it was you. Who else, could it have been? Hovis.Monk is hardly a good disguise. I'll just fill you in on a few of the salient points regarding my life, if that's O.K. with you? Actually, I don't care whether it is, or it isn't but here comes, 'All the news that fits.'

After the band broke, Poe and I rented a place in Manchester and everything went hunky dory for a while but like all relationships enduring loss, we were both on the rebound from the band and I reckon you know what happened next. We both agreed to stay in touch but that broke down and I've not heard a word from her in the past twenty years, or more.

How are you doing? How's life been treating you? Married? I am. Partnered, or kid's? I have two. You'll have to fill me in on the facts of your life. Write back soon and I'll see you around, Man?

It was electronically signed,

Preston Lancashire.

"Three down plus me, makes four and in only two days! Wow! After spending a mere thirty years in the wilderness, it's quite unbelievable," he said with a genuine sense of wonder, in his voice. "Only Allan to get in touch with and then The Fester's are back in town-nah." He emphasised the last extended syllable, purely for the Mark E Smith connotation.

Much as he would have liked to, Hovis knew that he couldn't sit around playing daft buggers with the machine all day. There was the finite matter of leaving No.37 to consider and he didn't have so many days left. He'd sorted the sticky problem of finding a place in the middle of nowhere, that was both him and Cheech tolerant but the thought of his log cabin being destroyed by machines, then fire, on the orders of The Company, somehow didn't sit right.

"Company Arson," he grumped and then, as if to give his frustrated declaration a little more weight, he repeated it but much louder the second time.

"FUCKING ARSON!"

Cursing done, Hovis got back to his real task of sorting out his affairs in readyment for the impending, Grand Departure. There was much to do and he was just adding to the ever-lengthening list with this Fester's thing, that Ken 'bloody' Alexander had instigated. For thirty plus years, the lifeless corpse of The Fester's, had lain peacefully decomposing in the wet earth. Now that inconsiderate sod, had just, on an apparent whim of his pathetic fancy, resurrected the band. Hovis couldn't help but feel it was fate…., or karma… or something like that anyway.

Today, they were to be challenged by another, 'One hit wonder,' from around their era and it was a really good one this time. Having dispensed with Baccarat, remarkably easily, they were now up against 'Desire me,' by The Doll, which like The Fester's, 'I Want you, love,' was a much-loved track by those who knew. In fact, Hovis had always considered, 'Desire Me,' to be a bit of a phenomenon. Back in 1979 he'd bought the 12-inch version of the song and he still had a much-played copy of it on his iPod. This challenge was going to be a hard one and he felt a rush of nervous energy ripple through his body.

'Don't think that there's anything in the rules, about not voting for yourself, again,' he mused and set about contacting the other extraneous members of the band and informing them, of the vote. "Loading the deck," he sneakily whispered. "Nothing wrong with that, eh Cheech?" he looked for support from his canine friend who opened one eye to reassure him.

Hi Guys,

Tune in, to The Ken Alexander Show, on Radio Two after 11 o'clock, today. They're playing our song and pitting it against The Doll's, 'Desire Me.' Third appearance, let's see if we can't vote to make it more....

Hovis

That done, he turned on his radio and kept a tab on the goings on at Radio Two Central. He was met with the undiluted garbage, which someone called Kerry Monkeith, was wilfully pouring out onto the airways.

"Remember to stay tuned, for the Ken Alexander Regatteaux, which will be along shortly," Kerry sarcastically implored his listeners, *"but first this one, from Adele,"* he continued, over-running

the intro and clashing with the first couple of chords of the plump warblers' prize ditty.

Hovis had almost nothing complementary to say about nearly everything he'd ever heard on Radio Two but 'Someone like you' was relative quality and this gormless prat, had talked all over the beginning.

"Jesus H. Christ," he mumbled. "That, was the only Adele song, I can stand and you fucked it up. Seriously Man, how d'you ever get this job?" He disdainfully added, "You can't quite get over the sound of your own voice, can you? And as for working the panel, ……….. Well, I rest my case," Hovis folded his arms assertively, then laughed at his own hypocrisy. Adele's ditty finished and a cheap Northern Soul copy, by Duffy, was eased relatively smoothly into Kerry Monkeith's rather dodgy playlist, then clumsily faded out, just as the incredibly annoying music that introduced The News, began.

Hovis slowly rose to his feet and started shuffling towards the kitchen, so he could grab another couple of slices of toast and another top up, for his cooling mug of coffee. He made it back to his seat, just as the weather forecast was ending. Settling his bum comfortably in his leather chair, he prepared himself for further bad news as The Ken Alexander Show began. The show finished in a few hours but in the meantime, ''I Want you, Love.., Want me too, Love' and 'Desire me,' would be played every thirty minutes, so that the audience could make a supposedly informed decision, before casting their votes.

"Good morning Copenhagen and here are the votes of the Welsh panel," Hovis cynically said, as The Doll, being the challenger's, got the first bite of the cherry. Next, it was The Fester's turn and he had to admit, if only to himself, that 'Desire me' was the better tune but he was still going to vote for, 'I Want you, Love.., Want me too, Love…,' purely because of ego.

"There you go, vote cast, now let's get on with it," he said to Cheech, as he peered out of the window, at another day of steadily falling rain. "You reckon, that this shit's ever going to stop?" He enquired of the Red Setter, who also appeared to take a look outside and then flopped back onto the soft, warm, dry embrace of his memory foam bed.

"No, I don't either..."

*

You never could tell what was going to happen when 'Joe Public' got involved in anything. Sometimes, they would do exactly what you expected them to do but sometimes, just sometimes, these anonymous members of the general populace tended to throw, 'the man' a wicked curveball.

He'd sent the e-mail's to the rest of the band but he couldn't make them vote, that was entirely in their hands. Hovis was now feeling noticeably less stressed and it registered. Then suddenly, he received three incoming e-mails in rapid succession. They were from, Poe, Preston and Araf, all confirming that they'd voted and were indeed, looking forward to the result. It seemed, that just like Hovis they were all tuning in, just hoping that The Fester's would live to fight another day.

However, time was flowing along and listening to Ken Alexander wasn't doing much to ease the tension, with his constant updates on the running totals. Hovis realised he'd pretty much wasted the whole morning on Fester related issues. So, he promised himself that tomorrow, should The Fester's win this one and if it was still raining..., then he would dedicate a little of his quality time to start clearing the loft. Just not today, not with the latest tally being so close, he couldn't drag himself away from the ongoing tussle.

Not now, not just yet.

With only six votes between the two protagonists, turning the radio off was not an option. So, while the show cut away for the sports report and the weather, Hovis rushed off to the kitchen and grabbed himself a sandwich and a cold beer from the fridge.

"This one's a doozy," declared the discorporated voice, resident in his Robert's radio. *"Right now, there's only three votes in it and remember, matey's, there are no recounts onboard this sound-ship, so get voting y'all."* As much as this Ken Alexander character came across as a complete prat, Hovis just couldn't drag himself away from this inane, ageing faux pirate of the airwaves.

"The Doll have just taken the lead, ship mates," Ken Alexander revealed to his listening world. *"So, is this to be the end for The Fester's, or is there a silent well of untapped fandom out there, just waiting for the right moment to strike? Only time will tell. Remember, you've only got seven more minutes to give the station a call and register your vote. So, get calling!"*

On hearing this news, Hovis' heart skipped a beat and his mouth went unnaturally dry. He had no idea what the score really was and he only had this trashy D.J's word that at this precise moment, The Fester's were teetering on the very edge of a rapid return to oblivion.

"Oh, come on people, it can't be allowed to end like this," he pleaded and raised both of his arms towards the heavens for divine intervention. Then, recalling the joke rendering of Michelangelo's Creation of Adam by God's lightening finger, he optimistically turned towards the grey monocloud and looked for a sign in the sky.

The next few minutes seemed interminable and then, just as the allotted time ran out, the voice of Ken Alexander reinserted itself on proceedings and declared the result.

"Close one today shipmates, it could have gone starboard or larboard," he said in his appallingly fake neo-piratical voice. *"However, we do have a winner and I'll bring it to you, right after this word from our sponsor's."*

"For God's sake, get on with it," cried Hovis and impatiently drummed his fingers on the tabletop, as though that would do any good.....

"Well, as I said, it was as tight as a sailors' knot today and it could have gone either way………, but the final score, was two hundred and forty-seven, to two hundred and forty-five, in favour of………The Fester's! Well done guys!"

The sound of a ships bell clanging and cheers, from a rather short loop now filled the cabin, *"That's three you've seen off so far but tomorrow you'll be up against a really tough one, which is going to be………………,"* At this point, a pre-recorded drum roll rudely interrupted Ken and for a brief moment the air crackled with anticipation, *"Which is going to be………,"* he repeated, *"'Happy, by Ned's Atomic Dustbin!' So, shipmates, here's to another golden battle tomorrow and remember, it all depends on…"* Once again, he was sailing a little bit behind and he only got as far as, "it all depends on," when the show ended with a jarring silence.

"It all depends on what, dickhead?" Shrieked Hovis. "Shit!" He continued in the same pitch, "That's not fair, The Ned's were on Top of the Pops, we weren't," he said with childish indignation and pouted, sulkily.

'Christ, how old are you, Man,' he justifiably enquired of himself, then chuckled as the nostalgic excitement overpowered any logic floating airily around in the ether.

Hovis, simply couldn't resist informing the others of their good fortune, just in case they'd missed the result of the vote. As he did so, another, far more radical idea began to form in his furtive mind.

Chapter Eighteen

The Loft of Souls.

s the alarm clock rang, Hovis could hear another, rather soft but insistent drumming sound, emanating from somewhere outside of his bedroom.

At first, he simply lay there, looking up at the rose patterned Anaglypta ceiling, attempting to put his head back into a state that could loosely be described as, 'Hovis mentis'.

"Oooh," he groaned as his spine clunked back into place, after he'd slept far too long in the foetal position. 'I really must try to move a little more often,' he thought, as the possibility that he'd been in the same position all night, crossed his mind. Slowly, he turned his head, trying to see what kind of day it was, then snapped it back almost instantly, when he confirmed the steady drumming was just rain, falling gently on the window.

"This doesn't look good," he called to Cheech, who as usual was lying on the rug, at the foot of his bed. "Seems like it's another day not to go out," he sighed as he turned again to watch the relentless rain on the bedroom window. "Sorry boy but we're going to have to wait until this dreek weather passes," he flopped over, splayed his arms out like a crucified man and farted loudly. "Cheech you monster!" Hovis falsely claimed and hurriedly sat up on the side of his bed, in readiness for another day and to escape the inevitable creeping aroma of his own 'Bum Gas'.

"Aargh, too late," he cried as the acrid scent invaded his nasal cavities. Cheech's nose twitched, as the invisible cloud enveloped him, eliciting a dirty look at Hovis and a swift exit from the bedroom.

"Ye Gods almighty!" Hovis exclaimed as the full horror of his own making, smothered his olfactory nerves. 'Christ, what did you eat to produce that?' He walked rapidly over to the window and opened it wide. Only now that it was too late, did the memory of last night's supper crawl its way back into his revolted consciousness. 'Chorizo Bean's on Toast,' he disgustedly recalled. 'Bean's on bloody toast, that's what caused this,' he groaned loudly. 'Could have something to do with the Guinness on top, I suppose...God will I never learn?' He knew full well that the next time he needed something tasty in double quick time, he'd reach for the nearest can of Mother's little Bum Gas Generators, in their trademark rich tomato sauce, thereby automatically avoiding any promise to abstain from committing yet another aromatic crime against humanity. Then, just as those thoughts crossed his mind, another loud and mellifluous cloud burst forth, unfettered into the clear morning light.

"Jesus, I've got to get out of here," Hovis said, as another scented intake of breath, proved that his personal biological nerve agent, was flooding the bedroom. Hovis woozily wobbled, barely conscious, towards the shower. "Medic, Medic," he murmured as he entered the cubicle and turned on the hot water tap. The cascade of water somewhat nullified the imagined 'toxic' nerve agent and inside it's protective veil, he could breathe more easily. As the scent of soapy vanilla graced his nasal passages he began replanning his day.

The dreek rain was still falling slowly after breakfast, but with an intensity that he knew would soak through to your skin almost the instant you stepped out into it. So, the promised trip out on Dennis was definitely cancelled from this morning's schedule. The Setter didn't seem all the bothered though; if Cheech had any such concerns he would have been right there, in his eye-line, looking impatiently at him and tapping his tail on the ground. Well, that's how Hovis interpreted what he called 'Cheechspeak.'

*

The room which Hovis called "The Loft," was in fact just a spare room in the eaves that could, if you so wished, become a child's bedroom. However, many of the employees of The Blue Yonder Mining Company had chosen to use the space as a den.

Johnny Geralitus, chose to use the space as his private 'Bar,' or "G's Place," as he called it. Everybody who knew him, was aware that he always kept a bottle or two of his favourite tipple, which in Johnny's case happened to be a rather fine Cognac, hidden behind the taps, only for "the chosen few" to partake of. As Johnny's oldest BYM friend, Hovis considered himself to be one of these preferentially, 'named' drinkers. Many was the night he'd sat in 'G's Place' and drunk himself into a state of abject oblivion. A fact, on reflection, he'd done on too many occasions for his own wellbeing.

In that hallowed room, all the problems of the world had been easily remedied, in only a few minutes. It was just a pity, that come the morning, almost nobody who frequented 'G's Place,' could even remember what the original question was, let alone the answer.

Memories of that room over at Johnny's ex-cabin, filled Hovis with melancholic thoughts, ones which seemed to be getting worse, as his own D-Day drew ever closer. When he considered it, he couldn't quite decide whether it was simply a matter of losing all these long-term friendships; ones that had sustained for years, despite the pressure that Blue Yonder Mining had applied. Or, was it more the passing of an era of his life that disturbed him? Thinking about such things never played well in his head and could make him moody. Hovis considered himself to be a generally easy-going guy but with D-Day approaching faster than he could cope with, he found that he had less control of his emotional state, it just wouldn't play by the numbers.

The wooden rail felt warm but unyielding in his hand and gradually he realised that he was still stood at the bottom of the loft steps. He'd put this off for as long as possible. Truth was, The Loft and its contents, presented him with a myriad of memories; some happy, some sad but all of them carried a resonance of a time gone by and a person, or in some cases groups of people, that he would never see again. It was an emotional rollercoaster he was reluctant to ride.

Hovis steeled himself to enter The Loft of Souls. Placing his foot on the bottom step, he set his jaw and growled,

"A man's gotta do, what a man's gotta do."

At the top, Hovis stopped and reached for the door handle, one which he knew would give him unfettered access, to god knows what long forgotten angst.

Fighting with the desire to cancel the whole idea and put it off for yet another day, he hesitated and paused for a very pregnant second, before he depressed the handle and pushed the door decisively open.

Almost every object in The Loft carried some, or all of his subconscious recollections along with it and as the door opened, letting the outside light in, it gently illuminated different parts of his past life. From the plywood soldier he'd illicitly acquired from a lamp post on The East Lancashire Road, in the dawn of an early Summer's morning many years before, to the head of the Esso Extra Petrol Pump, which he could, even after all this time, clearly remember stealing.

He was eleven years old when they temporarily closed the petrol station at the crossroads for remodelling. For years he'd admired how the petrol pumps lit up at night with their glass tops. He particularly liked the yellow Shell sign and the Esso extra. He'd already witnessed the destruction of the first set of pumps and been shocked when they just smashed the tops along with everything else. In a fit of youthful outrage, he determined to save the last two.

To that end he sat on the opposite side of the road, close to home, working out the vehicle flow. The traffic light system was such that for a couple of seconds, everything seemed to more or less stop and take a breath, before it all started to flow again. If he timed his heist perfectly, any pursuit would be almost impossible.

He watched the flows intently until he reckoned that the perfect time to make his escape with the booty, was just as one set of traffic lights turned amber and the cars coming from the direction of Liverpool slowly stopped. Then, there was a moment when no traffic was moving and if he struck without hesitation, he would never have a better chance of making an unimpeded flight with his prize. By the time anyone could react, he would be crossing the last lane of the dual carriageway. The traffic coming out of Manchester, would be revving up their engine's, ready for the lights to change and if he took the ginnel route only known to the local kids, it was unlikely that anybody could follow him.

Next, he checked how the glass signs fitted onto the pumps. There were two metal lugs, front and back. The rear ones could be removed with a spanner but on quick inspection, young Hovis realised they were rusted in place. So, how to release his prize? He mused for a while before settling on tapping the rear flange of the glass with a toffee hammer, so it would break and he could ease it out from under the front lug.

With his devious plan carefully worked out, Hovis waited until the evening rush hour as the light was fading, then crossed the road at the traffic lights and casually made his way towards the pumps via the footpath, his heart beating hard in his chest. The workmen were busy closing up for the day. Hovis, his hood up, ostensibly against the cold, slowed his walk and grasped the hammer firmly in his anorak pocket. Looking left and right, judging his moment, his heart beating like a piston, he dodged behind the Esso pump and gave the flange a quick whack with the hammer. With a satisfying 'dink' it cracked. He reached up and grasped the sign, tilted it forward, then yanked it back, free of its pump and set off at a run to catch the still moment in the traffic.

Just then there was a shout,

"Oi, what you doin' you little thief?!"

It was too late, Hovis was already across the four lanes of static traffic and heading off down the ginnel, breathing hard, flushed with success. Even now he could recall that moment of youthful triumph and he chuckled out loud. The next day he had pulled the same trick and gotten away with the beautiful yellow Shell sign. Looking back now, he thought the workmen had probably let him get away with the second, amused his youthful criminal ambition.

Hovis flicked on the strip light and spotted its yellow lustre in a corner under the eaves,

"You two are coming with me," he declared.

He had made off with the Glass Pump Heads, purely because he liked them but the plywood soldier, was acquired for completely different reasons.

There was an army recruiting drive down on Platt fields; to promote it, they had attached a whole load of army targets to lamp posts. These had a charging soldier with a machine gun and concentric target rings emblazoned upon them. Every boy wanted one. Every boy needed one. Hours of critical survival practice shooting gats, arrows, darts, air pistol pellets and knives were theirs, literally for the taking........

To this end, early one summer Sunday morning, he'd been walking quietly by the dual carriageway, cutters in pocket, when he'd heard the sound of multiple grumbling engines somewhere in the distance, heading in his direction. The sound was so unusual, that he'd stopped and listened to their approach. He brought one hand up to shield his eyes from the light and peered into the distance, trying to make out exactly what were all those tiny dots on the horizon.

They were quickly becoming clearer as they approached his position. Now the mystery was solved, they were a horde of huge motorbikes along with their leather clad riders. Later, he discovered they were called 'Hogs' by their seemingly enormous owners, who were all draped in American flags and dusty leather. As they rumbled past, he noticed two identical words that they all, without exception, had emblazoned on their backs.

'Hell's Angel's'.

Curiously, the apparent leader of this group, wore what seemed to be the head of a bear, for a helmet and just looked imperiously past Hovis, as he and his passenger, a girl with a definite resemblance to Cher, growled ominously by, on their way to Liverpool, or somewhere that was more fittingly exotic, he'd supposed.

As they rumbled past him, several of these curious strangers looked over in his direction and one, or two of the female pillion passengers, gave him a cursory wave, using only their middle fingers to register his existence. He remembered thinking, 'It's probably, just an American thing,' and to be polite, responded to their greeting, in kind. The rider's seemed to respond positively to his like-minded greeting and shouted what he supposed were other American style felicitations, as they thundered past.

Hovis smiled, remembering his eight-year-old childish naivety and his crush on Cher......

Anyway, a few years later, he would hear about a guy called, Sonny Barger, who people called 'The Bear.' He discovered the uncomfortable truth, that he was 'the head honcho' of The Californian Chapter of The Hell's Angel's. For years after, safe in the knowledge that Mister Barger was an ocean away, he would happily accept a drink and tell the tale, of how he,

"Once, flipped off Sonny Barger and lived to tell the tale."

Cheech's cold nose brushing against his arm, brought Hovis back to the present, with a jolt. Memories of motorcycle gangs quickly departed as he stroked the dog's head and sighed.

"You are right Cheech, time for lunch. We can do some more later....."

Hovis picked up the glass Esso sign, flicked off the light and headed back down the steps.

Chapter Nineteen

"Mr. Hovis Monk, on Bass Guitar."

"IWant you, Love.., Want me too, Love,' came to its inevitable close and after Ken Alexander had almost ruined the whole experience, with another splash of his unfunny, outdated, piratical sea dog styled banter, Hovis felt an unquenchable need to retrieve 'Jezebel,' his trusty Bass guitar and give it another go.

'Giving it a go,' may have seemed like a simple enough idea but all the years of punching the tabs on a keyboard, had hardly kept his digits in the prime condition for doing 'finger runs,' on his Gibson eb3. In truth, he wasn't even sure that he could remember all the segg building and sinew stretching finger contortions required to get the old girl to 'sing' again.

When he'd joined Blue Yonder, he'd sworn an oath to whichever God was listening at the time, that he was going to, "Stay in tune" and play Jezebel at least twice a week. That promise had only lasted seven weeks, before an accounting error, which had eventually turned out to have originated in the usually reliable Australian Head Office, sent the Agamemnon Building into an unnecessary fiscal panic and had eaten his habitual playing hours.

When he'd decided to buy a new bass instrument with his share of the advance the band got from Deaf Bunny Records, Hovis had followed a well-trodden Mancunian Muso's path and gone to see Murray, at The Light of The World. He'd been ushered secretively into 'The Retrievals Store,' which Murray claimed held the finest, rarest and generally most expensive second-hand models of musical instruments in Greater Manchester.

"I've got a Gibson eb3 that I'm reliably informed once belonged to Jack Bruce, of 'Cream' fame," he proudly stated. "I'm told, that he had left the instrument in an unlocked Transit van, while he was 'entertaining' a lady in the rest room of the Rosendale Masonic Theatre. A guy told me that another dude had liberated it, while Jack was otherwise engaged after the gig."

A few doubts started to emerge at this juncture, mostly due to the devilishly low price of £666 that Murray was asking for the classic Gibson. As he further elaborated the tale, the validity of some of the more salient points became ever more dubious.

Nevertheless, the grace and the balance of the instrument felt good in his hand, he slipped the strap over his shoulder and she sat comfortably, like an affectionate lover.

"You can plug in over there….," Murray pointed to a classic Vox amp.

Hovis played a few runs, tuned the strings, played a few more, she had a great sound. He had to have her! Who cared if she wasn't really Jack's knocked off baby, it made a good tale but he was going to knock the price down a bit,

"I'll take it…., for £600 though, including the hard-shell case," announced Hovis confidently, as he laid the guitar on the counter and stroked it for good measure.

Murray stroked his chin, "Hmm ok, maybe it's a deal."

"Well, I'm not exactly convinced, that Jack Bruce's fingers have ever been close to this beauty but the wear and tear suggests she's been a well-loved instrument, so what the hell…" Hovis slapped the last tenner down on the counter. Murray studiously kept his eyes on the notes and said nothing.

"C'mon, if she really was The Bruce's bass axe, then no player worth his salt, would turn it down, so how come she's so cheap?" Hovis raised a quizzical eyebrow, a half smile on his lips as he pushed the money over. Murray picked up the pile of notes....

"I don't know, what you could possibly mean," responded Murray defensively, starting to count the notes in his acquisitive fist.

"Get real," Hovis spluttered. "Christ Man, even you couldn't have believed that the Dobro you tried to fob off on me last year, was the same one that Mark Knofler played on the 'Love Over Gold' album."

"Well, it could have been," Murray slipped in for good measure, then knowingly chuckled.

"No, it couldn't," corrected Hovis, "and you knew it!" Then, just to cap the argument, he quoted the price that Murray had asked for it. "£500 for an almost perfect steel Dobro, that according to you, had impeccable prescience, I mean, come on, pull the other one," Hovis snorted as he closed the lid on the 'hot' eb3's sturdy case and made for the door to The Light of The World.

"Say, what's the name of your band...," Murray casually teased as Hovis stepped through the door.

"The Fester's!"

"What's that, The Fizzer's.....?" He jokingly called to the departing Hovis, who just gave him the stiff middle finger with his free hand in response.

With that final gesture he'd become the proud owner of Jezebel, or she took ownership of him, he was never quite that sure.

*

When the band had folded, Hovis promised himself that he would keep up with his Bass playing, for when the next band came along. When nothing happened and he landed the Blue Yonder job, he'd dreamt of growing old, sitting on the porch of his log cabin, playing The Blues with a faithful dog close by. Sadly, that dreamscape evaporated as the art of numbers consumed his world. As the years passed and the memories of The Fester's faded, Jezebel was restricted to an existence in the silent twilight zone beneath his bed.

Until today.

Today, she was going to be retrieved from her resting place.

Hovis knelt down and reached under his bed, his hand soon located her scuffed, black, hard-shell case and grasped its handle. Pulling it out made him sneeze as the dust of years was disturbed. He used his sleeve to wipe the film of grey detritus off the case, then lifted it onto the bed.

Hovis carefully unfastened the catches and reverently opened the case. He gazed down on Jezebel as she nestled in her velvet lined case, Hovis smiled. Distorted memories of several Fester's gigs flooded into his mind and the bands imagined triumphs, played again in his twisted memory. A jumbled mass of perceived past glory's, the drink, the drugs and the girls swamped his mind and he smiled as he bent down and stroked, then picked up his lady Jezebel.

Hovis hurriedly attached the plaited leather strap to her superbly balanced figure and slung it over his head and tightened the strings.

A quick rendition, of the Bass lines in Led Zeppelin's 'Whole lotta love,' which had always been his warm up, sort of followed but there was something very wrong this time, he was left plucking at invisible strings.

"Bollocks," he cursed, as he attempted to both play and shift himself within Jezebel's Cobra like grip. The body of his guitar, was strangely sitting just under his chin. Considering just how ludicrous this must have looked, he began to smile pitiably.

"This must be what it's like, being a fat guy trying to find his dick in the dark," muttered Hovis, under his breath, as he carried on attempting to extricate himself from Jezebel's stifling embrace. Good intentions were one thing but the years had mitigated against such actions. After a prolonged struggle he managed to undo the strap and extended it so Jezebel sat comfortably at pelvic level.

"That's better, eh Cheech?" He looked across to the Setter who just gave him a dirty look and closed his eyes. "Bah! You're no help...now where's that amp?" Hovis paused, then headed to the spare bedroom wardrobe. "Yes! You beauty, come to daddy....."

He rolled it out of the wardrobe and plugged it in, then scrabbled about for a lead. Finding one at the back of a drawer he connected up and started to play 'Whole Lotta Love' again. He soon realised it wasn't just the fact that Jezebel was out of tune, or that he had a belly. No, it was because his fingers had grown fat, slow and stiff, just like Ken Alexander.

A bit of tuning and a lot of posing was no substitute for getting his fingers working or growing a new back. Jezebel felt heavy across his shoulders and he sat down, lifted her off, then carried her, determined, into the bedroom. He was going to have to practice, practice, practice!

He laid her carefully in her case, closed it up and as he carried it into the lounge the radio bleated,

"Argh, matey's it's time to set sail for tomorrow and remember, this is Ken Alexander, bidding you all a calm sea and a fair wind until, next time."

Chapter Twenty

For Tokyo's Sake…..

T he first thing Hovis saw when he finally resumed his loft explorations was the half completed plastic versions of Count Dracula and Frankenstein's monster. He'd persuaded himself to buy them under the total childish self-delusion, that once painted up, old Drac and The Baron's abomination would be valuable addition's, to the decor in his proto-teen bedroom. Not content to own just these two pieces of illusory, grey moulded polymeric material, Hovis recalled that all those uncountable years previously, he'd bought all five of the models in the range. Somewhere nearby and subtly hidden within this Time Machine of Memory, were the others. The Wolfman, The Mummy and for some unknown and long forgotten reason, Godzilla. He'd already unearthed Franky and The Count, so logically, the other's must be somewhere close by. Granted, The Lord of The Night was looking a bit dusty these days. However, Hovis reluctantly had to admit, the dude was still classically menacing. Franky was in good condition too. 'Hmm,' he thought, 'maybe these could fetch a few pounds if I can find them all? OK, they haven't got their boxes but you never know…'

Hovis stood still and scanned the loft for the other figures. Out of the corner of his eye, Hovis spotted The Mummy and The Wolfman hiding behind some old books, which seemingly hadn't moved for decades. Godzilla's location, was still undiscovered and must be lurking somewhere within this organised but fashionably chaotic jumble.

"Best find him quickly Moriarty, or he may escape these confines and destroy Tokyo for sure," declared Hovis, in his finest pretentious English Broadcasting accent.

On the conclusion of this one-man conversation, he moved a few more steps into the wastelands of the loft, to retrieve the two wayward figures. They were heavily dust laden but seemed intact.

"Four out of five. Where are you Lizard? Come out, come out wherever you are," he muttered as he stretched over a pile of dust covered Encyclopaedia Britannica's and blindly fumbled around behind them, whilst holding the other two potentially valueless pieces of plastic. These two proved slippery characters and Hovis almost dropped them several times.

Detritus had coated every nook and cranny in the deepest realm of the loft, attempting to hide the events of previous time, from the gaze of the present. He'd intended to keep it clean and organised but over time he'd just fallen into opening the door and stashing stuff in anywhere he could. The years had casually slipped by and his once sharper memories, had naturally faded but as he slowly worked his way through the layers of the long-kept debris in The Loft, his recollective power's increased and a touch of clarity began to emerge. Things began to fall into coherent pathways that had real memories attached to them, like spiritual sign posts. With all this mind furniture whirling around in his now bizarrely organised cerebellum, dates, times and places began to make themselves clearly known to him.

'Whoa, in the zone, dude,' his giddy mind silently cried and went to look for somewhere to sit down for a while.

It was a strange state of melancholia that was stalking him in here, deep within the grey dust of some distant memory-land recollections. They were delaying the progress of finding Godzilla and whatever else it was that he was attempting to do. To try and break its spell, Hovis looked around for something to focus his gaze upon to prevent his mind from wandering further into some nostalgia fuelled netherworld.

Cheech, sensing his masters' distress, pushed his head under Hovis' hand and Hovis began to subconsciously stroke him.

"Well, it's all got to go with us to Llanbadrig, or it's going to be ignominiously consigned to the destroyers fire and that's all there is to it," he said to Cheech, then sighed. "For Tokyo's sake, I'm hoping that your presence here is preventing Godzilla escaping from this loft and wreaking havoc, in the real world below." Said Hovis, almost as if he meant it but the first twitch of a smile was already making its presence felt. Then, the image of Godzilla stomping around his kitchen trying to make toast shattered, his resolve and he began to laugh, almost uncontrollably, the tears running down his face. Cheech got excited and began jumping at him, then gave him a face wash with his tongue. Hovis spluttered,

"OK, OK! I love you too! Now calm down, we haven't finished yet!"

Everywhere he cast his eyes, he saw something else that carried a really strong and lasting memory. At this rate, it was going to take far too long to sort this shambles out.

"This needs the touch of 'Fearsomely Decisive Man,'" he declared, melodramatically punching the air with both hands like he was Rocketman, about to take off and rescue the girl, who in his mind's scenario was curiously tied to a rail track with an express train bearing down upon her. He held that position for the full fifteen seconds that some fitness guide he'd read claimed was essential for any callisthenic benefit of such posturing.

"Wow! That feels good," he involuntarily declared and ruffled the fur on the top of Cheech's head. "Must remember to do that again, sometime soon......There are few things in this world, as fulfilling as a physically relieving stretch and a good old fashioned blaspheme," he declared to Cheech as he caught sight the old Liquid Lens Projector.

"Christ, I'd forgotten all about that thing," he offhandedly commented to the Setter, who did his usual and very passable impression of Clement Freud. "We used to use that ancient 1960's Light machine, to make it seem the Festers were out there, on the edge of space, time and reality." He stopped talking after that, it seemed the less embarrassing option.

Those few words, carelessly spoken, propelled him back thirty plus years, to the time when The Festers were indeed, attempting to climb up the Indie Chart.

"I think, that it's time to change the subject," he offered. "There's too much to do and too little time, to do it in," he croaked, through his dust affected throat. "If I'm not going to lose all this stuff in a rather indiscriminate blaze, I'd better get a move on."

The liquid lens, came from Murray's place in Stockport, 'The Light of The World.' The Fester's had rented it for the entirety of their infamous, '3 weekends in 2 weeks' tour but in those 14 days the band had been on the road, 'The Light of The World,' went out.

On returning to Manchester, after a rather successful three-night stand at The Matlock Pavilion Garden's, Hovis had attempted to return the psychedelic light box to its rightful owner's.

That Monday morning, Hovis had gotten himself up early and grabbed a couple of slices of toast to eat on the way, before rushing off to Stockport, with the now 'only slightly soiled,' Liquid Lens Projector. He'd made this great effort, purely due to the fact that he and the other Festers, didn't want to pay any of the not inconsiderable financial penalties the company imposed on any tardy returnees of their equipment. These extortionate 'late' charges kicked in on a Monday at exactly ten o'clock, so Hovis had been up at the unmentionable hour of seven o'clock. Amazingly, the drive into Stockport was uneventful and he'd made good time.

As he drew up to The Light of The World, he noticed that there was a parking meter space almost right outside the depot and he resolved to take it. 'Just remember the patent method to avoiding any unpleasantness, should anybody object to you taking their spot.' He reminded himself and promptly applied it to this present situation. 'Remember, use the thousand-yard stare and put a stupefied grin on your face,' he thought as he began his manoeuvre. 'They'll have you down as crazy and nobody wants to be seen fighting in the street with the mentally challenged.'

He fed all his usable cash into the ravenous meter beast to buy an hour's grace from the browsing parking warden. Glancing over, he saw it said Closed on the door to the shop and he glanced at his watch. Only 8.55am and the store didn't open until 9am. He climbed back into his car to wait.

He spent the next five minutes, watching with amusement as two elderly ladies tried to park their vehicle. One of them got out of the car to try and guide the driver, who was having difficulty seeing the world through a reflected image in a rear-view mirror.

"Stop, stop! I signalled left woman! Are you deaf, or what?!" Screeched the director, in desperation at the driver, who was these days in less than pristine condition. A combination of arthritis and dementia were taking their toll.

"Listen, we'll be here all day at this rate. D'you want me to have a go?" The female director asked hopefully, only to be forcibly rebuffed.

Smiling to himself, Hovis got out of his car, glancing over at the two ladies who were now tussling over who should be in possession the car keys. As he turned towards his car boot, Hovis' money was on the driver.

Murray, an itinerant 'Hippie' and the owner of 'The Light,' as the bands called it, did a fine line in reconditioned, knocked off equipment, that half the Indie Bands in The Greater Manchester area used. It was only a few months previous that Hovis had secured his Gibson eb3 from him. Reaching into the boot Hovis grabbed the heavy light and made his way to the front door. It was still closed and he checked his watch again, awkwardly, 9.02am. It was then he noticed the rather blunt and hastily written note, stuck on the door below the closed sign. It read;

'Blame The Man. This journey's over and we won't be back.'

"Short and to the point." Hovis shook the door for a second and then, third time without success, whilst struggling to hang on to the heavy light.

"So, what exactly am I supposed to do with this thing?" He enquired of the locked front entrance, thrusting the Liquid Lens at it, as if that was going to do any good. "I want my Thirty-Five quid deposit back!" He pleaded to the unwilling door.

"Bollocks" he said under his breath, as he put the Lens down and pondered. Just in case. For the next few moments, he just stood there looking at the cold glass. Thoughts of throwing the piece of ageing technology at the doorway to gain entry and retrieve his deposit crossed his mind, then were instantly dismissed. If the place was bust it wasn't likely to have any money left lying around to refund his deposit. Hovis picked up the Liquid Lens and made his way back towards his car. At least the lens was worth more than his deposit, he reasoned and returned home with the beast.

Now, some thirty odd years later, he was looking at the damn thing in the fluorescent light of the makeshift store.

"I suppose I could attempt to sell it, in a car boot sale……," he said with a resignation that spoke of a man who was running out of viable options. The flames were beckoning and D-Day was approaching rapidly. One question kept recurring in his mind, 'But, who in this day and age, would want a slightly soiled, thirty-year-old, psychedelic light machine and be willing to pay for it?'

The Savings & Loan debacle had created this 'dash for cash' in his mind. There was just one problem, it was difficult to clearly define in today's world, what was actually a piece of worthless junk and what wasn't?

'Fuck it' he thought, 'I can use it to give atmosphere!' He grinned at Cheech,

"Now where is Godzilla?"

Chapter Twenty-One

Festering.

There was still no word from Allan Exit, although involving the other three in the search, had been a good idea.

Hopefully, it would give them a sense of belonging. So long as The Fester's kept winning these Ken Alexander face offs', they would all remain dedicated to a common cause. Today's win against Ned's Atomic Dustbin's 'Happy' had been easy despite their appearance on Top of the Pop's. Ken's latest choice of opposition was still bugging Hovis as he sat down to compose a congratulatory e-mail, that he would dispatch to Poe, Preston and Araf.

*

Ken thought his audience, which generally was made up of middle-aged trendies who had missed the whole Indie, Second Summer of Love thing but had heard about it from a friend, would enjoy this trip down faux memory lane. When the Second Summer of Love had emerged, they'd been too busy building careers and having children, which demanded that they kept working hard, leaving them very little time to appreciate the finer points of life. Now, after years of societal conditioning, 'alternate' anything that could possibly threaten their fractious work-life balances, posed problems requiring far too much time to work out amicably. So, any considerations regarding childish acts of rebellion, were extinguished in favour of conformity and it was this very conformity that Ken had been relying upon to keep his idea on the road. Unfortunately, his audience seemed to have developed a rebellious streak.

He'd been a little surprised when The Fester's had won the initial vote-off but as he said on the air, he'd always had a soft spot for their, "psychedelic,ic,ic zoundsssss." Unbelievably, The Fester's had been victorious over the two Spanish vixen's, Baccarat, granted it was only by a narrow margin but it had bothered the Station bosses enough to order Ken to,

"Pick something stronger and let's have done with this psychedelic throwback band and their stupid song."

With what was left of his true character, the ageing DJ protested and managed to convince the executive's, that jumping from one hit wonder's to let's say, Madonna, was too great a leap of faith and that in these days of a more sophisticated listener, the process had to be subtler to succeed.

After a break for consideration of Ken's salient points, the gang of Suit's returned with a typical compromise and a few stray biscuit crumbs on their expensive jacket's.

"O.K. Mister Alexander, we'll give you some time to arrange this transition, as you called it." That seemed reasonable to Ken but then, came the rider. "You've got three more days...."

The time scale had resonated like a 'done deal' and his control over his show seemed to be on the line. He desperately needed to get the train back on the tracks today. He'd picked 'Desire me' by The Doll, as the opening transition track but surprisingly the Fester's had beaten it, though by an even smaller margin.

Then, he'd selected a song he was sure nearly all of his unadventurous listener's, had at one time or another, either bought, danced to with their partner's, or God forbid, had sex with while it was playing. He'd been confident that Ned's Atomic Dustbin's, 'Happy' would see off The Fester's, sending them to the darkest graveyard of history, the suits in the back room could relax and he could sail on as Captain of the airwaves. What Ken had overlooked, was the fact that his 'Shipmate's,' as he called his audience, were punishing him for all the awful music he forced them to aurally consume. One safe hit, after another safe hit, was all he presented them with these days. Maybe once upon a time he'd been something of a rebel but that was long ago, in the days when his youthful exuberance, had led him into the world of Pirate Radio.

Ever since then, his loyal listeners had been getting increasingly disillusioned with his musical choices and now they'd decided they wanted something edgier. Unfortunately, 'The Captain,' had missed the sea change in his audience. They wanted something that reminded them of being young and as it happened, The Fester's with their brand of naive sounding, jingle jangle indie rock, just fit the bill. They had nothing against Aphrodite's Child, Baccarat, The Doll and Ned's Atomic Dustbin, they simply liked, 'I Want you, Love.., Want me too, Love,' more. If he'd taken a poll regarding this phenomenon, he would have discovered that it was simply because it made them smile.

Ken Alexander and most of the big cheeses at the station, were stunned by the ongoing success of this little-known band from the North West. They couldn't for the life of them, understand what was happening to what they thought, was a tame and captive audience.

*

While Ken Alexander fretted over his future with Radio Two, Hovis Monk was also thinking about The Fester's but for a totally different reason. He was considering the possibility of a short reformation of the band and maybe doing a couple of live dates, if the demand was there.

"Purely for old time's sake, of course," he quickly added and then furtively checked over both shoulder's in turn, just to be certain that Cheech hadn't heard that rather weak excuse.

"What do you reckon?" Cheech raised one of his eyebrows and looked directly at him. "Yeah, I know," Hovis said, hoping that his apology, would placate the wise, 'oldish' Setter. "Dreams of youth, that's all. Nothing will probably come of such plotting's but there's no harm in dreaming....." Cheech slowly closed his eye again. "Tell you what," said Hovis, Cheech opened both his eyes in anticipation, "while this rain persists, I'll have a few words with the others about a get together, maybe talk about it." Cheech's head dropped. "So, I'll get back to you on that one, when I know a little more, if that's okay with you?"

Cheech closed his eyes. This lack of enthusiasm from Cheech gave him pause for thought. "Yeah, you are probably right...wait until after the vote today....."

*

Across town, five stern looking men were sat around an obviously expensive Conference table, just waiting for the show to begin. When Ken Alexander had originally approached them, with his 'New' idea for an audience participation section, he had confidently claimed in his presentation to The Board, that it would add some 'mild drama,' to the quieter moments of his show and gain some much-needed telephone revenues for the Station.

"What d'you reckon," asked Carson Sinclair doubtfully. "Do you think he even understood the deal?" With that question left hanging in the air, Colin James rudely butted in.

"He seemed a little slow in the head, to me," he said and looked around the table, for any subtle signs of agreement from his colleagues.

"I was dubious from the start and if it wasn't for the falling listener figures, I wouldn't even have given him the time of day," Carson commented, nodding his head purposefully as he made the statement. Around the highly polished table, all five of the executives present copied his action, like nodding dogs, some added a few grunts, to signify agreement on a higher tribal level.

"He promised so much, with that reheated hippy conceptual stuff. All that crap about equality and the like, well he may have sounded relatively sane in 1968 but now....," Colin tailed off into a shrug.

"Alas, that particular idea of audience partition is just so, yesterday's man," interjected the unfortunately named Max Sheane. His name was another unfortunate victim of parents who were very much, 'In, with the in crowd.' He was secretly angling to replace Ken Alexander with a young female of his personal acquaintance, a certain Sarah Buckley.

So, ever looking for 'the main chance' to gain an advantage and promote himself and his desires in the process, Max had originally instigated, then backed Captain Birdbrain's crazy idea, hoping all along, that it would fail miserably. Then, a few choice whispers here and there would clear the way for him to promote the rather horny looking Sarah Buckley, to replace him.

However, for her part Sarah was a smart girl, who knew exactly the roll that she was playing in this farce. Her naked ambition relished the game. Any advantage from a short skirt and a little too much cleavage, to a roll in the hay was all part of her plan to succeed. She knew well her power over men. At the age of sixteen, she noticed her Uncle Raymond staring at her legs, when everybody else was watching 'Strictly Come Dancing.' On impulse to explore this newly discovered power, she had purposely crossed and uncrossed her legs, exposing more and more of her thighs. The more Sarah enjoyed her Uncle's undivided attention, the more he encouraged her. When she noticed the growing bulge in the front of his trousers, she had resolved to see how large the swelling would get, if she purposely encouraged his stares.

Initially, Sarah had been somewhat intrigued by this male reaction but that feeling had quickly passed as she rapidly learnt how to use her sexual influence. Over the next few years, she exploited this male weakness to her advantage and steadily climbed the corporate ladder, legs first.

Max was just imaging climbing those legs himself when Carson broke the spell with one of his pertinent observation's,

"Well anyway, I think we are all agreed that Captain Birdseye has until the end of today's show to be rid of that awful piece of crap that keeps on winning, or as far as I'm concerned he'll be another 'Gone Dude,' to use one of his dated expressions and he can paddle his own canoe up the canal of obscurity."

A hush fell over the room, Max tried hard not to smirk as they all just sat and waited to hear what 'Last year's man,' had chosen as today's contender for that top spot.

In his booth, 'Captain Birdseye' was about to get todays show on the road.

"Land Ho," cried Ken Alexander. "Well Shipmate's, we're getting ever closer to Weekend and today The Fester's are matched up against, Anne Peebles, 'the undisputed fox of the dance floor' and her biggest hit, 'I can't stand the rain.'" The first few bars of the latest challenger filled the airways.

The Fester's had reached day five as 'the song to beat' but the crowd still seemed to be with them. Today, Ken Alexander came across as being a little more serious as, unbeknown to Hovis, if he didn't get rid of The Fester's today, he might be looking for a new gimmick next week.

What had seemed like a good idea last week when that weasel Max Sheane had suggested he needed some 'band battle, phone in thing,' had just turned into a Pandora's Box of trouble. The Fester's had even made it onto Channel 4 News, when they were mentioned in a report on the increased sales of vinyl records, both new and rereleased. During the four-minute report, 'I Want you, Love.., Want me too, Love,' was played on two occasions. Once, as the report was beginning and then again as it faded out.

'I Want you, Love.., Want me too, Love,' made another appearance on the television, a little later on but this time it starred in a rather negative report on the spread of Crystal Meth, which for added impact, the Reporter kept referring to as, 'Killer Ice.' Perhaps a touch dramatic but it made its point. Unfortunately, the point the Suits and Station advertisers saw was the link between The Festers and drugs, which was exactly what Max Sheane had hoped they would when he'd suggested using the song to his sister, Satin, who'd made the report. He'd taken great delight in showing it privately to Carson earlier this morning, who had immediately noted the potentially negative affect on the station's advertising revenue and surely sealed Ken Alexander's fate.

*

Hovis was sitting there, sipping his coffee and tapping his foot to a song that in its day had been referred to as, 'The now sound,' by some now nameless pop pundit, who had hopefully retired long ago and was probably sitting in the garden of his nursing home, tapping his right foot and trying to remember the name of this vaguely familiar beat combo.

'As soon as this thing's over, I'll get on to the other's and float my idea,' Hovis said to himself but a case of instant superstition had overtaken him. It had probably happened when he'd indirectly disturbed the gods of fate, directly after The Fester's saw off their second challengers. From that point on he was to be bound by the ancient rules of consistency, they needed to win today, a full DJ week, before he could consider it worth a meeting.

He recalled an occasion way back in his schooldays, when he'd not worn his lucky Oxford Brogue's before the football team travelled to Liverpool to play St. Kevin's Grammar School, in the final of the Lancashire Schools Cup. Suffice to say, his only lasting memory of the day, was one disastrous back pass, which went straight to their centre forward, who banged it in the net, leaving the score 3-2 in favour of St. Kev's. Oh, the ignominy! That pass had haunted his memory and approach to life, ever since.

Smiling ruefully, he realised this Ken Alexander character was reviving all these hidden memories of the long-disbanded Fester's and their break up, amidst torrents of razor-sharp shards of vicious acrimony. Their ending had been so unforgiving, that one of their number had simply marched off with his precious guitar and caught a passing bus. Poe, Preston, Araf and Hovis had simply stood there and watched as Allan Exit, had vanished on a bus that was last seen heading off towards Newcastle. The remaining four members of the band mumbled obscenities and threw a few V's, while Preston contributed the stiff middle finger, as Allan's bus disappeared into the distance.

"Fuck you, man. Fuck you!" Araf called out, as he climbed back into the Transit and took his usual seat up near the front. "We're better off without him," Araf angrily growled and turned his head to look out of the window. "He never could keep time and anyway, adequate rhythm guitarists are ten a penny, you just have to shake any overhanging branch and three will just flop onto the ground in front of you."

Preston, simply looked at him and quietly answered his claim,

"No, they're not. Your brother might not have been the most elaborate guitarist on the planet but he certainly knew a thing, or two about keeping the rhythm. Mark my words, Araf, he'll be a hard gap to plug."

It never came to that, as by the time they got back to Manchester, they'd decided that the best thing was for each of the band members to go their own way for a while. Vaguely, they'd agreed that when they'd had time to rest up from the tour, the remaining Fester's would get together and decide on their future.

Time drifted and no one seemed inclined to contact each other. With creditors at his heels, Araf took a job that he'd been offered by Len Morris, to drive one of the families Big Top Circus equipment truck's, on the summer tour of the South West. With both Allan and Araf gone for the foreseeable future, things stagnated and before they knew it, The Fester's moment had passed. Poe and Preston, disappeared next and then, when Hovis bagged his job with The Blue Yonder Mining Company, the dream seemed to be over.

*

Six months or so later, there was a small financial gain from all this slightly renewed interest in The Fester's only hit, as all the members of the band eventually received a royalty cheque, to the value of £18.90, in lieu of latent sales, downloads and whatever of, 'I Want you, Love.., Want me too, Love.'

Chapter Twenty-Two

Victory!

"Right then, it's time to get on with it, 'cos if I don't then nobody else will," said Hovis stridently and reaching over to his company computer, scrabbled around for his Mouse, finally caught hold of it and navigated his way to the mailbox.

'O.K, so how do I begin this?' he considered while moving the curser to the right position for his intended next move.

'Same message for everyone, I think,' mused Hovis, as the words began to form up in his conscious mind. 'I don't think that an accusation of favouritism would be a good start. Christ, how long has it been?' He paused for a moment, tried and failed to figure the numbers, then took a very deliberate deep breath.

"Well forever, in dog years," he mumbled and cast his gaze towards Cheech, who was at this point, fast asleep. Hovis meekly smiled at the old dog, as he almost twitched in time to some nondescript piece of Pop garbage, that Ken Alexander was "laying on," his listener's. Vaguely, he realised he was talking to Cheech or himself more and more as his isolation continued. 'Christ I really need to get out more.....,'

"I recall the first time I heard that gem," squirmed the ageing DJ trying to ingratiate himself with the rapidly diminishing audience. *"I'd just emerged from a really torrid night at the old Wigan Casino, when this really hot chick just appeared out of nowhere and so, given the circumstances, yours truly made his move......."*

"Yeah, yeah, good for you, ya daft prick," Hovis said dismissively and returned his attention to the e-mail, that he was supposed to be writing.

'Cheech was right, best not to over-face them with possibilities of revivals or meetings, not just yet, let's see if we win today first.' He began with the oft used but always reliable,

Hi y'all,

Hovis often used this Americanism when he was writing to the many, instead of the few, or the one. He felt that it intimated a touch of friendship, and he'd been using it since watching, 'Fear & Loathing in Las Vegas,' at an art house cinema, one Saturday night, too many years ago for accurate recollection.

Are you still keeping an ear tuned into The Ken Alexander Show? Things are getting quite exciting. So far, with your help, The Fester's have seen off all comers, Aphrodite's Child, Baccarat, The Doll and Ned's Atomic Dustbin but I'm getting the feeling that we're not wanted by the station. More so, every day. Fantastic, I know but today we're up against Ann Peebles and it's close. However, we are still ahead but only by 4. So, make sure you vote. We're going to lose in the end, they'll make sure of that but let's just eek it out for as long as we can.

Hovis the Bass Man

The amount of support they were getting from the listener's simply couldn't be ignored. After all these years, the psychedelic sounds of The Fester's, joyously rang a long-silenced bell and a goodly number of Ken Alexander's audience, had woken from their long slumber and danced in the sunshine.

The emails sent, he quickly got back to the day's most pressing question, easily prioritised over clearing some stuff ready to move; would they be victorious today, matched against Ann Peebles? This was their toughest task yet. Today, they were trying to overthrow a cult classic. 'I can't stand the rain,' was still a monster hit on the dancefloor.

"Not fair," he growled. "This is a fix," he complained vehemently, as images of the original promo short, flitted across his brain pan. 'Jesus, if we make it past that woman's overly active hips, I'll bet we get Marsha Hunt's Walk on Gilded Splinters next,' he cynically snorted. 'Then, we'll be moving into the realm of ex-young boys' fantasies, with added cleavage…..,' he stopped there for a while, as his brain entertained itself with a series of images involving Miss Hunt, bumping and grinding to the aforementioned song.

The show followed its usual tried and trusted routine, which Hovis had quite gotten used to over the last few days but Ken Alexander was becoming ever more annoying. Anecdote, followed anecdote in Kenny's sad, sick world and just where he'd got this incredible idea that he was god's gift to women from, was a complete mystery!

Kenneth Winston Alexander, was never a model child, in any form that you would have wished on your worst enemy. His parents were possibly the wealthiest couple in the village of Stoatsfield. This indicated you'd passed the line between just plain rich and fucking loaded. His Mother was solidly convinced that the family was somehow related to The Churchill's of Winston, Randolf and the rest of that crowd. That presumption was not based on hard evidence but on a set of spurious rumour's, which resulted in too many male children having either Winston or Randolf as their middle name, alongside a number of pet dogs. In the case of a few of the dogs, Randy, was the shortened version grudgingly accepted. Then in 1928, Martin St. John Winston Alexander and his American wife, Clarissa, had a daughter who was christened, Randie. The family's outrage was legendary and thinking about it still made Ken laugh. Some supposedly humorous anecdote about the trials of a girl called Randie, would undoubtedly be dredged up whenever he reached a low point in the show. To make matters worse, for any regular listener's, Ken had a terrible taste in 'oldies'.......

'How does this guy, keep his job?' Was something that Hovis had been asking himself for days, as yet a satisfactory answer eluded him.

"I'm just going to keep on listening, until 'I Want you, Love.., Want me too, Love,' gets beaten, I can't stand this prick for much longer," Hovis explained to the sleepy Red Setter.

Ann Peebles completed the second rendition of her classic. The more he compared it to The Fester's offering, the more convinced he became that today was going to be the end of days. That analogy made him laugh, as he sat waiting for the latest running total.

"O.K, matey's the tally now stands at 51 for The Fester's and 47 for Ann Peebles. The next play for these two mighty tunes, will be in roughly twenty-five minutes and remember, keep voting for your favourite song."

At this point, Ken played a Station advert running into another thing by Demis Rousoss and Hovis promptly lost interest.

*

Ken was sitting there in his studio, sweating profusely. "What is it about this tin pot band and why do the audience like them so much?"

"Perhaps it's an expression of their discontent," proposed his engineer, with a wicked grin on his face, never for one minute supposing that his facetious suggestion might have contained more than a grain of truth.

"You really think so?" Retorted Ken, acidly.

"About what?" His engineer queried, absentmindedly.

"About this expression of discontent, of course."

"Oh yeah, absolutely. You want to hear what your supposedly loyal listener's say behind your back."

"Like what?" He asked, not really wanting to know.

"Are you sure you really want to know?"

"Absolutely," said Ken boldly.

"You're not going to like this," cautioned Billy, as he lined up the next track.

"Go on then, hit me," Captain Birdseye prepared himself for a few potentially ugly revelations to come his way, fresh from the streets, courtesy of his unfortunately named cohort, Phillip 'Billy' Kidd.

"For starters, nobody says 'hit me,' any more. That's like saying 'Far Out, Man,' when something surprises you and to put it rather bluntly, nobody is surprised that much by anything these days."

Now he had the floor and after all these years of awkward silence, Billy wasn't going to relinquish this position without a fight, so he just mercilessly tore into Ken.

"Did you honestly think, that them up there," he nodded upwards, towards the offices, "would agree to a daft, oh so sixties, dumb ass 'Battle of the Bands', idea if they wanted you to succeed?"

Ken simply sat there, behind his console, looking incredibly crestfallen as Billy's sobering words sunk in, confirming his worst suspicions.

"I'd say that you've got today to replace The Fester's, with something that 'them up there'," he said nodding upwards in their direction once more, "can see as the light of God, leading this poxy radio station, to a bright and glittering future, or.....,"

Ken looked utterly crushed, as the blatantly obvious dawned on him.

"You mean," he stuttered and looked at Billy with a certain disbelief in his eyes.

"Yep, you've finally got it..... You are meant to blow it, or to put it another way, you're fucked all ways up."

"But.........," said Ken, lost for words as he burst into tears.

"For Christ's sake, stop being such a big girl's blouse and either do something constructive, or just hand in your notice before they sack you," was the acid advice dispensed via his headphones, from the other room. "You didn't read the memo about the advertiser, did you?...... Shit Ken, sometimes you can be such a dick," muttered Billy, as he faded up the intro music to the latest progress report and replay of the two tracks that were in competition today.

Ken Alexander had been doing this job for so long, that the consummate professional was always there, just below the surface and he drew upon that experience now,

"Welcome back Shipmate's, it's time to see and hear," drawled Captain Birdseye and pushed another button to start the review of the morning's proceedings. "Once again, first up to the plate, it's your reigning champions, The Fester's with their four-time winner, 'I Want you, Love.., Want me too, Love.'" In his booth, Billy was shaking his head disconsolately.

"Jesus Ken, stop giving them another chance to identify with the bloody Fester's. We want them to lose, remember?"

Next door, Ken was oblivious to his engineers' wise words and if he could have been just a touch humbler, he might have read the circular that his co-worker was now incoherently bleating on about from behind the thick studio glass. Instead, he'd just dispatched it to the rubbish bin of history.

Years ago, during a holiday he'd taken to the USA to see Elvis Presley, 'Live' in Las Vegas, he'd impulsively bought the entire, 'Dr. Karl Schwartz, Deluxe Office Basketball Set.'

In that long-lost past, he imagined having endless years of fun with the 'very reasonably priced,' plastic reproduction of the LA Laker's endorsed, 'Hoop & Bin' novelty refuse container. Unbelievably, for once he'd been correct. Using the contraption, which came complete with a set of assembly instructions in Chinese, Captain Birdseye soon realised it wasn't much use for flat sheets of paper, which floated, this way and that, or even paper planes which seemed more likely to veer off anywhere but into the bucket.

No, the paper had to be screwed up and thrown, Basketball stylee, either directly through the hoop, or when he got the hang of it, off the backboard and through the hoop into the waste bucket.

With each successful 'basket,' two more points were registered on the electronic scoreboard, which came with the assembly. His highest total so far, before he had to change the cheap battery and the scoreboard inconveniently reset itself to zero, was 96 baskets.

It was clear to see, that many of his screwed up 'basketballs' had either missed their target, or bounced back, out of the trash can. 'Captain Birdseye' though, thought it was entertaining and anyway it passed a little time on a slow show. He was, after all, still aiming for his century. Sheila Cragthorpe, the studio's cleaning lady, thought that Ken was a dick and a bloody untidy one at that. One who with his childish antics created work, where none was required.

'God, if I ever hear this damned song again, I think that I'll go stark raving mad,' he thought as Araf hit the last chord and he wiped his tears of self-loathing away.

"O.K. shipmate's you've heard the present champions, now it's time for the challenger," Ken proposed, as he slid the volume up a few notches and the first chord of, 'I can't stand the rain,' funked its way into the ears of the listening audience.

Billy, who was now content with the demolition of the old dog, who in his opinion should have been put out to grass years ago, stuck two fingers' up towards the still teary Ken and then, stepped out of the darkness, smiling.

"Did you hear that?" Ken was anxious. "It's been so long since I had to control my emotions on air, I wasn't too sure I'd got away with it. How did it sound?"

"Groovy. Far out and solid," responded the engineer rather sarcastically, as he sent the running totals to, in his opinion, soon to be retired Captain.

"Argh, shipmate's here's the tally so far," he said as Ann Peebles faded out. "There's been some heavy voting today and as we go into the last few leagues of today's voyage, the totals are as follows............ 'I Want you, Love.., Want me too, Love,' by The Fester's, 113 and 'I can't stand the rain,' from Ann Peebles, 110. It's getting closer people, so keep voting," pleaded Ken as he played another insipid piece of Cowboy Folk Rock.

In the studio, Ken and Billy we're both smiling, but for very different reasons.

*

Upstairs the executives were wringing their collective hands and plotting a dismissal.

"It seems to me gentlemen, that we have a problem," said Roland Westlake, scanning the room for signs of agreement or dissent, as indicated by the body language on display before him. Content with the unified nodding of their collective heads, 'Roley' as he was creepily called by most of these sycophants, continued with his point, "How can we dump Ken Alexander and get away without a costly day in court?"

The awkward but inevitable question, had now been asked. Roland relaxed, sat back in his plush leather chair, rested his arms on the front of his chest and prepared to consider ideas.

It was Max Sheane, the station's headhunter, who spoke first.

"I can see, or should that be hear, why we need to shake up the presentation but at the same time,".......He stopped there and appeared to be steeling himself, before he aired the next part of the sentence. "I feel that I must ask, by doing so, are we just pissing into the wind, or do we have a duty to our, until recently, loyal audience, to liven up the whole concept of this show?" The overwhelming silence in the room, left little doubt in Max's mind that the other Board Members were short on idea's, so the ball was now squarely in his court.

"Please elaborate," said Roley and everybody turned their gaze, from him towards Max. For an elongated second or so, Max slowly and purposefully scanned his colleagues, looking for anyone who was showing even the slightest signs of protest at his original statement. On first inspection, all seemed well, so after placing both of his hands on the tabletop and stretching his arms out before him, Max began to speak.

"Ask yourself this," he enquired forcefully. "How much Radio have you listened to in let's say the past fortnight?" He peered around pointedly at his colleagues, as if daring them to lie in order to currie some transient favour, with either Roley, or their inquisitor.

"I listened to Craig Chamberlain on Saturday afternoon, while I was driving back from IKEA with Elizabeth and that seemed fine to me but I have to admit, Ken Alexander is sounding a little tired these days," said Alister Graves and then continued obtusely, "I don't know how many of you are aware of it but there are many out there, who refer to him as Captain Birdseye." Having said his piece, he pushed back in his chair and chortled to himself, almost inviting somebody else to 'testify'.

"I don't like the pervie way he keeps on referring to the listener's as 'shipmates' and his over use of the word 'matey,' really winds me up," offered Colin Goodway, the station's ad hoc Treasurer. "We all know that the days of the pirate radio stations are long gone and if Ken Alexander is an example of what we lost with their demise, then all I can say, is good riddance! As Roley say's, we must find a cheap way to rid ourselves of him."

"So, we're all agreed on that score then," Carson butted in, "but I am more curious about what Max had to say regarding the future direction of the show."

The whole of The Board, was now looking at him as if waiting for Max to deliver them from evil.

"Gentlemen, I appreciate your collective faith in me but what I am about to say may appear to be the exact opposite of our originally stated goal," he paused a moment then continued, "that being, the removal of an annoying relic from a bygone age. Well, for the past few days, I've thought of little else and there is a way for us to get him off the airways and at the same time, give Captain Birdbrain the impression that he is being promoted."

There was a quiet mumbling, amongst those assembled and a fair amount of barely disguised faux soul searching was being displayed amongst the other Board Member's, who were now hanging on Max's next words.

"How so?" Carson encouraged, ever the Inquisitor but before Max could even draw breath to answer the pertinent question, a small reedy voice, from somewhere at the other end of the table, suddenly interrupted proceedings. Everybody involved turned their heads to see what Leonard Siskin, had to say on the matter. He very rarely said anything at the meetings but when he did, you would do well to heed his words. There were indeed, some newer members of the executive Committee who had never heard him speak.

"I defer to my wiser colleague," Max meekly commented and silently waited for the most senior member of the executive, to enlighten them.

"We offer to promote Mr. Alexander, to the position of Executive Producer on a special trial contract and then, when he blows it, which he will, we very sympathetically release him with an insincere, 'Thank you.' Throw in a small gratuity, coupled with a nasty gold watch and all this manoeuvering will have cost us very little. Particularly compared to the cost's that would be expected to accrue, from any legal proceedings if we sacked him outright before his contract ends."

The simple clarity with which Leonard Siskin explained his ideas, was legend at the station and you went up against him at your own peril. Ken Alexander, being so vain, would undoubtedly fall for this subterfuge and happily accept the offer. At Sixty-Four, he only had one more year on his contract and at this stage in his career, a promotion from plain old Disc Jockey to Executive Producer, was too tempting for Ken to turn down, even if the monetary return was somewhat diminished. After all, they were going to sack him from the show anyway, so any spurious life raft would seem better than a protracted legal case.

The distinct hum of anticipation went around the room and Carson nodded his head in acknowledgement. Max was relieved, Leonard had come up with an even better plan than he had and now he was sure to be rid of Ken without exposing his machinations any further.

"I take it, that all are in agreement but purely for procedural purposes and to make it all legal, I'll take a show of hands."

A few seconds of silence then followed and a couple of the member's throats were cleared, to offer the occasion a degree of gravitas, which this sordid deal barely warranted.

"All in favour," Carson, as the Chair of the Executive Committee called and then looked around the table, to see if there were any dissenters. None were obvious, so he called the vote,

"Unanimous!"

He brought his Gavel down hard on the desk top.

"Now, has anyone any ideas who we replace him with?"

*

In the studio, Captain Ken was just about to announce to the world, that Ann Peebles, had crept another vote closer and now the

196

tally stood at 207 for The Fester's and 205, for the sleazy miss Peebles.

"Just one more chance, for you guys out there to depose the current champions and remember, it's all up to you Matey's, so come on, take a moment and give the show a call......., or risk being disappointed," gushed Ken, with faux bravura. He was blissfully unaware that the board had just conducted their own voting and by a unanimous execucite, had decided that there would be no telephone poll on Monday. Ken's sometimes rather slurred tone's, would be "moved upstairs" and thankfully never heard again by his rapidly dwindling audience. At this moment, only they knew this was his last show ever.

*

With the final tally of the Fester's vs. Peebles battle about to be announced, back at No.37, Hovis was growing increasingly tense and he peered over at the clock, for the nth time to check how long was left before his old band would either be declared the winners of another day's challenge, or dismissed to the waste bin of outrageous fortune.

In the Board Room, things were getting equally tense. "If those damned Fester's win today, that'll be the whole week and who knows what damage that's doing to our advertising stream," said Max. "It's a good thing Sir, that you've chosen to replace him with Sarah Buckley. I think she'll make an excellent change, a far better face and sound for the Station and our advertisers." He couldn't help smiling smugly. He'd achieved exactly what he'd wanted from the start of these machinations, even before the last vote. Max was letting his mind roam into the lascivious areas that he could extract from Sarah to show her gratitude; she was just about to......, when

Carson reached into the centre of the mahogany table and turned the volume up, jerking him from his reverie with an ...

"Ugh!" As his knee hit the table.

"Sshhh!" Commanded Carson, he wanted the whole board to hear the broadcast, so that there could be no misunderstanding when it came to dealing with the ageing disc spinner, downstairs in Studio One.

The sound of Ken Alexander's voice gave nothing away but he was doing himself no favours by feigning a rather ham-fisted drum roll, on his desktop. Then, the rather dodgy drum roll stopped and Ken prepared to speak.

"Ahoy there shipmates," he crowed. "Here be the final score," he said mixing his metaphor's in a ridiculous Pirate voice, which he had been using for decades. "Ah, Jim lad. It be close today and there's only one vote in it. Arrgh."

"Oh, for God's sake, just get on with it," said Carson and impatiently began to rap his finger's, as he waited for the next statement from the already condemned disc jockey.

"Pieces of eight, pieces of eight," chirped the sound effect that Billy had set up for this very moment. Then, in a dark brown distorted voice, Ken announced the result. "402, to 401. Yes, that's it, you heard that right, matey's, it went down to the wire today," said Captain Birdseye "And the winners are,".............., he said leaving a suitable gap to allow the faux tension to rise to a veritable crescendo,

"The Fester's! Can you believe it shipmates?! An independent band from Manchester, have beaten all comers for a week and who knows, what the next one will bring?"

'Speak for yourself Birdseye! Unfortunately for you, I do know what's going to happen next week and you're nowhere in it,' thought Max, smirking cruelly to himself.

Meanwhile, Carson calmly picked up his phone and informed Billy, that he wanted to see Ken Alexander, upstairs in his office.

"Immediately."

Chapter Twenty-Three

13 & 31.

"Wow! Cheech! We won………again! I bet The Fester's are more famous now than we ever were back then….," Hovis commented, gazing out the kitchen window. He smiled when a woken Cheech nuzzled into his hand to cop a bit of attention from his happy sounding master. Hovis absentmindedly stoked his head as he watched two Stoat's fighting over a piece of meaningless stale bread. Standing there, looking down the valley, past the burnt matchstick hulks of former cabins, Hovis was naturally considering what he was going to do with the rest of his life and just how monetarily poor he would become, once the company benefits ceased. After the initial shock of the loss of all his Save and Loan assets had worn off, he had focused his mind on the basics of life. He had some cash to play with in his current account but nothing like enough to stretch out over God knows how long into the future, before he got another job or could access his pension. Being 'the last man on The Hill,' sure gave him a different perspective of the future.

"Look at all those shadows on the ground," he sighed to Cheech, who out of mere courtesy, blindly stared at his owner for perhaps twenty seconds, then flopped down to drift back into his dreams of doggy youth, so rudely disturbed by Hovis.

"Shadows from the past, never to be whole again," he commented rather ostentatiously. 'Christ did I just say that?'

"Shadows of the past."

"Shadow's," he plaintively chimed, as the ghosts of many memories played across his mind. 'All those people. I wonder, where they are today and what they're doing?' A sudden and profound feeling of loneliness and futility swept over him. It was a moment or two before he realised that he was staring blankly at 'the shadow' on the ground where Dave Bryant and his partner, Kay had lived. Hovis had no worries about either of those two. Both of them were born into upper middle-class money and all four of their parents had passed away a couple of years prior to them both being made redundant, at Easter, a couple of years back. Only a few months before they had been laid off, Dave had mentioned to Hovis, they were thinking of leaving Blue Yonder and striking out on their own. He'd mentioned something about opening a bar in Greece but Kay had butted in at that point,

"St. Lucia," she'd insisted and Dave responded with,

"Yes, that's what I said."

It didn't take a genius to deduce that The Bryant's were bound for the West Indies but the sight of the dark rectangle where their log cabin had once stood, carried all sorts of memories, both good and bad, within its scorched confines. 'I liked Kay but God knows what she saw in him?' He asked himself for what seemed like the thousandth time. There were however, precedents for this less than favourable portrait of Dave. He was legendary for the amount of Guinness that he could 'put away' and still walk home. Tales of Dave drinking twenty pints of the Black Stuff, before ordering and eating a '12 Inch Bombay Blaster,' were often whispered in dark places.

The Bombay Blaster was a concoction that could only loosely be described as a Pizza. It was conceived of by Raj Petalli, an Italian Indian whose Father relocated to North Wales, after being demobbed at the end of The Second World War, claiming that he had pulled the trigger on the weapon that dispensed with Benito

Mussolini. Luigi Petalli had been part of a communist resistance cell who'd sent information to the British and Americans, so he was known to both of their secret services. After the chaos that ensued with the Italian surrender and the German pullback to their defensive positions in the Apennine Mountains, Luigi applied to settle in Britain. Whether or not he truly had anything to do with Mussolini's demise was a moot point that no one was particularly interested in disputing. So, nobody checked on Mr. Petalli's story and he was waived into Britain, with a certain amount of notoriety riding in alongside him. People hid their lips behind a blocking hand, whenever they spoke of his deeds in The War.

"Don't look Johnny but that's the man who shot Mussolini in the head," was a statement that was commonly heard, when he walked down the streets of Bangor.

Anyhow, Luigi also became famous for his pizzas. At first a complete novelty in 50's Bangor but soon gained such success that Luigi got married and bought his own home. His wife, Sharnaz, introduced him to the world of curries and Indian cooking. Soon after, Bangor had its very own Indian Curry House…, unfortunately named after Sharnaz's favourite book; A Passage to India. The Petalli's thought it sounded classy, a step up from Luigi's pizza parlour next door. It was a huge success, particularly with the pub and club goers and university students on a night out. Unfortunately, most people at the time, although they loved the taste, had a hard time digesting such exotic spices and pretty soon it became affectionately known as 'The Back-Passage to India' and eventually just, 'The Back-Passage.'

As the years progressed Luigi gave way to his son Raj, who was asked for more and more kinds of toppings for his pizzas, until the fateful day when someone asked for a curried pizza. This was the opening for a marriage of the two cooking styles, which Raj went

202

on to perfect from his mild Chicken Tikka Pizza to his renown, toe curling, Bombay Blaster favoured by Dave. Hovis shuddered at the thought of Kay kissing Dave, as he crawled all over her, demanding God knows what sexually. He'd had a good few conversations with Dave regarding sexual tastes and proclivities and very little of it could be described as, 'everyday normal'.

Kay, for her part, had a penchant for a rather fine Single Malt and sitting there at home, alone, she didn't skimp on the measures. In the pub, after every fifth pint, Dave added a Whiskey Chaser to his order and downed it in one, with a hearty cry of, 'She Blows,' as he poured the firewater down his throat. This action was most often followed by a licentiously rendered, 'and she swallows,' whereupon he began laughing loudly.

Back in the log cabin on The Hill, Kay was getting equally as drunk but she had more decorum. He went straight from the Pub, to the Pizza Parlour, Kay only got herself a new drink when the advertising breaks allowed and she went to bed, when there was nothing else worthwhile to sit up and watch. Most often, she made sure she was asleep long before he blundered home and therefore unavailable for him to drunkenly ravage or berate, dependent upon his mood.

Hovis looked wistfully at all the dark rectangles that had once been his neighbours homes, as they marched off around the corner of the now 'greening' road surface.

"Okay, that's enough of that maudlin shit. It's time to get on with something useful," commanded Hovis stridently, as he pulled himself away from the window and marched over to the computer in its usual position, on the far end of the table, which acted as an improvised work space.

*

He'd discovered years ago, that being mentally in tune with a space, was more important than the space itself. Even looking back to his days at University, he could remember how he'd had a certain amount of difficulty getting fully immersed in his course work. His two other house mates were, to put it mildly, 'Loud,' so concentration was at a premium. What had started as a 'real' student lifestyle, littered with girl's, drink and drugs, soon developed into a bloody nuisance roughly around the end of the first semester, when getting your course work completed, became a little more important than notches on a bed post and falling over.

One night, which his dubious recollections placed at the start of December, he'd been trying to complete a rather important paper for Mr. Painter's winter's graduation, when 'Blond' Bob and 'Red' Robert, his increasingly annoying roommates, were whooping it up as usual. They'd both finished their last Paper's earlier that day and didn't give a damn about his need for peace and quiet. He remembered how he'd eventually stomped off to study in the library, five miles away.

At first, Hovis had found it slightly disconcerting to have two guys with the same name living with him. He could easily see the potential for trouble rising up and biting him in the bum. The problem became obvious whenever a strange girl came to the door, desperately seeking 'Robert.' On those occasions, Hovis would have to ask her for a description. As this was not a viable long-term solution, Hovis had tried to take charge of the situation. Luckily, one of the Robert's was blond and the other was a flaming redhead. From there, it was a simple task to allocate the names of 'BlondBob' and 'RedRob'.

However, that did not avoid the major bone of contention. Getting any work done, was more of a conceptual matter for Bob and Rob, who both found partying to be the far more enjoyable option. Knuckling down and studying was a mutually consensual activity and their consent only lasted until their social lives overpowered either, or both of them. In a pinch there was always the library a few miles away, though what really caused the problem was that they were bloody noisy, nearly all the time. He could hardly go and bivouac in the library,

"I'll get used to them. Just give it a little time," he'd initially surmised, trying to convince himself of his logic. However, with BlondBob and RedRob, reason went straight out of the window. They were incorrigible and as far as he could see, the only way to get a little peace and quiet was to shut himself away somewhere. So, Hovis purposely sought out the smallest, quietest room in the house, excluding the throne room of course, to set up as his 'study space.'

He looked everywhere in the old, three storey rambling property that Bob had somehow found. He'd started right up at the top, in the small attic room, which had boarded up smashed windows and a curious aroma to it. To his over-fertile imagination, it smelled as though the room had once had a body hidden in it. Hovis had sat for a moment, to see if the 'essence of death' faded in his nostrils but alas, it only got worse and then he began to feel another presence. This small, dark room, was definitely not going to be his, 'Fortress of Solitude,' he would have to look elsewhere for that sanctified space.

He experienced a noticeable sense of relief, both in himself and in the intangibles of his psyche, as he quietly stepped out onto the landing. The all-encompassing and intrusive feeling that something was watching him, as he'd moved around in the room, lifted when he passed through the narrow doorway. He silently closed the door, never to enter again.

As he descended the rickety staircase to the second floor, Hovis thought that he could hear somebody else on the stairs behind him and once, or twice, felt compelled to stop and look back.

Exactly what he would have done if the horror that his imagination had concocted was actually there, was open to question.

All the rooms on the second floor had become their private bedrooms, so he headed on down to the ground floor. 'No chance of a meaningful escape on this level either,' he grumbled, as he stepped off the last riser and crossed the hallway. 'Just one more sub floor to explore,' he thought and reached out to open the cellar door. The old stone steps didn't exactly look inviting as they descended into the all-encompassing darkness but a convenient light switch on the wall, soon rectified that situation and with a simple 'click,' an until now, undiscovered world appeared before him.

"Better luck, this time," he said with faux optimism, as he took his first step down the substantial stone staircase.

His first scan around the dust encrusted place, didn't fill him with much hope. Then, as his eyes adjusted to the lower lighting level, he began to see that this wasn't as he'd surmised, simply an old storage facility. Down towards the far end of the cellar, between the empty paint cans and the damp cardboard boxes, he thought that he could see a small doorway.

"Looks like nobody's been down here for a while," he murmured almost silently, as he set off for the tiny door. On each side, he encountered old Edwardian style chairs, which appeared to have been down there, gathering dust since, God knows when and upon examining one, he could see why. 'Not exactly built for comfort,' he observed as he sat in one of the high backed 'straight jackets'.

"And remember Hovis, chew each Pea thirty-one times, before you swallow it," he sternly stated, in a voice that was nothing like his Old Aunt Emily's but it would do for this purpose. He laughed at the thought of a bunch of children taking forever to eat their evening meals, counting religiously as they masticated.

'Jesus, they can't have had much to occupy themselves, back there, in those days,' he mused as he reached for the key in the door's lock, just waiting to be turned.

He'd expected a little more resistance to his bid for entry. Perhaps a rusted key in a rusted lock, or at least something similar but on that score, Hovis was to be greatly disappointed. The key turned effortlessly and once unlocked, the door simply swung open, inviting him to step inside.

It was love at first sight and within second's Hovis was placing some of the Edwardian furniture from the other cellar, exactly where he wanted it in order to create an almost perfect study area. It seemed to have been an old cold store pantry, probably unused for that purpose since refrigeration was invented. There was grime everywhere but it was,

"Nothing that a little elbow grease won't cure," Hovis postulated, nodding his head in total acceptance of his lot. "Well, it's either them or me, and I suppose that a little solitary confinement is a price worth paying," he muttered under his breath. 'It's either that, or go stark raving mad and I haven't really got the time for those complications just now......' So, he'd spent that first college Christmas, covered in antique dust and needing to wash his hair regularly.

While Hovis was otherwise engaged with his 'study pantry,' BlondBob and RedRob, continued deflowering as many of latest intake of female students, as they could. During that three-year period, Hovis and the two Robert's, gradually grew apart until at the end of it, the animosity had reached such a crescendo, that snide comments were all they had in common.

"You do realise, that when these three years are over, you'll have fuck all to remember them by," was a common statement from one of 'The Bob's', as Hovis increasingly referring to them. To which he would bite back, with something like,

"As may be but at least I'll have a degree and a future, while all you two will end up with, is a sore dick and a nasty rash!" Their relationship had deteriorated from, "High Man," to "Bye Man," in a remarkably short time.

Thinking about it now, after all these years, he couldn't help affectionately smiling. He hadn't heard from either of The Bob's since he'd left uni and he knew, that this was simply another case of fond nostalgic bullshit breaking into his consciousness. If he stopped and thought about it, a far more factually based reality blossomed; he recalled quite clearly, 'decking' BlondBob, on more than one occasion and in truth, it had felt good. 'Should have hit him harder,' he retrospectively considered. 'It wouldn't have done the little shit any harm and who knows, it might have done him some good but enough of this rubbish! I've got an e-mail to write and time, as we all know, waits for no man.'

Chapter Twenty-Four

The Perils of Stout, Mushy Peas and Chips.

When Hovis considered, who's name to place in the main box and who to CC, Poe came out way in the lead, she always did. Previously, on the rare occasions whenever he remembered the old band, it was her that he thought of first and today was no different.

Howdy Y'all,

He began and went on to think about the possible ramifications that might construe from this unexpected reinvigoration of what he'd thought was a long dead band.

How do you guys fancy getting together for old time sake? He wrote, then deleted it and checked his Inbox, to see if there was any trace of Allan but there were no apparent 'sightings' of the guitarist. 'Looks like Araf is having difficulty finding him too,' he considered. 'Never mind, I'll just get the ball rolling first and then we can take it from there.'

He looked blankly down at the table top, wondering how and where to start this epistle? His fingers hovered over the keyboard, twitching, but the words didn't come easily.

"To Fester, or not to Fester? That is the question," he said but yet again, nothing was actually written and it wasn't for the next few minutes.

'Can't just sit here like this,' Hovis thought with frustration. Then, dissatisfied with a silent protestation, he clenched both of his fists and yelled into the air. Thoroughly invigorated, he got up......, to make himself yet another coffee before he began......

"Howdy Y'all,"

Brown Slice calling Planet Earth.

We won guys! Don't know about you but I'm going to listen, until something knock's us off our perch. Yeah, the D.J's a dick but he's the dick who's resurrected The Fester's!

Question: how d'you fancy meeting up for a good, old fashioned blowout of music, food, drink and whatever else, at my place here in the Welsh Mountains?

I can put you all up, so no worries there. Go on, be a set of devil's and take a chance. I guarantee you'll have a really cool time.

How's about next Friday? You can stay for the night or the weekend if you want. Let me know and has anybody heard from, Allan?

Hovis, then read through his communique again and signed off with his normal, well thirty plus years ago, monicker.

Hovis. The Bass Man.

"Well, now we just sit back and see what happens, eh Cheech?" Then he laughed at the thought of five neo-geriatrics, whooping it up at the local hop. "There it's done," he said purely for his own benefit. "Remember, Cheech, when the world's looking dark, try to spread a little light on the matter," he pontificated, more to the ceiling than his ever-tolerant Red Setter, as he stretched his back against the spine of his 'No.1 Computing Chair.' He let out a long, relaxed groan, which mingled easily with the tremendous feeling of self-satisfaction he was experiencing at that instant.

'Now here's a thing, another mid-afternoon and nothing to do,' Hovis sarcastically mused. 'Lot's to do in fact, just not enough time to do it in,' his sensible mind countered. 'Yeah but there's no point in starting anything right now, it'll be tea time before you know it and there's a Rugby League game on tonight, so whatever it is, it's going to have to wait.'

*

This love of the thirteen-man code began when he was four years old and his Grandmother, at a loss as to what to do with him on a quiet Saturday afternoon, had for some reason known only unto herself, taken him to watch Swinton RLFC and he'd loved every minute of it. He didn't know what it was but he was hooked on it, for life. He'd often wondered about his ongoing addiction to Rugby League. In the modern era, the mere thought of doing anything on a Friday night until the game finished on tv, was a definite no-no, as far as Hovis was concerned.

Right now, his optimism was high. Surely Hull would see off the hated Wigan Warriors in the game tonight. Although he was and always had been a Swinton supporter, for this and many other similar nights, he was quite willing to lean towards anybody who could dent 'The Cherries' title, or Challenge Cup hopes. Anyway, no matter the result of tonight's clash, there was always tomorrow.

Even at this distance from the action, there were certain rituals which had to be followed on 'Rugby Friday's,' as he'd been calling these nights since he subscribed to Sky TV. The timing of the evening's meal was generally geared to the match and it more often than not consisted of a Meat and Potato Pie, far too many chips, a portion of Mushy Peas and two, or three cans of Draught Guinness. This evening would be no different; Hovis was nothing, if not a creature of habit. This evening would find him sat in front of the television screen, wearing his childhood Blue and White Swinton RL scarf, hoping that a team decked out in Black and White, would soundly kick the ass of another team, who played in Red and White hoops.

The evening went remarkably smoothly, with no upset's, or unusual happenings. Hull defeated Wigan, thus stretching their lead in the table to four points, a happy Hovis ate and drank too much. The win meant it didn't stop at three cans of the black stuff. After all, the defeat of Wigan needed celebrating, so it was much closer to six cans and Cheech, as usual, got his rations.

His loathing of that one team, Wigan, had begun many years ago when they'd slaughtered Swinton on a regular basis. Over time it had just settled into a deep immovable rut, which was only bolstered by the team's ridiculous amount of success on the field and number of trophies they won. Since 1965, Wigan had, in any chosen season, been more successful than Swinton had ever managed, even if you combined their whole fifty odd years of existence and squared the result.

Next morning, both he and Cheech were somewhat hungover and hence, they both overslept. Back when he'd acquired the dog, Johnny G had told him about how his Setter liked a tipple but he'd neglected to mention, just how much that tipple was and it had been left for Hovis to discover the actual extent of Cheech's alcoholic depravity. What had started as a splurge from a can of Guinness, had over the intervening years, expanded to a whole can. It would have been more if Cheech had his way but Hovis wisely set the limit at one can, when it became clear to him that Cheech was a potentially ongoing sot.

Hovis had a special glass for his rugby Guinness. One which had been produced by the company for some anniversary, or other and Cheech had a Swinton RL Pyrex bowl, that Hovis had bought expressly for their special rugby night's in together.

However, hangover notwithstanding, on this bright morning Hovis had something rather important to do. Rousing himself, he slipped silently past the sleeping dog and made his way to check if any of the other Fester's had got back to him regarding his invitation. On first inspection, there was only a single reply and that unsurprisingly, was from Poe.

"God, she's efficient," he said as he opened her correspondence.

"High there Brown Slice, I'd love to come up to your place. Please send me more details ASAP."

Hovis, read the message again and was just about to reply, when another one came in. This second message, was from Preston and it said much the same as Poe's original, except it was more irreverent and began with,

Howdy, y'old fart.

The rest of the message stated his present location in England and requesting information on the when and where's of the proposed meeting?

"Wow! Two down and two more to go," he cried with joy and instinctively began playing air-bass, making bum, bum, bum noises.

'I wonder what is happening with Allan? Maybe Araf will have some news soon........,' That idle train of thought was rapidly interrupted by Cheech, who lazily farted and then casually grunted, as he rolled over and changed his position on the floor.

"Jesus man, where did you drag that one up from," cringed Hovis and shot an accusatory look at his dog, rapidly flapping his hands to disperse the cloying stench. "You're not giving me the one eye now, are you?" He picked up his rugby weekly magazine and continued wafting.

"Christ, a little warning would be nice next time."

On the floor, with his back to his owner, Cheech's tail wagged just the once and then remained perfectly still.

"I saw that," Hovis snapped, "and don't think I don't know you're awake," he remarked as the acrid odour began to dissipate. "What would you reckon if I cut your Stout ration down and no chips on the side, eh? You wouldn't like that, now would you?" Hovis smiled, as Cheech's red tail unavoidably twitched in response to the half-hearted threat.

Turning back to his computer he started to consider his replies to Poe and Preston. They were easy to construct and by using more or less the same words in both e-mail's, he was able to get over all the information that he felt needed to be imparted to his two ex-colleagues.

Araf, when or if he got back to him, wouldn't be so easy. He'd always been a little spikier but nothing like as difficult as his brother. With Allan, you always had to watch your words, Araf was at least reasonable, whenever he grasped whatever it was that you were talking about. Unlike Allan, he didn't see everything as an attack on his integrity, which needed to be furiously defended. The only times that Hovis could recall having anything more than what he referred to as, 'Fuck off conversations' with him were when the subject of politics came up.

After the Fester's broke up, Allan, unlike his more personable brother, had become a furious Welsh nationalist, whom Hovis would later learn, was a member of, 'The Sons of Owen Glyndwr.' Under their misguided auspices, he had done some time in prison for a blatant act of arson against a property, which he wrongly believed was an English owned, second home. In fact, the cottage that he and his dodgy mates had set ablaze, was owned by a Welsh speaking Estate Agent, called Ethan Parry, who himself was a long-standing member of Plaid Cymru.

However, right now Hovis was unaware of these facts.

Chapter Twenty-Five

The Manx Dragon.

Having spent the whole of yesterday just messing about, strumming Jezebel and waiting for any of the Festers to get back to him, Hovis had blown yet another day.

"Maybe only Poe and Preston are coming to your Festerval. Maybe it's only you who really gives a damn about the band....... And last week was just a bit of fun on the radio...,"

As Moanvis the Usurper, his negative inner character, spoke those last few words, the awful realisation that he might be right, struck the bullseye in Hovis' brain. As usual, he turned his gaze towards Cheech, asking the dog for its opinion on that last conjecture. His words elicited the usual response from The Setter, who merely opened one eye for a moment and then closed it again.

"Hmm," Hovis vibrated, echoing a general agreement that he read into Cheech's response. "I suppose until Ken Alexander played the damn thing on his stupid radio show, I hadn't thought about 'I Want you, Love.., Want me too, Love,' in almost thirty years …… perhaps I'm just grasping at straws," he stated as Moanvis' head slumped forward, in victory.

He hung there for what seemed like an age, his chaotic thoughts and memories intertwining in a disordered soup of emotions, the all-pervasive silence in No.37 seeming to hold him in its thrall. Hovis just stared blankly, waiting for something to happen. Then, just as he was about to give up on this whole email thing, 'Fliss' suddenly sprang into life.

"You have mail," she softly said, courteously waiting for him to decide on the next action. His machine's soothing words brought him back to the present with a jolt, like waking from a dream. For a few moments he found it difficult to truly locate himself in time and space. His inbox said there was one unread message awaiting his attention but before he could do anything about it, another message popped up, accompanied by the usual announcement from Fliss.

"You have mail," she seductively said, in her rather deep, privileged and Felicity Kendal sounding accent.

"Wow, two in as many minutes, aren't you the popular one," he facetiously quipped then quietly laughed at his presumptive statement. 'Probably just a couple of pieces of scatter gun advertising for something I don't want, n can't afford....' Moanvis surmised, mentally preparing for disappointment, but checked anyway.

The first one was from Preston who needed instructions on how to reach the 'Festerval' and the later email, was from Araf who graciously accepted his impromptu invitation to spend the weekend with him and the other Festers at No.37.

Much cheered, Hovis prepared to send copies of the details he'd started for Poe the day before.

The instructions, regarding the location of No.37 were simple. Well, it was if you had a rudimentary map of the area washing around in your head but unfortunately, most people didn't. What seemed like a bunch of simple instructions to Hovis, proved to be anything but when he attempted to convey them to a potential visitor. After much rewriting, editing, rewriting again, he finally dispatched his Route to Festerval.

*

The Company D-Day, which conveniently fell at the month end, would give him a good week after his planned Festerval, to finish getting his house in order, ready to depart.

Blue Yonder liked to be the bearers of the torch that lit the way to a clean break, after all, what better manifestation of that power could there be, than fire? Hovis, as the last employee on The Hill, felt that he owed it to all those who had departed before him, to take a resistant stance, no matter how futile the effort may turn out to be. Too many times he'd seen the company's men come in and smash a cabin then light the flames, even as the departing worker and his, or her family were driving away down the Rat Road. In the face of this statement of power, he was determined not to just meekly roll over and die. Not now, not after the Save and Loan rip off!

Hovis was determined to strike his blow for all the worker's who'd been cheated out of the future that The Blue Yonder Mining Company, had so earnestly promised them. He just wasn't quite sure how......

*

The directions, which had seemed simple enough to him, appeared to be causing some degree of consternation to Preston, Poe and surprisingly, Araf, who was after all, Welsh by birth. 'What can be so difficult about these instructions?' He pondered and then read them again, to see if they could be made any easier to understand.

"I can't see what the problem is ....," he said absentmindedly and read the instructions a third time, just to make sure that he wasn't deluding himself.

"In Bethesda," he almost incoherently mumbled, "take a left onto the A470 and then travel roughly 10 miles, until you are flanked by two gigantic mountains. These are The Glyder's, Fach on your right-hand side and Faur, to your left." Hovis stopped there, while he considered the words he'd just muttered, then with a nod of his head, he continued. "As you pass the sign for a Youth Hostel, on the right, you will get your first view of Snowdon, in the distance. A little further along the road, you will see a lake, to your left. That's Llyn Garon."

From here the instructions did in fact grow a little hazy, as picking out the Rat Road, was no easy task for the uninitiated. A small sign, that was mostly obstructed by a random overgrowth of vegetation pointed the way to The Blue Yonder Mine. The turning was easily missed and Hovis started to consider how to mark the spot independently, so that his intended guests could more easily find their way to No.37.

'Well, seeing as how there's only me and Cheech left on The Hill, who's going to complain if I make a sign of my own and stick it on the bottom of the road, pointing the way up to our place?'

"Nobody that's who," he quickly replied in response to his silent enquiry and continued with this one-sided dialogue. "I'll be long gone before anyone notices it and in truth, who actually gives a fuck anyway," grumbled Hovis, bitterly.

Even in this potentially splendid isolation, he just couldn't resist adding a touch of his once apparent artistic temperament. The sign, which had originally begun life in his imagination as a simple white board, with a black arrow pointing up the sloping Rat Road, had creatively become a Welsh Dragon. It was still white, thus making it easy to see against the green of the over growing foliage but more importantly, it stroked his creative ego.

Happy with this idea, he turned his mind towards the creation of the White Dragon and the tools required to complete the task. It was whilst he was considering the pointy angle of the tail that it dawned on him he needed another sign at the junction between his cabin track and the Rat Run, or his guests could end up disappearing inside the Agamemnon Building Complex.

'Best get the bloody things made then, so I can send them all another set of instructions with photos.' A few minutes later, after rummaging in the shed, he lifted the ancient Jigsaw onto his equally aged Black & Decker Workmate and began to sketch the lines of his vaguely artistic dragon onto a chunk of old plywood. He planned to cut one and use that as a template for the second. The old rusty blade, once so accurate, now tended to tear raggedly through the slightly damp plywood he'd found for his Dragons. His design intended to use the Dragon's tail as a pointer, to guide the driver in the right direction.

His mind bubble picture of the beast's tail swirling around and pointing in the direction of No.37, was sound enough, in theory. However, on the second dragon, when he was trying to be too clever with the rusty blade, it caught a weak spot, tearing away the last few inches of the tail.

"Oh, bugger!" He gasped as the 'pointer,' dropped unceremoniously to the floor, creating a Manx dragon. With no more plywood, Hovis would have to settle for something a good deal less impressive than his original concept.

"Oh well...., just a quick sand and a dab of paint, a bit of hammering and 'hey presto,' the job'll be a good 'un," he casually said in his darkest Mancunian accent. Five minutes later he was using an aged, stiff paintbrush, to apply another dollop of Dulux white vinyl gloss paint, to the freshly cut Manx Dragons.

"Well, it would have looked good, if it had worked," he said as he painted a crude black arrow on the belly of the beast of his second failed artwork and laid it on the floor to dry, before final construction could begin.

At this point, Hovis was unaware of the obvious error in his planning. The two Dragons weren't exactly what he had intended, but surely, they were good enough for the purpose of directing the other Fester's to his abode on The Hill?

"Not bad, eh Cheech?" He stepped back to view his handiwork. "Pity the tails didn't exactly live up expectation but what the hell, they'll do. Now it's just simply a matter, of placing them....., when they're dry."

*

A while later than he'd anticipated, Hovis confidently set off with his Dragons tucked under his arm. The first one, at the base of the Rat Road, was easy to place. Hovis was glad that he'd fixed a post to the main body of the Dragon, as there was nothing else in the vicinity to anchor the beast. Leaving it unattached, at the mercy of the unpredictable weather, wasn't an option he wished to explore at this time of year. The seasonal winds and the occasional monsoon like rain storm that the mountains could throw up out of nowhere, easily trashed most things not bolted down.

He'd even remembered to cut the ends of the post's into semi points, like a real DIY Dude, to aid him as he hit the tops with the old rusty lump hammer he'd dug out from the back of the shed. He picked out what he hoped was a good spot and began hitting his post.

One last whack and Hovis stood back in order to admire his efforts.

"Oh yeah, that's how you do it," he said for nothing more than his self-aggrandisement, folded his arms and nodded his head in total agreement with the sentiment. The White Dragon stood out clearly against the deep green of the background vegetation and the hastily added black arrow, clearly indicated the direction to travel to No.37.

His euphoria, would only last for as long as it took him to see the glaring error in his plan but as yet, that delight was still to come.

"Come on then, let's get number two done and then we can relax a little," he said to the Red Setter and with a click of his finger's, set off up the hill, Cheech in tow, to place the second of the two White Dragon's at the fork in the Rat Road. This split in the road was the key to locating No.37, or continuing on into the Blue Yonder.

At the mines inception in early 1979 there had been a rather classy hoarding, which proudly proclaimed,

'The Blue Yonder Mining Company Head Office, straight ahead 500 yards.'

That long lay broken into countless tiny shards, scattered in the bushes that lined the incongruous two-lane highway leading to The Agamemnon Building. It had been replaced in the 80's with an even grander one giving directions to each area of the site. However, the last long, windy and wet winter, had taken its toll and with Blue Yonder closing down, there was no incentive to repair the damage when it had become detached from its moorings and flown off to who knew where, on one of the wild winter storms.

It only took him a minute, or two to reach the split in the road and Hovis was still congratulating himself on his cut-out Dragon's. He still hadn't noticed the obvious and glaring error in his construction method. An arrow pointing the way, straight up the Rat Road, was one thing but it didn't allow for any twists 'n turns. In fact, Hovis hadn't allowed for any changes of direction when he'd painted the arrows on his two Dragon's. Unfortunately, the second Dragon should have indicated that after the fork, a sharp left turn was required, as continuing straight on from that point, only looped back to the main front entrance of The Agamemnon Building.

As Hovis approached the divide, he proudly held out the White Dragon and prepared the lump hammer, for its single appointed task. After halting, to consider the positioning of his second Dragon for a moment, Hovis confidently stepped across the junction and prepared to beat the sharpened supporting post, into the yielding earth. It was only as he was about to deliver the third blow, that he became aware of the mistake he'd so confidently made, when he'd painted the black arrow on his Manx Dragon.

"Oh Crap!" He gasped desperately, when the error of his ways became obvious to him. "You see what happens, when you think y'know what you're doing? Now I'll have to paint over this black arrow and start again," mocked Moanvis. "Or will I?" Hovis defiantly thought out loud, as he considered his options. "A little judicious use of the black paint and everything should be tickety-boo," he gleefully decided. Having thought of an alternate option to repainting from scratch, Hovis was unwilling to allow the number two Dragon to delay him any further and he gave his impromptu sign another whack with the Lump Hammer, just to be certain it wasn't going to fall over, while he located his aberrant paintbrush.

*

"Oh bollocks, where the fuck are you?" He complained as he rummaged about for the brush in the bin. On several occasions, he was within inches of the damned thing but his natural, blind impatience wouldn't let him stop for a second to take a longer look. Eventually located, the rest of the process took no time at all to complete. It was just a simple matter of extending what had originally been a straight line, at a right angle to the left, adding the arrow head and painting 'No.37,' above it, to ensure there was no confusion about what lay at the terminus of these instructions.

"Perfect," Hovis mumbled as he took a couple of steps backwards, to fully appreciate the culmination of his late morning's work. "Come on, I've got a few e-mails to complete 'n send......and Jezebel awaits," he said to Cheech, as he purposefully set off in the direction of home.

Chapter Twenty-Six

Trampled Underfoot.

S even hundred and forty-eight paces later, they reached the front gate of his log cabin. "Seven hundred and forty-eight metres," he repeated a few times for no apparent reason. For a moment he seriously considered putting the number on the sign that he'd just erected but dismissed the idea as being too pedantic, even for Accountant Hovis.

He opened the familiar front door and held it ajar for Cheech, who entered at his usual laconic pace, then followed him indoors and quietly closed the door. The rhythmic ticking of the German skeleton clock on the wall and the gentle beat of Jennifer Paige's, "Crush," on the radio, which nowadays, was permanently playing in the room with him, just in case The Fester's ever appeared on it again.

He'd spent so long getting the White Dragons sorted out, that he'd completely missed The Ken Alexander Show, so was unaware that he'd been replaced by the unethically ambitious Sarah Buckley. When the Fester's released 'I Want you, Love.., Want me too, Love' in 1984, she hadn't even been born, just a passing and yet to be fulfilled fancy in her father's rather upper-class trousers. Because of this heritage, she had something of a retarded musical background alongside the dubious privilege of being the youngest DJ that Radio Two had ever employed. Generally, the station didn't give that kind of responsibility to any old 'gad fly' who would be 'Here today and Solid Gone, tomorrow,' as Ken Alexander liked to say, because he incorrectly assumed it made him sound hip.

Ignorant of this, Hovis was now at the mercy of Pete Greaves and his "smooth afternoon vibes." Unlike Ken, he was trying to keep up with his audience's amorphous and ever-changing tastes, quirk's and all. In truth, very few people tuned into his show for the musical adventurism on offer. The audience only tended to tune in for roughly thirty minutes, which was around how long it took them to take their post prandial nap.

"Enough of this Tom Foolery," he gasped and flipped his iPad open. Now ready to type, Hovis took a deep breath and started to write this potentially important e-mail to the remaining three members of The Fester's.

"Good day in Hell, eh Cheech," he unthinkingly commented, as the first few letters of his missive, made it onto the blank page.

After a quick intro, which consisted of the usual 'Hi, how you doin',' kind of stuff, Hovis carefully re-read his latest additional set of directions,

When you see 'Llyn Garon' on your left, keep your eyes open, for a White Dragon, on your right-hand side and take that junction to turn up the Rat Road. Half a mile further on, another Dragon, on the left-hand side of the road, will show you the way to No.37.

He reread them and once satisfied that they couldn't really be improved upon, he attached photos of the White Dragons in situ, snapped earlier from his iPad. After a final read through he sent a copy to each of the known remaining Fester's, with a personal touch added to each mail.

To Preston, he enquired as to why he was still in the country, after all these years? Poe, got a question about her penchant for curious means of transport and he showed a touch of sympathy in Araf's note, asking about his brother Allan's wellbeing.

Once that was done, Hovis got up to make himself a drink, flicking the television on as he passed by it on his way to the kitchen.

"Right then Cheech, let's see who's threatening to plunge us into a Nuclear Winter today," he sat down on the settee and took a tentative sip from his bone china mug.

"Hot, hot, hot," he gasped, as his lips came into contact with the steaming liquid and he almost dropped the whole ensemble on the floor. That outcome was only narrowly avoided by the convenient closeness of the occasional table, which he mostly used to put his feet up on at night.

Hovis had a penchant for awful Horror movies whose inept plots usually sent him to bed laughing. Occasionally, he misjudged them and instead of laughing, the damned thing would make him cry, which only served to further disrupt his sleep pattern. When that happened, it often took Hovis several days to recalibrate his circadian rhythm and get back to something resembling normalcy.

*

His mind drifted back to an offering called, 'Odd Thomas'. It sure did sound like a madcap comic horror movie, possibly concocted by the Cohen brother's or Seth Green, perfect for the end of a particularly hard week. One which had resulted in a totally depressing set of sales figures, undoubtedly leading to even more men being laid off by Blue Yonder. If he'd ever needed something to cheer him up, it was sorely required on that rather warm, heavy Friday evening. Sleeping wouldn't be an easy state to achieve in those oppressive temperatures anyway. The late forecast had indicated that a thick band of cloud was coming in from the continent and for a few hours during the middle of the night, this would trap in the heat of the day, in both air and stone, raising the overnight temperature to an uncomfortable 28C.

"Jesus, that's all that I need," blustered Hovis, knowing that sleep was probably going to evade him again that night, so he'd begun to plan for an alternative night of viewing. It was then he spotted this movie called, 'Odd Thomas' and instantly been drawn towards it.

"Nothing better than a good laugh to herald sleep," he stated confidently but oh, how wrong you can be to judge a film by its title!

Having got himself settled on the settee, wearing nothing more than his jockey shorts, Hovis had prepared himself for a night of laughter and a little sleep. Before him on the coffee table were a selection of cooling aid's, including an ice bag containing six can' of chilled Draught Guiness, a family sized tub of 'Cherry Garcia', his favourite flavour of Ben & Jerry's Ice Cream, some Ice Cubes and last but certainly not least, a portable fan that he'd picked up for a knock down price at a jumble sale, some years earlier.

"O.K. Let's get on with our evening's laughter and start the movie," he said to Cheech and locating the 'der-der,' turned the television on. It didn't take Hovis long to realise this particular film was not in the least bit funny and was instead, quite a decent example of the horror genre.

'Odd Thomas,' was in fact about the scary harbingers of death, who were in themselves, dead. They couldn't speak to the living when crossing over between the two states of existence and the story was quite tenderly handled. It was captivating and not at all what he was expecting. In the narrative, 'Stormy,' Thomas' girlfriend and the female protagonist, was almost too perfect. She was every young lad's dream of a girlfriend, smart, funny, concerned and understanding. She was totally dedicated to Odd and it was made clear, that she would make a perfect, long-term partner for him.

Then, just when Hovis had invested himself totally in the story and he was hoping for a happy ending, the scenario turned sour and he had ended up 'six can's drunk,' in tears, wallowing in self-pity over his love life, or lack of it. He spent the remainder of that night, looking out the French Windows, listening to a selection of his favourite Classical Music Meloditties' as he called them and just remembering his past glories of being a younger man.

*

Come this new dawn, Hovis was convinced that he hadn't slept a wink but the ache in his neck, indicated differently. He was having great difficulty in moving his head at all, without a sharp pain shooting through his neck and running all the way down his spine. Sleeping on the settee was not recommended. For some relief from the pain, he rested his heavy head in his hands and closed his eyes once more. He could feel himself slipping away and his weary mind was offering no resistance to the overpowering inclination. Then he was snapped back into this world, by 'Fliss,' proclaiming that he had mail. The words made him jump and he dropped his head,

"Oooh ouch," he squeaked as his chin bounced on his chest and he woke fully with a start.

'Fliss,' declared that it was from somebody who went by the familiar call sign of OnceanAbutnowaP and for an instant, Hovis just looked quizzically at Cheech, who was barely awake, while he tried to put his brain in gear.

"It's from Poe," he yelped and hurriedly opened it, hoping to God that it wasn't a pull out.

Hi there, Brown Slice. Got your directions last night and I'll be there as requested on Friday afternoon. Not exactly sure when I'll get there, Gertie has her own ways,

Thanks for the invite.

Poe

Hovis punched the air, like he'd just scored the winning goal in the F.A. Cup Final.

"This is all going spookily well," he informed Cheech. "Something's undoubtedly going to go wrong soon enough but please God, not yet!" Then his brain added, 'I think we'll know more, when and if, Preston and Araf reply.'

This conversation was purely for his own benefit but it made Hovis feel better, even if it was only until he once again, started worrying about the silence from the other ex-Fester's.

Araf never had all that much to say unless it was some bile directed at his sibling and Preston had never been one for small talk, only speaking if he had something pertinent to contribute. Unbeknown to Hovis, that trend had been getting worse since he and Poe had split, all those years ago. It wasn't until then that he really missed her but their break up had been on such a fundamental level, there was no conceivable way back. Preston had missed her at curious times of the day and always at night. If he'd been smart, he would have fled back to The States, but the memory of Poe had held him captive in the UK.

As for Allan Exit, there had been no word from him in almost Thirty-Five years and for all that Hovis knew, he could well be dead.

"That's something that I really will have to verify with Araf," he almost silently muttered, then went back to thinking some more about the move to their new home at Mrs. Dugdale's old Crofter's cottage, just outside Llanbadrig.

*

A deal of time later, Hovis picked up Jezebel and started playing, amp turned up loud. He really pushed at it, forcing the stiffness out of his fingers as he played the bass line for Trampled Underfoot, as loud and dramatically as he could.

As he swung Jezebel in a dramatic sweep, he caught his foot on Cheech and began to fall. In that slo-mo moment, the full horror of landing on top of Jezebel, smashing her beautiful neck, played out in his horrified mind. Instinctively, he twisted mid-flight and landed, flat on his back, with his precious Jezebel held up above him like some offering to the gods of music.

"Oumphhhh!"

He lay there for a few moments, gathering his senses and figuring if anything hurt. Cheech, was staying out of it, shouldering the guilt for tripping his master up. 'Nothing broken' he thought, then laughed at the ridiculous figure he must have cut; chubby, balding, middle aged guy hammering his guitar to recapture some semblance of youth, tripping over his dog and going down like a sack of rock 'n roll spuds. It played out in his mind as a series of amusing snap shots and then it dawned on him, only Poe had furnished him with a recent photograph of herself.

This prompted Hovis to get up and take a good look at his head and shoulders in the hall mirror.

"Not bad for a man of my tender years," he commented as he tipped his head back and pouted, like he was an older, balder and still living, Marc Bolan. "You sad fuck. You look more like Steve

Priest from Sweet!" Moanvis countered. Undeterred, Hovis grinned back at the image in the mirror, blew himself another camp kiss and then dissolved into uncontrollable guffaws of breathless laughter, as visions of the two failed rock stars, filled his mind. 'God knows what they'd look like now, Jesus even I don't look like I thought I would,' he looked blankly away into the middle distance, lost in rose tinted thoughts of things the way they never used to be, reconstructing his image from some dubious data mined in an indeterminate past.

'Selfie?'

"Nah."

Chapter Twenty-Seven

Memory Maze.

"I suppose I'm going to have to ask Araf if we can expect Allan to join us for this little soiree," he offered to Cheech, while at the same time dreading just how he was going to couch the question, diplomatically. It was Poe and her rejection of Allan's rather clumsy and often crude advances, who was the trigger for the volcanic exchange on the Fester's tour bus and eventual destruction of the band.

"You know Cheech, when I come to think about it, it might be better if Allan doesn't come to Festerval. He was always the awkward one and Araf at least had the decency to respond to my Facebook enquiry......."

Logic said that time was the healer in cases like this but Allan Exit was not your average kind of guy. He had a propensity for holding on to the merest of slight's and once the dye was cast, that was it, as far as he was concerned.

"Araf, used to refer to him as 'Dumbo'," he said to Cheech, as an aside, like the dog wanted to know such a thing and as usual, the only recognition that Cheech gave to Hovis' monologue was the opening and subsequent closing of one eye. 'Dumbo,' wasn't a reference to his lack of intelligence, which was obvious, but a derisory comment on the size of his nose and ears; together with his elephantine memory for the slightest of slur's.

After a brief pause in proceedings, he realised that no matter what he wrote it could be seen as inappropriate by the analytically picky Araf, so he just set about it.

Howdy Araf,

*Any news on Allan? Should I be preparing for a
surprise guest appearance by the mystery Welshman, or do you
know something a little more relevant? I've heard nothing from him.
You, Poe and Preston all replied quite quickly but nothing came
back from your brother. Hope he's alright and simply doesn't wish to
partake in the reunion bash. You know better than me, I'm just trying
to ascertain numbers, before I get on with organising the get
together. Let me know if you could.*

Thanks man.

Brown Slice

He gauged this moniker would give his missive a lighter
touch, which hopefully would be more likely to illicit a response. He
decided if he didn't get a reply in a day, then he'd just prepare
enough food and drink for four guests and maybe pump Araf for
more info. when they met.

"Think that I'll wait and see how it goes," he mumbled as he
got up and flicked the kettle on.

'Right, lots to do and obviously not enough time to do it in,'
he mentally commented as he switched his iPod on, flicked the
volume up to Max, or as they used to say back in the day, 'Eleven on
the dial'.

The sound system stayed at that volume, as Hovis frantically
tried to prepare No.37 for Festerval, practice on Jezebel and organise
his imminent departure. Many time's during this period, he asked
himself if this was a wise thing to do. How he was going to find the
space to give them all a bed for up to two nights, and then there was

the small matter of toleration to consider. He couldn't imagine Araf and Allan, if he turned up, wanting to be anywhere near each other overnight. The only outcome from that unfortunate pairing would be an increased animosity in the morning, that is unless one of the brother's hadn't murdered the other during the night. On top of that, it would be somewhat insensitive to put Poe and Preston together in the same room.

'Look Man, you can't simply keep on imagining that they're just the same as they were before. That flame probably went out years ago and as far as you know, they haven't even seen each other since then,' he silently reasoned with himself. His lips were moving but there was no sound coming out from between them. It was indeed a conundrum. 'I haven't got sufficient information,' Moanvis complained. 'I should have asked more questions......' He chastised himself, growled his self-disgust and his shoulders sank, in sympathy.

"Still, these larger log cabins were built for families to live in......." Hovis said to Cheech, who was now pretending to take an interest in what he had to say. "Three bedrooms and possibly five people to accommodate. How do we solve this one, eh lad?"

However, in reality, Hovis knew that he wasn't going to get any practical answers from his Red Setter, as Cheech had already closed both of his eyes and lowered his head, which indicated that he'd lost interest around the "five people," bit of his speech and his words fell on deaf doggy ears.

Fliss broke his reverie,

"You have Mail!"

As hoped for, the response from Araf had come back quickly enough but hardly cast any new light on the situation,

Don't know. Don't care.

Araf Slow.

"Great! So, I'm on my own with this one," he muttered and began measuring up his options, for the rapidly approaching weekend. 'If I put Poe in the 'box' room and stick Preston and Araf in the spare bedroom, then that will leave me in the main bedroom that should work....... Allan can sleep with me if he turns up.' Here he paused, 'Yuk!' Then shuddered slightly and switched tack to another far more appealing thought; that of Poe sleeping with him, in the master bedroom.

"Funny, I don't recall these pants being so tight," he chuckled and took another look at her photo that he'd stashed on his Desktop, for occasional masturbatory purposes. "Well Poe, Siouxie Sioux's got nothing on you," he commented and then returned to the real world, after another swift look at his fantasy picture.......

*

Cheech nuzzling at his hand with his cold nose, snapped Hovis out of his world of perhaps' and maybe's, back to this quiet, indifferent mid-afternoon. All this dealing with the past had brought back some rather curious memories and at this point, Hovis realised that he was going to have to take a little time to accommodate some of them. They seemingly contravened previous recollections he'd mistakenly held as gospel truth's for years. It appeared it was time to reassess sections of his life that he'd almost forgotten, as he'd plunged heedlessly into the pursuit of monetary acquisition and all the goodies it could buy.

With that life now in ruins, it felt like he'd spent too many decades deluding himself. There was no metaphorical Oz, waiting for him at the end of this illusory Yellow Brick Road.

*

With a hum and a buzz, the fluorescent light burst into being. Suddenly, all the things that he'd earnestly started but failed to finish, were illuminated. His eyes fixed on the Airfix Scale Model of the German Second World War battle cruiser, 'Scharnhorst,' which had been sitting up there in the attic for thirty or so years, looking as if it was in dry dock for a refit. Then other moments of his life began to rear their ugly heads, demanding some kind of reassessment, in this artificial light of a new day….. or dinge of the loft. On reflection, he considered that The Scharnhorst represented his need for a more serious approach to life, that his newly acquired position at The Blue Yonder Mining Company had merited.

He'd only bought the 1:72 scale model because he'd been reading about the ship's run up the channel in 1942. For some crazy reason it had struck him as a romantic, yet pointless story of foolhardy bravery in the face of inevitable defeat.

Today it just seemed to suit his present circumstances perfectly.

"It would have looked good, fully painted and sitting in triumph on the mantle," he said as he looked at the grey plastic remains of the once proud warship, the original being somewhere on the seabed off the Norwegian coast. She'd gone down on Boxing Day 1943 and this model, with many of the missing parts now lost forever, was probably not in much better shape. "You're bound for the bin," he determined. Then shut up, as visions of an alternate fate developed in a mindbubble.

"Deuchland, Deuchland uber Alles," he sang but couldn't contain his vision mirth any longer, gave a Nazi salute and dissolved into laughter. 'What the fuck am I laughing about,' he thought and as the desperation of his circumstances overwhelmed him, he started to silently weep, the tears streaming down his face.

"Thirty God knows how many years and for what?" He asked the wooden floor, receiving no answer, he repeated the question but louder this time.

"For what?!" Hovis cried venomously. "No job. No partner. No home. No money worth talking about and at my age, no fucking future!" He wailed through the increasing flow of salty tears. At this point, he tried to sing another verse of the anthem that Hyden wrote in one of his cheerier moments but his broken voice was having none of it. No matter how hard Hovis tried, he couldn't hold a note.

"Oh, what are we going to do, Cheech?" He whispered. The dog, lying in the hallway below, could sense that he was upset, so climbed the steps and laid his head in Hovis' lap. A damp hand connected with his soft fur and at that moment of shared melancholy, Cheech burped.....

*

Mr. Exit, had other things on his mind. His wife Ellian, was trying to divorce him after suffering twenty-two years and three months of married disharmony, which had entailed being a mother, several more times over than she'd planned, all because he wanted a son to "carry his family name into the future."

However, it seemed that all he could produce were girls. Allan was quite willing to go on having children that neither of them wanted, if eventually Ellian gave him a boy, whom he fully intended to have christened, Owen Glyndwr Exit.

Some might have said and many did, that he was insane but that didn't matter to Allan, he was a proud but violent Welshman and that was all that there was to it.

"What's so wrong with Llewellyn?" Ellian had the temerity to ask. "Why does it have to be Owen Glyndwr Exit? Surely the pseudonym Exit, was just an affectation from your Punk period?

You were born Allan Glendining and you should be proud of that name and hand it on to your son...., if you ever have one," she'd snidely added, then ducked in anticipation of Allan's response, which was as usual delivered with the back of his hand.

It was the frequency of actions similar to that, which had led Ellian to the Royal Courts of Justice. In fact, they were due before The Court this month, to finalise the divorce.

Allan had already made it clear to his Advocate, that if Ellian got 'nasty' then he'd be wanting all of his daughters to live with him, on his rather unproductive small holding. In that unlikely scenario, Ellian would be left without a home and she would be required to move out of the family residence.

That in itself was not a problem, as David Sinclair, the man who she'd been having an affair with for the past eighteen months, had been kept fully apprised of the situation and both she and the girls were happy to go and live with him. The fact that he was English, was in itself something that she'd chosen to withhold from Allan, purely for safety's sake. Ellian deemed that her violent husband's reaction to that news would be unpredictable but negative. So, she opted for 'the non-disclosure clause' and hoped that when and if he ever found out, she and the girls would be long gone, beyond his reach. Of course, he could always do the considerate thing and simply die but he was far too vindictive for that.

When Hovis had contacted Araf and enquired as to the wellbeing of his brother, his initial response of ignoring the request, had gradually softened. So, out of consideration for an old friend, he'd forwarded Hovis' e-mail to his estranged brother and left it up to him to sort out.

The mail had been received by Allan but was still sitting in a pile of unopened correspondences, that at present, numbered over one hundred and twenty. Mr. Exit was not good with e-mails and in most cases, he simply deleted them as they arrived and whenever they built up, he had a lazy habit of mass deletion, regardless of their content.

*

The calm quietness of The Hill, which generally used to pacify Hovis when life's trials and tribulations got him down, was now annoying him intensely. He was actually seeking constructive answers to what appeared to be intractable problems. This had resulted in a form of semi paralysis. Even addressing the cabin directly had been of no use and he soon ran out of patience waiting for any advice emanating from the big logs.

"Fat chance," he cried with a touch of defeat in his voice and cast his weary eyes once again about the cabin and cursed himself for ever believing that any job was for life. "What kind of a fuckin' moron are you, Boy?" Said 'The White Devil Slavemaster,' in his subconsciously uncontrollable American Deep-Fried Southern accent, mostly garnered from Martin Sheen in the three-part production of 'Gettysburg.' His long-held fascination with The American Civil War had originally been prompted by his interest in collecting the cards from inside some rather foul-tasting bubble gum, some opportunist company had issued to see if they could make money from naive children the world over. They'd further sweetened the pot, by including fake Confederate bank notes of varying denominations, which for one or two summer's in the 1960's, served as legal tender in the kid's eyes. The same company also published 'Mars Attacks' cards and Hovis had collected those as well. These random boyhood memories, almost instantly put the smile back on his face and any frowning was entirely due to him being unable to recall which came first, 'The Civil War,' or 'Mars Attacks.' Either way, it didn't matter, he was smiling again and the remaining days, that he and Cheech had left at No.37, somehow seemed longer.

There was no less to do but he now felt things would magically sort themselves out and a cohesive pattern would emerge.

Chapter Twenty-Eight

Druids Drop.

With so short a time before Poe, Preston, Araf and possibly Allan, were due to arrive, Hovis discovered the fault in his life plan, which was; magic is no substitute for effort and those sheets in the loft needed washing for his Festerval guests. In a number's panic before going shopping at the hypermarket in Bangor, he dashed off another risky e-mail to Araf, pleading for news of Allan's intentions.

As I said last time, I don't know and I care even less. I am not my brother's keeper.

Araf Slow

"Oops! I think I'd better leave it at that," he said offhandedly to Cheech. "I reckon we'll just have to see who arrives......" His voice tailed off into a semi whispered drone, liberally spattered with obscenities. Cheech hadn't heard a word of Hovis' polemic and only ventured to open the single 'watcher's eye,' when Hovis rose to make himself yet another coffee, and clumsily knocked a previously used mug into the desk lamp.

*

The alarm clock woke Hovis as the sun rose on Friday of the Festerval. He soon found he couldn't help himself, he was just faffing around, straightening the books on the coffee table for the third time and blowing invisible specks of dust off the keyboard, before positioning it 'just so,' in his workspace. He turned the radio on and then turned it off again. He tried listening to his iPod but that just didn't do it, so he turned that off as well.

"Christ, I'll be insane long before lunch time comes around and nobody's due until ……… whenever?" He said in a whispered voice. 'Still, whatever time that is, I've definitely got a good few hours to kill…..'

"Hey Cheech, it's not raining so what do you say about getting Dennis out and you and me go for a last ride past the Agamemnon Building 'n up the path, towards The Druid's Drop?"

Cheech didn't know exactly what Hovis was talking about but it sounded exciting enough to warrant a 'tail wag,' which seemed to please Hovis, who set off for the back door and clicked his fingers expecting the Red Setter to follow.

'The Drop,' as the locals called it, was a jaunt they'd both taken many times, mostly on summer evenings. It was said that the beauty spot got its name after the Roman's arrived in 43AD, or so and set about brutally 'pacifying' Wales. The heartland of the old religion was Anglesey but there was a strong Druidic presence around the Snowdon area too, and they were the first to feel the wrath of Rome. The 9th Legion were dispatched to Wales, in order to put down any spark of Druidic rebellion - and put it down they did, with a brutal show of force. The Druidic Army of The Mountains stood no chance of defeating the power of this new invader and chose to make their stand, at what later became known as The Druid's Drop. A high plateau with sheer cliffs on three sides. After what in fact turned out to be a gallant but futile last stand, the Druidic forces were driven to the point where they simply ran out of options and their world was reduced to a rather deadly game of Shove Penny. The Legion rhythmically advanced and the defending Welsh were forced to back up, until there wasn't enough room to go any further and men began to fall off the edge. Death by Roman Gladius, or suicide on the jagged rocks below became their only options.

The drop itself, was a sheer fall of three hundred and forty-eight feet, onto an array of uncomfortable shards of volcanic rock.

With every second, the men at the front fought bravely, dying as their guts spilled onto the ground in front of them, the cold steel gladius ripping them apart. Those remaining members of mountain Druids, threw themselves off the edge, choosing a few moments of the sensation of bird flight, before a swifter end, impaled on the stones of their land.

From the lip of Druids Drop, on a clear day Ynys Mon, the mother of Wales, sat like a jewel on the sea and invited the way forward to the commanders of 'The Bloody 9th.' They hadn't required asking twice. With the demise of their enemy, the 9th Legion, moved on to Anglesey and did the same thing to the Druid's of Ynys Mon, destroying them alongside their sacred glades of oak.

"Come on then," he called and Cheech, who, like the Roman soldier's didn't need any more asking, happily tagged along as Hovis slowly made his way on Dennis, towards the Rat Road. When they reached it, he stopped and made sure everything was still in place. His makeshift dragon directions had not been vandalised or removed by one of the remaining company, 'jobsworth's'.

"Looking good," he informed Cheech, who was busy scent marking the post that held the second White Dragon.

"The place sure feels different," he whispered as he and Cheech made their way past The Agamemnon Building, on their way towards The Druids Drop. Over in the distance, he could see someone who'd just popped out for a quiet cigarette, amidst all the chaos of the final winding up of the company. Whoever he was, he waived at Hovis as he cycled slowly past the main entrance and purely out of politeness, Hovis acknowledged the stranger, with a nod of his head. The stillness and autumn warmth of the day washed over Hovis as he slowly made his way on up the slight gradient, with Cheech lolloping closely behind. At about half way, there was a small pull-in that in 'normal' times, people often used to break their journey because of the lovely view towards the surface of Llyn Garon, which on days like this, glistened invitingly in the soft warm sunshine.

"Take a good look Cheech, it's probably the last time that we'll be coming up here," he said and after a slight pause, added, "After the Festerval, if the weather holds, what do you say about that last trip up The Kid? We could have a bacon butty at the top if you like and an Ice Cream, if the van's there, how's that sound?" As usual, Cheech just wagged his tail, which Hovis took as a gesture of consent. "Okay, it's a deal but first, let's get on with today, tomorrow will come soon enough."

The rest of the ascent was conducted in silence and Hovis took every opportunity, to take in the beauty of the lower slopes of the great mountain. In the years he'd been here, he'd taken the landscape for granted. When he started cycling it had quickly become all about the numbers. How fast he could accomplish a route, how far he had cycled, what his heart rate was, how many calories he had burnt; but now numbers had betrayed him, or freed him, it was something he was working on. He drank in the vista like a thirsty man.

*

Back from his cycle ride, the shower on this auspicious day took a little longer than usual and he spent what seemed like an age, pratting around in his green hooded bathrobe, deciding on what to wear for Festerval. He cursed silently, 'Should I go for the typical retro look, or be subtly stylish in a present day, casual outfit?' He silently enquired of himself. 'As we were back there in the day, or as we are now?' His brain fell silent after that, baffled by his own indecision and totally lost in a morass of clueless thoughts.

"I wonder what Poe'll be wearing," he said almost totally subconsciously as his mind's eye wandered off and he saw her on stage, leather clad and almost naked, winding up all the young, inexperienced boys, who stood gawping below her.

'They'd probably call all that bumping, grinding and thrusting, Child Abuse nowadays,' he thought and laughed out loud. For some unfathomable reason, The Doll's old single, 'Desire me,' suddenly reappeared in his mind and his dressing gown slowly began to bulge in a particular way, at the front.

"Down boy," he commanded. "I can think of better things to do right now," he reluctantly stated as he slipped his dressing gown off, reached down for his Cargo pants and struggled into them, with the horny thoughts of Poe still redolent in his mind. 'Why, after so many years, does she still have this effect on me?' His mind failed to answer as his T-shirt started to fight back.

Chapter Twenty-Nine

Happy Trails.

P oe, on the other hand was at that same moment, trying to decide what to pack into her bijou, fake crocodile skin, travelling case. Since she'd split from Preston all those years ago, she'd drifted from one failed relationship to another, with an alarming regularity, even experimenting with a few female affairs along the way. This trip to see Hovis, or 'Brown Slice,' as she called him, was the most exciting thing that had happened to her in years. She hadn't seen, or heard from any of the other members of the band since Preston had walked out on her, following her decision to move to Sunderland and take up the offer of a job, as a stripper in the North East.

That job had bitten the dust when it's demands became too extreme. It was one thing taking her clothes off in a provocative manner but when it came to offering the punter's an array of salacious 'extra's', she quit. The AIDS panic had just hit the headlines and the world of the sex worker, suddenly seemed like a far more dangerous occupation. There were metaphorical icebergs all over the place. They appeared regularly on the television and it was hard to move about in that world without bumping into one and she had no intention of becoming another passenger on this latter-day Titanic. It simply wasn't worth the risk. Her initial attempts to contact Preston after he left, had met with a deafening silence and she didn't know where the other Fester's had washed up either. So, Poe Pouree, sexually provocative lead singer of The Fester's, had fallen back into the real world and for all intents and purposes, had disappeared from rock and roll sight.

In the mundane world of secretarial work, having a great body only caused her problems. It wasn't the acquisition of employment that was the problem, it was the maintenance of the positions that caused major difficulties. She would get the temp. job but then lose it, when it became clear to her bosses, 'That she didn't come across,' in the added extra's department. Simply because she looked like she might, didn't necessarily mean that she would.

A great many disappointed partners had come and gone and life was never as exciting as it had been, when she was the female singer in The Fester's so, as time passed, Poe missed those days more and more. Her blog on Performance Art had a good following, but it didn't compare to singing live on stage, how could it?

Then, out of the blue, Hovis had put the post up on Facefuck and somehow the dark veil of time was lifted. Incredibly, The Fester's were getting airplay on the radio again. It was Hovis who'd informed her about the Ken Alexander Show on Radio Two and she'd voted every day, as he'd requested. In truth the show wasn't all that good, just a jumble of old pop tunes and some newer stuff that probably had a shelf life of around twenty seconds, but hearing 'I Want you, Love.., Want me too, Love' again, was cathartic.

The years had fallen away and then, to cap it all, Hovis had invited the entire band to his place in the Welsh Mountains, for a nostalgic Festerval weekend. She could barely contain the excitement she was feeling inside. She'd dispatched a rather cool 'Selfie' to 'Brown Slice' and waited for his response.

As expected, he didn't let her down and promptly responded to her first contact e-mail but disappointingly, there was no photographic attachment. So, she had to imagineer his features from previous memories. She'd always got on with Hovis but a 'reunion' with Araf, Allan and Preston, was something quite different and it made her nervous. All those years must have wrought some enormous changes to their personalities and physical appearances, which gave her something else to worry about.

She'd always kept herself fit but she was well aware that men had a habit of 'letting it all hang out,' which generally led to big guts and bald nuts. Still, if she really wanted to know what had happened to the rest of the band, the only way to find out was to follow Hovis' somewhat enigmatic directions and take a trip into the mountains of North Wales. Hovis had mentioned that the other Fester's, with the possible exception of Allan, had all agreed to be round at his place and after what had seemed an interminable wait, Festerval was almost upon her. Sitting on her crocodile weekend case to close it, she mused about her travelling outfit. 'A vision of 'then,' or a view of present-day reality?'

"Then, or now," she searched through her wardrobe and in the end, chose neither and yet both. "Tight black leather trousers and a Paisley shirt?" She tentatively offered, then, with only a little deeper thought, agreed with herself.

On the way out, she took one last look in the hall mirror. Now, doubly satisfied with her choice, she blew herself a kiss and automatically reached up and grabbed the leather flying hat, which, as usual, was sitting on the very top shelf. She always wore the hat when she was driving somewhere special in 'Gertrude,' her vintage Messerschmitt KR200 three-wheeler.

She'd picked up the hat years ago at a branch of Wakefield's Army and Navy Store in Garstang, or it might have been Lancaster but anyway, it was back when she was still with Preston. Back then, she'd bought 'Gertrude' for a pittance, with her final share of the money the record company had forwarded to the band upon their demise. The leather flying cap, just topped off the whole ensemble of flying jacket, scarf and aviator sunglasses, beautifully. 'Gerti,' had cost her the grand sum of £180 and seriously needed more than a little tender loving care. After the band, Poe found she had loads of time to spare, just no more money.

As time passed Preston had left but the little Messerschmitt stayed. Slowly, Gerti was restored to her former glory, including being resprayed in authentic Second World War Me.109 camouflaged livery. Disappointingly, Gertrude had no wings, so there was no room for the much-feared machine guns. Still, it was an awesome craft, whether it was airborne or not. Frau Gertrude, was soon quite used to receiving compliments from other motorist's, whenever Poe took her anywhere. A few years ago, she had been offered £8000 for Gerti but had turned it down, she simply couldn't bear the thought of being without 'mein leiber.'

"You and me against the world, baby," she often said to the old car. Even when her finances dipped again and something had to go, it was her other car, an old Datsun Cherry, that was sold. "Don't worry, Mein Lieber," she told Gerti, "no matter what, you and me are forever!" With that thought in her mind, Poe slipped on her head gear and took one last look at the Philip's Multi-scale map of Britain, resting open on the rumble seat, along with a print out of Hovis' instructions, just to be sure of her route to Wales. Satisfied, she turned the key in the ignition and Gertrude sprang into life. Letting the engine idle to warm up, she automatically reached over, turned on her iPod and began to carefully select the music to enhance her long drive to North Wales.

"No."

"No."

"Not likely," she muttered as she methodically scrolled through the playlist of her favourite driving songs, called 'Route 66.' Like all her trips out in Gerti, finding the perfect accompaniment for her drive up the West coast to Snowdonia, would take some time. Woe betide any passenger who ever showed even the mildest irritation or impatience about how long it took to select a playlist. "These things really matter if you wish to make the journey in a conducive state of mind. The slight delay is well worth it if you want to arrive at your destination with a smile on your face, then the music has to be right! If you don't like it you can always get out and walk, " she'd forcefully say and it was hard to argue with that kind of logic.

"You've got to be joking," and "You're kidding me," Poe almost predictably spluttered, as she worked her way down the chosen playlist. Then, finally, "Ahh yes! Perfect!"

Lastly, she made absolutely sure that all the vibes were aligned correctly within the confines of Gertrude, before she pressed 'play' and the sounds of Rescue by Echo and the Bunnymen flooded over her as she finally set off to North Wales with a smile, for what she fully expected would be The Fester's last ever 'gig.'

*

While Poe was beating out a solid piece of Pete Defreitas drumming on her Bakelite steering wheel, Preston was quietly 'Raving on,' to 'The Theme from Morse' and selecting which shampoo to use in his shower. Yesterday, he'd been tinkering with his classic 'D' Series Mercedes Benz, preparing it for the journey from his home in the rural North Lancashire village of Scorton, to Hovis Monk's place in Snowdonia. There were still a few traces of oil on his hands and he scrubbed them hard, worrying he may inadvertently get oil on his expensive Italian designer suit.

For some reason, the prospect of meeting the other members of the band after so many years made him very nervous, which he didn't quite understand. Yesterday, when he'd been T-Cutting the Merc, just so that she would look her very best for the sole purpose of impressing the other's, he'd been a picture of calmness but this morning he was quite the opposite. He used to say to anybody who'd listen, that he was never going to end up like his Father but the passing years had proven that to be a lie. He'd ended up far more like his old dad than he cared to acknowledge. If the truth be told, he was also a lot more like his despised brother, Leyland, who lived in San Fran-disco, as Preston called it. His big shot lawyer brother lived in a designer house with an automatic, ornate metal gate, which, when they thought that he couldn't hear them, his neighbours described as ostentatious.

The only real difference that could be discerned by any casual observer, between Preston and the rest of his family, was that over the years, he had gradually become more of an English gentleman, than an American cowboy. On several occasions he had seriously considered taking dual nationality and gradually, over the past thirty years, that option had been growing ever more appealing. It was merely a matter of taste, Preston preferred his long gravel driveway and his well-manicured garden, to his brother Leyland's sun-bleached city-scape and his futuristic house in Marin County.

Even as a young child, Preston had been drawn towards music; a fact which didn't go down too well with Daddy, who was only too willing to relentlessly tell his elder son, "There's no future down that path, law is a much better life long career choice."

Whereas his sibling, Leyland, ever the one to curry favour with anyone in authority, chose a career in Law, making their parent's very happy but they were less pleased with his city of residence, as they dreaded the 'Big One.' Leyland, like all the other San Franciscan's, never mentioned the San Andreas Fault. He simply hoped that he'd be out of town, or dead, the day the 'Biggie' happened.

Perhaps it was the prospect of having to make polite conversation with a bunch of people that he no longer had anything in common with, or perhaps he was afraid of having to justify his present circumstances to those whose lives had turned out less fortunately than his own, that was unnerving him? Hovis, it seemed, had done alright for himself but he always gave off the air of a successful guy. Araf, it appeared, had made quite a go of his farm but Allan was a different kettle of fish.

He always was.

Allan was the most consistently belligerent member of the band and on giving it a little more thought, Preston realised that in his memories, he hardly knew him at all.

The Allan Exit that he was acquainted with all those years ago, was a complex character, one who had a world of psychological problems spinning around in his head. To cure him of these societal difficulties could easily be beyond the scope of any one man, or woman for that matter and if the infrequent bits of hearsay that came his way were to be believed, Mr. Exit had gone completely off the rails and become a crazed Welsh Nationalist. In whose cause, he'd burnt some house or other down, then spent some time in prison for his deluded activities. According to the story, he'd been out of jail for quite a while now and it appeared that Mr. Exit was keeping his head down and his nose clean.

Preston had heard this tale from an ex-member of 'The Alarm,' who he'd bumped into some years ago, quite by accident at a children's pop festival he'd attended with his youngest. The Alarm guy reckoned that he'd heard it from one of the blokes in 'The Manic's.' So, as was to be expected, the veracity of this information got thinner as it was passed from person, to person. Preston had simply stored it somewhere in his head, in the 'Interesting Rumour' file and put it away in his mind's library, for possible future verification.

No, it was the impending meeting with Poe, who'd been his live-in girlfriend for a while, that was really unnerving him. How would she react to him after so long? Was she still angry, or bitter about their break up? Or, had she forgiven him, for bailing on her because she became a stripper? As he'd walked out of the door of their flat, all those years ago, Poe had hurtfully commented, that it was O.K. for him to walk out on her because she,

"Never wanted to fuck his dad, anyway."

His response, to that somewhat barbed comment from her, had been a rather childish, "Fuck you then" and with that, he'd just angrily turned and walked away, slamming the door in the process. He was still embarrassed by the fact that he'd slammed it so hard that it sprang open and he'd gone back to close it properly. The last thing Poe had heard, as he walked off down the pathway, was him muttering something about her apparent lack of morals and something about him wondering why kids today, had no respect?

Preston now considered that maybe she was right and this was the first disturbing evidence of him becoming even more like his Father, than he was willing to admit at the time.

Yes, that was it!

He was frightened by the prospect of having to meet Poe Pouree again and the public tongue lashing, that she could if she so wished, give him. During their time together, she'd dished out a few of them and he wasn't looking forward to another one……

Hovis Monk, on the other hand, was just a nice guy and after all, it was Hovis who had put them all in the picture regarding The Ken Alexander Show and the resurrection of the Fester's one and only hit song. Otherwise, he and probably the rest of the band, would never have been aware that, 'I want you love,' was being played anywhere in the world, all these years after its release. Plus, it was Hovis who'd invited them all round to his place in the mountain's, for one last weekend of poignant memories and nostalgic recollections.

When he first received the invite, Preston had been doubtful whether he'd attend the proposed get together. It had been over thirty years since they'd last played together as a working band and nearly as long since he had so angrily stomped away from Poe in an ugly welter of recriminations and snide comments. Then, after a particularly boring day at the office was followed by a row with his wife about nothing in particular, he'd taken the plunge and agreed to Festerval.

*

Araf Slow was the complete opposite of his brother. He was perfectly normal for a livestock farmer. As usual, he'd been out and about since the first crack of dawn, tending to his growing herd of Aberdeen Angus Cattle, who were the mainstay of his financial income and feeding his prized flock of rare Balwyn Sheep. His ewes would have to be brought in for the winter any day now, as the weather had just started to turn for the worse and they could be susceptible to an early sharp frost.

Araf still sometimes played one his Rickenbacker guitars for fun and to entertain himself on cold, dark nights. It depended if the mood took him and the evening had just the right vibes.

Vibes, had become very important to Araf.

Even though he was happily married to Cerys, who he'd met in The Cold Eagle public house some 23 years previously, Araf still occasionally missed those long-lost days when he'd been lead guitar on stage with The Fester's. Although he would never admit it, he sometimes wished that he could travel back in time and do it all again. O.K, so the band had a few rough times but …… the biggest problem was his brother. Allan had always been troubled. His temper could flare up and get 'fisty,' remarkably quickly. In truth, Araf always blamed his brother for the acrimonious demise of The Fester's. Although, in later years he'd had to admit their lack of success, which in turn led to an absence of funds, was a contributory factor. Once or twice after the break up, he'd accepted invitations to join new bands looking to benefit from his experience but that exercise had invariably come to nothing. Araf, drifted for a while, going from job to job, with no real future in mind. Then, when the opportunity to buy the old and decrepit Talyn Bach Farm for a snip, arose, he'd jumped at the opportunity to try something new.

His Uncle Aneurin, had been a singularly successful Pig farmer, who's major claim to fame was his ability to get rare and difficult breeds to flourish in particularly unpredictable, Welsh highland conditions. So naturally, Araf thought that if he could just pick his uncle's farming brains, he'd be onto a sure-fire winner.

Sadly, as usual, Araf had tried to run before he could walk. He failed to use the correct fencing procedures. His uncle may have known everything that there was to know about Pigs but he was totally in the dark when it came to the nature of ruminants and Aberdeen Angus. Consequently, thirty-seven of his nephew's prized first flock, simply clambered over one of the badly maintained walls and wandered off, never to be seen again.

That was twenty odd years ago and not long after that, he met his wife. Then, in short order, his two children were born and for all intents and purposes he was settled as a farmer, for at least the next twenty years or so. Gradually, his skills in animal husbandry improved and along with help first from his wife and later his children, he'd made a relative success of his farm.

This invitation from Hovis was the first opportunity that he'd had to 'chew the cud,' with some old compadres from a time, long ago, when he was still a 'free man.' For nigh on twenty-five years, he'd been dedicated to creating a secure future for Cerys and his children and after all, it was only for the one weekend. Although, he was considering driving back on Saturday if it didn't go too well. That way he'd still have plenty of time to get the sheep away down the mountain and into the relative warm conditions of the lower pastures, before the winter set in.

Every year, the older local farmers promised a cold one but Araf had learnt that the colour of a Robin's breast, or the date of the first departure, regarding a flight of the Greylag Geese, didn't necessarily mean a thing. Old Bill Reese, the last living relic in the valley, had over reacted a few years back and delayed the sowing of his crop until the Swallows arrived. However, they were late that year due to an unusually low and tight pressure system, which slid almost unseen across the Atlantic and settled in the general area of The Mediterranean basin. That cold front delayed the migration by only two weeks but that was enough. Old Bill, was just about to book the Combine Harvester for the cropping, when the rains started and they didn't really halt until late into September, his crop was ruined.

Araf, had the shortest distance to travel to get to Hovis' place on the lower slopes of Snowdonia and on top of that, he had the greatest knowledge of where he was going. It was only eighty, or so miles as the crow flies, from his front door in Powys, to the knocker on the door of No.37. He reckoned that in leaving after lunch, he'd have plenty of time to get there, even if he ran into a little unseasonable traffic inspired chaos, which sadly, was always on the cards. It only took a breakdown, a lost tourist, or God forbid, a slow-moving tractor, to block the A470 for miles in any or all directions. Even taking all this into account, by 2pm, all three of the travelling Fester's were on the road and heading for Snowdonia and their Hovis inspired reunion.

Only Allan was missing...... but perhaps he always had been.

Chapter Thirty

On the Road Again.

Even though he'd started his journey from the closest point as the crow flies, Araf's route was on the slowest roads, so it was taking some time for him to reach Hovis' makeshift, White Dragon direction indicators. Also, he'd had to make a critically necessary detour to stop off at his favourite, 'Joe's Greasy Spoon Cafe' on the A55, to purchase a 'Sausage Mary.' The 'Mary,' was a kind of sausage meat burger, smothered in tomato sauce and could truly be described as delicious. It was a legendary trucker's breakfast, originating in Scotland, which had spread rapidly throughout the land.

The Sausage Mary, was one of those things of which drivers would say, "Once tasted, never forgotten" and in Araf's case, that statement was entirely true.

One cold morning, some years back, while taking some of his Aberdeen's to market, he'd noticed a brand-new establishment called 'Joe's Greasy Spoon Cafe,' which had tentatively opened in a lay-by by the side of the road. He'd set out early that morning so as not to be late for the auction but the traffic had been light and he'd made good time. He decided to try the new place, to sit and have a cup of Coffee. However, he didn't get more than a few steps inside, when the most delightful smell overwhelmed his olfactory senses and that was it, Araf was hooked. He ordered a single 'Sausage Mary' and ended up having three. From that auspicious day, to the present, he could never drive even near 'The Spoon' without calling in for a quick coffee and several Mary's.

Cerys constantly worried about her husband's ever-expanding waistline, especially as all the diets she put him on had little to no effect. Some years earlier, after Araf had been talking in his sleep about, 'mmmmMary,' Cerys had written to a famous agony aunt and mentioned both Mary and Araf's waistline. She asked her, "Was it an indication that he was being fed, and maybe appreciated somewhere else besides home?" In her usual non-committal way, Auntie replied asking Cerys if he came in late smelling of another woman's perfume? When she wrote back, stating that Araf was usually asleep by 9.30pm, stank of cows and sheep and rarely went out, the correspondence suddenly dried up. Which put her mind at rest, although she never did find out who 'Mary' was?

*

Poe's Messerschmitt, Gertie, fared little better, time wise. She'd made good time on the motorways but once she turned off onto the A roads, she'd been hindered by other road users. Especially travelling the route from the climb up to The Heads of The Valley's with their plethora of old mining villages and on up to Builth Wells. At some point a transit van had seen it necessary to attack a JCB coming in the opposite direction. The result wasn't pretty. After that, the other drivers seemed to get their shit together and stopped nearly colliding with each other. So, she'd managed to regain some of the time she'd lost sitting motionless in a long line of increasingly annoyed motorists. "Good job, I got the music sorted before I left," she said and patted her left hand, on the top of Gerti's dashboard. "Christ, I need to pee…."

*

Only Preston had an easy journey from his home in Scorton. Mainly because it had excellent motorway connections to North Wales. Plus, he had the best vehicle in which to make the journey. The trip was going smoothly and he was making really good time, so he eased off the pedal a little and just set about enjoying the drive. The last two things he wanted, was to be either the first, or the last to arrive, so a little time guesswork was needed.

Preston remembered driving along the A470 once before, years ago. It was on a holiday with his young family, he recalled the chorus of 'are we there yet?' emanating from the back seats. Frowning slightly, he turned left for Bethesda and headed confidently into the mountains. Following Hovis' directions was easy enough but it was the references to White Dragons, that had him confused. He'd missed the photo attachments on Hovis message, so images of mythical creature's pointing the way by the right-hand side of the road, with a lake on the left, seemed a little incongruous. Preston tried to dismiss his imaginings and just let things ride until he saw whatever it was that Hovis was going on about. In fact, it was much easier than he'd expected and when he saw the water of Llyn Garon, sparkling in the pale sunlight, he slowed down and kept his eyes on the right-hand side of the road.

The traffic was almost non-existent and a quick glance at the clock on the dashboard, informed him that it was 2.07pm. He hadn't seen another vehicle for quite a few miles, when in the near distance, he caught sight of a gaudy, white 'something' by the side of the road. Drawing closer he noticed it pointed the way along an obviously well used side road, disappearing uphill.

Having discerned that the 'white something' was possibly a Dragon, whose tail and arrow was pointing up the incline, Preston followed its instructions. He soon met another White Dragon with an obviously broken but poorly repaired tail, whose arrow also pointed the way but with a further turn indicated on the rougher looking road. He blindly obeyed the Dragon's instructions and drove on along the now 'greening' tarmac track. After about half a mile, he saw a single log cabin, which on closer examination had a sign in its well-kept garden, which read No.37.

He'd arrived!

He stopped the car, turned the radio off and got out, stretching as he did so. Looking remarkably like a man being crucified, he let out a loud groan and raised both his arms above his head, as if he was reaching for the heaven's and waiting for the spear.

"Why hast thou forsaken Me, Lord," he wheezed with a snort of derision, before relaxing his overly melodramatic posture.

*

The sudden intrusion of a vaguely familiar voice startled Preston,

"Want a drink? Tea, Coffee, or something a little stronger....," asked the voice.

It struck Preston that this was not the voice of Jehovah calling out to him but his host.

"Hovis?" He responded, turning and lowering his arms, cocking his head inquisitively to the left and squinting slightly.

"Well, who else is it going to be?" Came the friendly reply, "It's not exactly crowded up here, in fact I'm the last man standing of a once mighty army, that in days of yore bivouacked all over this hillside," he said, offering his hand and laughing. "Preston, how you doing man?" Then looking at the car, added, "Pretty good I'd say, if the motor's anything to go by."

"Am I the first here?" Preston frowned slightly, releasing his grip.

"Yes, you win the prize!"

"What's that then?"

"The choice of what music to play…" Hovis smiled. "Come on in…." He replied leading the way up the path to the cabin.

The Preston of olden times, would have been wearing Jim Morrison style leather pants, or a pair of faded Levi jeans but this latest incarnation of The American Fester, was wearing a rather expensive looking, loose fitting Italian cut, chocolate brown, pinstriped suit with cream silk open necked shirt. Instead of having a pair of old and rather beaten up Converse Allstar's on his feet, he had a pair of rather comfortable and expensive looking beige leather loafer's. Seeing this modern, snappily dressed version of Preston, with his obviously receding hairline and the carefully manufactured touch of grey around the temple's, was almost enough in itself to crush any of Hovis' proto-fanciful dreams of reforming The Fester's, even without Allan.

"Thanks for putting me on to that guy Ken Alexander's useless radio show. It sure was weird hearing 'I Want you, Love.., Want me too, Love,' again after all this time, and before you ask, yes I did vote and every day. You can't just let an opportunity like that slip by," Preston smiled widely at Hovis as they entered the cabin. "And wasn't there something about a drink, mentioned....,"

"Oh yes sorry," said Hovis obsequiously. "What's it to be?"

"I don't suppose you've got a Single Malt, have you," he casually asked and promptly turned a full 360, as he fastidiously appraised No. 37 like some realtor. "That drive, was harder than I thought it was going to be," he continued and then fell silent again.

"Funny you should say that, unfortunately not but will a wee dram of Johnny Walker black do, as a poor substitute? I've plenty of Jack though if you'd rather......"

"Well, I suppose that beggars can't be chooser's, the Johnny Walker will be fine," said Preston, still smiling. "Music, my choice, right? Got any Adele?" He asked without even blinking as he parked himself on his host's settee and took a one gulp hit, which emptied his glass. "Her new stuff's really good," he added, without even blushing.

"Sorry again," said Hovis, handing him the bottle. "Best I can do is a Cowboy Junkies playlist I compiled myself. It's very popular with the YouTube crowd, so you might like it but I don't really do Adele," he added, somewhat sheepishly. This wasn't going as well as he'd hoped it would and now he was already starting to dread meeting whoever, or whatever showed up next.

He didn't have long to wait before another vehicle could clearly be heard drawing up outside. The door of the new arrival slammed shut and somebody could be heard cursing in Welsh, with a good deal of English thrown in for good measure. Hovis cast his curious gaze over to Preston,

"Araf, you suppose?" Hovis smiled and shrugged his shoulders, while slowly rising to greet his next Fester.

"I just hope it's not Allan," offhandedly added Preston, as Hovis reached for the door.

Tentatively opening it he peered out. There was a shambling mess of a man, shuffling up the path towards him.

"Araf?" The man stopped and looked around, as though he was genuinely startled, then smiled.

"Yep, sure is and you're Hovis..., correct me if I'm wrong," the grinning stranger replied and stuck his arm out to shake his potential host's hand.

"Good to see you again, man. How're you doin'?" Hovis grasped the large meaty mass firmly but in truth, he was shocked; before him was a rather large grey-haired man, whom it appeared was around five stone overweight. He was driving an old, mud splattered Land Rover and it appeared that he'd just finished work on the farm and was coming inside for his afternoon panad.

"Who's the flash Harry?" Araf cocked his thumb at the glistening, dark blue Mercedes Benz.

"That's Preston's. He arrived about half an hour ago but Poe's not here yet, we're still waiting for her to arrive. Come on in…, shut the door. Preston's inside, having a Whiskey. D'you want one, or maybe you fancy a Tea, or a Coffee?"

There was a long and heavily pregnant pause before Araf replied, so long that Hovis turned back, beginning to wonder if Araf had heard him.

"Got any beer?" He enquired, "I could murder a cold Guinness," he said taking another step inside the cabin.

"Sure thing, a man after my own heart."

As Araf approached, the faint smell of rurality penetrated Hovis' nostril's and he was already dreading the moment his two old band mates met. Preston smelled of expensive Aux de Cologne, while Araf appeared to be wearing 'Farmyard pour L'homme.'

It was clear to Hovis that these two houseguests were worlds apart and disaster was staring him in the face...... and Poe wasn't even here yet!

*

For her part, Poe had just turned onto the A470 and was trying to make up the time she'd lost trying to get through Bethesda, where she'd encountered an upturned motor home, which had flipped over trying to take a bend much too fast. That incident had held her up for at least an hour and the desire to get to Hovis' place quickly, had led her into taking a 'short cut,' which now seemed to be littered with false hopes.

"Why can't you just stick to his directions and stop trying to cut corner's!?" She railed at herself. 'You left early enough this morning, that's for sure and now you're probably going to be the last one to arrive. Typical! Maybe now you'll learn that short cuts make long delays and you'll stick to the direction's instead of thinking you know better.....,' she admonished herself, then laughed as she realised she could hear her mother saying the exact same thing to her father, many childhood years ago.

The deserted nature of the A470, with the Snowdonian foothill's passing sedately by, calmed her nerves and she began to enjoy this last leg of the journey. The Chills Pink Frost, struck up on the stereo and she belted out the lyrics. The previous hundred and something miles, with all their unexpected obstacles, had seemingly been sent to try her patience but when the two imposing Glyder's with the road winding between them, reared up before her, Poe actually felt a strange kind of thrill and a childish sense of excitement.

"Bugger being late, this is soul food and it should be fully appreciated!" She turned the wheel and applied the brakes, bringing the Messerschmitt to a grinding halt in a small lay-by. "Shit, I should have remembered to bring my camera," she cursed and opened the side window. 'I'll make do with the iPad' she thought and took some snaps, then got ambitious and shot a pano.

She must have sat there for at least another ten minutes, just absorbing the scenery, before she drove on, having checked Hovis' directions for the umpteenth time. "Right now, keep your eyes open for a White Dragon, on the right-hand side of the road and a lake, that should be on the left," Poe commanded herself. 'No short cuts!'

Not long after, she caught sight of a lake, silently glistening over to her left, through a patch of trees. Then, to the right and slightly obstructed by the overhanging foliage, she spotted something white about fifty yards ahead. As she neared it she saw it was indeed a vaguely fashioned White Dragon and she turned onto the Rat Road, full of confidence.

A confidence that soon dissipated as she considered that Preston and maybe Araf too, were most likely already there, ahead of her. Hovis had let her know it was highly unlikely Allan would be coming and that was something of a relief. His crush on her in the past had been the cause of many arguments. Meeting Araf, if he was anything like he'd been in the days of The Fester's, she could easily handle. Hovis was 'Brown Slice' and he always was a really nice bloke, who from his mails seemed not to have changed much. After all, it was Hovis who'd invited everybody round to his place …but Preston…!!!!

Poe, bit her lip and turned her thoughts to the road ahead.

A swift turn to the left, then a left bend directed by another of Hovis' makeshift White Dragon signs, led her directly to No.37 and there in the driveway, she observed three cars parked.

"Late again," she said as Gertrude came to a halt. She climbed out, not sure if she was ready for whoever appeared to let her into, 'The Hovis Loaf' as she'd instantly dubbed the log cabin, which at this moment was grooving loudly to the sounds of the Cowboy Junkies.

'Hmmm, Ring on the Sill,' nice choice guys, she thought to herself, as she approached the door. Hesitating momentarily, she took in a deep breath, before taking hold of the knocker and giving it a good hard rap on its strike plate.

Chapter Thirty-One

Festerval.

"That'll be Poe," Hovis said, his heart beating a little too rapidly as he rose again to answer the knock. The vision in Paisley and Black Leather which met his eyes, literally took his breath away and momentarily left him speechless.

"Poe?!" He both asked and exclaimed in the same breath, while for some idiotic reason, he held out his hand for her to shake.

However, she was having none of that and simply ignored his hand, pushing past it to put her arms around him and hug him warmly. Then Poe kissed him first on each cheek, then surprisingly passionately on his lips, with her lips lingering a little too long on his.

"Wow," gasped Hovis and Poe kissed him again. "What's that for?" He spluttered and stepped back into the cabin.

"Just making up for lost time," she replied and smiled at him as she stepped inside.

"Preston and Araf are in the lounge but more importantly, would you like a drink of something wet," he asked her, seeking emotional sanctuary by reverting to his role as the perfect host.

"Got any Cognac?" She looked around her, appraising her surroundings in one quick glance and smiled. Hovis, who was feeling more confident after her surprising kiss, led the way into the kitchen and Poe happily followed him.

"Cognac it is," he replied and then picking up a Brandy Bell, prepared to pour her a large one. "Courvoisier, all right," he asked and without waiting for her answer, began to dispense the warming brown spirit.

"Amazing place you've got here," she commented while still trying to take in the Hovis Loaf. "How long have been here?" She enquired, "I'll bet this place, set you back a few Bob," she added before he could answer, then took a large sip of her drink.

"Come and meet the other two, they're expecting you," he said, ignoring her question and reached for the handle of the lounge door.

"Just a sec," she mumbled and finished her Cognac in one slug. Hovis was impressed.

"Want another?" He asked, sensing her anxiety.

"Go on then and please, make it a large one," she said with a touch of desperation in her voice.

"Don't tell me you're nervous," he said softly, taking her glass and slowly refilling it. "Preston's still Preston but ..... different."

"Different how?" Poe frowned a little.

"Well, he professes to liking Adele these days, God help him and Araf's just what you'd expect from a Welsh farmer." Poe's puzzled look cried out for a further explanation.

"How so...,"

"I'll take it you saw the Land Rover in the yard on your way in, well he looks just like what you'd expect to have climbed out of it .... Let's just say, he's got a rustic aroma about him." That explanation made Poe smile easily for the first time since she'd arrived. Hovis melted and the years slipped away as her eyes sparkled, revealing and a side of her character she kept hidden, except from a chosen few.

"Should we go in then?" He pushed open the lounge door, holding it ajar for her to make an entrance. Surprisingly, Poe just stood there, frozen to the spot. Hovis let the door swing back, "Tell you what," he proposed while picking up the cognac bottle, "I'll go in first and announce your arrival, so that you can really make a real entrance, how's that sound?" Poe said nothing and still didn't move. "Don't tell me that you've got stage-fright?"

"No, yes....," she answered, "well it's just that I've not seen Preston for about thirty years and we parted on such an ugly note....., and it's even longer since I've seen Araf!" She weakly explained; then tossed her head back and moved with determined elegance towards the semi open door, saying just these three words,

"Let's do it!"

*

"Poe!" Exclaimed Araf, standing up as she entered. "Not seen you for however long it is," he spluttered. "You're looking good girl, I see that time's been kind to you." She smiled, quickly hugged him, then sat down on the opposite settee to the one Preston had parked himself on, without saying a single word.

Preston, for his part, offered nothing and Hovis could see that breaking this long-frozen ice wasn't going to be easy. Preston and Araf had relaxed a touch since they'd arrived and were occasionally laughing at a few shared memories of the olden days and some of the stupid things, that they'd done in the interim. Now, except for a couple of nods of acknowledgment when she arrived, Preston and Poe remained absolutely silent.

Araf exchanged a couple of words with her but the animosity that existed between Poe and Preston, seemed suffocating. Whatever had occurred between them, seemed immutable and Hovis could see his ridiculously premature plans, evaporating.

"Anybody want another drink, or a top up?" He asked as the room grew ever more silent.

Then, in what was obviously a calculated move, Poe stood up and after pouring herself another Cognac, sat herself down next to Hovis, blatantly putting her hand on his leg. He instantly flashed a look at Preston to gauge his reaction but saw no perceptible change in his demeanour.

'He can't have missed this seating alteration,' Hovis thought and looked again at his old buddy. 'She must be doing this on purpose,' he mused but did nothing to remove her hand. He'd forever dreamt of this set of circumstances but never imagined it would come to pass.

Araf, who'd proven to be the most gregarious of the bunch, began a prattling conversation, which Poe didn't seem to mind but Preston said little, or nothing. He just sat there and after his fourth large Johnny Walker, drank from his own hip flask and sank a little further into his chair with each moment that passed. Hovis had stocked up on bog standard Jack Daniels, anticipating Preston was still favouring the American drink he'd previously loved but how wrong could he be about that? He was having none of it, never showing the slightest inclination to partake of the bourbon and having demolished half a bottle of Johnny Walker, now appeared far happier, drinking the contents of the hip flask he'd brought with him.

The late afternoon, was drawing on and the light was beginning to fade, when Poe suddenly just put her arm around Hovis' shoulder and pulled him towards her. 'It's the Cognac,' his mind said but he hoped that he was wrong. This was just impossible to comprehend.

Poe was hitting on him.

He looked at Araf, to see what his reaction was and then, back across the room towards Preston. Neither were batting a single eyelid. Araf was far away, lost in the music and Preston was studiously ignoring anything that Poe did, to seemingly upset him.

Hovis was just about to suggest that they should all perhaps go to the rooms that he'd prepared for them and have a rest before the evening meal was served, but he didn't get the chance. It was at this juncture that Araf became expansive in his telling of a tale of one of his Aberdeen Angus, flung his arms wide to indicate the horns and knocked Preston's open hip flask into his lap creating a widening stain on his crotch.

"For Fuck's sake!" Shouted Preston and before Araf could apologise he'd wobbled his way to the bathroom. Ten minutes later, Preston reappeared with an even bigger wet patch on his Italian designer suit. Grabbing his jacket, he announced he had,

"Something else to do," mumbled that he was very sorry but he'd have to go.

"You can't drive in your condition," Hovis vaguely protested, while Araf sonically laughed,

"He thinks he can do anything. I know because I've been talking to the idiot all afternoon and I can tell you, he won't be missed, even if I never see him again. What a stuck up, capitalist prick he's turned into."

Poe just laughed, while Preston, for his part, simply frowned and tutted, as he wound his way towards the door.

"Thanks for the invite and the Whiskey," he said to Hovis and shook his hand firmly and very business-like. "We'll have to do it again sometime," he said and stumbled over the step heading towards his Mercedes, righted himself with difficulty and then slowly opened its door. "See you again someday," he said blankly, as he climbed into his machine and started the engine.

"Not if I see you first," blurted out Araf, rather too loudly from behind Hovis, then dissolved into a fit of insane laughter.

"Couldn't have put it better myself," added Poe, her arm slipping over Hovis' shoulder, then snarled, "What a self-serving dickhead."

As Preston's Merc disappeared from view they all headed back inside.

"I had no idea that you two parted with such animosity," said Hovis, visibly shaken.

"That's nothing," she commented. "That guy's a real schiester," she spat. "He came on like a rebel, hah! He was anything but. Good old Preston, revealed himself to be a typical Yank when pushed. In private, he was a real Johnny Appleseed...... It's what broke us two up in the end," she said and emptied the last drops of Cognac, from her glass. "I mean, Christ did you see that flash suit and that fucking car, he's full of it," she venomously offered.

"And here's me, thinking that we might possibly get The Fester's back together, after the success of the single on the Ken Alexander show," said Hovis. "Fat chance," he hopelessly added, laughed ruefully and sat down heavily next to Poe, on the settee. "You will both be staying at least for the meal, I hope," he said to the two remaining guest's and they both nodded their assent. "Good," he declared. "Well, there's someone else, that I'd like you to meet," he got up again and walked over to the bedroom door. He opened it and Cheech leapt out and jumping up, put both of his front paw's on Hovis' shoulders,

"Meet Cheech," he said wheezing under the strain and then lost his balance, ending up falling backwards onto the seat that Preston had vacated, laughing as Cheech mercilessly licked his face.

"Okay," said Araf, feeling how the vibes were going, "but then I think I'll be getting off and leave you three alone," he said, genuinely smiling. "I could really do with being home tonight to tell the truth. I've got to bring the sheep down off the mountain and the weather's closing in fast......" Then added, "What's for tea," He said it so facetiously, that Hovis and Poe just dissolved into laughter.

Chapter Thirty-Two

Minus Preston Keynes.

T he meal that Hovis prepared for Araf and Poe to enjoy, consisted of freshly cooked Lobster's, New Potatoes and an assortment of vegetables. It went down really well and the table conversation was convivial in the extreme. Once the initial awkwardness was overcome by Preston's departure, it was as if The Fester's had never split and they were meeting in preparation for starting their next album. They all relaxed and the word's flowed easily between the three of them.

"Shame about Preston," Hovis said shaking his head.

"Not really," added Araf. "All the more for us!" He looked up smiling, then continued, "Okay, maybe we should extend a little understanding in his direction, I reckon that he's got an ongoing problem with 'The Juice'. I mean, Christ, did you see how much he drank, it was like he needed the stuff simply to get by. That was not a well puppy.....,"

"Yeah, he sure was knocking it back," added Hovis thoughtfully and put another spud in his mouth, chewed then continued, "Was he like that, when he was with you?" He asked Poe, who, after a short pause while she swallowed another mouthful of the delicious Crustacea, answered his enquiry.

"Drink was the least of his problem's," she said indifferently, while busily reloading her fork. "After the band broke up, he was fine for a while, simply bog-standard Preston but then, as the money got tight, he started to get really weird. Curiously, he became more and more like the Father he claimed to detest and at the same time, refused to get a job. So, when out of sheer monetary desperation, I took the stripping gig in Sunderland, he just exploded. He called me every name under the sun, even accused me of wanting to sleep with every Tom, Dick and Harry! Then, not content with that, he said that I had no moral's, packed his bags and stormed out of the flat, leaving me with all his bills to pay."

Hovis' face was a picture as Poe revealed these secrets to him, "Jesus, I didn't know....,"

"Fuck me," said Araf who was equally surprised, "d'you reckon he had a nervous breakdown, or something?" Poe just looked at them both and paused before answering.

"No, though it did cross my mind at the time," she said, "I think that the real Preston Lancashire, just showed himself. Put under pressure the demon leapt out and sadly," she added, "it seems it's still in charge. So, it's probably just best to say that the fun guy we all once knew, has left the building."

Hovis and Araf, just looked at each other. "I knew something was wrong from the get go but I was too stupid to say anything," said Hovis. "The car and his demeanour were yelling at me but I just ignored them. I thought he was just a little nervous at the prospect of meeting up with us again......."

Now it was Poe, who was looking at him and shaking her head.

"You're missing the point, the Preston Lancashire you thought you once knew, if he ever really existed, is a long time dead. He's been demolished, replaced by Preston New Town, which you might as well call, Preston Keynes."

That broke the spell and they all laughed.

"Where did you learn to cook like this?" Poe asked and slapped him on the shoulder. "And what other little secrets are you hiding?" She batted her lashes, looked coyly into his eyes and smiled.

In turn, Hovis looked at Araf and smiled, a knowing man-smile and Araf smiled back, nodding his head in acknowledgement.

"You can tell me later," she said, catching the exchange, then casually returning her attention to the lobster.

"How's the guitar playing these days?" Hovis enquired of Araf, just as Araf loaded up his fork again and shoved it into his enormous salivating orifice. Then, seamlessly transferring his attention to Poe, continued,

"You know, sometimes I surprise myself. I got this recipe from my Mother's old copy of Mrs. Beaton's. She swore by it 'n told me I wouldn't go far wrong if I followed 'Ma B's instructions. Seems she was right, at least this time." He shoveled another forkful of lobster into his gratefully open mouth.

"So, you don't murder Lobster's very often then?" Poe chimed in.

"No, to tell you the truth, I've never cooked a Lobster before, in my life. I was just trying to impress you guys with my culinary expertise," he shamefully admitted looking over to Araf, who was silently giggling and trying rather unsuccessfully to hide the fact from him but the uncontrollable jelly like shaking of his gigantic bulk, gave him away. Hovis looked down the table at Poe, hoping to see a little more support coming from her direction but she too, was on the point of explosion. "Yeah, Ok... I'm a pretentious dickhead, I admit it!"

"Hey, you've got nothing on Preston Keynes, boyo!"

When the laughter died down, he foolishly asked, "Does anyone require a top up from this rather fine, if I do say so myself, house white?"

"Oh yah, make mine a double," Poe replied, in her 'poshest' accent and Araf, just lost it, spitting microscopic morsels of Lobster into the air.

"Classic boyo," he said in his finest Welsh accent, "just fucking classic!"

Poe, dissolved into uncontrollable belly aching squeals.

"Next thing, he'll be offering us some Ferrero Roche, you watch," added Araf, then gripped his jiggling stomach.

"Oh, Ambassador Hovis, you spoil us so.....," wheezed Poe.

Hovis was laughing too, then he feigned a sense of hurt.

"If you don't stop, someone's going to die," cried Poe, as tears ran down the side of her face. "Oh, now look, you've made my mascara run," she continued and put both of her elbows on the table and dabbed at her eyes.

"Oh Man, I haven't had this much fun for years," gasped Araf, "but I'm going to have to go for a slash, or I'll wet my pants." He headed for the toilet, leaving just Hovis and Poe at the table.

Cheech, who was now lying by Poe, raised his head and watched as Araf made his way to the 'John,' only lowering it again as the wobbling stranger vanished behind the closed door.

"You don't mind, if I do stay for the night, do you? Only I wouldn't want to be driving Gertie in this condition," Poe said smiling and gripped his hand, under the table. After the initial surprise of her touch had receded, he recalled some of her other actions during this meeting. Initially, he'd them put down as kicks against Preston, but he was long gone. Hovis slowly realised, it was just possible Poe was interested in him. His hopes lurched as he considered the idea.

While hoping to impress her with his laid-back attitude, Hovis made a few consensual grunts and said, "Yeah, that's O.K with me, it's what we had planned, so feel free. I'll show you your room later on if you like but there's Lemon Meringue Pie and Cream for you to try yet."

"Ma B, again?" Poe grinned wickedly.

"Yep," replied Hovis, trying not to melt completely.

"Did I hear the magical words, Lemon Meringue Pie, or was that my stomach lying again?" Commented Araf as he exited the lavatory.

"No, you weren't just coming down from an overwhelming sense of relief, those were indeed the words spoken. Sit thi' sen down, lad and prepare to be amazed." The childish look on Araf's face made the whole thing worthwhile. Little did he know, that Hovis had made one of these things several times before and perfected his recipe. After a swift trip to the refrigerator, which only delayed him for a few seconds, he returned carrying the pie, laying it before them with a flourish, while Araf faked a drumroll.

"See, told you we didn't need Preston," Poe cried.

"Females first," Hovis stated, as he carved a huge piece of the confection and placed it in front of Poe. "Cream's on the table," he indicated towards a white porcelain jug.

"Thanks, but I'll never eat all this and I've got a figure to take care of," Poe remonstrated and just to prove the point, she added, "A girl has to be careful with things like this, Lemon Meringue, like hot buttered toast, goes straight to my pie thighs." However, her warning carried little, or no fear for Araf,

"I'll have yours then!" He grabbed her plate and dived straight in. Then, after a moment's hesitation, to give it The Faux Connoisseur treatment, he scooped another huge spoonful into his gaping maw before pronouncing, "This is fucking brilliant," as he slavered and shoveled yet another gigantic spoonful mouthwards.

"I think he likes it," giggled Poe as Hovis gave her a smaller slice, then she placed a far more reasonable amount of Meringue, delicately into her mouth. "It is excellent though," she mumbled with her mouth full.

"Dead right," Araf interjected. "You'll have to give me the recipe, it's just darling," and then he just burst out laughing and as previously, sprayed the air with tiny wind-blown morsels.

"Feel free to have some more," said Hovis, laughing and shielding the pie.

"Don't mind if I do," responded Araf as he cut himself another huge portion.

"He's a true wonder to behold," said Hovis, looking at Poe.

"You could say that. D'you reckon he's going to eat the lot, or will he pop first?"

"Just let him eat his fill, there's another in the fridge and he can't carry on eating forever. At least, I don't think he can......Now, who'd like a good strong Coffee, to wash it down?" Hovis smiled at Araf.

"Oh champion," came the reply. "Man, that was good," he said, belching. "You two really must come over to my place, sometime. Cerys, would love to meet you, especially if you bring one of those killer pies with you. Though I take it you'd have no objections if I don't invite Preston Keynes."

Hovis looked at Poe, waiting for her response to Araf's invite with its conditions attached and she peered back at him, not knowing quite how to respond.

"If it goes down as well as this, then maybe we could make it an annual event," Araf added without blinking. The pregnant pause from both Hovis and Poe gave him the opportunity to elaborate his argument. "Listen, this has been a really good day. Even though we've not seen each other for millennia, it feels like only a few months ago and that must be worth something. It's a shame about Preston but fuck him. It'd seem a pity to let it drift for so long again." He fell thoughtfully silent.

Poe seemed to consider his words, then looking directly at Hovis,

"You're right Araf. Well, you can count me in, it would be cool to stay in touch and meet up again. You in Hovis?"

"Yeah, that'd be really cool....," he replied, lost in her eyes.

After a polite gap, Hovis raised himself from his seat and moved towards the kitchen. "Coffee's all round, wasn't it?" He asked as he departed the table.

There was no reply, or objection to his rhetorical question and now he had time to consider the events of the day, while he waited for the kettle to boil. Festerval had given him the opportunity to break out the Cafetière that he'd purchased several years previously but never had call to use.

It was indeed a shame that Allan had failed to show and Preston had proven to be such a dick, but Araf was far easier company than he recalled. While Poe, was everything that his memory had conjured up, only more. On top of that, she wanted to stay over, so he could spend a little more time with her. Hovis smiled. Araf's invitation, hopefully meant that he would be seeing more of her in the future.

While Hovis had been in the kitchen, Araf and Poe had moved themselves back into the lounge and for some reason, were discussing the benefits of farming Aberdeen Angus Cattle, while listening to The Thirteenth Floor Elevators first studio album on Hovis' iPod, wired up to his Quad Stereo system.

"Great sounds, Man," Araf said as he picked up the Cafetière of specially bought Java Lava and poured out a cupful of the rich brown liquid. Poe looked up and nodded inquisitively toward the Coffee.

"Java Lava," answered Hovis, sensing her question. She made him feel ever so sophisticated and cultured, he was starting to believe she could become a true presence in his life.

"Oh lovely," Poe murmured, as she took another sip of her drink and smiled demurely.

"Now call me crazy but when I heard 'I want you love' again, after all this time, my fingers began twitching to the beat and when you started singing," Araf said nodding towards Poe, "I was right back there, on the stage at The Reccy Rooms in Toddy, counting down to the first note of the first chord," and with that, he made a totally incongruous, Pete Townsend like swirling arm movement. After all, I Want you Love was played with a jingle jangle Rickenbacker sound.

Poe laughed and clapped her hands, "Hey, you still got it Araf!"

Even though any idea of the band ever getting back together for a gig had gone out of the window long before Preston had departed, Hovis was still excited by the idea of playing. Araf's Townsend impression had him thinking of playing Bass, his fingers ran a few chords on the table top. His mind's eye shot back in time to a much younger Hovis in skin tight black jeans, his favourite red spotted shirt, Cuban heels and strident attitude, grooving with Jezebel. That mind bubble was suddenly burst by an ageing, fat, balding creature, covered in an unpleasantly skin tight, bright red coating, with baggy knees.

"I've got my mini amp in the jalopy and Rhonda is always ready for a few sweet bars, so what do you say to doing one last killer version of 'I want you love' and committing it to history?"

They both just looked at Araf and saw opportunity knocking. "We could stick it on YouTube if it's any good," Hovis bleated, looking directly at Poe.

"It's been a long time," she noncommittally observed, but her eyes flashed with excitement. "We might sound like shit guys....'n what about the drums?" Her caution was undoubtedly honest but those who heeded her warning, at this moment, numbered zero.

"Let's just put it on the stereo! We can play 'n sing over the top….," grinned Hovis.

"Ahhh what the hell! Let's do it!" Poe was beaming with excitement.

"I've still got Jezebel and a tiny practice Amp but I've hardly played a note in anger for God knows how long...," Hovis lied, hoping to cover for his one week of practice, while playing a little air-bass.

"Well, I've got nothing, we vocalists don't tend to carry a microphone around with us, in the off chance of a gig," interjected Poe and she took another sip of her 'fire water.'

"Ah, yes but I've also got.....," said Hovis, leaving the most pregnant of pauses.

"You've also got what," snapped Araf, impatient to hear the end of this unexpected proclamation.

"I've got...........a Karaoke microphone and its speaker," said Hovis triumphantly. The look on Poe's face was priceless,

"So, we can do it," she squealed and clapped her hands together, like a child.

"Sure can," answered Hovis and he moved towards the spare room. "You go and get your shit and I'll just fetch mine, then we'll be ready for The Last Re-Festerisation."

*

"One, two. One, two, three, four," counted Araf and struck the first chord, as the liquid lens from the Light of the World, drenched the room in Psychedelia.

"I see you on the dance floor," sang Poe as she slowly slithered towards him and Hovis played a funky if somewhat flat Bass run, which could hardly be described as flowing but served its purpose.

Poe could still sing well and Araf was still able to crack out a lick or two but Hovis was struggling. Well, he wasn't but his fingers were. The strings hurt as he slid up and down the frets and his knuckles ached as he tried to deftly dance around on Jezebel's smooth neck. Luckily, most of his faux pars were drowned out by the recorded version playing alongside.

Then, he broke a string and then a second and he stopped playing for real but fingered along until the end.

"Sorry guys but I've got no spares," said Hovis apologetically and he put Jezebel down. "It sounded, sort of O.K. to me," he said and looked pensively at the other two, who were grinning ear to ear as the liquid lens coated them in sliding colours.

"Did you get it on your iPod," Poe asked.

"Sure thing," Hovis replied and pressed the 'Play' button.

Chapter Thirty-Three

"They're here...."

"I'll just drink this and then I'd better be getting off home, I've some ewes to shift in the morning......," Araf looked at his watch, then mumbled something like, "..... and you two, will want to be on your own tonight, if I'm not mistaken." He gave them a knowing look and chuckled. Hovis imperceptibly nodded and Poe smiled, one of those smiles that was worth a thousand words.

"Hey," said Poe, "does anyone know what happened to Ken Alexander? After we won for a fifth time he just seemed to disapp....."

"Yeah, it's someone called Sarah Buckley now...." Interjected Araf and they both looked at Hovis, who just shrugged,

"Don't know, but it seems he's not coming back and they've just dropped the band contest....."

Later, as he was leaving, Araf embraced Hovis then said,

"Drop me a line sometime, Man. I'm sure that we can work out the date thing, there's no rush, let's just get it right and stay happy." With that comment, Araf turned to Poe and gave her a hug and a peck on her cheek, before heading for his Land Rover.

"You make a great couple," he called back to them, as he climbed inside. "Cool dog as well," he yelled through the open window and waved as the vehicle accelerated, turning left, onto the Rat Road.

As he dropped out of sight, Poe gave an enormous sigh and put both of her arms around Hovis.

"We'd better be getting inside, before we freeze," he said, taking hold of her receptive hand and leading the way. "Well, it's only ten past eight, so what do you want to do for the rest of the evening?"

"Oh, I don't know...., it's nice just being here, fantastic views, when it's daylight."

He looked at her and for a lack of anything better, fell back on the mundane, "Well, if I was on my own, I'd sit back and watch a movie, have a beer, or two and then go to bed. That's about right eh, Cheech?" He asked the dog, who wasn't really listening but wagged his tail once, in recognition of Hovis' question.

"Sounds good to me, what shall we watch?" Poe patted the vacant space on the settee by her side. Hovis didn't need a second invitation and removed himself from the armchair that he'd just that minute sat down in and shuffled over, to sit with her.

"Depend's what you want? Living this far from civilisation, I've garnered quite an extensive collection of films. They range from lush sentimentality, like 'On Golden Pond' or 'Fried Green Tomatoes at The Whistlestop Cafe,' to good old 'Blood Fest Horror,' as I call it, 'n pretty much everything in between."

The Blood Fest category intrigued her the most, so Poe requested some further clarification,

"Like what?" She waited patiently for his reply.

"Okay, further categorisation coming up," Hovis mysteriously declared. "Now just let me see," he said, rubbing his hands together like some mad professor. "Well, there's Ancient and Interesting. That category include's classic's such as 'Nosferartu' and pastiche terror, or 'sci fi terror flix,' such as 'They Came From Outer Space,' 'This Island Earth' and 'When World's Collide.'"

"Too much information," Poe said. "You choose and I'll just lie here and enjoy it," she added and dropped her head, snugly onto his shoulder.

"You do know, where this is leading I take it?"

"Yes," she placed her hand, gently on his thigh.

Now he couldn't think clearly and there was an uncomfortable lump, forming in his trouser area. He'd been imagining a situation like this occurring for three decades and he didn't want to blow it now, by being too pushy or picking the wrong entertainment for the occasion. 'Nothing too freaky but nothing too intriguing either,' he thought to himself as he began scrolling through the movies stored on his tv hard drive. Amid the ensuing browsing confusion, 'Poltergeist,' raised its head.

"Alright, I hope this suits Madam's mood, for this evening," he pompously announced, as if he was her private Butler.

"Ooooh, Poltergeist. I love this movie. Great choice," Poe appreciatively declared, as The Star's and Bar's played out onscreen. "They're here," she added and then fully relaxed, to watch the now ageing Spielburg Classic. He felt her jump slightly, when the spectral hand reached out for Carol Anne and he felt her sigh deeply, when that moment had passed. He felt the warmth of her body, as it pressed against his and he automatically squeezed her close to him, as the movie continued.

"I must have watched this thing at least twenty times or more, 'n it never gets stale," Poe observed quietly, "and it's a perfect first course," she added, stroking his thigh.

Hovis' head was spinning, 'This is getting ridiculous,' he thought, 'if we were younger, then perhaps it would seem natural but we're both in our fifties!' He didn't know about her but he'd been technically celibate, for longer than he cared to recall. Until she'd sent him the amazing photograph, Hovis had no idea what had happened to Poe, or even if she was still alive but he certainly imagined, that if she was still taking up her place on the planet, she was probably married with a couple of kids. Or, failing that, happily living with some lucky guy and was totally indifferent to him, or any of the other Fester's. Women like Poe didn't hang around, they didn't need to and yet here she was, snuggled on his settee, with her beautiful head in his lap. 'This can't be really happening to me,' he thought perhaps a little too loudly and she stirred, as he gently stroked her hair.

On the TV, Diane Freeling had just fallen into the half-dug swimming pool and Poe perceptively tensed, let out an almost silent moan, and gripped his leg a little tighter. The climax of the movie was approaching and soon, Hovis feared that he would have to make out that this kind of a situation was a common place occurrence. He really didn't want to disappoint her by coming over as a born-again novice. 'It's best, to be honest with her,' his head argued but telling her that he hadn't been with a woman for years, seemed just a little too honest......

Unbeknown to Hovis, identical thoughts were racing around in Poe's mind as well. Her day's with Preston and her time at the Strip Club in Sunderland had somewhat put her off men. Apart from a few brief relationships, mostly doomed from the start, she'd also been technically celibate, for many long, lonely years. She may have appeared to be a picture of 'The Girl Around Town' but she leant heavily on her memories of yesteryear and now here she was, alone with a guy who she'd briefly known, for just a short while, some thirty years ago.

As the credits of the film scrolled up on the television, they'd both reached the same conclusion. It was just best to be honest.

"I've got a confession to make," Hovis hesitantly began.

"So, have I," admitted Poe.

'Oh Christ, she's married,' he thought.

"I haven't been with a man in years," she quickly added, almost apologetically.

"Neither have I," he said and then blushed a little, at the statement's possible connotations. "Well, not a man.... but you know what I mean."

Poe, just looked at Hovis and burst out laughing. He was still the same man she remembered from all those years ago and that in itself, was tremendously comforting.

"What do you say to going to your bedroom and making fool's out of ourselves, eh?"

"That sounds like a plan to me," Hovis said smiling as he stood up and proffered a hand to the lazing Poe. "Come on then Miss Pouree, let's go to my room and give it a go...... I mean, what could possibly go wrong?"

"Well, let me see?" Poe jokingly said and grinning widely, took his hand. "Lead on, 'til morning and let's just damn the candy torpedoes, eh Brown Slice," she playfully added, pulling him to her, then she kissed him warmly on the lips.

"Wow! Just a minute...., how about a bit of mood lighting...." Hovis reached over and flicked a switch.

Suddenly, the room-was full of liquid colours.....

Chapter Thirty-Four

The Kid.

P oe happily stayed at No.37 for the next thirty-six hours, or so
but when Hovis awoke on the Sunday morning, she'd
disappeared, leaving only a note. It was lying on the pillow
next to him, just waiting for him to wake and find it. He sleepily put
his arm out to feel for her but finding nothing, his foggy head cleared
rapidly.

Hovis was confused. He thought that everything had gone so
well. Ok, so they were both a little out of practice when it came to
the finer points of sexual congress, but he thought they'd got on like
a house on fire.

"Maybe I was just fooling myself, eh Cheech," the Setter's
head rose at the sound of his name from his usual overnight position
at the foot of the bed. "A lot of use you were," Hovis complained. "If
she'd been a thief, she could have stolen just about anything before
you woke up." Cheech, just looked at him for a second or two and
then closed his eyes, lowered his head again and went back to sleep.

"I thought you were my friend," Hovis whined and fell back
onto his pillow.

A lasting vision of Poe remained in his mind's eye and he
realised there was no chance of more sleep in his present state of
distress. Feeling a hopeless sense of disappointment, he picked up
the neatly folded piece of paper with his name on it, well in so much
as 'Brown Slice' was his name. After a few more moments of
reflection and courage building, he began reading her words,

I'm sorry Hovis, I didn't want to disturb you as you looked so peaceful. I had to go early, because it's a long drive back to Bridgewater and I have another appointment later today. I had a really good time this weekend and you were a perfect gentleman. Thank you. We should have done this year's ago and I hope that you feel the same way, about me. If you don't, it's no matter and at least we gave it a go. Stay in touch, I'd love to come back to stay again some time... but you may not want that?

Oh! I nearly forgot, Cheech is really cool too.

Love Poe

He had to read it again, just to be sure he wasn't dreaming.

"She likes us," he joyously cried to Cheech but immediately began thinking of all the things he hadn't told her. The whole of the time from Araf leaving to waking up that morning, had passed in a sort of dream. Both he and Poe hadn't really spoken much about their lives. He didn't know anything about her job in Bridgewater and he certainly couldn't remember mentioning the fact that No.37 would be a heap of smouldering ashes, in just a few days' time.

He recalled Poe had mentioned something about it being a brilliant home and an even better place to live, with great views of the mountains. He definitely hadn't told her those circumstances weren't going to last for much longer. Soon he'd be out of work, with no home, no income and stuck, renting an old Crofter's Cottage in Llanbadrig. That was hardly a selling point. He seriously doubted that Poe would see that as a reason to give up her job, doing whatever it was that she did in Somerset, to come and join him and Cheech, in some kind of Welsh netherworld.

"This is hopeless, what've I got to offer her? Not bloody much," he declared. "Nothing, zilch, nada, zip, sweet fuck all in fact," he desperately whined to the lonely distant peaks.

"I need a miracle," he said to the Setter, "humph! Some chance!" The whole sense of loss was weighing in on him and he began to sink under the weight of his seemingly hopeless situation. 'I had a dream dangled in front of me for a weekend….., but my present shitty life has pretty much crapped all over any chance I might have had for happiness in that future. Jesus, thing's don't come any crueler….'

"Perhaps I did something awful in a previous life," he said to Cheech as his head dropped and he sighed. 'Ahh, yes but at least I know my dick still works!'

"Come on," he said to Cheech, smiling. "It's no good mooning over Poe and what could have been, the rain seems to have backed off for the moment, so let's get ourselves out there and take that last ride up 'The Kid' that I've been promising you. What d'you say?" The furious wagging of his tail, told Hovis everything he needed to know about Cheech's answer to his proposition. "O.K, well let's do this thing properly then, just one more time……"

The sound of a life or death struggle soon emanated from within No.37 and when Hovis finally emerged from his bedroom, hot and sweaty, some fifteen minutes later, he was once again ensconced in Miguel Indurain's Flame Red, World Title Winning, Timetrialing Onesey, and he was ready for action.

"Flame on!" He heroically declared, striking a Superhero pose. "Now all we need is Dennis and we can set off to conquer the evil monster that goes by the name of……, The Kid," he said in a dark gravelly voice and struck another pose, this time more reminiscent of He-Man.

After mounting the Red and Black striped pedal powered machine, he pushed off and thrust an arm forward, crying,

"By the Power of Greyskull!"

Cheech shot past him, heading for the Old Road which ran up the side of The Kid. The turning was located on The Rat Road, roughly half way between the A470 and No.37.

At this time of year, the road surface was still fairly trustworthy. The green slippery film on the Tarmac was rideable, until icy, then it became treacherous. Just as he set off, Hovis heard the sound of that big truck heading for The Agamemnon Building, to pick up some more of whatever it was they were removing. 'Sunday working, hope he's getting paid well for it,' he mused. Soon enough, it would be heading the other way with its load and The Blue Yonder Mining Company in Snowdonia, would be that much closer to liquidation.

Hovis kicked hard to gain a head start on the mystery vehicle. It could get pretty tight on the Rat Road when something was trying to pass you. Cars, were bad enough but meeting a truck and a large one by the sound of it, could be potentially very dangerous, especially when going downhill.

A couple of years previously, a big Scania had only just missed killing Cheech by a whisker. The driver didn't see the dog until the last second, so swerved violently and ended up running through a number of the new Silver Birch saplings, growing on the edge of the last piece of ancient woodland, about halfway down the hill. Ironically, the Saplings had only been planted around five years previously, in an attempt to protect the ancient trees from destruction by automobile.

Prior to that, the roadway by the turning for the Old Road, had been getting wider by the year until you could almost fit a full-sized roundabout at the turning, naturally causing the ancient forest to retreat. It was caused by tourists and other road users slowing at the foot of the old climb up The Kid and Blue Yonder's impatient office employee's honking their horns and undertaking at that point. Eventually the Welsh Environment Agency instructed the company to plant the line of new Silver Birch saplings, ironically the ones their own truck tangled with just a few years later.

"Whoa there Cheech, there's big trucks about! I've only got two wheels, not four legs, so slow it down boy," cried Hovis as he chased in pursuit of his dog.

When they reached the corner of the Rat Road, Hovis stopped and listened out for any sounds of approaching vehicles. Satisfied that all was clear, he and Cheech set off down the slope. From the apex of the junction, he had no problem in seeing the road ahead of him and on the descent, he had an unobstructed view all the way to the turn for the Old Road, which led up to the summit of The Kid then on beyond towards Deeside.

The climb up the Old Road, started gently enough but its gradient increased steeply, as it switched back on itself several times. Long bends curved their way up, and two thirds of the way around The Kid. From the elevated position at the top, the tourist was offered a clear view down the entirety of the Nant Franken Valley and on a clear sharp day, Cader Idris, was visible, away in the distance.

The pull in at the summit of The Kid, was occupied by a small cafe, which because of its elevation and unobstructed views, chose to call itself, 'Cafe365.' Of course, that was only true on clear, dry days, there were many times when due to low cloud, you could hardly see your hand in front of your face. Cafe 365, shut its doors at the end of September for the winter and didn't reopen them until the following Easter. However, during the annual shutdown, a small one-person snack's van was located at one end of their car park, to cater for the few unseasonal tourist's and truckers who ventured up its slopes.

The snack's van was generally run by a young girl, who occasionally served up a Bacon Butty and a steaming mug of Tea, or Coffee to a passing driver. Normally, at this time of year, the traffic was very light and the van was often closed, purely because permanent part time staff were difficult to find and their turnover was naturally very high, due to the cold, isolated location and poor renumeration on offer. To cover for this blotchy service, Hank Lowengrin, the owner, had installed a self -ervice drinks dispenser, which kept running out of cups. So, fairly often the unfortunate customer just stood helplessly by as his, or her piping hot beverage poured itself down the drain. The abuse meted out to this machine was relentless and caused even more breaks in service to occur. Sometimes, it was so long between visits from the owner or van worker, that the slots became blocked as irate customer's attempted to cram their loose change, into the already over full slot, invariably jamming the mechanism. No amount of jabbing at the return button proved to be of any use. At this point, the 'Dispensorama 90,' usually got a good kicking for its troubles and all the creepy mechanical voice said in response was,

"Thank you for you patronage, please call again," which did little to placate the infuriated customer and usually resulted in the machine getting a second going over.

However, at this moment Hovis and Cheech were quite a distance from the The 365 Cafe, its Bacon Butty van or the Dispensorama 90. He was more concerned with the condition of the road surface, trying to judge the fastest speed that he could take the bend and remain upright. The truck that he'd heard come up the Rat Road this morning, had put a lot of slippery mud on the road and

Hovis felt the back wheel of 'Dennis' slip away from him, as he turned the first corner onto the Old Road but he righted his balance almost immediately and carried on up with Cheech in tow.

"Close call," he cried to the dog, who just ignored him and continued to lope on up the gentle gradient.

Over to the left, the view across Llyn Garon appeared and the mountains beyond, beckoned. Hovis stopped here, in the first small unofficial parking alcove, to take a possible last look at the lake and the hills behind.

"I'm going to miss this," he almost whispered to himself and took in a deep breath, before he slowly scanned the horizon. The beautiful autumn colours shifted, rusts and yellows, reds and purples flaring in the sunlight as the clouds blew past. A strong wind was running at altitude but the only sounds that he could hear, were some Crows who were busy squabbling over the last few morsels of a discarded Corned Beef sandwich, which some passing motorist had thrown from their vehicle.

Hovis remained motionless, observing the Crow's, with Cheech sitting by his side for a breach in time, before he moved on. He was trying to drink in every detail of the countryside that he'd lived in for over thirty years and never truly appreciated. Now it was almost too late and here he was, trying to make up for all those years of missed opportunities.

The Old Road, cut a narrow path around the slopes of The Kid, almost like the slideway of an aged Helter Skelter. It had long slow switchbacks that wound around two thirds of its girth and offered spectacular views over the whole of the Snowdonian Range. Originally, it was the secret ancient pass route out from the valley, one which The Welsh Armies had used to keep their movements hidden from an oft superior force of invader's.

There were two of these original tracks wending their way around Snowdon, which The Druids managed to keep secret for many centuries. Then, when The Romans came to conquer Wales in 48 A.D, their locations were betrayed for a not insubstantial amount of gold, by some members of the poverty-stricken local populace. It was this betrayal which culminated in the merciless slaughter at The Druid's Drop, some years later.

However, Hovis and Cheech weren't there for a history lesson, they were on the Old Road to bid it farewell and another reason, less esoteric. So far, they'd only reached the first switchback lay-by. Each switchback gave the road user a chance to pause and take in the wonderful vista's but there were another eleven to negotiate before they reached the top and Cafe 365 with its dysfunctional Dispensorama 90, drinks machine.

'I hope the van's open, I could go a bacon butty…..' Hovis could almost smell the bacon sizzling as he kicked on upwards.

There was a Snowdonia Views Calendar, that was produced around Christmas, which always featured at least one shot from The Kid. Each year, the public were invited to submit any photograph they'd snapped during their journey to the summit of The Kid. If their photograph made it into the calendar, they were eligible for the end of year 'shoot out' as it was dubbed, which gave them the chance to win £500, just three weeks before Christmas.

However, due to the advertising for this ongoing competition only being available in Cafe 365, many of the entrants were misled and they foolishly submitted a selection of rather bizarre shots of their children, stuffing their faces with Burgers that they'd just purchased from the cafe. Some of them were actually quite good and certainly didn't lack for inventiveness but that wasn't quite the idea of the competition.

'Snapper,' which carried the by-line; 'The on-line magazine that keeps *you* in the picture,' had the task of picking the winner every year. Many was the time that an office junior wanted to award the cash prize to a small-minded cameraman, who had taken yet another vomit churning photograph of some open mouthed, spotty faced urchin, with the half-chewed contents of their meal in full focus. Often the management of Snapper had to remind competitors, that 'mouth open' shots, would not be considered for the calendar, or any prize money. However, this wasn't enough of a deterrent for some who jokingly continued to submit ever more revolting pictures. One particularly infamous shot, had a whole family of Mother, Father, The In-Laws and Seven horrendous children, all posed smiling, their mouths full of well chewed Bacon Butty's. It was taken in August 1998 by the Jackson family from Shrewsbury, one of whom resubmitted it to the competition annually. At Snapper H.Q, it was thought that one of the revolting children featured in the original, had a grudge thing going on and hoped they would eventually tire of trying to subvert the magazine's rather lofty self-opinion. There had been some close calls but as yet, 'Open Wide,' as the snap was known in house, hadn't yet made it to the winner's podium but the fear at Snapper H.Q. was, that one day it would.

Hovis had never entered but now, as the axe was about to fall on his time at No.37, he was going to try it. This was why he'd popped his camera in his saddlebag. To get some shots for himself and maybe win £500 to boot. He sure could use it.

"Time to go," called Hovis and Cheech pricked his ears up. "If I remember correctly," he said to the Red Setter, "on a day like this, the best views are probably to be had, a little further up the hill, looking west," and with that he pushed on.

The air, which in the sheltered glade at the bottom of the climb, had an ambient Autumnal warmth to it, had now taken on the essence of a chill, which was coming down from the peak of, 'The Big Mountain' as Snowdon was colloquially known. If you attempted the ascent of The Kid at this late stage of the year on a bicycle, you had to be prepared to cross the 'thermal barrier,' where the temperature suddenly dropped by several degree's in only a few hundred yards.

Hovis had experienced this rather uncomfortable phenomenon several times during the decades that he'd been employed by Blue Yonder. The first time had been something of a surprise but after that, he'd always been fully prepared for The Kid's, Mother's icy breath and anyway, this time he was wearing The Big Mig's flame red onesey and no passing breeze could penetrate its protective, man-made, stretchy skin.

Most of the tourists having gone home, he was alone on The Kid and he didn't have to be so aware of Cheech and any oncoming traffic. At this time of year, he'd be lucky to encounter anybody else on the climb and even if he did, he would have quite a while between hearing the engine of the approaching vehicle and its passing of him and Cheech. Occasionally, when he was on the right side of The Kid, he thought that he could almost discern the faint sound of voices emanating from the yard of the Agamemnon Building far below, but it could have just been the wind.

As he continued up the slope, the gradient gradually increased and his progress slowed as the muscles in his legs began to complain. 'At this rate, I'll be out of the saddle before the fourth pull-in,' Hovis thought to himself and his determination to remain in the saddle, at least until he'd reached that point, was reinforced. He planned to take a 'killer' photograph at the fourth pull-in because he knew from previous experience, that on days like this, it gave the cameraman the best view down the length of the valley.

He reasoned that the inherent cold of October and the low Autumnal sunshine, should afford him the opportunity to get a shot of the thermal interchange barrier, with the loftiest peaks on each side, poking out above the mist layer.

"Giving us a competition winning photograph," he sneakily said to Cheech, like a man with an edge he wished to keep secret. Cheech laconically looked up at him, somehow disapproving of his master just blatantly using 'local knowledge' regarding the weather conditions, to win the £500 prize. Hovis responded with a matter of fact,

"We need the money."

Hovis pedaled on around the next section of the seemingly endless right-hand bend.

Suddenly, the distinctive blast of a rather large air horn, could clearly be heard as it rose up the sides of The Kid and announced the departure of an obviously rather large truck, from The Agamemnon Building. It was Glen with his special pick up for the Company.

'That'll be the bugger that I heard this morning, coming up the Rat Road, heading for the main office,' Hovis considered.

"No problem there," he dismissively concluded, so pressed on up The Kid.

On bright blue mornings like this, everything seemed possible and the view when he reached the fourth pull-in didn't disappoint, he stopped and dismounted Dennis. He called to Cheech and corralled him in the semi lay-by with the bike.

"There, we should be safe here now, should anything come down the road," he said and patted Cheech on the top of his head, ordering him to "stay." The dog knew the routine and simply lay down, back against the wall with a view up and down the road.

Hovis reached into the bulging saddlebag at the back of his seat and withdrew his Nikon, which he slung around his neck and peered out down the misty valley. This was exactly what he had hoped would happen when he'd stepped out of No.37 this morning. The Nant Franken Valley looked for all intents and purposes like it was having a dream and he was an intruder. This photograph was just crying out to be taken and there was apparently nobody else on The Kid, this morning.

"Perfect," he said and was just about to take, what he considered was probably going to be a winning shot, when the sound of a climbing truck, could be heard approaching his position from below. 'It's carrying some weight by the sounds of it,' Hovis thought as he attempted to judge how long it would be, before it reached his position and he would have to become critically aware of Cheech and Dennis, so that none of them got run over. Maybe it was the blower of the horn he'd heard earlier? If so, it was also logical to assume, that it was the mysterious truck he'd heard approaching and departing The Agamemnon Building. Hovis decided to wait before taking the shot. He stood by Dennis with Cheech behind him, patiently waiting for it to pass by, his left hand gripping his dog's collar. He could tell by the increasing volume, that this was going to be a tight squeeze but there weren't many better places on the climb to stand, when a truck was passing. Dennis acted as a shield for them both and Hovis figured that if Dennis got himself run over by the approaching behemoth, then nothing would actually be lost. Granted, he'd be walking back to No.37 with his Red Setter in tow, but that was a minor inconvenience, when the alternative was considered.

"No bike, or no dog?" He asked himself out loud. "No choice," he answered and moved Cheech back another foot, or so, up against the drystone wall, as the roar of the truck's engine grew ever louder. It sounded huge. Anxiously, Hovis shuffled his feet back another few inches and his grip on Cheech's collar, grew a bit tighter. Dennis on the other hand, now looked somewhat exposed, with his wheels sticking dangerously out onto the tarmac of the Old Road but there was nothing Hovis could do, the behemoth was almost upon them. It was only a matter of seconds before it would be roaring around the bend. Hovis could hardly believe the noise being made by the monster's engine and he was imagining an absolutely enormous fanged beast bearing down upon him.

Chapter Thirty-Five

W900.

He saw the thick black smoke spewing from its twin exhaust pipes, only fractionally before he laid eyes on The Beast itself. The driver, Glen, was forced to drop a gear, just as it came into view; the monster's voice dropped another menacing octave and dark gases billowed from the two tubes as he reapplied force to the drive wheels. The engine screamed as the huge machine clawed its way up the incline towards a wary Hovis and a quivering Cheech. Hovis was looking intently at the leviathan, desperately trying to judge if there was enough space for it to pass without running over him, the dog, or the prostrate bicycle.

It's massive chrome radiator grill reared up at him like metal teeth, seemingly hell bent on gobbling him up. He quickly reckoned it was going to be a close shave, but if the truck maintained its present trajectory, it would just miss them all. The noise was deafening and Hovis felt Cheech shiver and snuggle further into him as the humongous rig drew within a few feet and then, right on the crown of the bend, dropped another gear. Hovis could feel his whole body vibrating as the Burgundy and Gold beast reached the point of perigee and the surging heat of its straining engine, enveloped him like a diesel sauna. Yet, instead of his life flashing before his eyes, all he could think about was the ridiculous concept of;

'This must be what it would be like to face the Washington Redskins front line.'

Spellbound, he stared as the front wheel of the behemoth missed Dennis' rear wheel by a couple of centimetres. Casting his gaze back up to the sleek machine, he fleetingly observed a chrome plate passing within inches of his face, it read:

W900, and it had the word;

Kenworth, written in smaller letters just below it.

The little sense his panicking mind could make of that name, was an incongruous connection with food mixers. Yet, this vehicle was hardly something that anybody in their right mind would keep on their kitchen worktop.

"No idiot! That's Kenwood!" Hovis yelled at the departing engine, and although his voice was drowned by its roar, he felt re-empowered for pointing that out to himself...., so loudly.

Its twin chrome exhaust pipes were like tall fumerols, belching menacing smoke, which nearly choked Hovis and Cheech, as it continued to power its way on up the incline.

Within W900, Glen breathed a sigh of relief as he checked his side view mirrors and saw he'd just missed the guy, his dog and his bike. 'Shit, that was close! Think I'll light a cig at the top.....'

Behind him, when his heart rate and breathing had slowed a little, Hovis would deduce that the words and numbers he'd seen had something to do with the make and model of the enormous unit, but for now they remained a mystery, due to a distinct lack of interest or knowledge on his part.

From the sound's it had made, Hovis had expected a forty-foot, articulated lorry to come around that bend, but what he'd seen was technically a Class 3 vehicle with a huge engine, that was obviously carrying a heavy weight. He assumed that whatever the load was, it had been picked up from The Agamemnon Building. For some curious reason, the driver was now using the back roads, in preference to the A470.

Hovis watched the monster eat up the Old Road and disappear round the next bend, towards the summit of The Kid. The sound of its huge engine gradually faded away to almost nothing, as it climbed ever higher.

"Phew! That was a touch too close for comfort," he bleated as he turned to check that Cheech was alright. "You O.K?" He stroked the still shaking animal and immediately got his answer, the Setter licked his hand. "Right, I'll just let the air clear and then I'll take this damned picture," Hovis commented under his breath, and having released his grip on Cheech's collar, began looking for the best shot.

"£500 is still £500 and right now we could do with getting our hands on that kind of easy money," he declared and continued scouring the horizon for that, 'perfect shot'.

To the South and East, he could see for miles and as the mountains gave way to the open plains, he was able to look out all the way to the English border, God knows how many miles away. To the North, he could make out the haze, caused almost entirely by Liverpool, Chester and Wrexham. Just a little further to the South, there was the first Midland City of Shrewsbury. To the west Ynys Mon lay like a green jewel against the autumn sea. At this altitude, on a day like this, only the curve of The Earth prevented Hovis from seeing much further.

Looking west the valley simply faded into the mist and gradually disappeared, as the sun heated the land and the haze increased. He was left with a wealth of opportunities to snap the potentially winning photograph to submit to the Snapper, including his original idea of the shot down Nant Franken towards Ynys Mon.

"Stop pissing about and take one of everything," he chided. "Then you can choose later, submit the best one and trouser the money." It all sounded so easy but something far larger was troubling his mind and it wouldn't let go.

Not for the first time today, thoughts of Poe crept into his consciousness and he got an icy jolt of a cruel reality. She had seen the best of him, with all the things that working for The Blue Yonder Mining Company for all those years could provide, but now that safety net had been removed and very shortly, he would almost be a pauper.

"And what difference is £500 prize money going to make?" He asked the sky. "Not much, to be honest," he retorted indignantly.

*

The road was particularly quiet and apart from the monstrous Burgundy and Gold truck, he hadn't seen another vehicle all morning. So, as far as he could discern, they were now alone on The Kid. Hovis, with his desperate thoughts of Poe and how he'd almost won her hand and Cheech with thoughts of a bacon butty hopefully waiting at the top of the climb.

"Come on let's get going, or we'll never get there," he called out and clicked his fingers. That was all Cheech required to get him moving, he jumped up expectantly and was soon there by Hovis' side, matching his pace.

They'd been climbing for roughly ten minutes, when the faint sound of a speeding car caught Hovis' attention. After the unexpected encounter with the monster truck earlier this morning, he wasn't exactly in the mood to tangle with some 'Boy Racer,' who was more than likely still hung over from the night before. However, it seemed that despite the continued sporadic squealing of tyres in the distance, he still had a little time to reach the next mini pull-in and make sure that everyone was safe from the lunatic approaching from higher up The Kid.

The screeches grew louder by the second and Hovis began to pick up the pace to reach the next pull-in, before the 'whatever it was', made an appearance. If the driver carried on at this brake neck speed, he could easily mow Cheech and himself down, leaving their bodies in the road for somebody else to find. Hovis didn't care if Dennis was hit but Cheech was a very different story and for an instant, Hovis found himself weighing up the possibilities of him taking the blow, instead of his dog. His perceived loss of Poe, after being so close to the prize was influencing his thoughts at this point, while the mad guy who was careering down the hill, was getting closer with every passing second.

Suddenly, a mint green convertible, that looked like it had been designed and built in the 1960's, came screaming around the bend. Its tail drifting on the loose gravel as it approached his position on the outside wall of the left-handed curve. Hovis skidded to a sharp halt, grabbed Cheech by his collar and leaned hard into the wall. A split second later the mint green speedster, screeched past, peppering them with flying pellets of hard grey granite, which stung something rotten as the vehicle's rear bumper grazed past them by only a matter of inches. The sound of The Rolling Stone's 'Let's spend the night together,' blared out of the open top and the driver, seemingly oblivious to the presence of any other road user's, just gripped the wheel with clenched teeth and appeared to have his eyes closed.

Hovis watched intently, as the mint green sports car slithered past and the sound of The Stones 1967 hit, faded as it barely negotiated the next corner. To his surprise, the Boy Racer had been anything but an adolescent boy. The driver was balding and what little hair he did have was white and appeared to be attempting to escape in the wind. Hovis only got a very brief look at the driver's face as it flashed past but he instantly deduced that he was 'drunk, as a skunk' and literally in a blind panic.

"You do know, you're going to die?!" Hovis shouted after him, as he disappeared round the next section of the downhill curve. "Oh well, it's not my life," he said and set off up the rise once again, with Cheech in tow. "He'll be lucky to see tomorrow, if he carries on like that," he barked and shook his head ruefully.

'Wonder what he was running from?' Pondered Hovis but instead of anything sensible, he imagined some kind of Welsh Yeti, just springing out from the rock face and startling the ageing racer.

"There can't be any more crazies out here.....," he quietly muttered, as his right foot pressed down hard on the pedal and he, Dennis and Cheech made their way around the next bend.

They didn't meet anybody else on the road, between there and the last part of the climb, which culminated in the makeshift Car Park, just outside the closed Cafe 365. Both he and Cheech were hoping the 'Bacon Butty Van' would be open when they reached the top, otherwise it was just a hopeful hot chocolate from the Dispensorama for Hovis, and nada for Cheech.

As he turned the final part of the uphill bend, Hovis saw a scene of total devastation stretching out before him. There, on its side, lay the gleaming Burgundy and Gold Leviathan that had almost killed him and Cheech earlier. Steam rose from it like a wounded dragon.

'You don't look so tough now,' he thought and for an instant considered leaving it for somebody else to phone in and report. Then, a slight moaning sound, which seemed to emanate from the cab, drew his attention. On closer inspection of the stricken vehicle, Hovis discovered that 'W900' had a driver, who was trapped inside the smoking drive unit. The truck seemed to have collided at some speed, head on with 'The Rock Sausage,' flipped over, hit the cafe then mashed through the mercifully closed, Bacon Butty Van. Hovis checked his phone but there was no sign of life, then he realised he'd been so distracted by Poe that he'd forgotten to charge the thing.

'The Rock Sausage,' as the local drivers called it, was a long section of exposed granite, which sat just outside Cafe 365 and prevented most collisions with errant vehicles. This was a common problem, as often drivers failed to brake quickly enough when in desperate need of the toilet facilities. So, without the Rock Sausage the now legendary 'Trucker's Breakfast's,' would have been a particularly short-lived phenomenon.

Just how W900 had ended up in the condition it now found itself, remained something of a mystery to Hovis but he considered it may have something to do with the crazy driver in the vintage mint green convertible. However, other matters were more pressing; if he didn't get the driver out of the cab pretty sharpish, it was possible the whole thing could go up in flames. He tried the door but it seemed that the impact of the accident had damaged the handle and for now, the heavy door was staying shut.

"Christ, what's this thing made of? It weigh's a ton," he gasped and jumped down off the huge cab. He tried kicking the windscreen but just hurt his toes. "I'm just going to see if I can find something to force your door open, or smash the window, hang on a minute while I see what I can come up with," he called to the obviously injured driver.

"O.K........ I'm bleeding....... quite heavily......," came the whispered, breathless reply, tailing away.

"You just hang on mate," said Hovis, anxiously. It didn't look good, from what he could see through the blood-stained glass it appeared the driver was impaled on the steering wheel and bleeding heavily.

As he got around the back of the vehicle, he noticed something gleaming, coming from the inside of the flipped over Burgundy and Gold wagon. All thoughts of the driver's safety vanished from his mind, as he opened the sprung rear door and took a look inside.

Chapter Thirty-Six

Speak Friend.....

F urther down The Kid, a car appeared to have gone through the retaining barrier and plunged into the ravine below. A climber had called the Police and reported that there was "a fresh, car sized hole" in the once beautifully built drystone wall, that lined the Old Road at that point. That section of the wall had been built in the mid 60's, after Lance Percival crashed over the edge to his death. Back then there'd been plenty of money about for quality constructions like this, it was built to last and up until today, had fulfilled its purpose admirably. The caller had reported that there were some rather large skid marks on the road, along with a good deal of broken glass, a few chips of what the he'd described as,

"Light green paintwork, on the walls broken structure, a broken plate dedicated to some cyclist and a C90 Panasonic cassette of the Rolling Stones."

However, the caller could not see any vehicle and was unclear when the damage had been done but he said he'd heard a couple of loud bangs and crashes not long before. As there was a police patrol vehicle just going past Hovis' white dragon sign on the A470, he was dispatched to take a look.

Arriving in his squad car, P.C. Carlisle had given the scene the once over but could see no vehicle in the forested ravine, deep below. He'd taken a few photos and measurements, such as the length of the skid marks to estimate the speed that the presumed vehicle had been travelling, when the incident occurred. With only this limited information readily available and no way of him getting down to the bottom of the ravine without specialist equipment, he reported his findings to Head Office and requested a specialist road accident team to attend, then remained on the scene to await them.

*

Back at the top of The Kid, Hovis grappled with the rear door of W900.

"Open Sesamee," he said jokingly, as he peeled back the burgundy doors and entered Aladdin's Cave.

When Glen's truck had reared up on 'The Rock Sausage,' its structure had warped and several of the internal compartments had involuntarily sprung open, spilling their contents around the back. There were gold coins and large denomination banknotes everywhere but what especially caught his eye, was a still unopened secure section containing gold bullion. If he could get in there, then it may be possible to reimburse himself and recover, granted by illegal means, the return of his money stolen by the Company and their crooked Save and Loan scheme.

OK, so it was illegal but wasn't stealing his money in the first place? Revelling in the delicious irony of it and the feelings of re-empowerment now washing over him. All thoughts of assisting the driver were lost in the sudden realisation of how this could change everything for him......, and for Poe.

"Stay calm and take your time," Hovis advised himself as he gazed around, what was in effect, the vault of this mobile bank. It was obvious to him that Company Security may be arriving fairly soon, as trucks like this one, were usually in constant contact with their security headquarters. It appeared that the crash had probably been caused by the drunk driver in the green sports car he'd wrangled with on the way up. Logic said that guy was unlikely to call the Police and as the truck was taking this back route, it was obvious the company was trying to keep this shipment secret. Indeed, he'd been their main accountant at Blue Yonder and he'd had no knowledge of this secret stash of wealth. With only a couple of security guards left on duty at the Agamemnon Building, Hovis figured it would be a while before anyone arrived to take charge. Just so long as no other driver appeared, he had the van vault to himself.

Gaining entry to the inner sanctum of this injured leviathan, was proving to be a lot more complicated than it appeared in the movies. He'd tried many of the obvious passwords on the locks electronic keypad without success and was beginning to get frustrated and anxious. Time was running fast, the was a scent of hot oil and he was starting to sweat.

"Think laterally," desperation resonated in his voice.

"What would Gandalf do in this situation?" He childishly bleated. 'He'd come up with some clever elven phrase, or something like that,' he answered silently and his head dropped in the expectation of impending defeat.

The tight, Flame Red Onesey he was wearing, rendered the stuffing of a few handfuls of gold coins, or wad of bank notes down the front of it too obvious, yet he was beginning to think this was his only option. 'The time limit must be running out on this deal,' he thought and then it struck him.

"Okay, let's talk about stupid, it's not Gandalf you idiot! Its Frodo and the password, you're looking for, is 'Friend.'"

'Yes, as may be, but.............' Moanvis countered.

Falling back on tales of fantasy for any solution when confronted with a real-world problem, generally didn't work. However, the 'Moanvis but' didn't matter in this case, because he'd no sooner pressed the 'D' key, than the lock clicked and miraculously, the door swung open.

"What?" He gasped, "That never works......," then he finished with the rider, "well not often, anyway."

The inner door was open and now, just like 'The Fellowship' when they chose to step into The Mines of Moria, the stakes had shot up. There was no going back if he touched the shiny things inside. He figured that he would be able to plead that the door had been sprung open by the crash, his cycle gloves covered him there but if he left any evidence inside, his number would be up.

Hovis was looking at a king's ransom in gold. There were ingots of several sizes, ranging from the thin 100 gram make weight's, to the enormously valuable 50k variety. He was fully aware that The Blue Yonder Mining Company owned all of this wealth and they would know the gross value of every last gram and would weigh it, when the truck was recovered.

"Wearing this onesey, was perhaps not the greatest idea You've ever had," Moanvis complained and he began to seriously consider his option's. He didn't really have any but as his Uncle Horace used to say, 'It felt better if sometimes you pretended really hard.' Hovis knew the reality of the circumstances he now found himself in. 'It's got no pockets and every bulge is obvious. Now, if I was a superhero, it might look good in a certain light but I'm not....,' he chuckled at the image in his mind. 'Shit! Concentrate Hovis!'

Suitably self-admonished he closed his eyes and took a deep breath, then coughed at its smoky taste. 'Smoke! Quick man, secrete enough of this shiny stuff somewhere to make it worth your while! But where.....?'

It was fast becoming the time to pretend really hard.

His choices were predestined by the limited options at his disposal and he soon realised it was simple, he only had one choice to make. He could hang his camera around his neck and fill his saddle bag with one of the big ingots but he was going to have to hide the thinnest Gold Bars inside of 'The Big Mig's' time trialing outfit, but how?

Hovis put a big ingot to one side then, in desperation, he recalled something that he'd once read; that men in particular, look first at a stranger's crotch in an attempt to understand them. So, the first place he hid a 100 gramme, gold sliver, was over his newly reactivated penis, then a second for balance and in order to give a good impression to any random onlooker.

"Okay, now to create a six pack, so let's get more of these bugger's inside this bloody onesey," he mumbled and reaching down picked up a few more of the 24 Carat mini ingots. Starting with his imagined six pack he swiftly began to construct a totally false torso. The rippling stomach muscles were the most difficult to fit down the onesey but once that was constructed, things got incrementally easier and it wasn't long before Hovis was equipped with a totally new superhero upper body. He looked down at this heaving chest he'd created and apart from the occasional lump, that only a practiced sculptor would notice, this was as good as it was going to get. Considering the fact that he'd had to wing it due to the pressing time factors involved in this impromptu heist, it was pretty clever.

'This is your chance, so either take it, get yer arse on y'a bike and just cycle away. Or, put the stuff back and risk getting collared by DNA for something that later you'll only wish you'd done.' He knew he was convincing himself to commit quite a serious crime, then realised he'd already made the choice, turned and clunked his way out of the truck.

Banging the door as closed as he'd first found it, Hovis stepped back. The smell of burning oil was getting stronger. 'Ahh, good...when this baby blows she'll take any evidence with her....' but then his failing memory and overactive conscience kicked in and made him reconsider for a second.

'Oh Shit! What about the driver?!'

Now here was a problem that in his lust for gold, Hovis hadn't reckoned with. The last he'd seen of the driver, he'd seemed in a pretty bad way, volunteering the fact that he was trapped and bleeding profusely. 'He hasn't made a sound since, so maybe he's bled out..........?' Hovis mused, hopefully.

No, he couldn't just leave, not if the driver was still alive! He wasn't a monster! However, if he was dead, well that was different and questions concerning his own getaway, came into play...... but right now, Hovis needed some clarification.

"What kind of a beast d'you think I am," he mumbled to his inner voices as he clanked around the back of the wagon towards the unfortunate driver.

"You still with us?" He cried but got no reply, so he tried again.

Silence.

"I need to go and get some help. Will you be ok in there?"

Again, nothing came back from the driver's cab. This was not looking too good for the poor guy in the truck. Hovis told himself, that these things just happen and he should be glad it wasn't him. Peeping in through the blood-stained cab window, Hovis could see that the driver was lying in a pool of blood, still impaled on the steering wheel, eyes wide and glazed, an unlit cigarette still between his teeth, one hand still clutching a lighter, the other his smashed mobile phone. He appeared as dead as a door knob. Hovis shouted and banged on the reinforced window, just to salve his conscience…, the driver remained dead.

As he was clonking back to the rear of the 'Cash Wagon,' Hovis noticed increasing clouds of black smoke, coming from somewhere deep within the engine. His brain was telling him something and his subconscious self, was in total agreement.

"Come on Cheech, we're going, this thing's going to go up at any moment and we don't want to be here, when it does," he yelled.

"Come on, let's go," he screamed urgently, and stiffly clanked off across the empty Car Park, like some resurrected Medieval Knight in skin tight, red Lycra. The sudden rush of agitated movements, settled the 100 gramme ingots more smoothly in the interface between his body and Miguel Indurain's Flame Red Onesey.

It registered with Hovis immediately.

Moving around was suddenly much easier and there were noticeably fewer pinch points. "I could get used to this," he joked as he clambered aboard Dennis, thrust the large ingot in the saddlebag and settled the camera around his neck. Hovis and Dennis, with his tyres noticeably flattened by all the increased weight, slowly scrunched off across the gravel clippings which made up the surface of Cafe 365's car park. As he hit the Old Road's surface and headed off towards home, there was a low booming sound and the crashed truck set ablaze. In the distance he could detect the first wailings of a siren, approaching from the opposite direction. Disturbingly though, he could also hear, what he thought were faint screams of agony coming from the driver, who seemingly was not dead and whose feet were just about to catch fire.

'But he was dead! ……. He was Dead!' Hovis kept on repeating, over and over in his head, but that pathetic mitigation wouldn't hold up as a defence if he got caught with all this illicit bullion, secreted about various parts of his body.

Chapter Thirty-Seven

Deja vu.

B ehind him, Cheech was having a great time. These crazy runs back down the hill, didn't happen often enough for his liking and he was enjoying this romp, as if it was the very first one.

'He was dead, he was dead......I was sure he was dead......I couldn't save him anyway,' kept on repeating in Hovis' head, as Dennis picked up speed. It was like an insane mantra, chanted in pedal perfect synchronisity. The intrusion of P.C. Carlisle into the equation, was both unexpected and unwelcome but there he was, standing bolt upright, with his arm outstretched and his palm, directed straight towards him, silently commanding him to stop.

A million stupid, 'Things to do, if you're ever stopped by The Law,' flooded through his brain but right now, none of them seemed all that practical. There was nothing else to do, he squeezed the brakes but failed to account for his greatly increased golden weight, so almost nothing happened. Quickly, he crushed down hard on the bake handles.

The smell of burning rubber and a good deal of smoke rose from the tyre rims, as the unflinching P.C got closer and closer. At last he began to slow down and, in an act that could be explained as either, 'Superb Bikesmanship' or 'An amazing act of good luck,' he managed to stop Dennis, precisely in line with, 'The Dark Blue Stranger.'

"Problem Officer?" Enquired Hovis, trying to sound as though he was simply a passing tourist. He could see that the cop was looking over his shoulder at something that was interesting him. 'Cheech,' he thought and then quickly added, "You'll have to excuse the dog but I thought I'd give the old boy a good run out as the road seemed almost deserted......"

"Yeah, yeah, whatever," cut in P.C. Carlisle. "I don't suppose that you saw anything unusual this morning but we've had some poor sod go straight through the retaining wall and then off down the ravine."

'This guy doesn't know about the overturned wagon by Cafe 365,' thought Hovis and he patted Cheech, who had taken up residence by his right leg, gently on the head.

"Not really, just a guy nearly mowed me down in an old pale green sports car when I was on my way up. Is it him?"

"I couldn't say sir. Did you go all the way to the top?"

"No, I just went up to switch four to get some photos." Hovis touched the camera around his neck, casually adding truth to his lie.

"O.K. Can I just have your name and contacts in case I need to speak with you again." It was not a request, so Hovis complied and the cop wrote the details in his little black book. "Thank-you Sir, you stay safe now and keep your dog on its leash when you're out on the open road in future. People can get awful jumpy sometimes and we wouldn't want there to be another accident, would we?"

"I will, thank you, Officer," said Hovis, released the brakes and began to roll away. As an overt display of relaxed good citizenship, he raised his arm silently, as a friendly gesture of goodbye.

"Nice outfit, that must be have cost you a few bob," called the P.C in response. As Hovis picked up speed he casually threw out a cheap platitude behind him, aimed directly at the cop's head.

"You wouldn't want to know," he yelled, as his momentum put some distance between himself and the 'Boy in Blue.'

Gradually, Hovis began to breathe more easily. He felt a strange sense of relief, as if he'd made it through Customs with some contraband and was home free.

"I think we got away with it," he declared to the air. 'Now it's just a case of getting back to No.37 and getting this onesey off.'

The error in all this smug self-congratulation now revealed itself, as he tried again to apply the brakes on the next switchback. Barely making it round, he desperately began to weave, trying to slow down his momentum enough to negotiate the last switchback. With only centimetres to spare, he swept around it, only to be faced with the almost ninety-degree bend, where the Old Road met the somewhat newer, Rat Run.

There was no hope of making it.

Realising the inevitability of a calamitous end to this unexpectedly rapid descent; Hovis began to make contingency plans.

*

Back up at the summit, the company security services had arrived by helicopter and were struggling to douse the last bits of the fire, which may have taken the life of the unfortunate driver. At least it seemed that way to The Company's own, on the spot emergency assessor's:

The destructive blaze started when a single lick of flame from engine oil, ignited by the heat of said engine, set a load of large denomination banknotes ablaze.

The sealed and insulated, box-like structure of the vehicle's haulage area acted independently and totally accidentally, like a furnace. During the destabilisation of the vehicle, the rear door's buckled very slightly and allowed a small amount of fresh air into that particular compartment. The already burning engine compartment, sought out the source of this infusion of oxygen and rapidly spread to The Secure Area, where it wreaked havoc amongst the contents.

All that could be salvaged from this accident is an indeterminate amount of Gold, much of which has equally indeterminate amounts of melted Kruger Rand's of a differing Carat, plus various metals and plastics amalgamated within the body of the metal.

Therefore, it is our considered opinion, that the original owners of this now amalgamated mass, namely the Blue Yonder Mining Company, would be well advised to consider it as a write-off and claim directly for the stated and not the actual contents. The amalgamated metals could work as a sweetener to the insurance company, leaving them to undertake the not inconsiderable costs of re-purification. The Company's subsidiary trucking enterprise should claim for both the truck and the loss of the employees' life.

There is no evidence of any third-party involvement at the scene.

Recommend immediately contacting police and company insurers to report accident with attendant loss of life.

Please advise further action, awaiting your response.

*

However, at this point Hovis was ignorant of the existence, or ramifications of any future crash reports. Right now, he had a couple of far more pressing problems to deal with. The first being the fast approaching turn off, and as he banked into the last few yards, he could clearly see the Rat Road beckoning his demise.

The old concept of, 'If you're falling, you might just as well flap your arms,' entered his mind as he just kept pumping on the brake handle's, knowing full well that it was utterly useless. The last facsimile of anything even resembling rubber, had departed the pads long ago. There was no way to prevent the oncoming and inevitable crash from happening. He considered if he should leap off the bike, but figured he would still hit the road at the same speed. It made not one bit of difference and besides, he now had a death grip on the handlebars. Pain was rapidly and unavoidably approaching, all that Hovis could do was choose the location of its administration.

At this critical point, the zone of slow motion overwhelmed him.

There were only two 'safe' options open to him. He could, bear left or alternately, right. So, in his usual manner, Hovis thought too long and acted far too tardily to affect the outcome of this white-knuckle ride, and chose neither. He went straight on, putting his fate in the hands of pure chance.

He cut right across the junction at high speed, clinging on for dear life, as he rocketed towards the line of maturing Silver Birch's and the forest beyond. Steering Dennis on this overgrown and rutted surface was impossible and unable to slow himself down, Hovis simply closed his eyes, clung on and hoped for the best.

Had he dared to open them, he might have seen the fallen tree trunk that lay directly across his path, but he didn't. He collided with its stubborn wooden bulk at almost the same speed as he'd originally sped across the ever-widening junction. The initial impact with this heavy organic object, burst the front tyre on Dennis and his wheel buckled. Hovis lost his death grip on the handlebars as the jolting blow propelled him up, over and downwards, crashing heavily into the damp earth, where he lay immobile and gasping for breath.

As Hovis was heading for the leaf strewn earth, Dennis was playing his part in this example of somebody or others umpteenth law of motion. The one that says;

'Every action, has an equal but opposite reaction.'

So, as Hovis was rapidly moving groundwards, Dennis was heading skywards.

He lay flat on his back for a minute or so, trying to make some kind sense of what had just happened but the sporadic snapshot images, coupled with his suffering a slight concussion, were not helping. Slowly, he became aware of a cold damp patch, spreading along the length of his back, almost demanding that he should get up. Then Cheech was in his face snuffling him, checking he was ok.

"Ummph! Yeah, I'm ok, I'm not dead....., just a bit banged up....." Hovis stroked Cheech's head, to prove his words to him. Satisfied, Cheech stepped back and barked at him,

"Woof!" Setter equivalent to 'get up!'

Hovis tried to sit up but just flailed like some upturned red beetle. Failing miserably, he began to push himself up slowly with his arms, his extra golden weight fighting back.

"Ouch!" He complained as he became aware of his cut n grazed elbows.

"Shit!" He exclaimed as he realised not only was he bruised, cut and bleeding from both knees, his right hip, shoulder and elbows but that the onesey was shredded. Remarkably, his camera was seemingly intact and still round his neck, trying to garrote him. Loosening the strap, he took a deep breath, his next thought was for Dennis. He had no idea where his trusty steed had gone after the crash. A cursory seated scan of the surrounding area, revealed nothing. How could a bike that he'd been riding until a few moments ago, just disappear into thin air? It didn't seem possible, but confusingly, it seemed to have happened. He struggled slowly to his feet and wobbling slightly, stood there like a broken toy, trying to locate his wheels.

Miraculously, although Miguel Indurain's onesey had rips, they were in places which had not, on first inspection, disrupted the stash of Gold Ingot's, which seemed more or less intact. He patted around areas and assuring himself there were no ingots lying on the ground, it just left one question still outstanding. Where on earth, was Dennis?

Cheech, on the other hand, having assured himself Hovis was still alive, found the whole incident incredibly exciting. He was wildly and indiscriminately crashing around in the unkempt grass, furiously wagging his tail and jumping up at Hovis. The insane ride and run down the hill, with him chasing hard after Hovis, was a thrilling event. When seamlessly combined with the frantic end result, this was one of the most exciting morning's he'd ever had!

"It's grand you're finding all this really amusing but I don't suppose you've got any idea where Dennis is, have you? ......No, I didn't think you would ..... But then I don't really think you've any idea what I'm talking about, have you?" He said directly to the Red Setter who just jumped up and barked again.

"Ahhh, who knows where the bugger ended up." He said and shielded his eyes against the low glare of the autumnal sun. Cheech barked to draw his attention and as Hovis looked over, he saw the Setter was staring up at the top of one of the maturing trees, lining the edge of the cliff. Following Cheech's indications, he soon noticed Dennis, whose final repose was some 30 feet up, apparently hugging the upper reaches of one of the only Horse Chestnut trees in the whole glade.

"Oh brilliant," Hovis gasped "and just how am I supposed to get you down from there?" An overwhelming sense of déjà vu, was pervading the air and Hovis' shoulders sank accordingly.

'It's Gwendolyn all over again,' he creepily thought and involuntarily shuddered as he looked up into the tree's branches, then plaintively sighed at Dennis. His front forks had spookily wrapped themselves around the trunk, as if it were afraid to let go, for fear of falling. There was something rather alarming about this almost carbon copy event and his mind raced back to his much younger days, when 'Gwen,' had ended up in a similar position, in another tree, where she resided to this day.

He instinctively passed his hand over the ingot's, checking they were still secured down the front of the onesey and just to check again, that he hadn't shed a few in the crash. It appeared on this further inspection, that one had been lost and where that had happened, was anybody's guess. Right now, Hovis wasn't going to set about looking for it.

"Never mind," he grumped, "one day somebody will come across it and think that their birthday and Christmas have come on the same day," he smiled at that thought. Then he remembered the large ingot hidden in the saddle bag. He couldn't leave that! He took a closer look at the captured Dennis and realised the saddle bag was no longer attached. 'Must have come off in the crash...yes! My lucky day! Just gotta find it....'

Hovis clanked his way around the crash site, calling to Inspector Cheech,

"Fetch the saddle bag, boy!"

The next moment his foot collided with something hard and he swivelled as he tripped and ended up on his backside.

"Ummphh!" He cried as his already bruised backside connected hard with the ground. Then,

"Yes!" As he realised the tripster was the saddlebag he was looking for. "Oh, you beauty! Come to Brown Slice!" He hugged the heavy bag to his chest, kissed it and clanking merrily, levered himself up again. Following another quick check of himself and the area, he scanned around to see if he'd been observed. Satisfied he hadn't, he called Cheech over and they set off walking the half mile, or so, back to No.37.

Chapter Thirty-Eight

Le Coque d'Or!

As Hovis trudged, clunking and counting every step up the gently inclining hill, Cheech still pranced around giving the occasional yip of encouragement. The gold that he'd secreted inside of the now ripped and torn, skin tight onesey and the saddle bag ingot, were beginning to register as quite a considerable weight. His knee joints complained and he visibly flinched, when he stupidly tried to scratch an itch on his badly grazed hip bone.

"Oooh, shit! That hurts," he squeaked, as his fingers collided with a few tiny pieces of finely splintered wood from the fallen tree trunk, which had decided to use his hip as a temporary pin cushion. He hadn't really investigated all his injuries...., he could walk, so he could get away with the loot. The rest could wait.

As the adrenalin ebbed from his system, his aches and pains became ever more obvious. Hovis just wanted a coffee and a sit down. As he was about to turn and clank his way up the garden path, Hovis stopped to catch his breath and took the opportunity to absorb the whole vista. For a few months after he moved into No.37, this view had given him a pronounced sense of entitlement.

He was going to miss this place when he left on Friday but unlike some of the other, 'Last Leaver's,' he'd resolved that he wasn't going to hang around and watch his home burn on Sunday, at the behest of the Company. That seemed far too much like a set of Pagan Funeral Rites.

The eviction notice had made it perfectly clear, that all the items of furniture that had been inside the property on the day that he'd moved in, were to remain in that location. There was even a check list of all the items that The Blue Yonder Mining Company had provided for him, in order to greater, 'enable the transition to his new lifestyle.' Any of those selfsame items that couldn't be accounted for by the occupant upon eviction, were incumbent upon the occupant to reimburse The Company, for their loss.

All of that nonsense, was simply another case of The Company power tripping. Hovis had noticed that when The Blue Yonder Mining Company repossessed one of these choice properties on The Hill, nothing was checked or removed before the Clearance Crew smashed it up and then torched the place.

Slowly, he made his way up the path towards the cabin's front entrance, but he couldn't help stopping every few yards and turning around, to fully appreciate exactly what he was being forced to give up.

"Three decades and for what?" He sighed, looking over at the rose bushes he'd been so lovingly cultivating for the last ten years, or in the case of his greatly prized specimen of 'Our Beth,' even longer. Then, there was the 'Anglesey Palm,' which he'd saved from an ignominious end by picking it out of a pile of rubbish waiting to be collected by a house just outside Bethesda. Hovis had retrieved the poor thing and planted it in, 'The Arboretum,' as he called the sunny space by the side window. This once tiny, miserable, pot-less specimen, was now a rather impressive, multi-stemmed twenty-footer, that wouldn't have looked out of place in a genuine Oasis, somewhere in a far more exotic, desert landscape. Instead, it had found itself here in Wales, with a death sentence hanging over it, like everything else in Hovis' garden. Silently, he resolved to cut back 'Our Beth' and dig out the root. It was worth a try to take it with him.

As he reached the door and clanked inside, Hovis stopped again and just looked around his home, "And the Company's just going to barge in and destroy all this," indignation coloured his voice. Cheech, who was clearly far more interested in having a drink, than hanging around while Hovis idly pontificated, pushed past him. "Okay, you're right, I could murder a Coffee, right now......, I've had cactus gob ever since that 'Copper' made us stop half way down that bloody hill." Hovis flicked the kettle on and put an extra-large spoon of coffee in the mug, then added two heaped ones of sugar, reasoning he needed the energy.

'Well, the question of what to do with the much esteemed, flame red Onesey, seems to have been settled,' Hovis thought, 'I really must get the Ingot's out of this thing. Then, I can get them weighed and sell them on.......,' he smirked silently to himself.

With the mug of Coffee in front of him, Hovis calmed down a little and perching awkwardly on the Washington Redskins bar stool, took a long-awaited sip of the brown liquid.

"Oh, I needed that," he volunteered to Cheech and fell into a few moments of silence, while he attempted to reorder his life, now that he'd managed to make off with the stash of gold bullion.

"Save and Loan bankrupt!" He snorted, "Yeah! Pull the other one! The bastards were moving the money, *my* money, in secret!" He addressed Cheech,

"We just took what we were owed..., well ok maybe a little extra for all the hassle they've caused us, eh boy?"

Briefly, the screams of the driver invaded his thoughts but he shut them down quickly, 'He was dead, he was dead, he was dead......there was nothing I could do anyway...., if I'd had my phone and a signal.......'

*

The onesey didn't seem likely to put up as much of a fight this time and Hovis diagnosed it as fatally injured. He grabbed the sharp scissors from the kitchen drawer and stiffly headed for somewhere a little more comfortable.

Radio 2, with its constant diet of repeating news and never-ending bad music, had somehow become an everyday part of his rapidly diminishing life, here on The Hill. The new lunch time show with Sarah Buckley was decidedly too poppy for his taste. However, he'd found that its constant time checks gave him a strange sense of grounding. Since he'd become the last man on The Hill, he'd had a tendency, to let time drift, causing chaos with his schedules and right now, that was the last thing that he needed.

Every now and again, there actually was a bit of breaking news to report but the producer of the show, always had the final say on whether it was suitable for broadcasting; or if it needed a little modification, before broadcasting at this time of day. The public, it seemed, had to be protected from hearing anything about murdered or abused children while the kids were at home. Any mention of blood was suspended during lunch hour. All stories of demented crime involving any hint of 'Road Rage,' or anything else that could be linked to that particularly bizarre ballpark, no matter how tenuously, were religiously cut out of both the 'Rush hour' broadcasts. However, the station's news hounds were always quick to report on any positive item, that could, no matter how loosely, be connected to the Station.

Sarah Buckley, who'd apparently taken over Ken Alexander's slot, was about to start her show as Hovis made his way to his bedroom to complete the unburdening of the onesey with its golden contents. Once there, Hovis just couldn't resist taking a quick look in the full-length mirror but he instantly wished he hadn't bothered.

"Arrrghhhh" he groaned as the horrendous image was displayed before him in full technicolor. The knees had got even soggier and there were sections of the onesey that looked like they'd been fed into a shredder; there was blood and muck all over him and the onesey. His penis, with its dual ingots placed either side, looked like it was made of seamless Lego bricks and just for a moment or two, he seriously considered whether or not this was a good look?

Having decided to the contrary, Hovis now set about choosing the best place to start cutting. He didn't want to simply snip away without any plan, this Onesey had once belonged to Miguel Indurain and its unfortunate passing deserved to be treated with a modicum of respect.

Slowly, he made a couple of cuts to the tightest areas, which had been giving him the most pain but they both proved to be useless. The ingots just sagged a little and the outfit remained impossibly tight.

"This looks like another case for 'Ripperdude,'" Hovis announced and in a bold action, which was not all that dissimilar to committing Hari-Kari, he sliced across the belly of the onesey.

His guts of gold spewed forth like a veritable gelterfall. The release of all that 'excess weight,' was an immense relief to Hovis' back and he let out a great big, heartfelt groan, as the ingot's fell clanking onto the carpeted floor, followed by a yelp as a couple crushed his naked toes.

"Oh God!" He wheezed, rubbing his bruised toes, then eagerly snipped away at any area which still held an ingot or two, securely in place. The once proud Flame Red, Time-Trialing Uniform, now looked like a Swiss cheese, with only the crotch section remaining untouched. This was going to prove to be the most awkward of cuts and it required several test approaches before any material was actually sliced.

Somehow the presence of Cheech, who'd just pushed his way into the bedroom with his softie, settled his nerves and in one swift and sure action, Hovis exposed his Coque D'Or to the waiting world.

"Da dah!"

He declared, as the two supporting ingots fell onto the floor, just missing his hastily moved toes. Finally, he was free of the golden splints and he could scratch that incredibly annoying itch with impunity. Standing up he waggled his cock, no longer le Coque d'Or now a happy freeborn maggot. "Ahhh, much better...," he chuckled quietly to himself at the reflection of his vaguely S&M eroticised image, then jiggled his tackle, gracelessly from side to side.

"Yeah man, still got it..........., well mostly."

Cheech begged to differ, lay down with a loud, unimpressed sigh and closed his eyes.

*

Once bereft of its valuable cargo, the Onesey was just a sad and lonely shredded second skin. Looking at it now, in the mirrors' reflection, it seemed somewhat forlorn.

However, he reminded himself it had securely held all but one of the Ingot's in place during their hectic descent of The Kid and the crash at the bottom, so he deemed it a true 'Hero!' Observing the stained and tattered apparel in the mirror, the only thing that Hovis could think of now, was giving the poor abused suit a decent send off.

Nevertheless, all thoughts of a state funeral would have to wait, first he had to get cleaned up and dressed. Then, collect all the Ingot's and get them into The Volvo. What came after that was something of a mystery. He'd never done anything even remotely like this before and it would be only too easy to get it wrong.

"Ignorance is bliss and his best mate is Norman Naive," he said to Cheech "and don't you forget it," he added as an aside, just in case his dog was actually listening to him.

A couple more judicious snips and the onesey practically fell off.

"Hmm, well it sure beats last time," Hovis commented. Then, as he stood there, stark naked looking at his stash, the enormity of what he'd just done began to strike home and it was at this point that the idea of burning the slate clean, clearly entered his mind.

"There's no going back, so you don't have to play by anybody else's rules, or conditions. I mean, are they going to do the time if it all goes wrong? I doubt it...," he whispered under his breath. Somehow saying it out loud made the whole dreamlike scenario more real and a proto plan began to form in his mind.......

"Exactly," he replied loudly and emphatically to his inner chorus. His surprising change in decibel level was so unexpected, that Hovis felt he had to look both ways, surreptitiously, but even Cheech had his eyes closed.

He quickly showered, examining his wounds. They were mostly bruise's and grazes, he'd got off lightly. After drying, he rubbed a bit of antiseptic cream on his wounds and threw on a pair of ancient but much-loved chino's, any old shirt from his large collection of boringly similar item's and a pair of trainers, that appeared to have seen better days.

He needed to take another look at the detailed D-Day information the over-paid clever boys at Blue Yonder's Head Office (Australian Division), had e-mailed him last week, in response to his enquiry regarding,

At what time do I have to vacate my home, so that you can burn it?

The answer, which came back unnervingly quickly, stated,

The Blue Yonder Mining Company, expect you to clear the property by 12:00 pm (Midday) and not to attempt to regain entry. As a refusal, may cause offence.

Hovis read the response twice and slowly shook his head. He'd been undertaking a lot of this sort of correspondence lately, as his world had taken on a distinctly more surrealistic tone.

"Christ, these people aren't even nearly normal," he commented with disbelief to the dog, who at this moment was more interested in scratching his ear.

"Come on Cheech, we're going to the garage."

Chapter Thirty-Nine

The Boy in Blue.

T hey'd only driven a short distance down The Hill, when Hovis spotted the Police vehicle parked on the rim of the ever-enlarging intersection of the Rat Road and The Hill. A Police Officer, the one he'd seen earlier on the Kid, was looking at something shiny, which he was carrying carefully in a plastic bag, while talking to somebody on his radio.

A flash of insto-panic rippled through his entire body.

"Drive on, smile and give him a friendly wave," Hovis advised himself, quietly, while trying to appear relaxed and innocent.

"Officer," he 'me-mawed' as he drove sedately past, then said something inane to Cheech, to make it look like he was unflustered when truthfully, as Araf would say, he was 'shitting bricks.' The shiny thing the cop was holding, was undoubtedly the missing ingot and he was informing somebody higher up, of his discovery.

"Shit," cursed Hovis loudly and hit the steering wheel as he left the cop behind. "That's just great, that is. I'm the only idiot left on The Hill, or anywhere else for that matter and by some cruel trick of fate, P.C. Plod just happened to run across the only bloody ingot not accounted for! Godammit! Now he's going to come knocking, that's for sure."

The remainder of the journey to the garage passed in something of a time warp, as Hovis tried to anticipate everything that The Cop's might ask him regarding the ingot and how he might respond convincingly innocently, to their incisive questioning.

'And here's me, plotting another crime, while the first one is still whirling around my head! Jesus, what's it they say? In for a penny, in for a pound. How true.'

*

This unexpected turn of events had put everything at risk. The ingots were all still lying there, in a pile on his bedroom floor, while he was on his way to The Petrol Garage, known as Y Barn, for fuel. After much chewing, he deduced there was nothing that he could do about it right now, so the leaving plan was still on track, he just had a few things to do before D-Day.

Doug at the garage, was his usual friendly self and Hovis filled up the Volvo and a couple of Jerry cans.

"Getting prepared for the winter?" Doug asked, as he totted up the bill.

"Yeah, something like that," replied Hovis, as he paid cash and picked up the cans, "Oh, nearly forgot," he said as naturally, as you like, "I need some Zip Firelighter's and a box of matches." Doug reached down and without looking, grabbed a box of matches. Meanwhile, Hovis reached back a pace and grabbed the firelighters.

"With the matches, that's another £1.78, if I'm not mistaken," said Doug, with a smile.

"Hmm, well then, I suppose you'd better keep the change," retorted Hovis and handed Doug a two pounds coin.

"Wow, a whole twenty-two pence, are you sure that you can afford this kind of wanton generosity?"

"If you don't stop coming on all sarcastic, I might consider taking my custom elsewhere," said Hovis, faking a serious attitude.

"Oh yeah, like where," replied Doug.

"Touché," said Hovis and picked up his purchases, as he left.

"That's it, we've got the fuel, now all we need to do is manoeuvre our way around that nosey cop and we're home free," he said to Cheech with more confidence than he felt, as he turned onto the Rat Road and made his way back towards No.37. He'd expected to see The Cop mooching about as he approached the junction with The Hill but there was no sign of him, or his car. Well, not until Hovis turned for home and then, there it was, parked outside No.37, awaiting his return.

"Trouble Officer?" Asked Hovis, as he slowly drew up to the squad car and wound his window down.

"No sir but do you think, that I could just have another word, it won't take long."

He was trapped. He signaled compliance and pulled up in his driveway.

"Sure, won't you come inside?" Hovis heard himself asking as he made his way toward the door but as soon as the words left his lips, he started casting his mind's eye all around No.37. With relief, his mind gallery gave him no nasty surprises so long as he kept him out of the bedroom. The cop followed him inside.

"Would you like a drink, it's a long way out here and people get thirsty sometimes. Tea, or perhaps a cup of Coffee? I'm having one......To save you asking, the toilet's the white door down there," he said nodding, to a door beyond the kitchen whilst flicking on the kettle.

"Thanks, but no to the drink, I just wanted to ask if you've heard any unusual movement's during the last few days?"

Hovis nearly choked.

"Sorry, sorry. It's just me," he spluttered and then the Policeman, got it,

"Sorry," he repeated smiling coldly, "my fault, I meant Traffic Movements."

A fortuitous escape hatch had just opened up before him, with no subterfuge required to convince the listener.

"To tell you the truth, I've been hearing what sounded like a huge H.G.V, going back and forth in the last few days but when the latest one left it sounded like it took the Old Road for some reason and not the A470, which is further down the hill. I might be wrong because the wind here can play some really clever tricks but that's what it sounded like." Hovis shrugged indifferently.

"And how long do you say it is, that you've lived up here," asked the Lawman, obviously seeking to verify his interviewee's aural ability's.

"Only about thirty-two years," answered Hovis, almost contemptuously.

"Oh, right," muttered The Policeman. "Sorry, but we have to check up on these things, it's all part of the job." Hovis just pecked his jaw, to signal to the cop he understood.

That gesture of understanding by Hovis, mysteriously gave the cop carte blanche to continue,

"I saw you on The Kid before and you said that you'd almost been mowed down by a car coming down the hill, in a hurry…"

"Yeah, it was a vintage mint green sports car. The driver looked like he was in another reality," interrupted Hovis.

"Well, we're thinking that this car, the one that nearly ran into you and went over the edge a little further down the mountain, may also have been involved in another incident, higher up. You came from up there, did you see a truck at all?"

"No, like I said earlier, I set off for some exercise with the dog 'n to take some photos, *after* I heard the truck from Blue Yonder start growling up 'The Kid'. That's the only truck I've heard today. I didn't think anything more about it, until you mentioned it just now," stated Hovis, as sincerely as he could manage in these circumstances. "After the run in with the car I didn't go that much higher up The Spiral. Just a couple more pull in's, to number four, like I said, so I could get some good shots down the valley."

As if to press the photographic point home, Hovis deflected the conversation from the climb up 'The Kid,' to the camera, which was sat on the table. "I'm entering a local competition for the annual Snapper Calendar. Don't know if you've heard about it. There's £500 prize money if you are interested?" He offered but the Cop wasn't for shifting.

"So, you're certain you didn't see anything, or hear anything from above the point where you gave up and came back down?"

"No, nothing." Hovis confirmed and shrugged his shoulders again. "Sorry, I wasn't paying much attention, I was looking for the best pictures to submit...."

"OK then sir, sorry to bother you. This does seem like an open and shut case, but if we need you again we know where to find you...." He turned and headed for the door.

'Not for long,' thought Hovis as he waved the cop goodbye and closed the door, firmly.

The Cop stood at his car and looked piteously as Hovis disappeared from view. He was the last soul on The Hill and the isolation was probably driving him slowly insane, 'but at least he's got that flea-bitten dog,' he thought and smiled weakly as he leant forward and opened the drivers' side door.

When he got back to The Station, he submitted a report that hopefully covered all the bases and left no room for any doubts to grow to maturity. The truck crash was easily left at the feet of Ken Alexander for being a hopeless drunk, and judged to be an accident. Glen's unfortunate death, upsetting as it was, was also viewed as an integral part of this 'accident' and thus it allowed The Blue Yonder Mining Company to come out of the farrago, without exposing their subterfuge.

The private report stated:

There does seem to have been some activity around the junction area but apart from that single gold ingot, which I found lying on the ground in short grass, there was no other activity in the area. I undertook a thorough search but found absolutely nothing else to go on.

I'm pretty sure that the cyclist, one Hovis Monk, saw and heard nothing about, or of, the truck. He did however, see the mint green Sport's Car, that was being driven by Ken Alexander, erratically careening down the mountain. I think that we can assume the car driver caused the truck crash.

Accidental deaths due to dangerous driving.

Perpetrators demise creates a closed case.

*

Now that he was alone again, Hovis waited until his unwelcome, though informative visitor, was out of sight and then he marched over to his Volvo and removed the two Jerry cans. He didn't like the idea of having them in the cabin with him, no point in tempting fate. So, in this case, wiser council prevailed and the petrol was stashed safely outside, in the shed.

The next most logical step, was to get the gold into the car and get it covered up. Doing this at the front of the cabin was obviously too risky, so Hovis drove his Volvo round to the back.

Getting the gold from the master bedroom to the car wasn't a difficult task but it certainly took longer than it should have, because 'Accountant Hovis' insisted on counting and weighing them all. Then, when he tallied a far greater number of Gold Ingot's, than he'd originally estimated, double and triple checking totals and weights. Eventually, he agreed with himself, took them to the Volvo and covered them up.

Chapter Forty

Alexander RIP.

And so finally, it came to this. It was always going to happen, it was just a matter of how and when. He couldn't leave it until Sunday, so a few arrangements had been speeded up. This increased the risk of something going wrong but he had little choice, D-Day was a fait accompli.

With all of his personal belongings taken care of, Hovis stood with Cheech in the room that had, since he moved up The Hill, served as his operation's hub. It contained all the electronic items that he'd cluttered up his life with; from an Amstrad 'doorstop' that laughingly claimed to be a Word Processor, which he'd picked up in a jumble sale for next to nothing, to the really impressive Digital Radio, which due to the interference caused by the mountains, had never received a signal. All these items from previous technological times, had been sorted and judged wanting in a modern world. Most of the items were ensconced in a large cupboard that for many years had become known as, The One Day Pantry. As in 'one day, I'll get 'round to fixing that thing.' Sadly, for most of the ancient technology stored within, that day rarely dawned. It was only the items that were 'last year's model,' that had any conceivable purpose, but Hovis had always found it difficult to throw anything away. If a light came on when it was plugged in or it charged up, he kept it. 'You never know when it might come in useful,' was a commonly heard phrase in 'The Pantry.'

He'd put this off until last but now it was time to get ruthless and divest himself of this mostly useless tech. When he ran across an old burner phone, the delicious idea of filming the demise of No.37

for posterity and the whole world to see, occurred to him. He could create a permanent record of, 'This Final Solution.'

Yes, this idea was simply too wicked for him to pass by.....

"Okay, let's see if this thing still works," he said as he plugged its lead into the socket to charge. A little green bar lit up, sending a wave of devilish optimism rippling through him. Now, all that he had to do was wait until the thing stayed charged up, or it didn't. Right now, the jury was out on this one but while he was still waiting for some verification, either way, Hovis reached up on the next shelf and plucked an aged Binnatone Transistor Radio from the death grip of electric spaghetti cables. He plugged it into the mains and turned it on. After a few crackles n pops, what he heard stopped him in his tracks. It was a news report:

"It's been reported today, by Welsh Police, that they have recovered the body of Ken Alexander, the former Radio Two presenter, from the bottom of a ravine, in Snowdonia. Further details remain sketchy at this time. However, a spokesman for Mr. Alexander's family, commented:

"He went downhill from the moment that he first played that damn Fester's song, 'I Want you, Love.., Want me too, Love.' He championed it years ago in the face of Relax, which he still refused to play and it lost him his job back then and again last week. That song is cursed! Damn you Fester's!"

Hovis stood with his mouth open as the radio cut to a conversation between Sarah Buckley and Dougie Newton, regarding Ken Alexander and the discovery of his body. When they'd stopped sycophantically gushing about,

"What a pioneering figure of the Art of Broadcasting, Ken Alexander truly was," and how "he would be sorely missed by all those, who had worked with him during his extraordinarily long and varied career," there followed the obligatory eulogies from some of the stalwarts of Pirate Radio. They'd even managed to rope in Johnnie Walker on the deal, who waxed lyrically about the time that he and Ken conducted a two-man marathon of twelve hours on, twelve hours off, for a whole One Hundred and Sixty-Eight-hour week.

"Sometimes, things got a little stupid in those days," quoth Johnnie, with a distinctly emotional crack in his voice.

Hovis stood, aghast. So, it was Ken Alexander, or 'Uncle Fester' as he'd taken to calling him, who'd almost killed him and Cheech during his blind headlong panic down the Kid, before crashing to his death. He couldn't decide if his unfortunate demise was either an awful tragedy, or a suitably melodramatic end to a sadly declining pop media presence.

'Wow, who'd have thunk it!' Was all his mind could offer as he carried on listening, spellbound.

It wasn't until all the arse lickers had experienced their turn in the spotlight, that the report cut to a Police press conference. Chief Superintendent Franklin Williams, was imparting a few details regarding the incident, to the public:

"Last Sunday, Mr. Alexander was descending from the summit of what the local's call, 'The Kid,' due to its proximity to Snowdon. It seems, that he was simply going too fast as he tried to negotiate the always dangerous, 'Breakneck Curve.' His vehicle lost traction and tragically crashed through the drystone wall down into

the ravine below, resulting in his death. There was no one else involved in the incident."

"So, was there anything suspicious about the scene?" He was asked but evaded the question quite handily, choosing instead to talk about the dangers of driving on slippery roads at this time of year,

"There was some light green paint on the drystone wall, right by a rather large hole and some indications of a frantic attempt to avoid going over the edge, but there was nothing suspicious about the accident. It is a well-known black spot, after all it was where the cycling legend, Lance Percival, lost his life."

There followed a few more inane questions and some evasive answer's but between them, they did very little to shed any light on the circumstances of the fatal crash. With the rather perfunctory press conference concluded, Chief Superintendent Williams disappeared to a cacophony of reporters' questions.

It dawned on Hovis, 'I was probably the last person to see him alive! Wow! He really did manage to crash the truck and run himself off the road! Some going Ken! Thanks for the golden windfall!' Then he recalled how he'd cursed him at the time and felt a little guilty about thinking ill of the dead.

The next voice Hovis heard, was Sarah Buckley's. She was making a sarcastic comment about Ken's brother, Jason Alexander's polemic about, 'That damn song,' as he'd called it. From what she was saying, it seemed that Jason blamed 'I Want you, Love.., Want me too, Love,' for driving his brother crazy and by insinuation, causing his death.

"Yeah, Man," chimed in Dougie Newton. "Death by ditty, how Rock 'n Roll, d'ya wanna be?" Then added an old cliché, for good measure, "Jeez, whadda a way to go," in a rather poor Brooklyn accent and started laughing.

"Well, he was sorely missed for a whole ten minutes; Andy Warhol got fifteen but I suppose it's better than nothing," commented Hovis to Cheech, finding it hard to suppress a heartless giggle from rising in his throat.

"Anyway, enough of that soul searching, it's time to be getting on with the days business," Hovis snapped, as he looked into the One Day Pantry. He sighed, then after a moment thought,

"Bugger it! The rest of you are just not worth my time."

*

It was Saturday evening, time for action.

Hovis went to fetch the two Jerry cans he'd carefully stored in the shed, leaving Cheech safely in the Volvo. He opened No.37 for the last time and went inside.

There were certain things that had to be done first and then he could set about his final solution to the termination of his employment by The Blue Yonder Mining Company. He'd had second thoughts about the onesey. Considering its colour, it only seemed fitting that it should be consumed by fire. Hovis felt that Miguel Indurain would be pleased to know that the speeding onesey, had met such a fitting end.

All the stuff that was actually his and wasn't owned by The Company, had gone to Llanbadrig yesterday, including 'Our Beth'. He'd met his new landlady and officially moved into his new cottage. To her and the outside world he was there now, the lights were on, the radio was blaring, there was just nobody home.

Hovis was standing in the ravaged hulk of No.37 about to cremate its husk. He had this whole thing planned out, nothing that left any trace of his golden escapade was to remain and the conflagration itself, was going to be screened, 'Live' on YouTube. Remarkably, he'd left an old sim in the burner phone and there was still enough money on it to connect to the internet. How long it would last was anyone's guess but he was going to give it a go. Everything even remotely involved in his 'Golden Escapade,' was in the cabin and accounted for. Now, all that remained, was for him to liberally redistribute the gasoline around the place, light the blue touch-paper and get the YouTube, 'Live' link rolling on his burner phone, via his cunningly set up, fake welsh profile.

Putting down the cans, all that was left for him to do, was wait until it got even darker before starting 'The Show,' then heading off to get a good view, from a distance. So, in the meantime, Hovis sat in the Volvo with Cheech, at the back of the cabin, for what seemed like an interminably long time, playing bass finger runs, while they waited for the last dregs of twilight to fade.

Chapter Forty-One

Flame On!

T he first star appeared low in the Western sky but it was a while before any more showed up and he was growing increasingly impatient. It had been dry, for the whole of this last week, windy too but today had been clear, still and sunny, perfect for a good view of The Show.

Suddenly, he realised that despite all his careful planning, he'd never directly looked into the best way to set a log cabin on fire. Sure, he'd seen stuff on movies but this was real life. Not for the first time, Hovis found himself at a bit of a loss when it came to deciding what to do next.

'Do I spread the petrol about inside, or out?' That question alone stayed his hand and he put the petrol cans down while he considered his options.

In all the movies that he'd seen, fire always seemed to erupt more effectively if you doused inside, then threw a Molotov Cocktail through a window. After some deliberation, Hovis decided there didn't appear to be any measurable advantage to throwing a bottle with a flaming rag stuffed into its neck, through a window. Sure, the crash of breaking glass had a certain arresting sound to it but he reckoned that maybe this wasn't what he wanted......arresting that was. Though maybe it could work to light the fire....?

Holding the Jerry Cans, he boldly began the process of distributing their contents all over the most flammable areas inside the cabin. He concentrated on the wooden structural areas, such as the walls and doorways. Then, having given the kitchen units a good dousing, Hovis dribbled out the fuel, going around as much flooring as was possible and out the door, reserving a small amount.

Now the stage was set and there was no going back. The Blue Yonder Mining Company had lied to him from the start. They had promoted him, relying upon his greed and ego from the very beginning, then trashed his world and stole his money back! It was time for revenge! Not just for him but for all the others they'd manipulated, exploited and disposed of. He stood for a while and admired his late evenings work, before making his way back to the Volvo, to wait for the last glimmer of twilight to fade.

"Well, old son this is it! Now they get their just desert's," he affirmed to Cheech and took another look at his watch. Not that it made any difference, the same rules appertained to this undertaking as applied to the watching of a boiling kettle.

After a few minutes Hovis simply ran out of patience, got out of the car, walked over to No.37, opened the door, lit the Mini-tov Cocktail that he'd put together whilst he waited from the dregs of the jerry can. He'd fashioned it from a rather old and long empty 330ml bottle of Kinder Bier that somebody or other gave him as a gift following a trip to Germany, which he'd rediscovered in the glove compartment. An old nylon sock had been employed as a wick and as it caught light, he threw it through the temptingly flammable, open doorway.

Hovis propped a board in front of No.37, then assuring he was beyond its focus, set the old phone's camera going live on YouTube, so that the whole world could bear witness to his final triumph.

However, as he sped away from the scene, no trace of the impending firestorm could be seen on his YouTube 'Live link.' For all intents and purposes, it appeared that the seat of the intended blaze had fizzled out.

Several minutes later, parked in the pull in on the other side of the valley, Hovis was watching his iPad screen intently. As yet, he saw no signs of fire coming from his old home. All he could see in the dark was the sign he'd carefully placed to one side which read,

Sons of Owen Glyndwr

Free Wales ☐

When he'd initially done the guestiematics and logistics of this undertaking, he'd reckoned that 330ml's of petrol in the kinderbier bottle, would be enough to trigger the intended 'Towering Inferno'. So, foolishly distracted by images of Faye Dunnaway, he hadn't considered this negative possibility. He'd used all of the remaining petrol to thoroughly douse the interior of No.37. Then, whilst he was seriously considering the possibility of returning to relight the blaze with a fire lighter, BOOM! The whole place seemed to spontaneously, explosively, combust.

"Wow!" He squealed, as a tongue of flame shot out of the top of the chimney and the windows shattered in the percussive blast of expanding air. Safe in his Volvo, Hovis could observe his triumph from two different perspectives. One live but from a distance and the other seen through the eyes of the camera, which put the blaze up front and personal. Watching on the computer screen, he could almost feel the heat. More flames burst out through one of the broken windows and started licking at the roof timbers.

From the safety of the pull in, it seemed the whole hillside was illuminated by the blaze, yet there was no sign, nor sound of the Fire Brigade. Hovis had been careful. Unless they were watching it unfold on YouTube and recognised the location, which Hovis had been careful not to give away, the Fire Brigade, nor anyone else, would have any idea of where the blaze was. It would need someone who was close enough to see it for real, for any emergency services to be called.

Then, unbeknown to Hovis, as he was watching his old home burn, an unseen spark landed in an overly dry pile of wind-blown leaves, on the far side of No.37. After smouldering for a little while, they suddenly burst into flames. From his position on the opposite hillside, the major blaze obscured this development and as Hovis watched the roof of his log cabin collapse into the blazing mass below, something far more dramatic was developing behind, unseen, yet right before his eyes.

This newer blaze did what brush fire's normally do and proceeded to cut its own individual path across the hillside behind the cabin. Pretty soon, the undergrowth of dead bracken, leaves and heather was set ablaze. The area was now in danger of becoming one huge conflagration, spreading unchecked towards The Agamemnon Building Complex.

Hovis and Cheech, still sitting in the same spot that had claimed the lives of Ken Alexander and Lance Percival, on the other side of the ravine, were watching all of this unfold, blissfully ignorant of the extending inferno. In fact, Hovis was busy congratulating himself on thwarting The Company's desires to dictate this final act of power and Cheech, well he was sleeping on the front seat.

Meanwhile, the second fire was building and climbing its way along the hillside, spreading its tentacles down towards the Agamemnon building. The once diligently attended gatehouse was now feeling the first caress of the flames. With no one living on site there was no one to either see the danger or to raise the alarm.

Hovis remained observing events, grinning and raising a fist in salute,

"Yeah! Rebel yell!"

The old phone had just succumbed to the flames, when his vision of the black screen was rudely shattered by the sound of an enormous explosion. He hadn't got a clue what'd caused it but the resulting mini mushroom cloud rising from far behind his old home, didn't fill him full of hope. A second and third explosion, increasingly large, left little doubt in his mind. The Agamemnon Building Complex was being destroyed.

Looking at the red glow enveloping the sky beyond the crest of the hill above No.37, he got some insight into the scale of the blaze rapidly disintegrating the Blue Yonder Mining Company's Welsh Operation. Reaching for the ignition he remarked to Cheech,

"Oops! It's time for us to go......"

Epilogue.

"I 've just got one last important thing to do," Hovis said to Cheech as he pulled over, a safe distance from the guilty conflagration. The setter casually opened both eyes and looked inquisitively at Hovis as he brought the Volvo to a halt by a fast-flowing stream. He reached over into the mess that was cluttering up the back seat.

"Ahh, there you are!" He cried triumphantly as his fingers detected the uneven plastic frame of something lying under the old Candlewick bedspread he'd thrown over the crate of Ingot's, innocently sitting on the back seat, alongside the looted Shell and Esso Petrol Pump tops and his precious guitar case, containing Jezebel.

It was the incomplete model of The Scharnhorst.

He'd decided it deserved better than being carted around from place to place, just to be dumped into yet another loft, only to sink under the weight of future Hovis detritus melancholious.

"Not this time," he informed it, as he untangled its forward guns, from the possessive embrace of the bedspread.

"Time for you to sail one last time," Hovis affirmed as he got out of the car, flicked on his torch and carrying the Battle Cruiser under his arm, solemnly took a deep intake of breath and headed, goose-stepping for all he was worth, towards the full moon lit stream.

Upon reaching the tributary, he stopped and bending down, reverently lowered the 1:72 scale model into the flow and released it. Striking the Hitler salute, he hummed a particularly poor rendition of

'Deutschland, Deutschland Uber Alles' and watched respectfully, as his offering of an incomplete plastic replica of the Kriegsmarine's Battle Cruiser, Scharnhorst, slowly made its way into Llyn Garon.

Hovis watched silently in the bright moonlight, as it reached deeper water and inevitably began to sink. As it finally slipped peacefully below the waves, he clicked his heels together and saluted, Deutsche style.

Returning to his Volvo, he retrieved his smart phone from the top of the dashboard, saying just these seven words.......

"I think, it's time to call Poe."

For further information about Tom McNulty please visit:

My website: https://www.tommcnultyauthor.com/

My facebook pages:

https://www.facebook.com/tom.mcnulty.56679 &
https://www.facebook.com/Tom-McNulty-Author-
422056368538153/?modal=admin_todo_tour

Pinterest: https://www.pinterest.co.uk/tom54mcnulty/

Goodreads: https://www.goodreads.com/user/show/93339463-
tom-mcnulty

44909354R00211

Printed in Poland
by Amazon Fulfillment
Poland Sp. z o.o., Wrocław